LEAPING
INTO THE
UNKNOWN

D. C. LEWENS

CRANTHORPE
MILLNER

First published by Cranthorpe Millner Publishers (2022)

ISBN 978-1-80378-071-9 (Paperback)

www.cranthorpemillner.com

Cranthorpe Millner Publishers

Preface 1

The first step is the most frightening.

I looked at the scene before my eyes. It was breath-taking. A beautiful summer's day, not a cloud in the sky and a sea in matching blue. In front of me, half a million music fans, sitting in a huge arc on a hillside facing a stage centred by a piano and a lone female singer/pianist.

Behind me and to both sides were a sea of tents of every size, reminding me of the poor shanty towns seen throughout the world. All around me I could hear the sounds of happy groups sitting chatting and wandering about.

From what I could hear through the amplifiers, above the low murmurings of the crowd noise, the quiet blonde singer was not at all happy with the crowd. I was equally annoyed, as I was expecting to be watching Jimi Hen-drix. The sole reason for me being there was my wish to see Jimi in action, and to tease my father. He had told me on numerous occasions that it was one of his big re-grets in life, not having been here to watch him. Some-how, I'd missed seeing Jimi, but I had got something right – this was the 1970's Isle of Wight Pop Festival,

1

just not at the right time.

I'd materialised between two large tents just above the main slope on the brow of the hill, slightly out of view from the main crowd, who were all looking in the other direction. I checked my footing, soft grass, and took my first step forward, carefully avoiding the guy ropes. As casually as I could, I walked away from the tents.

I'd learned from past experiences, and chosen clothes that suited the period: faded jeans, a white T shirt and a pair of baseball boots, quite expensive. My most important possession was a 1960s-looking wristwatch, specially made for me. It did have a wind-up mechanism, but also a small button that enabled it to turn into an accurate stopwatch. It looked very authentic. I set it at thirteen minutes counting down to zero, at which time I would disappear.

I checked the watch again, counting down. It also had a pre-alarm that left me two minutes to find a quiet unobserved space. I edged forward towards a group of lads sitting on the ground, just ahead, watching the stage. They noticed my hesitation and moved slightly aside as if to let me through or sit down near them. They seemed a friendly bunch, so I decided to sit alongside them.

Talking was easy; I asked who was playing and where Jimi Hendrix was, as he was due on stage now according to my obviously poor research. They all laughed, telling me the whole timetable was a complete mess and other than Donovan and Tiny Tim, who appeared every five minutes – a little exaggeration – they had no idea, nor it seemed did the organisers.

Apparently, far in the distance, no side screens in those days, I was listening to Joni Mitchell (I learned later the correct spelling of Joni) who seemed a bit morose (bad tempered with the crowd). She was singing a nice song using a carousel as a metaphor for life in which the ride was life's journey going round and round through the years and the painted ponies going up and down being life's ups and downs – not quite right there, Joni.

In a quiet moment between songs, I looked around again. The whole scene was breathtaking, and unlike the modern festivals there were no children or older fans. Everybody seemed to be in their teens or twenties. Happy faces as far as the eye could see.

Peaceful and calm it truly was.

I checked my watch: six minutes left.

The lads let me know they were having a great time, apart from the toilets and a diet of burgers. They were happy they'd left the arena and moved to the top of the slopes with their tents. They had a really good view from there. The sound was good too, as the hills seemed to amplify the sound. The crowd below were fairly quiet, probably due to the number of acts they'd seen. They needed to be as the volume from the amplifiers in those days was very poor.

Chatting away with the guys was very entertaining, and one in particular was especially funny. His is the only name I can recall – Podge (what days they must have been, when we were not offended by an uncomplimentary nickname). I told them I was with friends, who had moved down to the arena for a better look, and we were leaving tomorrow, the last official day. They said they were heading home in a couple of days, when most of the crowd had left the island and it would be easier to hitch. I nodded but had no idea that hitch-hiking was an acceptable and reliable way of getting around in those days. I'd already learned that words and meanings can change slightly over the years and being here was very 'cool'.

Quick glance; three minutes left.

As if on cue, the guys decided to walk down to the main arena, to hopefully listen to a rock group due on, maybe. I declined the offer to go with them, and they moved down through the seated crowd, giving me a farewell wave.

I quickly moved back between the two large tents, waited till my watch said fifteen seconds left. I had no desire to leave, but right on cue, I disappeared.

Perhaps now might be a good time to explain.

On second thoughts, let me tell you the story from the start…

Preface 2

Picture the scene. A familiar scene to a lot of families in the recent past, when most lived close to each other and the fashion for moving away hadn't yet happened.

It's just another summer's Saturday afternoon at Granny's, and most of our extended family are having their normal get together. The grown-ups are laughing and chatting over cups of tea, the mums tending to drift together and the dads waiting for a bit of action on the large lawn.

Children of all ages are already on the lawn, waiting to be organised into team games. They are kicking a ball around. I wouldn't call it football, just chaos. An uncle had tried to get a bit of 'sides' going but had given up, until another turned up and between them they managed to get a loose game of cricket going, played with an old tennis racket. It was mad, joyful fun.

However, on that particular Saturday, I had a slight headache, and was quietly resting on a bed in a down-stairs bedroom with a cold flannel across my forehead and a bucket by my bed, just in case. Even though I knew I was missing the fun, I somehow drifted into a light sleep. I was nearly five at the time, with an older brother Ian, aged seven, who I knew would be in the thick of it on the lawn.

I hadn't long dozed off, or so I thought, when I found myself at the edge of the slightly raised lawn, just beyond the flower bed, watching Ian and his cousin Susan having a friendly squabble. Maybe a little jealousy, but I wished I was playing with them. They were really laughing and throwing dandelion heads at each other (in those days dandelions heads had the power to make you rush to the toilet if you got one in your mouth; sweet innocent times).

I got bored of watching them and started to walk back to the house. Nobody took any notice of me or asked if I was feeling better, which surprised me, but I guessed they were all too busy having fun. I went into the house by the shaded back door; everyone was crowded at the sunny front door with tea and biscuits. Before I could understand what was happening, I had somehow returned to my resting place, and found myself lying down with a dry flannel across my mouth.

Mum put her head around the door and asked how my head was and whether I would like a drink? I was feeling better so I took her hand and we went to the hall where everyone was congregating. The games had stopped for drinks and all the children were lining up for Granny's special orange juice, all clutching their straws in eager anticipation. Kids will be kids and before long they were all squirting each other through the straws. Bedlam.

Mum and I moved towards Dad and scrounged some chairs. I asked Mum where Ian was. I told her I had seen him having lots of fun with Susan earlier and asked whether he had swallowed any dandelions. Dad seemed to come alive at that, giving me an odd look and asked me how I knew that.

I told him that I had been watching them from the flower bed. He said he was nearby and hadn't noticed me. Mum said she had kept an eye on the bedroom door and she was sure it had stayed shut. I told them I'd really been watching them but they hadn't noticed me either.

It was then I noticed them give each other a funny look and Mum said to Dad she thought it might be an idea to contact Uncle Pete. I didn't know what she was talking about, nor did I take any notice. I was too busy with a jammy dodger. But looking back now, I knew this was only the start.

Lo and behold, the following weekend a kindly looking older man turned up at our door who turned out to be Uncle Pete (I later found out his real Christian name was Petrov). I had only met him a few times, and barely remembered him as I had been very young. I later learned that he was in fact my mother's uncle, a brother of my other grandmother, Sylvie (the family had escaped Russia for England in the 1930s). In he came with great flourish and sat having tea and biscuits. He seemed very friendly. Mum and Dad laughed at his old stories. After a while we were all at ease. Mum and Dad then left the room and Uncle Pete came and sat nearer me.

We talked a bit about general things and he brought

up the subject of my little dream from the previous week at Granny's. He told me not to be frightened or worried as I was one of a few special and lucky people who could have small dreams that seemed very real; little dreams where you kind of left your body and went somewhere else, but nobody else knew you were there, like a special hiding place. All very confusing at the time. I told him what had happened last week by the lawn, and he asked if I'd had any other dreams. I told him I didn't think so and asked if it would happen again. He said it probably would and not to be frightened; he said I should just tell my mum and dad.

I struggled to understand; I thought it happened to everyone. He said it was very rare and special, and the only other person he knew who could do it was his sister, my other grandmother. She was now very old and had also had the gift, as he now called it, when she was younger. He said nothing bad would happen to me. The dreams wouldn't come at night, he told me, only when I was having small naps during the day, and they would always take me somewhere nice.

It was very hard to understand, and I asked if I could get into trouble doing it and if I could get hurt. He told me nothing could happen to me; I'd just wake up and I wouldn't get into any trouble. . He said the only big important rule was that I must not tell anyone except my mum and dad, that was really important. I felt much happier and went to see Mum and Dad. I was very young and it's amazing I can remember it all so clearly still.

Everyone seemed happy and relaxed, and Uncle Pete

8

left, making sure to tell my parents that if there were any problems at all they should contact him immediately and he would come.

True to his word, Uncle Pete called on us regularly over the next few years; everything went smoothly, and I told no one. I began having these 'living dreams', as I liked to call them, from time to time, without any problems. I went to the swings a few times, watched people feeding ducks. Truthfully it was quite boring, but I didn't tell anyone.

Around the age of eleven or twelve, I had my first experience of somebody speaking to me... What a shock. Luckily it was a younger cousin, Isobel, saying something about her doll (at least that's what I thought). I answered her, wondering if she could hear me; she could. It scared me so much that I found myself instantly back in bed. When I told Mum and Dad what had happened they rang Uncle Pete and he was here within the hour. It seemed I had moved into the grown-up version of the 'gift' and now had to be a lot more careful, as I could now be seen. He again stressed not to tell anyone. He reassured me again that I couldn't be hurt, as I wasn't really there. I knew this to be true, as I could never feel my feet on the ground. Remember, he said, when you feel scared you just go back to your sleeping body. You are not there to frighten anybody, he said, least of all children.

The dreams carried on, but infrequently, and I always remembered not to tell anyone, and now the new rule: try not to get involved with what's going on. I'd already learned to keep out of sight if I could, and was always ready to move out of anyone's way. I'd also learned to understand time better, and my dreams would only last about ten minutes. However much I tried or wanted to, I couldn't stay any longer. I also learned how to leave the dreams when I wanted, and I always had a clear recognition of the dream when I awoke.

The years passed; I carried on with no major mishaps, some odd creepy moments (nothing I couldn't handle) and as I got older, I was having more varied and interesting dreams. Uncle Pete had tried to explain the lucid dreams I was having. They were based on a mathematical formula, a sequence of numbers. Something called the Fibonacci sequence: 1, 2, 3, 5, 8, 13, 21, 34, 55 and so on. I didn't get it. He continued, telling me the dreams related to a curve in time, very common in space and the natural world. Still no luck, though I did learn that the dreams would last only thirteen minutes, the rest would come in time and with experience, he said.

He went further; there was no stopping him. He said my type of lucid dreaming was very rare, unlike the lucid dreams that most people have occasionally, and was called pellucid dreaming. I liked to think it was named after me as my name's Lucy. He laughed at that suggestion.

I tried out the time travelling bit a few times – yesterday's rain, traffic accidents, that type of thing – before I had it slightly mastered. I didn't find out how far I could go back until a few years later, courtesy of Uncle Pete, who gave me a lot more information, distances, time, etc.

As you can imagine, this came in very handy at exam times (maybe more than just a few, to be honest). Example: I dreamed myself into a deserted staff room, hoping one or two exam papers had been left out. Occasionally, they had been just left across the desks, open at a number of pages, hence no real problems with exams. I learned that I couldn't move inanimate objects, and if I touched something alive, it sent a strange quiver through my body – and what I touched was also given some kind of static shock. This was a very rare occurrence. I kept well clear of people, and all animals kept clear of me. They definitely had a sense I was there and didn't like it. Most ran for cover.

As I got older, I visited the places I wanted to go, rather than let the dreams decide, but always following the rules. My most ambitious travel was just the other day to a rock concert in 1970 on the Isle of Wight – great success, apart from timing.

I had many good friends and boyfriends but was never tempted to tell. I had decided that Uncle Pete was right, they would never believe me anyway. He also said it might make my dreams stop if I told anyone, and although this wasn't true, it was another good way of ensuring I told no one.

I enjoyed my secret life and short, strange travels, but by the time I reached my early twenties, I was beginning to run out of ideas; it was hard to keep being imaginative. Back home from university, with no particular ambition and wondering what on Earth I was going to do, I spent less and less time dreaming.

But then… I got the call.

Chapter 1

I was hoping that I would get a marvellous view over the Thames from the SIS building on the South Bank, but instead I ended up in a completely white room, floor included, with no window, just a chair and a few magazines on a small table. It made me feel nervous and uncomfortable... perhaps that was the point, part of their plan. Either way, it was working.

Earlier I had followed my instructions to turn up at the building and follow the signs for the Visitor's Entrance on the riverside frontage. The pathway along the Thames was already quite busy with joggers and dog walkers. The last sign pointed the way to a black door with an adjacent smoked glass full-length window. I was exactly on time, nine thirty as arranged, and pressed the only button by the door with some trepidation. Almost immediately the door was opened by a fairly nondescript middle-aged man. I held my false press badge towards him.

He gave it a thorough look and said, "Follow me, Miss Firmin."

I nodded and followed. He opened an internal door

for me and gestured for me to go through. I hadn't known what to expect, but I certainly hadn't envisioned a long bleak white corridor with matching flooring. We entered the lift at the end of the corridor and went to the fourth floor, where he showed me into a small room, and without another word, he left. I entered the room and took the chair to where I am now.

The phone call a few days ago had offered me an interview for an unspecified position after 'they' (I had no idea who 'they' were) had been contacted by a relative of mine – Uncle Pete, or as he was known to them Peter Pashley, formally Petrov Pashovich.

It had taken me a few seconds to recover from my shock as it had never occurred to me that my Uncle Pete was involved with the Secret Service, but then again, I had never been interested in his life when he was not involved with me or the family. Perhaps I should have been, but it never occurred to me at the time. The caller hadn't given his name but suggested I might find it quite interesting (I had no plans for anything else at the time). He said he would explain more if I was happy to come along and meet him.

He'd said that the general public were always keen to see entrants into the building, something that would make it more plausible for me to enter, and that he would courier a pass to my home (my parents' home) in Guildford. I had just been about to ask him for a bit more information but as I started he'd interrupted me to say that all would be explained on the day if I was interested (who wouldn't be?). He'd finished by saying he would be available and looked forward to seeing me tomorrow (Tuesday) at nine thirty if that was good for me, and that was that.

Once off the phone I told my parents what had just happened, who confirmed to me that they had an inkling that Uncle Pete would be doing something concerning me with his previous connections. I tried to wheedle a bit more information from them but no help there. I also rang Uncle Pete who wouldn't say anything either – a mystery.

The 'press pass' in my name, Lucy Firmin, arrived as promised. I tried to not think about the meeting but as you can imagine I thought of nothing else. My parents refused to say another word.

The morning arrived, at last, and I was given a lift to Guildford station, still not a word said by my father. I caught an early train to London, arriving too early so I had coffee at Waterloo Station at nine a.m., tubed to the nearest underground station Vauxhall, and walked down towards Vauxhall Bridge where the building was on the right-hand side. I followed the Visitor's Entrance signs towards the South Bank. It all went very smoothly, perfect timing, and I now sat in the all-white room, waiting…

Not for long though luckily. The door opened and a nondescript middle-aged lady stated rather than asked, "Lucy Firmin.". She beckoned me to follow her and I did.

Just a short walk down the 'arctic style' corridor, she opened a door with just a number nine on it for me to enter, closed it behind me, and left. A much plusher office opened up in front of me with the view I was hoping for over the Thames. A man and a woman sat at a large mahogany desk, upon which sat a telephone and a buff file. They motioned me to take the seat.

In front of me sat a very well-presented man in what looked like a very expensive dark grey suit. Impeccable came to mind. He was in his forties, slim, with short hair and glasses, attractive for his age and seemingly upper class.

He stood up and with a little pomp said, "Good morning, I'm Alexander Ambrose and this is my colleague, Michele Douvrer. We would like to welcome you to the 'Services' for an informal chat."

Nervously I stood up and replied, "Good morning, I'm Lucy Firmin." I was tempted to say 'I guess you know that already', but thought better of it.

He put his hands on the file, slowly opened it, and said, "I suppose you're wondering why you're here, though you may have an inkling. Let me expand a little further and then we can answer a few of your questions. Your uncle, Peter, a long-time colleague of ours, now retired of course, has let us know that you also have a unique gift, that your maternal grandmother had. You have the ability to initiate controlled out-of-body experiences; some call it astral travelling, call it what you may."

I just nodded.

He continued. "It seems you have the extra ability to go back in time. Our Special Services, loyal to 'Queen and Country', have used these abilities from time to time in defence of our liberties."

He leaned back in his chair. That seemed to be the opening that his colleague was waiting for. She seemed a very dour woman, dressed well but in a dull grey. I would say in her late thirties, but her stern looks, mousy hair, stern-looking frown made her look a bit older. Again she spoke with a plummy accent, and I thought she looked and talked to me with a small amount of aggression.

"We have working for us a small group of 'fellow travellers' like yourself, and wonder whether you have sufficient abilities to join them. There may be others, we know not of, who use their gifts in frivolous or nefarious ways, but we take our people very seriously as a matter of principle." Michele leaned forward as she continued. "You are being interviewed by us here at MI6 as your uncle once worked here, but you would be under the umbrella services of MI5 if you joined us. Your uncle tells us that you have honed your abilities since childhood and have strictly followed his advice and never mentioned this outside your family. Is this correct?"

At last I had the chance to say something. "Yes, that's correct. My Uncle Pete has instilled the rule in my brain over and over since I was a small child, and he was always there to help me make sense of it."

Michelle replied, "I didn't imagine that you would have any idea he was involved with us. Since his retirement he has rarely spoken about you."

I confessed, "I never had a clue."

Michele (I couldn't quite remember her name) then attacked again. "You're certain that you kept it secret?"

I confirmed I had.

She continued. "Before we go any further we have to ask if you have any thoughts or ambitions in any other direction, or are you open to us? We would like to see if your abilities are good enough for us. Have you any objection to that?"

She had such a nice way and tone of putting things.

Mr Ambrose came in then with, "We have a small group with similar abilities who work in pairs for different contexts, who are always looking for extra help. If you're willing, I would like you to meet them. They will of course be the team who will have to check that you can do what I believe you can."

I again nodded.

He continued, "This won't be here or today as we have a separate unit for them in Covent Garden. It should only take a short time and assuming it's successful I will make arrangements to meet with you again to discuss the terms of your future here. How does that sound to you?"

"That sounds good to me," I replied.

On that note he stood up to leave the room, turned and said, "Thank you for your time. My colleague Miss Douvrer will give you the rest of the details."

Miss Douvrer then moved her chair to face me and said, "Are you free tomorrow?"

I nodded.

She then picked up the telephone and asked to be put

through to Cloud 10. I heard her get confirmation that tomorrow at two thirty was good. She put the phone down and said, "Okay, let's get going."

She then wrote out the address and a mobile number for a Darryl Harrison who I was to see – the person Mr Ambrose had spoken to.

"Cloud 10 is just off Langley Street and don't be surprised when you arrive at the frontage." She went on, "This time just go straight in and the receptionist will take it further. No further questions," she stated rather than asked.

As it was, I didn't have any, but I took it that she wasn't expecting to answer anyway.

She stood up, shook my hand hurriedly and had already pressed for the door to be opened before I had time to blink. It did immediately, and the same woman as before 'technically' showed me to the door. Before I had a chance to gather my thoughts, I found myself back on the train to Guildford with not a clue what to expect tomorrow.

Chapter 2

Tomorrow came as it usually does.

Following the same travelling pattern, but this time getting off the tube at Covent Garden, I soon found myself in a pedestrianised small square just off Langley Street in front of a substantial four-storey modern smoked-glass office block (at least it seemed all glass). The building fit perfectly in its surrounding. The only place on the ground floor that looked to have access was on the right-hand side of the office block, where a full-sized smoked (bronze) glass window was positioned adjacent to a door. I checked and could see I had the correct number and looked again at the fascia – CLOUD 10.

Walking towards it I could see behind the main window. There was a female receptionist at work, another computer, a couple of easy chairs and the usual office paraphernalia for the size of office – average.

With only slight reservation, I double checked the time – perfect. Then walked towards the frontage, stopping before the main window to read the company title to see if I could make any sense from it…

CLOUD 10
Cloud Support Resource
Strictly by Appointment ONLY

And below listed a telephone number and email address.

That helped a lot. I hadn't a clue what any of it meant but I was sure that would apply to most of the population.

The receptionist didn't look up until I moved to the door and pressed the buzzer. She then looked up, checked the clock on the wall, left her desk and stood before me to get a good look at my 'Press Pass', then touched a button to her left. The door opened, she moved slightly back to let me in and greeted me with: "That's good timing," and a smile. So far so good, I thought.

I stepped in; at least it was carpeted here. The door closed automatically behind me. Once I was in, but before I'd had any time to glance around, she moved and opened an inner door and shouted up the stairs.

"Darryl, your appointment's here."

A few seconds later, bounding down the stairs and through the door and completely unexpected came... The Darryl Harrison.

Yesterday had obviously tainted my view of the 'Services' so when this casually dressed good-looking young (about thirty) guy looking every inch 'a media icon' came through the door I was completely flabbergasted. My eyes must have almost exploded out of my head because he started laughing.

"Not what you were expecting, eh?"

Composing myself as best I could, I replied, "Not after yesterday."

"Come on up. I've got a couple more people for you to meet."

I followed like a lost puppy…

Through the door I could see a central staircase leading up to the top of the building, but we carried on and turned left into what looked like a company boardroom, with a window at the far end. Taking up most of the room was a large boardroom table and chairs, and sitting waiting were a friendly looking man and woman who seemed quite keen to see me, at least I hoped so after yesterday.

Darryl introduced them. "These are the company geeks, Kim and Henry."

They both looked slightly embarrassed at the obviously quite old joke

"I'll let you work out who's who. I'm the one in charge," he said with a little glee.

I'd caught his style of management right from the start and had a feeling nothing was going to change. I could sense already that maybe you could have a little too much of him some days.

Both Kim and Henry leaned forward and shook my hand with a brief hello.

I leaned across to meet them halfway and said, "I'm Lucy Firmin. Hello."

They sat together on one side of the table; Darryl took the head chair with me to his left. We sat and Darryl seemed to calm down a little and continued.

"Lucy, it's come to our attention that you may have the ability that we search for at this office. Before I expand on the role we undertake here, we would need to see a small demonstration from you. Is that okay with you?"

Neither Kim nor Henry added anything to that but just nodded and, for just a second, as there was a small pause, I thought the meeting had ended. However, Darryl carried on.

"We don't want to put you under any pressure per se, but it's our usual policy to go straight in and see what develops. Is it a bit early in the day for you? Are you a morning or an afternoon person?"

I wasn't sure if that was a joke or not; the shape of things to come, maybe. I answered as casually as possible "Now's fine."

Following that he said, "Kim, I wonder if you wouldn't mind showing Lucy to the sleep area?"

At that, everyone rose and dispersed to the corridor. Darryl wished me luck and with that bounded up the stairs. Henry had already disappeared and Kim showed me up the staircase, in the direction of Darryl, and up the next staircase to a room on the left-hand side. What I had been expecting I don't know, but it wasn't a large dormitory with three beds either side in a lengthways system. Not beds as such but platforms suspended out from the wall, a couple of feet off the ground, no legs but a small table and a chair positioned near each. They looked comfortable and were made I think from leather with just a pillow.

Kim told me I needn't take my shoes off, but I must have seemed a bit hesitant, which she picked up on.

"Why don't we pop down to the kitchen and have a cup of tea?"

Great idea, I thought. "Thanks Kim, I think I need to relax a bit."

Down we went again.

Chapter 3

It was another quiet morning for Neil Bland.

He sat in his usual chair in his lounge looking out of his front window onto the footpath. Not an unusual view, just young children walking on the other side of the wall beyond his small front garden, heading to school, laughing and playing. The sight of them always had the same satisfying effect on him; it was not their happiness or love of life, but the pleasure of knowing that for most of them this state was only temporary, and that a lot of them would lead miserable lives. It took a certain kind of person to get satisfaction from such things, and he was that person.

Now in his late twenties, Neil was very average to look at, with sandy-coloured shortish hair and maybe just too many freckles. All his life, at least how he remembered it, he had suffered from being the boy on the outside and he wasn't wrong. He had been singled out for teasing and ridicule as long as he could remember. It had been his first and worst mistake to tell his class-mates about his dreamworld. Of course nobody had believed him. Unfortunately, he'd had no 'Uncle Pete' to help and guide him through these difficult times, so he had just become the school 'oddball', and being the 'oddball' at school was tantamount to continual teasing and contempt.

As the years moved on, nothing improved, the damage had been done. When he started university, he was unfortunate enough to be joined by some of the kids from of his school year, so the ridicule continued, only this time even worse. He'd kept quiet for years about his dreamworld activities, but the memories remained, although faded. With the other students, the word went around the campus slowly at first, but soon grew, and the jokes continued .

The school children had now all passed, but he remained fixed to the chair, his mind struggling to accept yesterday's failure when he had tried unsuccessfully to dream himself into the SIS building by the Thames.

This was his first ever major setback.

In the last few years, he had managed to get anywhere he wanted to. Investment banks, many finance companies and the like. It had all been a breeze.

His main source for access and planning had been a well thought out plan to join a large office cleaning company that he knew had contracts in the main City of London. He joined as a lowly cleaner and in fact still worked for them, albeit less hours. This job had granted him access to all areas of many companies and, much to his disbelief, a girlfriend. Once he had the lay of the land in these companies it was relatively easy for him to return late in the day or evening, and this on a regular basis gave him enough knowledge to play the stock market and be ahead of some takeover bids – true inside information. His term for it: 'going fishing'.

With that mix of information, Neil had become a wealthy man. He'd started with small sums, and gradually his investments had increased and his finances had grown well enough to move from a shared house (still no real friends but a few more acquaintances) to a small modernised terraced house in Wood Green – a long way from Derby.

Perfect and nondescript house and area.

Due to his nefarious but successful habits over the last few years, he should have been quite a happy man, but he knew himself well enough to realise that any real pleasure for him was only gained by a challenge and the achievement that goes with a success. He hated losing with a vengeance and that thought brought him back to rethink yesterday.

The problem it seemed to him was not that easy to overcome, as no matter where he looked – magazines, the internet, you name it, he'd tried it – he was unable to find any internal details or plans of the SIS building, and without that knowledge he was sunk. He had sat in his car in a nearby multistorey car park and dozed throughout the afternoon without any success. One of the bonuses of his cleaning work was the very early starts on some days, so a little doze in the afternoon was not difficult. To travel, he thought, you must have a destination, and that was what he lacked.

This was his first major setback and he didn't like it.

He must find a way to see a plan of the building. It was a problem he hadn't come across before.

Think alternative, he told himself, and he tried. Just as he was about to give up, it came to him.

He had one slim lead...

Lefty.

Chapter 4

Kim opened the door to the 'kitchen'. I'd seen many things described as a kitchen but this wasn't one of them. A small area to the right had a kitchen area with a sink and a few base and wall cupboards, work tops, coffee machine and a microwave, overshadowed by a large, American-style double-doored refrigerator.

The remainder of the room was opulently furnished with small tables and chairs, and some comfy looking sofas and coffee tables, newspapers, magazines and coffee cups. Fully carpeted, with what looked like original abstract paintings. The receptionist, Nikki, I learned later, followed us in, and scampering past our legs, jumping onto what seemed like its favourite spot, was a very beautiful golden spaniel.

Again, further amazement. What sort of office was this?

Kim laughed at my expression and said, "Don't worry, Lucy, it's usually worse than this. This is a good day."

I shrugged in amazement.

Kim then turned saying, "You've already met Nikki,

our girl on the front line."

Nikki smiled and pointed. "Hi, Lucy, this is our office dog, Morry. I hope you like dogs."

Kim chimed in, "Darryl has an unorthodox way of running things; it might look at first sight a bit casual, but it's quite the reverse. We are a computer company operating and offering our digital and cloud services to those who need them, and do in fact have a number of clients for whom we can do no wrong."

At this, Nikki raised her eyes and chuckled.

"Enough of this," said Kim, "We'll give you the complete works later, I expect you came into the front office without noticing the dog basket behind Nikki's seat. Probably Morry had been taken out for a walk. There's no shortage of volunteers."

I had warmed to Kim, attractive-looking, well dressed (her office wear looked expensive), brown, perfectly trimmed hair. I made a note-to-self to find out where she got her hair done.

"Tea or coffee?"

I pointed to the coffee machine and added, "One sugar, please," and we sat down at a table near the sofas. Nikki took her tea, ginger, I noticed, and went back to the front office.

I wondered how many times Kim had done this before, perhaps she was a natural, as with her easy-going attitude she soon had me relaxed. She let me know she'd worked here for about five years after getting transferred (she didn't say where from) having heard the odd funny story about the branch. She'd been looking for a change from the regimentation that she'd got used to.

"Any questions pertinent to now?" she added.

"I've seen the dorm room. Is that where I go for my doze? And if I manage to 'travel' what's the plan as it all seems a little vague?"

"You've no worries, just relax, if you can. If you're successful and manage it, just try and appear in either Darryl's room or mine – you know where both those are – when you can. We've both got lots to do there for the next hour. Just a short time will suffice, just make sure you're noticed. Is that clear or is there anything else?"

I confirmed all clear and added, "When would you like me to try?"

At that, Morry moved to Kim, who couldn't resist giving him a stroke saying, "It was Darryl's idea to adopt him; he says it helps to keep things calm, having a dog around. Though he mostly hangs out with Nikki; she takes him home with her at night. You probably haven't got Darryl's name joke, have you? Morry is a shortened version of Moriarty, the villain in Sherlock Holmes. Only Darryl would think of that."

At that we left and started up the stairs. I couldn't help smiling, thinking of Darryl and his jokes as we went up the stairs, but my mind soon turned to other things. There was such a lot to think about.

As I parted ways with Kim I called out and asked, "Are they anyone's beds in particular or shall I just choose one?"

"Take whichever one feels right. There's a dimmer switch on the wall. I'll leave you to it."

I had a mind like a swarm of bees with all that had happened in the last half an hour. How they expected me to perform for them, I didn't know.

I chose a bed, put my handbag on the table and jacket on a peg, lay down, switched my phone off, dimmed the lights and hoped for the best. The room was completely soundproof with nothing to distract me – absolutely perfect – but twenty minutes later, I was as awake as when I started. I thought I'd give it a little bit longer, and just as I thought I was about to doze, I completely woke up. I felt a bit anxious about their reaction but really there was no point in hanging around, so I stood up, grabbed my bag and jacket, left the room and went across the corridor, checked which was Kim's door, knocked and went in.

She looked hard at work on her computer, head-phones on and concentrating.

She looked at me as I shook my head and with a smile said, "I'm not surprised to see you, with the morning you've had, all the stimulation. I would have been surprised if you had managed it. Go down to the kitchen, have a read of the mags. It'll soon be lunch and we can go out and get a bite to eat and you can try later."

Relieved was the word that came to mind "Thanks, Kim. I didn't know how you'd react. I felt I'd let you down, I don't want everyone to think I'm a fraud."

"No problem, really. That's what I was expecting."

With that I left the room, wandered down to the kitchen, picked up a magazine and tried to clear my mind. Before long the door opened and Kim came in.

"Let's get out of here before everyone else comes in," she said. "I know a little café nearby where we can get a sandwich or something."

And that's what we did.

In the café Kim kept off the subject of the office and I found out she was married (to Martin), no children yet, but hoping, and lived in Hemel Hempstead. She asked about me and I gave her a general background of my life as basically that was all I had. School, university, friends and family.

She laughed and said, "Things are about to change for you."

That was what I remembered most about the lunch.

General chit chat exhausted, lunch over, we were soon taking the short walk back to the office.

When we got back to the office, Nikki was nowhere to be seen and I was surprised when Kim put her thumb onto a pad beneath the buzzer and the door opened. So much for my previous powers of observation. We were careful not to let Morry out as he was in his basket, but he just lifted his head, looked at Kim and went back to sleep. Door safely closed, we went through and closed the inner door.

Kim motioned to the left saying, "Toilets, if you need them."

"Thanks, yes I do."

She waited patiently for my exit and up the stairs we went. I could hear quite a lot of noise coming from the right; lunch time for everyone it seemed. Another set of stairs then she went right and I motioned to her that I was going left – another try.

This time I felt quite familiar in the dorm and made myself comfortable in my 'usual spot'.

I was relaxed and after a short time, felt in my 'zone' and dozed off.

What should I do?

I thought about going to Kim's office but decided to impress them all and make my 'entrance' in the kitchen while they were on their break. I decided the wall by the window would make the greatest impact. So off I went...

Empty, or so I thought.

The next second, Morry had leaped off the sofa and stood in front of me barking. Everything happened as in slow motion. The door opened and in came a small crowd to see what the noise was all about. A couple of people I didn't know came first, followed by Kim and Darryl. They turned as if choreographed. Looked straight at me... and started to clap.

I'd passed the test.

On that high, I returned instantly to my body, opened my eyes, and with a large grin started towards the door, when Kim and Darryl burst in.

"Mission accomplished," said Darryl.

"Absolutely!", Kim followed with and then, "Lucy, well done. Welcome to the team. You're just what we need. Darryl, let Mr Ambrose know."

With a smile on his face, off he went. Kim sat down opposite me. I returned to my position and sat on the bed facing her.

She continued, "Now it all starts for you, Lucy. You'll need to go back and see Mr Ambrose as soon as we can set things up, later this week, I'm sure. He'll give you all the details of employment and terms, if you still want to join us?"

"Who wouldn't want to?" I spluttered, and we stood up together to leave the room.

As we did, she put her arm across my shoulder and said, "I just know you're going to have the time of your life."

I started down the stairs and from every direction, or so it seemed, I heard a chorus of "well done" "see you soon" and "congratulations".

Kim came with me to the front office where Nikki sat with an even larger grin on her face and said, "Lucky for you, Morry was there."

I couldn't have agreed more and went across to his basket and gave him a little pat on his head. "Thanks Morry,"

*

It all happened so quickly after that.

The next day I was back in the SIS building, sitting in front of Mr Ambrose and Miss Douvrer.

Mr Ambrose started. "Lucy, I offer you my sincere congratulations. They are a great team to join, and I can guarantee the work there is extraordinarily interesting and we feel you are absolutely perfect for it."

Miss Douvrer agreed with just a, "Well done, Lucy,

welcome to the firm."

Mr Ambrose got up to leave saying, "I'll leave Michele to go through the paperwork with you and once again congratulations to you."

"Thank you very much," was all I could come up with.

Miss Douvrer outlined the financial package (wow). I tried not to blink too much.

She then asked me to sign the contract and also the Official Secrets Act and enquired, "Are you happy to start Monday as we have lots to show you, lots for you to learn and the whole team for you to meet. I would just mention that although you interviewed at the MI6 building, due to your uncle, you will in fact be working under the auspices of MI5."

"I can't wait," was the best I could come up with.

She stood. It was obviously time to leave. She shook my hand and said, "Cloud 10, Monday morning at nine thirty."

Chapter 5

Daniel sat at his workstation along with his colleagues in a large open office in New Scotland Yard, trying to solve an internet issue and get into a people smuggler's personal account.

From the one enclosed office on his floor came a shout "Dan, are you there?"

Daniel stood up.

The superintendent shouted, "The commissioner wants to see you again. Now."

He closed down his computer and with very little enthusiasm – he'd been up there now for so many interviews and meetings – said, "On my way."

Here we go again, for the umpteenth time, he thought.

He left the room. No one bothered to give him a second glance; he'd been going up there for so long that now nobody was remotely interested. Up he went again, knocked on the door.

"Come in, Daniel, and close the door," said the commissioner.

He sensed this time it was different, normally a panel

would subject him to a barrage of questions and situations, but now there was just the chief and a very well dressed officious looking woman. As he went in they both stood up and the commissioner introduced the lady as Commander Douvrer, our liaison. Intriguing, thought Daniel. They shook hands and motioned Daniel to sit as they did.

The commissioner continued, "As you're aware we've been seeking a computer-savvy individual who can assist the Special Service in an unorthodox and clandestine operation, that may also assist us at the Met." Commander Douvrer just smiled as the chief continued with, "Commander Douvrer liaises between us at the Met and MI5 and MI6."

She looked him straight in the eye. "Daniel, you know we've been seeking somebody like you. We've interviewed many and you've distinguished yourself. Your degree in computer sciences put you ahead of some of the other applicants, plus we think your demeanour will fit in perfectly with our Cloud 10 unit."

What a remarkable turn of events. He was astonished. "I thought the post was for something unusual, but I had no idea it was with the Secret Service. I'm staggered."

"Fair enough," she said. "We must have got it right as we try to make it as vague as possible. Are you still keen?"

"Absolutely! I'm really sure I'd like to go ahead."

"In that case, before we go any further, I must ask you to read the Official Secrets Act." She passed him the document from her briefcase.

He took his time to read it carefully and signed.

She continued, "You will, for all intents and purposes, still be employed for the time being by the Metropolitan Police Force, but as we progress it's our wish that a transfer across to us will be necessary and when that happens you will find our terms of employment a substantial improvement on your terms here. Shall we say twenty-eight days just to confirm the arrangement works in all our interests?"

He replied, "That sounds perfectly reasonable to me. When is the initial transfer to take place?"

"Well, it's Monday morning now. How long do you think you'll need to pass over your ongoing work?"

Daniel replied, trying to sound positive but not too eager, "I suppose if I pushed it and moved it on to my colleagues, by the end of the day?"

"Okay, nine thirty tomorrow morning it is."

Both wished him the best of luck and that was that.

He went back to his office, looked at all his colleagues with a big cheesy grin and told them that today was his last day.

To say that left them speechless was an understatement, but the short silence was quickly followed by an equal amount of banter: "congratulations" and "traitor", and then question after question.

Something he'd wanted to say his whole life came next. Hardly able to keep a straight face, he was able to use the famous quote, "If I told you, then I'd have to kill you."

Daniel Montgomery was on his way.

Chapter 6

Neil's flash of inspiration had him on a high (which would be most people's normal) and he spent most of the rest of the day thinking about how he should approach Lefty. He knew it would be another eleven or so hours before he could see if Lefty was around, but as it was a Friday, he had high hopes. He needed to get him on his own; a cigarette break outside the pub was his best idea.

What to do for the rest of the day… he hated waiting. He considered cleaning up the house a bit, but he was generally a tidy person, a place for everything and everything in its place was one of his favourite sayings. Also his cleaner was due on Monday and she'd need something to fill her two hours. Reading, TV, or a bit of 'travel'? He wasn't in the mood for any of those. His first thought was the gym, but as it was such a beautiful day he decided to kill a big chunk of time and have a round of golf.

He'd joined Muswell Hill Golf Club a couple of years earlier at nearby Alexandra Palace. He'd taken a few lessons and found it had come quite naturally to him.

He rang the course office and booked a tee time for himself just after lunch. It had a good reputation for food, so he thought he'd have a light lunch there before the round. He'd never particularly taken to any of the other golfers he'd played with but knew enough of them to know that if he turned up, there was usually someone else looking for a playing partner.

He booked a taxi for eleven forty-five, got his clubs ready and put his golf gear on ready to go. He picked up a nearby book he was halfway through, Scandinavian Detective, Harry Hole. It was a slow read, just what he needed.

Lunch came and went, the golf round did the same, and for a change his playing partner was a bit of a character, a plumber who had been let down on a job at the last minute and not one of the usual 'old boys'.

Back home about five o'clock he changed into something more suitable for the evening – trainers, t-shirt, and jeans – checked his emails, grabbed a drink and a sandwich and tried to relax for the next couple of hours. Some chance of that.

Eventually, seven thirty came. He had decided to walk; it was a balmy evening. He usually taxied, but the walk would give him a chance to work out his pitch to Lefty. He knew Lefty usually drank at a couple of pubs on Hornsey High St, or when he was looking for a story with some of the 'arty' types at a pub in Crouch End. Both of the pubs in Hornsey, the Compasses and the Northern, were really good drinking pubs, real ale, as well as great food, but if one was a bit too popular or noisy, stag or hen nights especially, Lefty would drift to the other.

It was about a twenty-minute walk. He'd done it many times; it was not at all interesting. Over the canal and then a series of houses, takeaways, shops, takeaways, offices, takeaways, etc. Not that he had anything against takeaways, as he was a user sometimes, but it was just a rather repetitive route.

He thought he'd try the Northern first; it was the nearest. He knew there was usually a beer drinking set there, through which he'd met 'Lefty' a couple of years ago.

He reminisced as he walked. Nicknamed 'Lefty', Miles Rogerson, a freelance journalist, had written quite a few features for the local area paper, but was always submitting pieces to England's foremost left-wing paper; now and again he succeeded in getting one of his submissions published, but he always wanted more.

His political leanings were slightly to the left of Trotsky, but if anyone was going to help furnish Neil with the information he was seeking, it would be him. Divorced (bitterly) in his mid-thirties and going slightly to seed, he'd had the perfect start: public school, political sciences at university, but as is so often the case, his parents just didn't quite know enough of the 'right' people to get the connections he needed.

A quick look at Lefty's usual spot – he was a creature of habit – confirmed to Neil he was either too early or Lefty was at the Compasses. There was also no sign of his other band of buddies – Ray, a local builder, surname

Barrett, who drove his van proudly with the name Barrett's Builders on the side, trying to infringe on one of England's biggest builders, or Greig, failed music band member but successful session musician. They weren't his only two drinking mates but were the two most consistent.

Neil thought of having a quick pint in case he was a bit early but instead decided to go straight to the Compasses; he could always come back. Just a short walk across the road and success. Standing at the bar with a couple of guys that Neil only knew slightly was Lefty, deep in conversation.

Up to the bar he went as Lefty turned with a smile, "Same again, Neil, thanks."

Neil asked his two mates if they wanted another couple of pints but they both declined.

"I only popped in on my way home. 'Her indoors' will be goin' off the deep end," said one of them, to the usual bar laughter. They said their goodbyes and Neil took their place.

The two drinks arrived. Neil saw his moment and started to speak… just as Greig walked in.

"Better make that another pint, Neil," said Lefty who had also seen Greig.

"Same as usual please, Neil," said Greig, taking his jacket off. "I thought you'd be in here rather than risk another hen night."

Neil nodded.

The pint came as Greig shifted through the crowd and took the other seat. "Cheers, Neil!"

Like most pubs in London, the Compasses had been tastefully modernised, keeping the best of the character of an old London pub, yet making it a comfortable place to eat and drink. It had an extensive menu, plenty of seats, chairs and tables, a good area for those who liked to drink at the bar, a small outdoor garden, but differently to other locals, it also had a small stage in one corner with an open area in front for a band or singer. One night a week they had a resident band; sometimes Greig would sit in and play guitar with them. Another night, they would host an open mic – best avoided. In the fairly recent past, they'd had the odd comedian, but that seemed to have gone out of fashion.

Taking the first drink to the sound of "cheers", Greig followed by saying, "What a day I've had. I've had an all-day session with the latest wannabee pop stars; none could play an instrument properly and I wouldn't wish their singing on my worst enemy – well, maybe I would!"

Neil followed, "That's just the way it is nowadays, Greig, But you know, by the time the record comes out, it'll be sweetness and light."

"Probably true," said Lefty.

The conversation continued in this manner and drifted through the 'usuals', same old; moving on to TV, rubbish; football, not what it was; women, not what they were, and so on. Just a normal night.

Neil wondered if it would go on like this forever. He was getting hugely frustrated but holding it in.

After about an hour, Greig said, "That's it for me, got an early start and must keep my fingers knowing what

44

my brain wants them to do."

He said his goodbyes and at last Neil had Lefty to himself who said, "I'm off outside for a cigarette."

Neil said he'd come with him as he had something to talk to him about. They asked the barman to look after their seats and beer and off they went.

They went outside and Neil motioned to a table in a quiet corner away from the few other people out there. It was less of a garden, more of a smoking area, so not so crowded. Lefty noticed Neil had gone both serious and nervous and because of that, so had he. He had a feeling that he didn't want to hear what was coming.

They moved towards quiet corner seats. There were a few others out in the warmth, but mainly other smokers. Lefty took out a cigarette. He knew Neil didn't smoke and couldn't help but notice Neil had gone quiet and pensive.

"Are you okay, you look a bit worried?"

"I don't really know how to start, but I do have something to tell you, but if and when I do, I've got a feeling that you'll think I'm either mad or living in a delusional fantasy world."

Lefty looked at him, puzzled, but his reporter training kicked in, and he said nothing, motioning for Neil to carry on.

"What I'm going to tell you I haven't told a single soul in my life, but you're the only person I can think of that might be able to help."

Lefty stopped the smart remark on the tip of his tongue.

"Since we've met you've always been on the lookout for a great story and frustrated that they've always passed you by."

Lefty agreed.

"What if I told you that I think between the two of us we could cause a fair amount of trouble and it would be completely legal?"

"Carry on," said Lefty, thinking the worst of the worst, and how he could get back to the bar without upsetting Neil.

"I don't think you'll believe a word I say unless I prove it to you without a shadow of a doubt by tomorrow evening. Would you accept it might be true?"

"It depends, I suppose, on what you're going to tell me."

Neil, now in his stride, carried on. "It will be a life-changing moment for you. I'm completely serious."

Yeah, right, thought Lefty.

"It can help both of us, you've no idea. Just trust me on this one…"

"Fair enough," he replied cautiously.

Neil carried on with his thought-out pitch. "Okay, here's what we'll do. I need to see where you live and don't panic, just the kitchen. Tonight, leave the kitchen light on and put a piece of paper on a worktop or table, easily seen, with five or six random numbers on. Close all curtains or blinds, double lock all the doors to make sure nobody could get in or see the numbers. Tomorrow night, we'll meet back here and I'll tell you the number."

Lefty looked baffled and worried.

"Don't ask me anything else now, just do it, and we'll meet here tomorrow. It'll be worth your while, honestly."

They went inside, finished their beers in silence, Neil phoned for a taxi and went straight to Lefty's house (pretty impressive) in Crouch End. Neil asked the driver to wait for a couple of minutes.

Neil had a quick look at the kitchen, remembered the location of the house and said, "That's all I need. Do you want a lift back to the pub?"

Lefty didn't, saying, "No, don't need to go back, I've got an early start tomorrow, might have a lead on a story. Can we meet around seven tomorrow night as I've arranged to meet a couple of guys at the Small Mercies." On most weekends, Lefty drank in a couple of pubs in Crouch End. Known there as Miles, it was quite a different 'upmarket arty' set.

With that, they said their goodbyes, and Neil got back in the cab and went home to Wood Green.

Lefty had been bemused at first, but as the night closed in, he started to feel worried and uneasy. What had he let himself into? Neil, he thought, was only a cleaner; a failed womaniser, well, not lately, but he wondered what Tricia thought of him. He was a right miserable git nearly all the time. What could he possibly do for me, he wondered? He must be on drugs or something.

Still shaking his head, he sat and watched some TV, well, looked towards the TV, flabbergasted that he could have fallen for such a stupid story. Must be a prank set up by one of his competitors, he thought. He needed to trick Neil, whatever his plan. Instead of a number, he wrote: 'Do you think I'm a pillock, 007?' and went to bed, sleeping fitfully... thank you, Neil.

Neil went home and set the alarm for three a.m. Awake at the first ring, he went downstairs to his favourite dozing chair in the lounge, drifted off, and within seconds was in Lefty's kitchen, looking down on the paper and smiling – trust Lefty.

Memorising the note he instantly returned himself to his chair, wrote it down, went to bed and fell straight to sleep – like clockwork.

The day couldn't go quick enough for Neil. He was due to see his girlfriend Tricia in the afternoon and evening. She came round early afternoon and they decided to go to Camden Market and then for a walk along Regent's Canal and up Primrose Hill, always a nice afternoon on a sunny day. Neil had arranged to meet Lefty at seven p.m. at the Compasses and had a reservation at the Northern for a meal with Tricia at eight p.m. Tricia had fallen for Neil's tousled looks, and what she thought was his wicked sense of cruel humour, or so she thought.

In reality, most of his comments weren't meant by him to be funny, but she took them as being ironic. They'd met when both of them were on a fairly long-term contract at a large office block and somehow Neil had always made her laugh, unlike most of her previous boyfriends. She was a petite and quite attractive brunette in her mid-twenties and going nowhere. And Neil seemed a good guy to hitch along with, for the time being, which was her way.

She was happy Neil went off early; it gave her a

chance to change and dress up a bit. She told him she'd get a cab to be there just before eight.

It all seemed a perfect plan for a good night out, and so it turned out to be.

Neil arrived at the Compasses at seven p.m. as planned. Lefty was already on his favourite bar stool, beer in hand, as Neil sat down with the comment, "Not broken into then."

Lefty shook his head with a wry smile. Neil then made an overacting pretence to look through his pockets for the sheet of paper, muttering under his breath about being unable to find it.

"So, you think I'm a pillock do you, 006?"

The look on Lefty's face should have been preserved for posterity.

"What!" he spluttered. "How did you do that?"

"When I said I would change your life, I meant it."

"How?"

Neil was still laughing but then went a little more serious "Has that caught your attention? Do you really want to know, and if I tell you, will you believe me?"

Lefty could only nod.

"Remember what I said last night? You must never tell a living soul or write anything down. This must be our secret. If we work together, between us we can cause the establishment a fair amount of trouble, we can make waves, real waves."

A moment of silence then Lefty said, "Okay Neil, I'm a believer."

Neil took another sip of beer, moved towards him and

said quietly, "I'll explain it slowly and carefully. First, let me say, believe it or not, I am a very wealthy man and I have used my wealth to buy my house for cash and have many investments bringing in a nice lot of dividends. I initially used my gift for financial gain but now feel I'd like to move to new territories, and I think we can help each other. I assume in the back of your mind you're thinking, but he's only a cleaner, but by just being a cleaner, I was able to get easy access to places I could only have dreamed of, places that could change my life, and they did: banks, investment companies, top offices – you name it, I could get there. The information I gleaned has enabled me to start very small on the stock market, increasing amounts as time went on until where I am now, and all on the face of it, perfectly legal."

If Lefty's jaw could have sunk any further, it would have been on the floor.

Neil continued, "Serious question, Lefty, have you ever had what is known as a lucid dream? When you somehow know in your dream that it is a dream, and you can alter the outcome?"

Lefty thought and answered, "I've probably had one or two. Why?"

"Well, it's not that common for people to have them, but they do occur regularly to some, apparently." Neil stopped for another drink. "Well, you must promise again, although I don't believe anyone would believe, but that's not the point, when I tell you."

"Okay," said Lefty, "I absolutely promise."

"I can have lucid dreams at will, and not only that, I

have the ability to situate my dream wherever I want, and to sort of travel to that location, via the dream. That's why I could dream myself into your kitchen in the middle of the night, look at the message and return instantly back to my body, sleeping in my chair." Another drink, he needed it. "I'm not physically there, but some part of me is. I don't understand it, but I have been able to do it for as long as I can remember. My parents just thought I was making it up and, in the end, I just let them believe that. I've made a small fortune looking at trading accounts as I've already told you, but I want to do more and between us I think we could do it. I've always found you a fairly straight guy, on the side of truth, and I reckon we could make a great partnership. What do you think?"

"I need another drink, that's what I think."

Neil got the drink.

"Are you serious, Neil? Can you really do this?"

"As long as I have a plan of the room, or have been there before, I can do it for just over ten minutes, thirteen minutes to be exact, and I need to be very careful to make sure I am out of sight before I disappear." Neil could sense that, quite understandably, Lefty was still a bit unsure. "I'll tell you what, why don't I give you a demonstration? Something a bit tricky, say a print room or something. I have a wardrobe of clothes so I always look the part."

Lefty's jaw had reasserted itself in the correct place by now, and he said, "Can you really do this, Neil?"

"I really can, how do you think a cleaner got the

money to buy a house in cash on stocks and shares?"

"Are you the only person who can do this. Have you ever come across anyone else?"

"Not a single person ever, nor have I ever read about it, but then again, I probably wouldn't know as they'd just look like everyone else."

Lefty saw his life changing in front of him and held out his hand which Neil took and said, "You've got a deal, partner, with one proviso. Drop the Lefty, my friends call me Miles." He paused, then added, "Why me, Neil?"

"Well, as I said before, I think you're straight and I knew you knew people I would never meet, connections I could only dream of. I had my first failure this week, when I tried to get into the SIS building on the South Bank, but I needed some internal plans and tried everywhere with no success."

"That's because they've all been destroyed for security reasons."

"See, Lefty, sorry, Miles, that's why I came to you, you know things I could only dream of knowing."

"You're probably right there, Neil."

"So we're on the same page here, Miles?"

"Too right we are," said Miles, thinking his ship has just come in.

"Sorry to cut it short, it'll give you time to digest it, but I've got to meet Tricia over the road at eight o'clock. She thinks I'm here quoting on a private job. Think about another task for me."

They swapped phone numbers, agreeing to never

mention anything on the phone. They arranged to meet on Monday night at seven. Neil left the bar and left Miles staring into the middle distance before leaving to join his other friends. He felt as if he'd had ten pints; he could barely feel his feet on the floor.

Chapter 7

Monday morning train to London. A bit early for me, but I was sure I'd get used to it. The coffee helped, and the rhythm of the rails (nice title for a book) set me musing on the last few days.

What days they'd been.

Mum and Dad had been very pleased with my 'computer job' in London. My brother Ian couldn't quite believe it, how quickly it had happened after the time it had taken for him to get into banking.

I explained that most media digital companies were looking to expand and improve their image and were keen to encourage more women with a flair for computers and maths to work in the field. There were an awful lot of start-up companies who wanted to ensure that their company was made up of a diverse group and not just a roomful of male geeks and nerds. I told him I was going to be well trained, and that this job could be a steppingstone to more interesting areas of work. I dropped some further words I'd rehearsed: creatives, analysts, insight consultants.

It seemed to work, and in the end, encouraged by my

parents, he went with it.

I'd also taken the time to visit Uncle Pete for the first time in years. We talked for hours, and he recalled all sorts of escapades and anecdotes from his sister Sylvie's life; my grandmother had used her gift for all sorts of things over the years. He knew the people I'd met at the SIS well, though he didn't elaborate on his previous line of work, and I didn't ask.

All in all, it had been a lovely afternoon.

My thoughts of the weekend stopped suddenly as the train pulled into Waterloo. I wondered if every journey would go as quickly. Probably not. It was a quick trip on the Northern Line to Leicester Square, then a short walk, and before I knew it, it was nine twenty and I was looking through the window of Cloud 10. Nikki noticed straightaway, got up and let me in. I suddenly realised what actors meant when they said they had 'first-night nerves'. Why was I so anxious?

Nikki stood by the door. "Morning, Lucy. Let me show you the 'tradesman's entrance' so you know where to go next time. Can't have you using the layman's door every day."

We walked around to what I thought was the back of the building but was in fact the front. As we walked, Nikki, sensing my apprehension, asked me a series of questions about my weekend, travel etc., to try and calm my buzzing mind.

At the front of the building, in the centre, was the entrance to the two companies that used the building, the other being a music publisher. Once inside the smaller foyer, Nikki went to the left door, put in the first keycode and opened the door to an inner hall with a door marked Cloud 10.

"Always use this entrance; there are so many people using this door that it gives us a sense of anonymity." She pressed the keypad – 1610 I noticed this time – and at the same time pressed her thumb beneath. The door opened automatically and right in front of my eyes was a glass lift.

How had I not noticed it before?

She saw the look on my face. "You don't think we walk up and down those stairs every day, do you? I'll let Darryl know you're here."

We took the lift to the first floor and at Darryl's door, she knocked quickly, and put her head round the door.

"Darryl, I just thought I'd let you know that Lucy has arrived."

He didn't get up, but I heard him say, "Great, show her the ropes, but remember, Daniel is starting tomorrow, so just keep it general otherwise we'll have to go through the whole thing again. We'll do that with Henry, the full 'ins and outs' of the procedures once we've given Daniel the tour."

I followed Nikki down to the kitchen for a coffee and to meet up with Kim.

Once removed to the kitchen, waiting for Kim, I wondered what everybody else called this room. 'Kitchen' was not a good description.

"Nikki, I can't believe that you all call this room the kitchen. What's it's called by everyone here?"

She laughed. "We call it 'the galley', named by Darryl, because he likes to think of himself as a bit of a boating man."

We sorted out drinks and moved to a comfortable spot, sitting in opposite chairs. I took my jacket off and settled down. I had the feeling I was in for a bit of a session, and I wasn't proved wrong.

"Okay, now you're here, there is quite a lot to go through. While we're on names of rooms, my front office is called 'the front', as it is in the front and also, as you know, we operate the building as a computer company, so it works to camouflage what we really do. However, we do have computer clients as Henry will explain tomorrow. I'm going to go through some of the general office procedures today and how things work overall. As I just mentioned, Henry and I run the computer side of things and help out when needed on your side." She took another drink – in fact we both did – and continued, "You may have just gathered that we have another member of staff joining tomorrow, a Detective Inspector Daniel Montgomery from New Scotland Yard, but he will lose his rank as, technically, he has now left the police and he will be your 'partner in crime'."

She could see I looked extremely puzzled.

"Don't worry, all will be explained. You can imagine how it will be for him; he hasn't a clue about any of this. I'm only going to touch on the work you'll be doing today but now's a good time to let you know that we have another word to describe your gift. It's quite unusual but I think it works very well. What you achieve in your dream travels is a higher form of lucid dreaming. The ordinary version is quite common; for you it's like a leap into the dark or past. A previous dreamer, who left to start a family, coined the term 'leaping', so the sleeping area is known as 'the leap' and when you are on a 'leap' we call it 'to leap'. A lot quicker to say and if anyone overhears it just sounds harmless."

I laughed. "Nothing surprises me here, but that's a good idea. I must remember it."

"Oh, I'm sure you will, and by the way the beds are called 'hangers'."

That I could understand.

She continued "Our leapers are all assigned to different tasks, and currently we only have three leapers, including yourself. Each leaper works in conjunction with a non-leaping partner. You will work alongside, but not with, the other two. You'll meet them shortly. All fairly clear so far?"

I nodded again. "I think it's all sunk in so far."

"You'll work alongside Daniel on unsolved current cases. We have another pair, Grace, who leaps, and Hilton, who back-ups; they protect the royal family. We also have one more leaper called Jamal, known here as Jay, who works on terrorism, and we are in the process of recruiting a partner for him."

At that point Kim walked into the galley (got that one) and came to join us.

"It's a lot to take in all in one go," she remarked sympathetically. "How's it going?"

Not wanting to upset Nikki, I confidently said, "I

think it's going pretty well. Nikki has explained some of the general background and I guess as the day goes on more will become clear."

Nikki said, "I'm almost done now. We'll do a full tour in a minute. We are holding back on a bit of information but that's only because of Daniel joining tomorrow and for him it's going to be like stepping into a parallel universe. He'll probably be a complete disbeliever and I expect he'll need us to put on a little show for him."

Kim said to Nikki, "It's okay, Nikki, I'll do the rest of the tour. You go back to the office, probably time for Morry's walk."

"Yeah, he'll probably need a short one. Off to Phoenix Gardens again, I suppose."

With that she left the galley and Kim beckoned me to follow. We walked directly opposite into another large office, divided into two. Both offices had their own doors and were set out in the same format – large desk area with two chairs plus an easy chair, I guessed for clients. Both had the usual computers and paraphernalia. I was pleased to see something that looked a bit dated – a filing cabinet. I wasn't expecting that.

Kim explained the rooms. "These two rooms are only for the use of Henry and Nikki and their visiting Cloud clients. You might be surprised by how much genuine Cloud business we actually pick up."

I asked, "What do you actually do for them?"

"I'll tell you what, Lucy, let me show you an extract from one of our pamphlets."

She looked through a drawer and passed it to me, just

a single A5 sheet. Beneath the heading it read:

Helping businesses meet the increasing demands of today's world by aiding their digital transformation and movement to the cloud.

I must have looked as brainless as I felt after reading it. I had no idea what any of it meant.

Reading my expression, Kim said, "Don't ask me either, I haven't a clue, well, a small inkling. Probably all you need to know is data protection."

"Good enough," I said, and we left it at that.

"Henry is a computer 'whizz' and has taught Nikki enough that she can now help him with the more mundane aspects of the job. It takes a bit of pressure off him, not that he gets under pressure, I'll introduce him to you later."

We moved up to the first floor where she pointed again to Darryl's office and moved along to the next windowless room, which she introduced as 'wardrobe'.

"This is fitted with hanging space where we have, over the years, collected and been offered full sets of clothes and shoes, from the 1970s onwards. These are for you leapers, to make sure you fit in with the time period and don't stand out as different. There are also a section of good period-looking watches with totally modern workings, so you will always have an accurate timepiece."

It was impressive and I said so.

Across the hall were another couple of doors which

led to one double-sized office and one single. Kim continued the tour. "These are where you'll actually work with Daniel. You're unlikely to all be working in here at the same time. The other leapers rarely work set hours and I expect as time goes by it will be the same for you. One of these desks will be allocated to you and any bits and pieces you want to bring in, that's fine."

We closed the doors and left for the next floor.

Kim said, "You know this floor already. I have an office across there and so does Henry. He'll be back soon, and I'll introduce you, and of course this is the room with the hangers in." She opened the door to the room I already knew well.

We then headed up to the top floor, where I'd never been. There were four doors which seemed to be for identical-sized rooms.

"Let's go in one," she said. "They are all identical and the floor is just known to us as 'upstairs'. Any preference?"

"Any will do."

She opened the nearest door and in we went... again total surprise – a fully fitted-out bedroom complete with bathroom facilities. Basically a hotel with dark windows.

"Regrettably, Lucy, not all your leaps will be during a nine to five day; quite a lot will be out of hours, mostly in the evenings and unfortunately some during the night."

This didn't surprise me at all. I wasn't expecting anything else, but I wasn't ready for their professionalism – I should have been.

"In the case of late evenings or early hours leaps, it's

sometimes opportune for you to just stay on. These rooms should suffice for your needs. We also have a strict rule that partners to the leapers must stay on as well. It doesn't happen very often, and I hope it won't for you, but occasionally a leaper may return after having witnessed something unexpected, in a distressed state. It's rare; usually they just have important information to pass on immediately."

I picked up on the 'distressed state'. "What do you mean exactly by distressed state, Kim? I don't like the sound of that."

"It's very rare, Lucy. Just occasionally you may hear something or see something that you might find upsetting, for example, a car accident. It happens more to Jay, as he's dealing with terrorism; he may hear of a plot to kill someone, or worse. Let's hope nothing like that happens to you. It's very unlikely, honestly, as you're involved with crime cases and picking up useful information that will only be of interest to the police."

I wasn't totally convinced, but at this stage, what did I know.

Kim carried on, "Daniel will pass that information on and as far as the police are concerned it would be in the form of a tip-off, so nobody could ever trace it back to us."

We re-entered the corridor, turning left away from the stairs to the lift, and went down to the ground floor.

Kim noticed Henry just starting up the stairs. She caught his attention with, "Henry, have you got a minute?"

"Yeah," he said. "Now's a good time."

We passed Kim's office and once inside Henry's (roughly the same format as hers) Kim introduced me to Henry, who said, "Pleased to meet you, Lucy, you're here at last."

Kim then asked if he wouldn't mind giving me a brief description of his role in the department.

"No problem, Lucy," he began. "My chief role here is to help with the needs of the Cloud 10 clients, alongside Nikki. We basically help with their data storage to ensure they have complete security and secrecy that no hackers can breach. We give them confidence that nobody, and I mean nobody, can get to their data. I am putting it all a bit basic but I'd rather you understood. If that sounds rude, I don't mean it to be. It's probably all you need to know on that score – it's all everyone else knows."

Kim and Henry both laughed.

"You may see the odd person around here, from time to time. Just be polite and ignore them."

Kim said, "We're not just talking about Darryl"

More laughs.

I laughed too and told him that was fine.

He seemed pretty easy-going. If asked to describe him, I would say mid-thirties, average – I must improve my powers of observation otherwise I'm not going to last long here, I thought.

He continued. "My other, and more important role here, is assisting on your side of the business. For me, I don't get involved enough, but perhaps that will change with yourself and Daniel arriving. I won't go into it any further now, as I know Daniel, your partner, will be arriving tomorrow and I think it might be a better idea to go through it with him as well."

Kim stated, "Yes, Daniel will be in first thing in the morning."

Henry continued as if not hearing. "Let me just say, Lucy, if the past couple of years are anything to go by, you're gonna have some very interesting and unusual times."

Thanking Henry, Kim finished with, "We'll leave you to it and meet together with Daniel first thing." Looking at me she said, "No doubt the two of you will have a mountain of questions and Henry is just the man to answer them."

We said our thank yous and left. Where to this time, I wondered?

"I've got a few things to do, Lucy. Why don't you go back to the galley, make yourself comfy and I'll see who else is around."

I duly did as I was told.

Once in the galley, I picked up a paper, sat down with a drink, not quite in my usual spot but near enough, and tried to focus on the paper. Not a chance, my mind was a whirl of facts and not so important information. All too much to remember in one go, but I thought I had grasped the major points, the others would fall into place naturally I guessed.

I sat down in, not quite my usual chair, but comfortable, nevertheless, and tried to focus on all I'd been told.

64

Too much, really, to absorb in one go and rather than keep going over the same old things I forced my mind elsewhere to try and keep a little sanity. I drifted back to my last days at university when all my friends and I had decided to absolutely guarantee to keep in touch – none of us had, as far as I was aware. I knew a few of them lived in and around London and decided to contact some of them when I had the chance. No, I would do it now and wrote a group email there and then, rather than wait till the weekend. I hoped I wasn't the only one who'd managed to get a permanent job in just a few short weeks from ending my studies. I hoped their results were good and wouldn't dream of letting them know that mine didn't count for a fig. I let them know I would be difficult to contact directly till the weekend. I told them I was away, as I thought anything could happen in the next few days, over which I had no control.

That took all of ten minutes and then my mind raced back to life as it was now. I wondered how the weekdays would work out. As for time off, not a clue. I decided to just wait and see, what else could I do? I was just coming to terms with it and beginning to feel a bit like my old self when the door opened and in rushed Morry, followed by a young Asian man dressed in trainers, jeans, a pale, loose long-sleeved top and a maroon t-shirt. He was on the dumpy side, with a full beard, partly-shaved head and really piercing eyes.

"Hello, Lucy, I'm Jay. Kim told me I should pop in and introduce myself."

I stood up to shake hands and noticed I was just a

little bit taller than him. He must have been about 5ft 5in.

He looked up slightly, and in perfect English with no accent (why did I expect otherwise?) said, "My actual name is Jamal but all my friends call me Jay. I won't begin to start spelling my surname," he said with a hint of amusement.

"Hello, Jay," I said a bit formally.

"How are you doing Lucy? It's all a bit odd here, isn't it?"

"You can say that again, but I think some things are falling into place. At least, I think I know my way around the building," I joked.

"I'm still waiting for that!"

We'd got off to a pretty good start, but Kim cut short any more joking.

"Thanks for popping in here, Jay." Looking at me, Kim said, "Jay has been working here on his own for too long, but I think we've managed to find him an excellent partner and she should be starting here very soon."

"Not a moment too soon for me," he said.

"Okay, I know it's been a bit trying for you lately, but I think we've found Miss Right; you'll see Jay."

"I hope so, I really do. Apologies, Lucy, I'd like to talk more, but I'm on my way out to meet a friend. I'm sure we'll bump into each other soon."

"Okay, Jay, really nice to meet you. I look forward to working alongside you."

"See ya." And with that he was gone.

Kim remained holding onto the door, as if on her way

out. "There's not much on today. It will really start to-morrow for you, so why not just hang around for a bit and slope off early this afternoon. It's how we work here, quite loosely, but don't worry, it won't always be like this."

"Okay," I said. "If that's all right."

"Oh, I know, you could find any empty desk; you remember where they are? Make it a bit your own."

"Yeah, I'll do that."

*

Deed done at the desk, I returned downstairs and went out front for a chat with Nikki.

She was just about to take Morry out for a short walk and said, "Why not come along with us. It's a nice little garden park. Then go home.

"But it's not even lunchtime yet."

"Not a problem, this is Cloud 10."

So that's what I did.

Chapter 8

Miles, full name Miles Evelyn Rogerson, ruminated over Neil Bland. He'd had plenty of time to chew over his meeting with Neil on Saturday night. All in all, he remained plagued with doubts, and his journalistic career so far only added to it with all the disappointments there.

Something strange had happened, and although he tried not to be, he really wanted to be part of it. He needed it.

His usual meet up with his other set of friends was fun as usual and he made sure he laughed in all the right places. Jokes and anecdotes about some of the acting fraternity that lived in Crouch End always went down well, especially the pretentious actors; in their opinion, most of them were. Miles always liked to hear about failing actors as he considered himself a failing journalist. The breaks hadn't gone his way; the ones that might have led to more had been stolen and cheated from him by those with more power and clout. It wasn't only these actors and him, it was the way of the world.

He spent Sunday afternoon, after a couple of pints at

the Compasses, desperately trying to come up with the most fiendish plan to catch Neil out – nothing so far. He'd already decided that absolute cynicism was the way to tackle it. If he could catch him out, fine, if not, Neil would be the answer to his dreams. A top career, rather than a failing journalist; his life would go into overdrive, it could be payback time, big time. The saying 'revenge is sweet but best served cold' was something he could equate to. He hadn't forgotten any names. It really was a jungle out there and this could be his chance to be a top predator.

He thought himself senseless trying to come up with something and eventually just dozed off.

Monday came, still nothing. He was just sitting in his sunny garden when his mobile rang. It was Neil. In the short space of time till he spoke, he thought he knew Neil was just about to pull out of tonight…

And he wasn't wrong.

He answered with a positive voice, "Hi Neil, all good?"

"Afternoon Miles, up to much?"

"No, just waiting around till tonight, haven't got a plan for you yet, but I will have, don't worry, it'll be tricky, for sure."

Neil said, "Actually, about tonight…"

Miles' heart sank.

"You know, as a cleaner, Monday is one of the few days I have a really early start, and I didn't get back here till eleven last night. Plus Tricia stayed the weekend, so I'm really knackered."

Miles' heart sank even lower. "Are you saying to-night's off?" Miles said a bit aggressively.

"No, I suppose I could still meet you for a pint, but that's about all. I'm just dozing off and I thought I'd give you a call." Neil sensed Miles' disappointment. "Miles, you are still interested I hope, I think we'll be a good pairing, and besides, I've got an even better plan." Before letting Miles speak, he continued, "Where are you and what are you doing?"

"I'm at home waiting for tonight," was all Miles could think of saying.

"Tell you what," said Neil, "Lock your doors, stay in the garden or go and watch a bit of telly in your lounge. Whatever you do, don't go in the kitchen. The time's now a quarter to four. At exactly four o'clock go into your kitchen and sit down on one of your stools and don't move. Got it?"

"Yeah. Okay I've got it," said Miles, now expecting everything and nothing at the same time. "I'll sit on that stool as if glued."

Neil ended the call.

Miles wondered what he'd got himself into. He couldn't believe Neil was going to try the same trick twice. Why hadn't he thought of something else?

Fifteen of the slowest minutes in Miles' life eventually passed, and he picked up the paper, went to the kitchen stool and started reading.

Meanwhile Neil, sitting in a comfortable chair, had started to slowly doze. He kept an eye on the clock and at one minute past four he visualised himself sanding in

Miles' kitchen and materialised, right before Miles, who virtually fell off his stool.

"Jesus. How did you do that?"

Neil smiled and spoke softly and gently. "Don't move, Miles, we can speak easily from here. Any questions?" he said with a laugh.

"That's not possible, it can't happen, it must be a trick," he managed to gasp.

"There is no trick Miles. It's a superior form of lucid dreaming. You've heard of that."

Miles could only nod and shake his head at the same time.

"My body is sitting in my lounge asleep and I'm dreaming I'm here, talking to you. The difference is that in my form of lucid dreaming I can go almost where I want, people can see me and talk to me if I wish, and I can talk back to them, and they hear me. As far as I know I'm the only person living who can appear at will, but only for thirteen minutes."

Miles was still too shocked to say anything.

Neil continued. "You can now begin to imagine, with a bit of planning and luck, how I was able to achieve my financial status and what we can do together."

At last Miles seemed to wake. "Are you able to touch anything?"

"No, if I do, even accidentally, my dream body goes into a funny wobbly vibration and if it lasts for more than a few seconds the dream ends. I can feel what I'm wearing slightly."

"What if you touch anyone else?"

71

"Same vibration effect for me, but for them, they seem to get a small shock, a bit like static electricity. Something else interesting: animals can sense me; dogs will bark and cats will just look towards me. One last thing, I can only do present time, not future or past, future isn't possible; if I go back, it's just like looking at a TV screen with static."

"This is truly cosmic," Miles whispered. "We could make a fortune."

"I don't want a fortune, I've got one. But you could make one for yourself with journalistic scoops. Editors are going to be queuing up for you."

"You're right, Neil. Sorry for being so bourgeois."

"As I said before, Miles, absolute secrecy."

"Total."

"Miles, I'm going to dematerialise shortly, I can do it instantly or I can fade. I use the fading method if I've been seen where I shouldn't. It makes me appear like an apparition. Works well. People think they've seen a ghost."

And with that, he faded out. Miles had just witnessed a controlled out of body experience.

Miles did look like he'd seen a ghost. Virtually paralysed, just trying to absorb what had happened. Slowly he got his mind around it and went and had a large whisky. He knew there were no words to describe it easily and it seemed there were no words in his head.

He just sat and drank.

Back in Neil's house, Neil woke up, noticed he was still tired, and rang Miles.

Miles, by now on his second drink, just listened.

"Miles, I'm still shattered, would you mind if we move the meet to Tuesday, same time?"

Miles managed "Okay, Neil."

They both had plenty to think about.

Chapter 9

It was the day after yesterday,
The day before tomorrow

Freja Sarah stood in the soft golden air, like a celestial being upon her raised turret in the centre of the old battlements of her medieval manor house deep in the Suffolk countryside. From that vantage point she could survey the whole of her 'earthly' kingdom. There were only a few square miles of park land in sight; no other buildings other than her chapel; just a few of her flock in view, her 'watchers upon high'.

She had no need for further land or possessions, none were needed on her pathway to glory.

For she was the 'Chosen One'.

The new Almighty One.

She dwelt a little longer, enjoying her moments in the sun, thinking only of her quest. Now our time's here for we, the watchers, she thought. Our time is almost upon us.

She was young and ready, radiating youth and vigour with perfect light olive skin, her features well shaped, framed by long, soft, fair red hair over a swan neck. Raised on her podium she looked like a presence from heaven clothed in a long pale green dress, hair over her shoulders, with a slight figure, looking both fragile and strong. If she were to raise her arms you could be forgiven for mistaking her for an angel on Earth – a true apparition.

Her path to divinity was already well trod, it had attained its own life. She now had her own flock of pilgrims, each on a quest to convert non-believers.

To stop her now would be impossible.

Born Sarah Childrake just twenty years ago, she had added the name Freja, pronounced as the English 'Freya', as she had read that the name's meaning in original Norse meant goddess. Her path had not been without some sad sorrows, but there had also been joyous moments. She had been foretold of her divine destiny by a Lutheran monk, Brother Tobias, on one of her sabbaticals. Told of her Merogovian bloodline, through the Norman Conquest: seven hundred years of the Childeric dynasty, rulers of France to the small coastal fishing village near Marseille called Saintes-Maries-de-la-mer where Mary Magdalene had escaped with her daughter Sarah, after the crucifixion of her husband Jesus of Nazareth.

She thanked the Lord for her gift and her divine purpose.

Her close few, the Initiated, had swiftly turned a trickle of truth into ripples on a large pond. She felt she had been here forever just waiting, just watching for this moment to come.

'The New Beginning'.

But Sarah had a problem, and part of this problem was that she didn't know or have any comprehension that there would be a problem, and not of her making.

She believed, truly believed, that she was unique, God-given, the Chosen One, and it was beyond herself to think that mere fate would decide her destiny.

Unlike Lucy, Sarah believed her gift of dream travelling was her birthright from God .

Lucy knew better.

Chapter 10

Daniel lived with his wife Jill and their new baby Matthew in Barnet. As luck would have it, Barnet had the outermost station on the Northern Line. This led directly to Leicester Square tube station, just a short walk to his new place of work. He wondered what he was letting himself in for.

His first day ahead, he wasn't sure how Jill would cope with more uncertain hours; he felt sure it would be the norm. She was already a bit fed up with being a 'copper's' wife and all that went with it.

On the plus side, he needed a change. He'd enjoyed his farewell drink with his mates, short though it was, promising when he could to keep in touch.

He had dressed formally, suit and tie, not knowing the protocol, but wished he hadn't as it was already one of those really hot July days. Filled with apprehension, it wasn't long before he found himself in front of the Cloud 10 office, exactly on time.

Nikki had been keeping a look out for him and she let him in with a "Good morning, bang on time," showing him straight up to what he found out was Darryl's office, but there was no sign of him. Nikki said, "Take a seat, I'll let everybody know you're here."

Before long, the door opened, Daniel still standing awkwardly, as Darryl entered.

"Good morning, Daniel. Great to see you here."

"Good morning, Mr Harrison."

"No, no, no," said Darryl theatrically. "We're all on first name terms here. Are you a Dan or a Daniel?"

Now smiling and a bit more relaxed he answered, "Dan."

"Great," said Darryl. "Just one more thing before we get going, we're a bit of a dress-down outfit here, smart casual or even just casual. You'll soon catch on, especially on a day like this is going to be. Thank God for air conditioning."

Daniel took the hint and undid his tie saying, "Okay, sounds good."

"Okay, that's enough team talk from me for now, let's find the others."

They left the room and went to Henry's office where Kim, Lucy and Henry were already there and waiting. Everybody stood and Kim took the lead and did the introductions (he was now just Dan).

Kim again took the lead. "Right, Dan, where to start? I'm going to leave all the technical, more theoretical stuff to Henry. Henry will always be available for help, but you'll be working in a full partnership with Lucy, overseen by me. As you know, you'll be working together on unsolved crime cases that have hit the proverbial 'brick wall'. Henry will explain as best he can in as simple as possible terms. You are now going to hear things that will sound far-fetched and impossible to believe. Please try and keep your mind open – very open."

She smiled and left with a, "Good luck Henry, call me if you need backup or if Dan tried to escape the building."

Henry was about to take over when Lucy interrupted just as his mouth opened.

"Dan, just to let you know, a lot of what you are about to hear will be new to me too, well the technical stuff anyway. We waited for you to join before Darryl let Henry loose."

Another Darryl joke, thought Henry.

Henry tried again. "What we know on the science side is accurate but theoretical. How it applies to Lucy, however, we haven't a clue. If you don't fully understand the mathematics, I have a couple of screen diagrams to help." He turned his computer screen in their direction. A second or two's hesitation and then almost thinking out aloud he said, "There's a certain well-known mathematical formula called the Fibonacci sequence, where you add up the answers as you go along." He noticed that both Dan and Lucy looked like they were both beginning to switch off. He pressed a key and the screen lit up.

$$1 + 2 = 3$$
$$2 + 3 = 5$$
$$3 + 5 = 8$$
$$5 + 8 = 13$$

$$8 + 13 = 21$$
$$13 + 21 = 34$$
$$21 + 34 = 55$$

"As you can see, the numbers go 1, 2, 5, 8, 13, 21, 34, 55 and then 89 and so on to infinity. Once put on a graph the sequence turns into a beautiful spiral, as shown, seen throughout all space and nature. It is in fact a ratio of 16 to 10 minus 3 to 5; 5 to 8; 8 to 13 and so on." He stopped there and gave them a demonstration, held up his arm and said, "Forearm 16, arm 10, and this ratio goes all over the human body."

"That's quite a lot to take in," said Dan.

"Don't worry, there's no need to take any of it in directly, but if you're ever interested there's a whole bunch of stuff on the internet where it relates to artworks, nature and space. Okay, that's the technical stuff over. Any questions?"

Dan said "No, I don't think so, I've heard of the Golden Ratio in art."

Henry, looking a lot more serious as he knew the hard part was ahead, started speaking again. "Now I have to tell you how going through all that relates to Lucy. This is mostly for you as it's become the norm for her. Let me also say from the start, we, as a scientific community, do not understand how any of this is possible. It is still beyond us and many secret studies have been undertaken and we're still baffled. It will be as difficult for you to understand as it has been for our scientists. An out-of-body experience she has control over." He leaned back in his chair, speaking directly to Dan. "I assume you've heard of lucid dreaming, where you are in a dream and know you are?"

Dan nodded.

"We've discovered that there are a few individuals, very, very few, who have the ability – born with, we believe – to decide before sleeping, where and when their dream will be. For example, she can dream she is listening to the debate in the House of Commons that happened yesterday, and could tell me the order of the speakers, without prior knowledge, or she could just turn up in a park and tell us what dogs were there. We call this dreaming pellucid dreaming. Which means clear and transparent, and her dreams are just that."

In a slightly aggressive tone Dan said, "You're telling me, you're telling me Lucy can do this? She can turn up where she wants and when she wants? I just can't get my head round it."

"Yes, I am, Dan, with certain restraints. She can only do it for thirteen minutes, she must be within twenty-one miles of where she wants to go, but best of all, she can go back fifty-five years. Looking at the screen, you can see the numbers correspond, the number thirty-four is still unknown to us but we think we know what the five and eight relate to."

"I still just can't quite believe it," said Dan, head on his hands.

"Dan, do you really think you'd have gone through all those interviews and be here now if she couldn't?"

"Fair point," said Dan, still shaking his head.

"Our plan here for you two is to help the police solve unsolvable crimes by getting Lucy to the crime scene for clues. She cannot be harmed as she isn't really there, and if there are any problems she can instantly return to her sleeping body. No harm can come to her."

"I can really do this Dan, honestly. I was born able to do it. I'll show you this afternoon."

Dan, still in a mild state of shock, just nodded.

Henry continued, "Look Dan, you're now working for the Intelligence Services; it's serious stuff. I'll just briefly mention, we have two other departments like yours working here. One does anti-terrorism and the other focuses on the Royal family. They all have slightly different talents in timing."

"It's just such a lot to take in. Next week we'll be talking to aliens," Dan joked.

"That's tomorrow," replied Henry, laughing, then quickly, "Just joking."

After a slight silence from Dan he turned to Lucy. "It's just a pity you can only go back fifty-five years to 1964. If only we'd have met last year you could have solved the mystery of President Kennedy's assassination."

Relief all round, they all laughed a bit too loud.

Henry, still chuckling, said, "Shall we stop now and resume after Lucy's demonstration? I understand you've brought three police cases with you. Perhaps you can go through them with Lucy. Also, Lucy, can you give Dan a guided tour of the unit and enlighten him regarding some of our other eccentricities."

"Sure. Let's first go down to the galley for a tea or coffee."

"Galley?"

"Don't worry, that's just the start."

*

After grabbing a coffee each, they went straight to the front. Lucy introduced Dan to Nikki and also pointed out Morry, sitting in his basket behind Nikki's desk.

"So much for your powers of observation, detective," joked Lucy. "I knew you wouldn't have spotted the office dog, I didn't either. Apparently he's another of Darryl's ideas."

"I've worked in quite a few different offices, but this is a first for me," said Dan.

Nikki followed with, "It was one of Darryl's first ideas, to quote him, 'it'll give the place a light atmosphere, a good stress buster'. Anyone can walk him. He's good on a lead."

"Nikki, I'm going to give Dan the 'tour'. Can you remind me again of the entry code and do you know if my thumb print will work? I wasn't sure this morning so went in with Kim."

Nikki told Lucy it would, and gave her the entry code again. They then left 'the front' to go to the real front entrance. Nothing was surprising Dan now, he was ready for anything, or so he thought. Everything worked perfectly for Lucy. She explained the joint entrance with the other company and the reasons why it worked so well. She proceeded with the tour of the building, complete with all the eccentric names, the ones that she knew so far.

Again, the building was lacking in people; it felt quite empty, and there was no sign of any of the other 'leapers' who she had yet to meet. All in all it took about an hour, including another cup of coffee, this time with Morry in his usual spot, content to sit and play with a couple of dog toys.

Nikki came in with a lead, asked if they wanted to do the honours. They declined, saying another time they'd be delighted. They'd already decided next on their list was to have a look at the two ongoing crime cases and grab a spot of lunch at the café Lucy had been to the previous day.

They seemed to be on the same wavelength and getting on pretty well, much to their relief.

*

Their quick lunch over, walking back Lucy said, "I think it might be a good time for my demonstration. Are you up for it Dan?"

"As ready as I'll ever be."

They went to the second floor and both went into 'the leap'. Lucy had already decided that as yesterday's leap went down so well, she would repeat it. She found her 'hanger' and all ready to start said "I'm ready for the show. There's a lock on the outside of the door, so lock it so I can't get out."

"Hope there's not a fire, Lucy," he joked.

"Don't worry, this will only take about twenty minutes. You go back down to the galley and just relax."

Which is exactly what he did.

She moved to a hanger, closed her eyes and in a short time her body was fast asleep, her mind wide awake. Following her normal set routine, within seconds she was back in the galley, about six foot in front of Dan, his head deep inside a newspaper. She coughed slightly. Dan glanced up, saw Lucy and said, "I didn't hear you come in."

"That's because I didn't use the door. Look at me carefully, this isn't my body, it's an illusion like a hologram, my body's asleep upstairs."

Dan looked. "Don't be so ridiculous, you're here right in front of me, anyone can see that."

Lucy, inwardly enjoying every minute of the encounter, said, "Okay, get up, come over here and touch my hand."

She held out her arm towards Dan and he got up, with a huff, put out his arm to touch her hand. Instantly he received a short sharp static shock and jumped back, noticing that he had no feeling whatsoever of her hand.

"There you go Dan – told you."

Before he had chance to reply, the door opened and Morry scurried in, stopped in his tracks and started growling and barking.

Lucy remarked, "Dogs can sense my presence. I'd better go." And for good effect, she just slowly faded out.

Morry calmed down and so did Dan marginally, completely mystified by the episode. Total belief and disbelief at the same time. Morry turned and sat, Dan virtually fell into a chair, still staring at the spot where Lucy had stood before disappearing.

Then, to break the spell, the door opened and in came Nikki with, "Shall we go and let Lucy out, Dan?"

Upstairs they went to the locked door. Dan unlocked and opened the door, seeing Lucy sitting up, feet on the floor, smiling.

"Fair enough," said Dan. "I'm convinced." He sat opposite her. "How is that possible, how have you managed to keep this secret from the public?"

Nikki, just leaving the room, turned and said, "Dan, we are the Secret Service. I'll see if Henry's free."

A minute's silence later, Henry appeared and said, "Shall we resume this morning's meeting?"

Lucy and Dan nodded, and they returned to Henry's office.

Henry, with a smile all over his face, said, "Well, Dan, that was something, wasn't it?"

"I've never come across anything in my life, nothing comes near. It's like a kind of sorcery, magic – whatever."

"It certainly looks like it, Dan, but we do have two others who can do roughly the same and there will probably be others that haven't come to our attention. It does on the face of it look completely bonkers, but you do get used to it. Now you can see how you with your police knowledge and Lucy with her gift should easily make a good partnership. It will be down to you, Dan, to work out times and places and you, Lucy, to come back with the goods."

They all looked at each other; there was definitely a sense of agreement.

"What do you think?" Henry said, not really expecting an answer.

But Dan replied, "I think we are on to a winner here, Lucy, and I for one can't wait to start."

"I agree, Dan, let's give it our best shot."

Henry finished off. "There's no time like the present. Good luck to both of you."

Meeting over, they left.

Chapter 11

Unbeknown to Dan and Lucy, something very similar was happening at the same time just a few miles away at Neil's house. Neil had rung Miles that morning and suggested instead of meeting that night at the pub, with too many distractions, they should instead meet at his house in the afternoon, plenty of peace and quiet. Miles wholeheartedly agreed; he had spent some time whittling down his list of potential reprisals into Division One and Division Two.

Across Neil's desk he'd laid out two files, not trusting the internet. These two cases, he believed, had a fair chance of some success. The first was a sub-editor journalist who had given hints of false information about Miles and made him lose a good position and the other someone who'd taken all the credit for one of Miles' scoops which led him onto a TV career.

This, he hoped, was payback time.

Between them they chose the first. This was a case where the other journalist and Miles were on the shortlist of two for sub-editor of one of the 'majors'. Miles had gone in first and felt the interview had gone very well, to the point that one of the panel had given him a little aside as he was leaving: 'I'm sure we'll be seeing you soon'. Miles left feeling pretty confident and, as he left, he caught a glimpse of the next and final applicant, a guy he'd already had the odd tussle with; normal journalism.

What he later found out, in a press bar, from the person on the panel who'd given him the positive goodbye, was that the last person interviewed had let slip that he'd seen Miles leave. Instead of just leaving it at that, when he was asked if they knew each other, he'd been clever enough to say he knew Miles quite well and then made a clever little aside to the fact that Miles liked small boys. As it happened, Miles had spent some years in his twenties helping out in Outward Bound courses and the Duke of Edinburgh award scheme. This was all true but what he hadn't mentioned was that he helped out in these activities with his wife. He'd conveniently forgotten to mention her. The damage was done. Nobody wanted to employ anybody with a dubious history, however tenuous it was, and that put paid to Miles.

The other applicant got the job.

Miles had been hoping for years for his chance of revenge, and this was it, only a chance, but better than nothing. He wondered if Neil could find anything.

Neil needed to see the address where he lived and catch a glimpse of the inside and hoped for Miles he could find something unsavoury. He had a plan. Using his cleaner cover he would go from house to house along his road offering his services. Miles would then check when this guy was likely to be at home, and make sure they caught him when he was. He left that bit of planning to Miles. This suited Miles perfectly and he didn't bother with the other file, a well- known to the public celebrity, now a TV host. He was once a good source of information to Miles and often still turned up at the 'mercies', but that could wait.

*

Back at their office, Dan and Lucy prepared to look at the two cases Dan had with him. Unlike Miles, he had full confidence of the internet security where he was and the files where online.

The first, a kidnapping case – not public news – of a German businessman, kidnapped, ransom paid and released unharmed. Not really an important police case as such but the British police were keen to get this one solved, particularly to save face in front of their German counterparts.

The other, in the Brighton area, was a series of violent attacks on young women. They were pretty sure it was the same assailant, given the description. It seemed to be ongoing, and as the press hadn't yet put two and two together that there may be a serial rapist on the loose, the local police needed help fast to prevent further attacks and to stop it becoming a media circus. Lucy was drawn to the Brighton case and Dan agreed. Time was important here; the kidnapping case could wait.

Dan went to see Kim about how to proceed. She told

him there was no ceiling whatsoever on expenses. Her advice was to get a hotel down there asap and take it from there. Dan confided that he knew the times and places of the attacks from the file. They both concluded that if Lucy was somewhere nearby, out of sight, she could get a direction of escape or even a vehicle registration number.

Something would happen for sure, he was confident of that.

Now to break the news to Jill.

Chapter 12

Dark waters run deep
But soon we'll be crossing the stream

Sarah knew it was only about an hour or so before her midweek performance (as she now thought of them) at the manor chapel. A materialisation here and there, was all that her worshippers craved at this time. To slightly alter the service this week, she had decided to move from inside the chapel to the steps and lawn outside. The weather was calm and July perfect and she would take full advantage of the low sun, as the chapel frontage faced west. She surmised, quite correctly, that her shimmering appearance, enhancing her soft, strawberry blonde hair, would be awe-inspiring. The low sun would have no effect whatsoever on her eyes, which would remain fully open and mesmeric.

She'd already given instructions to a couple of her initiates, asking then to position two large crucifixes either side of the front doorway, as that was where she would materialise. She glanced again at her sermon, if you could call it that, just to make sure she would be word-perfect, but really she knew it by heart. It only differed slightly from the countless services that she had already appeared at. Finished, she then spent the rest of the time gently meditating and thinking of her plans for the future. Plan one was to find a new base in the City of London; it had been a perfect start, but it was time to move forward.

She'd loved her time here but wished her parents hadn't moved so far out of town, reminiscing about how she came to own it so young, aged fourteen. She felt nothing as she remembered the day that she had materialised in front of her parents' car on a tree-lined country road, causing them to swerve, lose control and hit a tree. The accident had killed them both instantly.

She felt no remorse. No remorse at all.

After all, it was the Lord's doing.

Jolted back to present time by a knock on her door; one of her initiates letting her know her congregation would soon be arriving. She called them initiates but knew they considered themselves disciples, which in fact they were.

Thanking the initiate, she walked towards the door, checking her appearance – only perfection, she thought. She then locked the door and moved to her chair in the corner, closed her eyes, and was asleep very quickly. She knew she had a good internal clock which told her when to go – five more minutes. Outside in front of the chapel, the seats were beginning to fill. Her flock eager to meet their messiah.

The gentle murmuring stopped immediately. She

slowly materialised with first a hushed sound and then a collective gasp coming over the forty or so members of the congregation – the effect she had was mesmerising. The golden sunlight enhancing her soft, strawberry blonde hair as she stood over them and gave her blessing. Her simple message to her worshippers.

Rejoice for you are saved
For you follow my path
To the days of enlightenment
To the keys to the light
Rejoice for you are saved

She waited just enough time for the words to have their desired effect.

For those who deny
I say beware
Take shelter
Take shelter from the coming storm

The flock murmured in agreement. Again, she bided her time, knowing there was a perfect moment to resume.

For I am not He
I do not wish to follow His fate
The fate of the Saviour of Nazareth
For this is the Final Coming
For I am the Chosen One

There was a roar of happiness, shouts of "Praise Freja Sarah", "Hail Freja Sarah". Her words had been perfectly chosen, the simple message, everything that they wanted. No hidden message.

There was no need.

For she was the Chosen One.

Once back upstairs, she moved from her chair, unlocked the door and moved to the window as Alina, one of the chosen few initiates, knocked and entered, saying under her breath, but so Sarah could hear, how glorious her appearance had been and that she would think of it forever. Sarah just smiled, knowing how well that and similar combinations worked for the flock; how they loved and needed them, no matter how many times they heard.

She needed a little refreshment now and Alina returned with what was required and left.

She summoned another of her inner circle, Andrew, who took care of the finances, and let him know she wanted to purchase a small private house in London. Some secrecy required and a lot of privacy.

Not surprised, as he could see things were moving now at a faster pace, he confirmed that it wouldn't be a problem financially as they were receiving huge amounts in donations and some bequeaths. Over the last few months, she'd arranged with her favoured few to appear at a number of small gatherings of potentially like-minded and well- heeled people. It had done the trick.

All at first had been shocked, then impressed and finally thought themselves unbelievably lucky to be involved. Her loyal and adoring flock was still in the low thousands, but rumours of her were beginning to circulate throughout the country and it was now time to move to the next level.

Freja Sarah knew her coming would be soon.

Chapter 13

We finished on Dan's cases, closed the paper files and computer just as Darryl popped his head around the door.

"Could I see you two for a couple of minutes?"

"Yeah, sure, we're all finished here."

Sitting before Darryl, I soon learned that this wasn't the Darryl I'd seen before. He had his serious face on – much more serious.

"Right you two, first, before you set off, I just want to go through what your plans are."

"Well," said Dan, "We're going to book a couple of rooms in Brighton and once settled go and check on the three places where the attack occurred and see which one of them might be the best for surveillance."

Darryl came straight in "Lucy, are you okay with staying away like this? I'm afraid it might be the only way forward in this case."

"Yes. To be honest I'm a bit jittery about it, but I'm sure as the day progresses, I'll feel okay."

"Dan," said Darryl, even more serious and leaning towards him, "You are the partner in charge of this operation. I want you to assure me that I have nothing to worry about, as Lucy's safety is absolutely paramount. Any, and I mean any, sign of a problem, abort immediately."

"I certainly will, Darryl, on my life. Lucy will be kept completely safe and I will be nearby, out of sight."

"Thanks, Dan," I said.

"Lucy, see Nikki about wardrobe, as I gather the attacks took place late evening so make sure you get fixed up with clothing to match the time and scenery. Also, Dan, what you're probably not aware of is that Nikki, in one of her many duties, is our office 'fixer'. She will arrange to book the hotel and car for you. When are you going?"

"I thought we'd go first thing in the morning. I've got to get my gear and run everything, well, run what I can, past my wife."

"Good idea, Dan. Lucy is that good for you? And have you any questions?"

"I haven't, really. Between you two you've answered most of them. I just need to start and see where it goes."

I thought I'd handled myself pretty well. I wasn't sure I was ready for any of it, who would be? Third day at work and already about to be thrown in the deep end. It was all happening so fast. I felt I'd only just left 'school', but they seemed confident in me and all I had to do was stand there and watch.

Darryl came back, "It's important, I stress important, that you, Dan, make sure that Lucy comes in at the scene after the act is over and not during or before. When the perpetrator is leaving the scene. Timing is everything –

I can't stress that enough."

I piped in, "I have told Dan that my personality affects where and when I can travel, sorry, leap. I couldn't watch any violence. I would just go straight back. Also, if I wanted to sound any alarm, I am not able to, and if my travel could affect the future again, I would just disappear instantly. I found this out when I was younger; it just ends and I have trouble remembering anything."

Dan spoke reassuringly, "Don't worry, Lucy, I guarantee to you that if I have any doubts on any part of the case I shall stop, but we must do what we can. This is an unsavoury case and we must do what we can to catch this guy."

Darryl, returning to his usual jovial self, spoke. "Right, I think we're singing from the same song sheet. The seaside beckons."

I couldn't help but smile.

We went down to the front where Nikki was ready for us.

"I've booked a nice hotel in the centre of Brighton. The car is also ready for collection, Dan, so you could just get it on your way home now, as you're virtually finished here, and you could pick Lucy up in the morning. It's Guildford, isn't it?"

"Yes," I confirmed, "Just outside. That would be great. Okay with you, Dan?"

"Yeah. No problem. I assume, Nikki, it's modern enough to have sat nav. I hope you've had the blue flashing light taken off?"

We laughed.

"I hope it works out nice and easy for you two and we'll see you next week. Lucy, let's go up to the wardrobe and see what we've got. Dan, here's the booking sheet for the car. As I said before, why don't you go and get it, and finish for the day. You're going to be away for a few days; probably got some explaining to do to your wife."

I gave Dan my home address, we both collected our bits and pieces from our desks, arranged a pickup time, said our goodbyes and he left.

Nikki showed me the wardrobe and between us picked out a selection of dark-coloured trousers, tops and trainers. She then threw in a balaclava and a pair of gloves.

"We're going for the invisible woman look, late in the evening," she joked, but she wasn't wrong.

With Dan gone, I hung around for a bit in Nikki's office, chatting about Morry. I could see she had some 'client' work to do and started to leave.

"Wait, you've missed your lunch. Here are a couple of muffins I've made for your journey," Nikki said, handing me a tupperware. "Vegan, I'm afraid, but see if you like them."

I took them and nibbled into one. It was delicious, to my great relief, and I thanked Nikki gratefully, leaving her to get on with her work. I tried to keep my mind off tomorrow on the journey home, though secretly I was quite excited.

*

Meanwhile, in Highgate, Neil was walking the streets in his guise as an upmarket cleaner. Miles had given him the address of their first target, and he was now just a few houses away. He had no other information about the person; it had seemed a good plan. He knocked at a couple more houses, both empty, left his leaflet, and knocked at the door of his target. After a short while, just as Neil was about to leave, it was opened by a well-dressed man in his forties. Neil went through his spiel and the man, a Mr Dutton, seemed interested, as his last cleaner had left a few months ago and he had been meaning to replace her. An opportune moment for Neil.

He offered Neil a look around, wholeheartedly accepted by Neil. It was a well-kept two-bedroomed typical London townhouse, already quite clean with the exception of the kitchen and bathroom. Neil was particularly pleased to see, inside the room that was used as an office, that the man was old school and strewn around the room were lots of handwritten pages and notes. Perfect. Neil offered him a couple of hours a week cleaning, with one of his female cleaners called Christina, and gave him a quote, asking what days was he likely to be there as his company preferred the owners to be there when the cleaning was taking place. Mr Dutton asked for his card to mull on it but as Neil started to leave, he called him back and told him he would take the quote. Neil already had what he came for, but as he already had a few prospective customers in the area, he thought why not. One of the girls he worked with on a Monday morning could do with the money.

He asked Mr Dutton which morning would be best and he came back with Friday. He would be there till noon and then usually left for lunch at his club and then called into the office. Neil pretended to look in his diary and then confirmed that was good and that she would be along just after nine this coming week and for him to pay her directly if he was happy.

They thanked one another and Neil made sure he was seen going to the next few houses for good measure. Neil's work finished, he called a cab and left the area.

What a result. As soon as he got home he went to phone Miles with the good news, but decided with a wry smile to let Miles stew.

But it didn't last. Twenty minutes later he was through to Miles, after having spoken to Christina, who was delighted and would meet Neil at the address on Friday. Miles was over the moon and they agreed to meet for a drink later.

Chapter 14

Happily positioned in a quiet area of the bar, Neil started to tell Miles how successful the day had been. When he'd finished, Miles couldn't believe his luck, but Neil said with mock modesty, "It's just a case of careful strategic planning."

Ignoring Neil, Miles just shook his head. "Marc Dutton. I've waited a long time, but I can wait a little longer."

"Actually, Miles, I thought he seemed like a nice guy. Are you sure it was him that did the dirty on you?"

"Yes, I'm absolutely positive, twice over. The information I received from my guy at the interview pointed the finger at him specifically. I even had someone else who worked with Marc afterwards make a joke about it to me – I put him straight."

"Fair enough, Miles, we've all done a few things we shouldn't have done."

"Coming from you Neil, that's a bit ironic."

Not wishing for the conversation to carry on in a sour way, Miles ordered a couple more beers and they both settled back to work out the next step.

Neil took the lead. "I've contacted a cleaning friend

who's always on the lookout for a bit of extra cash, Christina. She's very good and reliable, and not only that, another punter contacted me from the leaflet and now she's got two cash jobs on the same road on the same day."

"Good result for her then, Neil."

"What I'll do is go with her on Friday and introduce her to Marc and the owner of the other house, can't remember his name. With luck she can go direct from one house to the other. Also, while I'm at Marc's, I'll have another look around the house and suggest she doesn't clean the office or move any papers she sees around. Everybody always agrees to that. Maybe I can find out what other days he's out."

"Good thinking," said Miles approvingly. "I have no idea what you may find in his office; anything that looks a bit odd, take note."

"Will do, for sure, and we'll meet again later on Friday."

"At your house or mine?"

"I'll come to your house, Miles."

"Sounds like a plan, and we'll have a drink later."

At that point, good timing, in came Ray, full of tales of woe. What a week he'd had. How he hated the public. They both knew him well enough that it was just another week in Rays' life.

The pub was quite full with people eating, but the bar area was quiet. No sign of Greig tonight and the three of them just carried on with the usual chit chat. Ray cheered up a bit after his second pint and came on as usual to Maureen the barmaid, and as usual for her, she was having none of it – exactly what Ray was expecting; Maureen would take no prisoners.

Other than the start of their new venture, Neil and Miles didn't have a lot to talk about. Both of their weeks had been pretty boring so the conversation just meandered on aimlessly; even Ray admitted nothing that interesting or new had happened to him.

A couple of other guys they knew sauntered in and joined them for a while, but one by one they called it a night, as each of them had a few busy days ahead. For Miles and Neil, the next few days would seem like a fortnight – especially for Miles.

*

After an uneasy sleep, and with no appetite for breakfast, I tried to wait patiently for Dan to arrive, folding almost every piece of paper on the kitchen table into a paper aeroplane until at last I heard a car draw up outside. Mum was hovering around, so I remained seated, letting her answer the door to Dan. I was sure that as soon as she saw Dan, she would feel more confident about me going away for a few days. The last thing I needed was a worried mother constantly checking that I was okay.

I said hi to Dan, introduced him to my mum and gave her a hug goodbye. She was so much calmer now that Dan had come up with the right platitudes. I chucked my suitcase into the back of the grey saloon and off we went.

Dan put in the postcode for the hotel and with a big

grin said, "Here we go then. Our first case. Let's hope it's the first of many and successful."

I could only agree, but somehow Dan knew I was anxious and spent a while making light of any difficulties ahead. It was all planned out, he reassured me.

Keen to change the subject, I asked Dan how his wife had reacted to him going off for a few days to a hotel in Brighton with a female colleague.

Dan smiled and said, "I wondered if you'd ask about that. While I'm completely open with Jill about most things, well, as open as I can be, I thought this small detail was better left unsaid."

"Fair enough. I guess it makes sense; why give her unnecessary worry."

"Overall, she seemed okay with it; she's used to my unusual hours. Once I told her it was to do with a rape case, she was fine with it, and with our new baby, well, he's six months now, she has plenty to do."

Once we arrived, we parked the car in the hotel car park and checked in, heading up to our rooms to unpack. Nikki had made sure that Dan had a larger, business-style room, suitable for us both to work in, so I quickly joined Dan and we started studying the case.

The attacks had taken place over the last four weeks, all late evening, just before total darkness and not on set days of the week. The police had toured the areas on foot trying to come up with any information from any witnesses who were in the area; no one had come forward with any information – it was a complete blank. It was all very unsettling for the people of Brighton who wanted it cleared up and the rapist caught; they were fearful of another attack.

We decided to go through the attacks in chronological order. The first attack had taken place on the margins of a large grassy area north of the town, the second in the popular Queen's Park and the third in a smaller park with a sports and social area to the east. Our first plan would be to scout out the locations during the day and see if there were any obvious viewing vantage points for me to leap to. Dan had collated detailed maps of each attack, and exactly where the victims had been attacked first and then dragged away. It was upsetting to think about the fates of these poor women, but I was determined not to let my emotions get the better of me. We had to catch this guy.

Case reviewed, we left the room and collected the car. We had both dressed casually so as not to stand out – just summer tourists – of which Brighton was full. We didn't look too out of place as a couple; Dan looking quite a bit younger than he actually was when casually dressed.

Once we arrived at the first location, Dan parked the car on the side of the road, roughly opposite where the pathway led onto the grassy area Dan had the detailed map folded inside a tourist map he had acquired earlier.

I checked the map with him and we walked down the path taken by the first victim, stopping where the initial attack had taken place. It made me feel uneasy, and I said as much.

"I'm sorry, Dan, but just being here really upsets me."

107

"Lucy, you wouldn't be human if it didn't. I've had years in the Force and I've seen some horrible stuff. I still try not to think about it. If I do now, rather than get upset I get angry. Try to focus on the fact that what we're doing is stopping it from happening again."

"You're right. Let's go see where the rape happened."

Checking that there was no one around, we moved off the pathway, across an open space to an area of trees and bushes where the act had taken place; there was even the odd bit of police tape left behind.

Dan spoke. "He came up behind her, hit her quickly and pulled her into those bushes. The best and only description came from her. He was normal height and weight, around forty with greying hair. We don't know if he had any accent as he never spoke. The police have combed the area for clues and spent hours talking to the locals but have come up with zilch. No one saw anything out of the ordinary."

"But it was a warm summer's evening… nobody saw or heard anything? How could he have just come up behind her unobserved?"

We looked around the scene and both agreed that there was nowhere nearby to hide, only the road and perhaps in a car, but that was about twenty yards back.

"Let's come back this evening," Dan suggested, "and see what the footfall and traffic is like at the time of the attack. Let's go on to the next one in Queen's Park."

We drove off towards Queen's Park some way away in silence.

Eventually, Dan spoke. "I think we've got to assume

this guy has a car. It's not that easy to get from one of the crime scenes to another, especially not on foot. We have to assume he's motorised."

I nodded in agreement, still feeling uneasy.

Soon we were parked on the road near the second attack, similar to the first. Again, a busy path during the day lead off the main road at an angle. We walked the path.

"It's almost déjà vu, as regards the first scene," Dan said. "Nowhere to hide really… so similar to the first location."

"I wouldn't feel comfortable walking here alone at night," I offered.

"Very true, these parks look lovely during the day. I wonder what it will look like tonight." Dan paused. "Hey, how about I park my car facing the pathway, then you can sit low down in the back, car locked. Then, you can materialise in the car and see if he comes this way."

He looked so triumphant, I only just about managed to keep a straight face. "Dan, umm… I hate to break this to you but I can't magically transport inanimate objects with me when I leap so I'm afraid your master plan isn't going to work… I can only transport me. I'm basically a hologram, think Princess Leia in Star Wars."

We both collapsed into laughter.

"God, I'm so stupid," said Dan, eyes to heaven, shaking his head. "Well, on that subject, how do you do it?"

"The simplest way I can describe it is… it's a case of as I go to sleep, but I'm still a tiny bit awake, I kind of focus on the subject and then un-focus, and then it happens."

"It's beyond my understanding really. Forget I ever mentioned the car. Let's go to the last one."

We drove east across the town to the final park, which was even more open than the other two. I couldn't get my head around why this guy had chosen such open spaces.

It was around lunchtime and the park had a café so we stopped for a quick bite before heading straight to the scene. Again it was very similar, only this time the attack had taken place even further away, about a hundred yards into the park, off the path into shrubbery. Again, the girl had been hit first. Why had this guy risked attacking here? This park was even busier than the others had been, with loads of different play areas and sports facilities. No doubt it was a hive of activity in the evenings as much as it was in the day.

All the victims had said basically the same – the attack came from nowhere – and their descriptions had been vague. The police had done a thorough job and were still asking for any information from anyone, no matter how trivial, but nothing – a dead end.

Basic groundwork over for the time being, we drove back to the hotel to further discuss the case. Comfortable in Dan's bedroom-come-office, I took an easy chair, leaving Dan to sit at the table he'd turned into his desk.

"Right, let's go through these files again," Dan suggested. "Feel free to butt in at any time, no matter how trivial."

"Okay, I will."

"As I see it, these are just ordinary roads, not the sort you'd expect to see this type of crime on. Easy parking in the evening, just urban roads adjoining parks, like thousands of similar roads used by hundreds of people all the time. Why is he choosing these roads? I can't believe it's just 'access to easy prey'."

"I agree, there must be something we don't know about, or that we're not seeing. I just hope it's something I can spot."

Dan continued, "Let's go over the timings in each case; as you said the other day 'timing is everything'."

Just for a moment, those words made me start to think of myself as part of a real detective team – it was a good feeling.

"Looking at the cases in front of me, I can see that in two we have a pretty good idea exactly when they took place. The third is a bit messy." Dan shook his head.

"We're going to do the easy ones first, I hope."

"Correct. Okay, the most accurate timing is the very last one. The victim came out of the park in a terribly distressed state but had the sense to look at the pavilion clock. It was checked by the police and found to be accurate to one minute – it was ten thirty. Once at the station she was pretty coherent about timings. She reckoned it took her about five minutes to pull herself together and another five minutes to walk to the road to seek help and that's when she noticed the clock. She also said the rape was over quickly. So, allowing for her to be hit and dragged to the bushes, that makes it likely that the attack started at around ten, give or take a couple of minutes. She remembers nothing out of the ordinary before her attack. So, if you were in position at ten o'clock somewhere near the road, you could possibly see something, however small, that may be significant."

"Totally agree. A minute or two after ten would still have me watching till nearly quarter past; he should be past me by then if he goes that way."

"Great. Let's move on." Dan scoured the pages on his computer for a minute or two, just to confirm what he already knew. "The first attack is the most difficult to put a time on; not many people there as it's quite a way from the town centre, and from the information I have the timing is vague. There's a window of about half an hour or so – too wide. If we haven't come up with anything on the other two, we'll come back to this one."

"Suits me. I wouldn't want to see any details."

"The attack in Queen's Park appears to have good timing as well, as when the woman was first hit she fell down hard and broke her watch on the tarmac path. Her wristwatch smashed. But we're not sure that the time shown on the watch is accurate. Similar timing, the watch showed five to ten, and again, according to her, from when he attacked to when he left her it was no more than ten minutes. So, is you got there at around five to ten?"

I did my own mental calculations and nodded.

"If we don't make any progress with these two then we'll see what can be done regarding the first attack, but let's hope we don't need to. He seems to be working on an MO of around ten in the evening for whatever reason. Maybe he's a shift worker – who knows. Are you completely happy with these timings, Lucy? I've gone over them a few times to be sure, but if you've any doubts at all, now's the time to speak."

"Let's go with your plan and we'll see what comes of that. I can be there and out of direct sight. Hopefully, I'll come up with something."

Dan smiled, and we both agreed that we couldn't achieve anything else now; it all hinged on tonight. Dan said he would take the rest of the afternoon to double-check he hadn't missed anything in the files, so I decided I'd have a stroll around the town and seafront to clear my head, then meet him for dinner later.

Something had to be done, and it was up to us to make it so.

Chapter 15

The path still unclear
To where the quiet waters flow

Sarah had spent the last of her days at the manor waiting for her New Beginning, just in quiet meditation or meandering around her parkland estate, contemplating the next chapter towards her step to the great awakening – her second coming. She had passed a number of now derelict small cottages, once the homes of the estate workers when she was a child, who had since been driven by her to leave.

She remembered with a secret joy how they had left by her haunting the cottages. Dressing as a spectre, she had entered their homes dressed from head to toe as a ghostly being, a pale shroud appearing in front of them or haunting their small gardens. The fear and suffering she had caused, appearing and disappearing, gave her the first taste of what her power could achieve as an ethereal figure. How she hadn't caused a death amongst them she still found amazing; of course, not her fault, just God's spiritual work collecting some of his flock.

One by one the families had moved away, full of their experiences of the spirit world, her parents totally sceptical of their haunted tales. Slowly but surely, as the tenants weren't replaced, the estate drifted back to parkland.

Of course, Sarah had never haunted the manor house. She saw no reason to give her parents any idea of the truth and they remained oblivious to the knowledge until the day they died. After their death, she'd been comforted and looked after by the house staff when not being schooled, and as the years progressed, they had been replaced by her followers. She reflected on her difference, the fact that she'd been noted as the different one at school, never popular, just a girl they'd been forced to associate with. Perhaps she'd given off an uneasy aura, who knows.

Now she walked the grounds, in a carefully chosen Christian-style dress and veil, with authentic-looking aged sandals and a crucifix hanging from her neck. The effect of this appearance to her subjects was perfect – they were totally subservient to her; she was all that they expected. From time to time, she would pass some of her flock, and they would bow in a quiet way and murmur 'Freja Sarah, the merciful one, our Goddess', or something similar. The choices of salutation were many, so many that Sarah had stopped listening. A small regal bow was enough for them.

Her contemplation came to a halt when Alina appeared. She had news that Andrew was at the house and needed to speak to her. She returned immediately, expecting good news, and wasn't disappointed. He excitedly told her that he had been in contact with some of her more wealthy followers, already deep members of her 'watchers upon high' sect, and one of the most ardent members would be able to offer her a vacant fully-furnished house now, if she thought it was good enough for her. Andrew took out a photograph of a beautiful whitewashed detached house in Holland Park. It would be available to her in perpetuity. All he wanted was her blessing.

A more detailed description of the house from Andrew seemed even more perfect. Set on a corner walled plot, the main house had four bedrooms and an adjoining annexe featured two bedrooms and its own private access. The main house had plenty of parking with an electric gated drive. She told Andrew to cease searching, for it had been found. She and her four close initiates would move in tomorrow. The four would have complete access to the main house and she would have total privacy for herself in the annexe.

God was with her. She would begin the great awakening from there.

Chapter 16

It was a very different atmosphere when we parked the car at the first crime scene we had visited earlier in the day. The sun had drifted behind a row of trees and it was already getting dark.

"Why is it so dark here? Aren't the streetlights working properly?" I wondered aloud.

"A few years ago the whole country changed from bright streetlighting to this duller type. Some green initiative, I think," Dan informed me.

"Well, it hasn't worked at all well for safety; the dull light makes it almost impossible to see. What were the council thinking installing such poor streetlighting next to such a big swathe of parkland?"

Dan commented that he wouldn't be happy with Jill walking here on her own, and I had to agree with him. The attacked girl had left a friend's house nearby and had taken the path as a shortcut. She only lived about a ten-minute walk away and had previously always thought it was safe.

We walked past the spot of the initial attack and then about twenty yards past. The path was almost empty of people. All we'd seen so far were a couple of late-night joggers, a cyclist without lights, a couple of dog walkers… all the usual. We turned and went back towards the road, scanning either side, when Dan pointed out a tree set back a bit on the left-hand side of the path, close to where the path joined the road. The tree was in full summer leaf and had a large canopy, some of which hung low.

"Have a look over there by that tree," said Dan, and pointed.

I walked across and found a good position against the trunk, in a gap between two low-hanging boughs, with a decent view of a long section of the path,

"Dan, I think this is as good as we're going to get."

"You're right," he said, and made a mark in the ground.

"Dan, you can't make an 'X marks the spot' for three weeks ago," I laughed.

"I know that. Just force of habit," he replied, laughing along with me.

"We're finished here. Let's go back to the car and sit for a bit and wait and see who's still about."

It was just more of the usual suspects: cyclists, dog walkers, a group of lads on their way home or out.

"Okay, then, Queens Park, here we come. You've got plenty of dark clothes, a balaclava, gloves… I can't think of anything else you'll need. Are you up for giving it a go when we get to the park?"

"Absolutely. I'll feel at ease there; nothing to stop me taking notice of who's around, anyone looking slightly suspicious. In fact, anyone."

We arrived at Queens Park just after ten; apart from the lack of decent streetlighting, it was very similar. The happy, sunny park of earlier in the day now looked gloomy and menacing, though I couldn't tell whether that was just because I knew what had happened there.

We followed the same procedure, though this attack had taken place further into the park, where it was a lot more open. How had he managed it when there was no-where to hide?

Dan noticed the houses adjacent to the park had a very good view of the path. Directly opposite the path-way was a large, detached house with an established open front garden, small wall and open driveway. Dan told me just to go along with him as he walked up the path and knocked at the door. A lady opened it and he introduced them as the police, showing his badge. He told her they were just doing a follow up on the attack that had occurred on the park opposite a few weeks ear-lier. The lady at the door said she couldn't remember anything else on top of what she had already told the officers. She wished she could be of more help, but ex-plained that, in the evenings, she and her husband sat at the back of the house, watching TV.

I still wasn't sure what the purpose of talking to her had been as we thanked her for her time and turned to leave. But as we started to slowly walk down the drive, Dan pointed out a perfect place for me to stand, at the edge of the lawn, between two large shrubs. Just my head would be in view from the park. It was ideal. And there I was thinking Dan was bothering this old lady for nothing.

Back on the path, we double-checked the height of the gap.

"I think we can call it a day here. That's a really good spot, somewhere I'm really comfortable with. I'll see everything or nothing – who knows. I feel really sorry for the local residents after what's happened."

"So do I," Dan concurred. "And you're right, we've got two great locations. Let's go back for a drink before the bar closes."

"Good plan."

*

Back at the bar, Dan said, "Look, Lucy, I'm going to spend tomorrow at Brighton police station, checking on any new leads, as a 'Met' officer. Why don't you just go back home to Guildford for the day. There's a direct train from Brighton, I've checked, and we'll meet up here in the evening."

"Are you sure, Dan? That would be great, it would save me hanging around all day. My mum and dad are always happy to see me, and hopefully won't ask any embarrassing questions about the job."

Dan raised his glass. "That's our plans then. Cheers."

*

Dan woke the next morning eager for his day, opened

the bedroom window and noticed immediately that the hot weather over the last few days had turned decidedly humid. Just to check he was correct, he turned the TV on and waited for a local forecast. He wasn't wrong; a vast belt of thunderstorms were heading for the south coast, expected this evening. He knew that Lucy could leap in the afternoon, but he wanted to be careful – this was their first job together after all.

He shook his head, resigned to the fact that tonight would have to be postponed – so much for careful planning. Not knowing how storm atmospherics could affect Lucy, and to be on the safe side, he would call her after breakfast and move this evening's plan by twenty-four hours. He didn't want to risk putting her in danger.

Chapter 17

Friday came in many directions.

In the direction of Sarah, it meant waiting. Even the gods and goddesses, it seems, sometimes have to wait for keys like ordinary mortals, and that was the case for Sarah. At last, they turned up late Friday morning.

She and her chosen four – Alina, Sebastion, Judith and Lovage – had spent the last couple of days slowly packing in preparation for the move and were now eager to leave. All four, plus Andrew and the property owner, were sworn to secrecy. Only the favoured few knew of the destination; nothing must hamper the way of the clear New Beginning.

One of her followers had filled his van with their possessions. Sebastion would drive it to London, unload, return it to the estate and make his way back to London. She, and her three, would take Alina's car. They said their farewells to the remaining assembly. Some would remain and carry on the upkeep of the grounds and some were leaving to go back to their homes and wait for the awakening, ready for her calling. All had been assured they would be needed. All were delighted and expectant.

A few hours later they were pulling into the drive, the automatic gates closing behind them. The four were a little shocked as Sarah and her belongings moved towards the annexe, and clearly delighted as they moved into the main house. Sarah told them that the annexe was for her and her alone and completely out of bounds to them. She had been assured that there was an intercom between the two and insisted that it would be their only form of communication. That said with finality, her followers all spent the next few hours settling in, agreeing to meet for supper later.

Sarah wandered around her new home. It was perfect, superbly clean with nothing needed, everything thought of. She surmised some of the delay might have been caused by a super-clean instigated by Andrew, and she wasn't wrong. She tested the lounge chairs one by one to find the one most suitable for her travels, found the perfect one, and positioned it to a position beyond passer-by view in a far corner of the room. The room was warm, after all it was a hot day in July. But she didn't have to concern herself about the winter cold as her quest would be successful by then.

The general settling in had taken longer than she expected, and she took a little break to recuperate, startled by the buzz of the intercom, pleased that it was loud and clear. It was Alina letting her know that supper's ready.

She walked the few yards to the main house and couldn't help noticing that although the sun had not yet set, the moon was very bright.

123

Friday for Neil and Miles was the highlight of the week. It really was all they'd been waiting for, and waiting had taken its toll on Miles. For Neil, however, it was just another jump into the unknown.

Christina was her usual punctual self; at quarter to ten on the dot, outside what would be her second clean of the day, Neil introduced her to Mr Brown and let him know she would be along just after midday after she finished her first clean. That now organised, they moved to Marc Dutton's house. Introductions over, she was let into the house, equipment in hand, and Neil left for home.

It wasn't much of a wait till twelve thirty, so Neil just settled in his chair and watched a bit of daytime TV. That was enough to send him into a light doze, and before he knew it, his wristwatch alarm went. Ready for action, five minutes later, he was in Marc Dutton's hallway.

He hadn't fully materialised just in case there had been a change of plans and he was still there. He listened carefully – nothing. He decided to check out the bedrooms first. Nothing. Kitchen. Nothing. Lounge. Nothing.

He moved to the office, the hub of Marc's home world. One wall was almost totally just one large pin and white board, about eight foot across and four foot high; he'd leave that till last. He stood in front of the desk and slowly let his eyes run across it. He wasn't sure what he was looking for, but he hoped something would stand out, something odd. All Neil could see was a random selection of half-written letters, the odd bill, some scribbled notes and even a half filled out sheet donating money to a charitable cause. Marc had a habit of underlining in red what he felt was important to him, but even these notations were fairly nondescript. Neil took a mental note of them, but none seemed current or provocative. He moved on to the notice board, checking his watch for time: five minutes remaining. He scanned the board from left to right; nothing obvious. He decided to scan again. Nothing stood out, nothing in the news, no ongoing scandals or new possible new scandals – nothing. This is not going to please Miles, he thought.

Last chance. He noticed Marc had a well-worn wall calendar. Marc was away this weekend, on a short golfing break with some friends in Berkshire, back Monday afternoon. Excellent, Neil thought. He'd try again on Sunday to see if anything had changed.

Admitting defeat, he closed his eyes and was back home. Miles would be disappointed, but it was what it was. He rang Miles, but only getting his answerphone, left a message for Miles to come to his house when he could. Then he went to the kitchen for a quick bite to eat before sitting down to watch a bit of golf.

It wasn't long before the doorbell rang and in came Miles. Neil ran through the morning's episode and although disappointed, Miles took it philosophically. After all, they were having another crack at it on Sunday. Miles also had some news on the celebrity Lain Pederson. According to one of his sources, Lain was flying to

Paris on the twelve fifteen flight from Heathrow on Monday. Apparently it was a well-known fact that his wife always dropped him off and picked him up from the airport – something to do with the public and his celebrity status. Therefore, said Miles, a midday visit would be perfect. Neil didn't like the idea of such a short window, the timing was a bit risky, but in order to raise Miles' spirits he agreed to do it.

Miles knew where Lain lived, not too far away, and if Neil had time now, they could drive to his house, park nearby, and Neil could play the cleaning entrepreneur and get the lay of the land. Neil agreed, and off they went, and the plan worked to perfection. He didn't need a cleaner, they had one, which pleased Neil, but thanked him for his offer and wished him luck.

To Neil, he seemed on the surface another nice guy and it crossed his mind that Miles might well have misread them.

Miles drove him home, agreeing to meet at the Northern that evening; no shop talk at the bar, purely social chat, as it was Friday night and it would be crowded.

*

I was standing frozen to the spot against the tree trunk. It was deathly quiet here, only the sound of motor cars fading in the distance. It was an eerie feeling, knowing that, just a few yards away, a young woman had been attacked. I needed to pull myself together. Concentrate… concentrate, Lucy. It was a cloudy night, much darker than my last visit here, and the tree canopy offered both concealment and a good view over the small area. I was glad I had taken Dan's advice, particularly the balaclava; only my eyes were visible, everything else was black.

I had a good wide view of the path and road path, even though there was very poor lighting coming from a couple of distant streetlights. I darted my eyes from side to side, checking whether anyone was about.

Then, it was as though some invisible train had pulled up, and some train commander had yelled out 'all change please!'. A couple of well-lit cyclists came racing down the road and onto the park path, followed almost immediately by another cyclist, no lights, possibly female. They zoomed past an elderly couple with two dogs, walking along the road, and from the park path came a doddery old portly man with a small dog, who was walking with such difficulty I wondered if he'd make it home. A couple of young lads materialised, larking about on the road, and finally one more cyclist with modern flashing cycle lights. Then that was it. I wondered if any of these cyclists had come forward. Dan would know.

I waited a couple more minutes – no one else. I checked my watch – time's up. A millisecond later, I was back in my hotel room. Immediately, I rang Dan, and he was there in an instant, with his hopeful, expectant face. I was not so hopeful.

He was eager to hear everything, and I went through it exactly as it happened, omitting nothing, even the trivialities, and Dan wrote it all down meticulously. He was surprised by the lack of anything that could help, but to my surprise, he didn't seem to be that downcast, or if he was he hid it well. He asked me if there was any other little thing I thought might be relevant. There wasn't, so he left it at that. He told me he would contact the CID office and let them know about the cyclists, then proceeded to tell me about his time at the office. The police had re-interviewed the three victims: apparently, the attacker had made them face the ground on their knees (which was not going to make my job easier), and when the rape was over for two of the girls, he had put his foot on their backs and said in a gruff, nondescript voice, 'stay down'. Fearing for their lives, they had done just that. The other girl had collapsed anyway, without being asked.

Thinking ahead, Dan had decided that, as the attacks had taken place during the weekdays, we should go home tomorrow morning and return on Monday. He knew it wouldn't affect me and my travels, but he did know it would affect his wife, Jill, who wouldn't relish a weekend on her own. He would ring Kim and let her know that, due to thunderstorms and hoping for more leads over the weekend, their case would be delayed slightly, and would ask her to get Nikki to rebook the hotel.

We decided that he would check in with the police Monday morning and pick me up late afternoon. I was equally happy with the short delay, though I had strangely enjoyed my stakeout, and couldn't help but look forward to trying again on Monday. Maybe this was the job for me.

Chapter 18

To the pathway full of flowers;
Scented showers; blissful hours

Sarah loved the sound of the city. She found that surprising, in a good way.

She'd spent all her life in what most people would
have considered a rural paradise. Here, now, the sounds
and sights in every direction were immensely uplifting.

She must investigate. She looked in her wardrobes
and found some casual clothes: jeans, t-shirt top – today's modern uniform for anonymity – and left the annexe by her private exit onto the street, after remembering to turn off the intercom.

The street was busy with people going in all directions and she approached a friendly looking couple, explaining that she was new to the area, and asked if they
had any suggestions for a walk. They mentioned Hyde
Park was nearby, but someone overhearing said that
Portobello Market was fantastic on a Saturday. He
pointed out the direction and she was off, with not a clue
what to expect.

He wasn't wrong. Never had she seen so much life in such a small corridor. The atmosphere to her, never having been part of this city life, was electric, with hundreds of people milling around, market stalls offering just about everything with the traders in fine voice, each trying to out-shout each other. She was tempted by nearly everything, with their fine banter and clever jokes, but luckily for her, unluckily for them, she had no purse as she'd never needed money. It was wild and colourful, the best of humanity, and somehow, organised chaos.

She must get to these people somehow. Her well thought out journey up to this point had mostly involved the church-going well-to-do, and they had been generous benefactors. Here was part of another world, a more real and basic world, and she would make sure she would be included in it. How to do it... that was a question for another day. Today, she was just going to enjoy the spectacle as a spectator.

The different foods were one of the most impressive things for her; she had never seen so many varied and unusual foods from around the world. She had rarely left Suffolk, let alone England.

There was an open meeting this afternoon and she would bring this up. The meeting would be presided over by the very capable Andrew, who could easily handle it. It would be slightly informal in that any question could be asked by all there, which would be Andrew himself, the four, and her.

She wandered through the bustling crowds for just a little longer, savouring the memories, and then turned to go back to her new home. A thought flashed into her mind about tomorrow being Sunday and how happy and fortunate she was not to have to put in a performance at the manor chapel any more, as she was too far away. Never again, she promised herself. Things are going to be different, very different here in London.

She walked back home in the beautiful warm sunshine, taking in the sights and sounds of city life. Although old beyond her years, nothing had prepared her for this bright modern world. The thought of moving to London had thrown her slightly but now she knew it had been the right choice and she hoped her next plans would be as successful.

She saw ahead her walled house and let herself back in by key. She had made sure she had the only key to her private door at the side of the house, which led directly into the rear hall of her annexe. She had complete privacy to come and go as she wished. She turned back on the intercom and checked that everyone was settled and okay, and mentioned lunch. The buffet was prepared and ready to go, according to Alina. Lovage, who loved catering, had spent all morning in the kitchen and it looked ravishing.

Sarah changed back from her street clothes into the more appropriate outfit that the four were used to, one of her Freja Sarah outfits. 'Back to reality', she thought, but her mind now dwelt on her new reality, in this new environment.

The four were strangely relieved to see her. Andrew had not yet arrived, so they dived into the delicious lunch prepared by Lovage, herself overwhelmed by the kitchen compared to the one in the manor. Andrew arrived as lunch finished and they moved to a large room set aside for meetings, with a large central table and chairs. Andrew settled himself into the main chair at the end, and the others, including Sarah, sat with eyes facing Andrew.

Smiling at them all Andrew proceeded. He confirmed it would be an open meeting with any, however minor, questions. He set the ball rolling. "I want this to be informal but let me start by stating that any procedures that we had at the manor will just carry on as normal. We all have our roles and Sarah has already confirmed to me that she'd like things to be just the same as what we had there; it seemed to work well and everybody seemed happy. Any queries on this, no matter how trivial, just contact me, happiness is all here. I know on the surface it can seem like a big change, but it is not, just more of the same for us in the house. Any queries at all? Are you all okay with that?"

There was a nice general sound of agreement.

"I'm glad, that's all settled then, but remember, anything, just anything, contact me."

Sarah motioned by hand to Andrew and all eyes moved to her.

"Andrew, I haven't mentioned this to you before and you may find it difficult to understand at first, but it is important to me, very important. Can you tell me now, here now, roughly what my finances are? You have told me how magnificent my benefactors have been, and still

133

are, with regards to pledges and funding. They even gave the gift of this house."

If he was taken back by this, his accountant's mask didn't drop. She must have a plan, and I will follow, he thought. He took a little time for calculations and finally said, "At this moment you have currently £3 million pounds available and it's still growing."

There was a hush amongst the four as Sarah continued, "Good, I was hoping for something like that. Now I will tell you why. With that money, I wish you to very quickly buy, and gift to my initiates here, four separate places for them in nearby unobtrusive locations."

The four sat there, stunned by this revelation, but afraid they might have to leave this house, and leave Freja Sarah, but before any of them could say anything Sarah continued, "We won't be moving from here. This will be where our final battle for the great awakening of our people will take place, but as you know in battles for the truth, there will be turbulence along the way, and I do not wish my four to be embroiled in this turmoil. While none of it can affect me, I am concerned for my chosen. Let them have a place of refuge in times of trouble."

There was complete since in the room, some sat with dropped jaws.

"Do not concern yourself with the trivialities of money; find them homes worthy of my initiates. Let us hope they are never used, but let the safety of my four be paramount."

The meeting ended on that bombshell and Andrew

went to work.

*

The rest of the day was uneventful. Judith, in her role of chief organiser, suggested to Sarah that, as tomorrow was Sunday and the traffic would be lighter, and as she was really a stranger to London, it might be an idea to go to see some of the main tourist sights. Sarah agreed wholeheartedly, eager after her secret walk that morning. Sebastion was commandeered to be the driver. Alina and Lovage were asked also; Alina was delighted but Lovage declined as she needed to prepare the evening meal and she knew the sights well enough.

As they got in the car the next morning, Judith suggested to Sebastion a tour of the main tourist spots today and maybe tomorrow a closer look at the business skyline to the east.

Off they went, Judith in the front seat, in her role as guide, Sarah and Alina comfortable in the back. The roads were quite empty and the driving easy; Judith correct again. Before long they had seen and parked for a better view where they could, Piccadilly Circus, down past Buckingham Palace, over the Thames near Battersea Power Station. Crossed the river again, Big Ben and around Parliament Square, along the Embankment with good views of The Eye and The Shard, along to the Tower of London, left at Tower Bridge and back through the skyscrapered city and home.

Judith commended Sebastion that he had shown

them all the main sights in one large circuit. He said he knew London quite well and the traffic was easy. Had they enjoyed it? They all had, particularly Sarah, as she had only been to London once before as a small child and it was very impressive.

It had given her one or two ideas. She now knew this was the place to be.

Back home, Judith, always keen for more progress to the awakening asked, "What will you do next Sarah?"

"I'll wait for the Lord to tell me."

Chapter 19

A week of new beginnings. Well, that's how it felt at their new base for the four. The weekend over, they resumed their previous roles. It never felt like work for them; it was their calling.

All four of them were in the garden relaxing, taking a well-earned break in the sunshine. It had been a relentless couple of days getting to grips with their new working area and the buzz amongst them was only favourable.

Sebastion had installed and set up the computers, printers, phone system, all the paraphernalia necessary for modern life. He had been invited to join the group by Alina because of his expertise in that field, with Sarah's consent. He'd joined about a year ago when an invited guest had brought him along to one of Freja Sarah's earliest events and he had been blown away (his quote), by the experience. He was at a time in his life, mid-thirties, when he had been searching for a new direction. He had worked for various tech companies and a heavy discontentment had set in. Already quite spiritual, the move to Sarah's manor house was irresistible. He'd taken the vow to Sarah and it was beyond what he'd hoped for.

Already with Sarah was Alina, a long-time friend from college, who had been lacking any direction when she had met Sarah 'by chance' (all set up by Sarah, who had recognised a soul mate). She was innermost to some of Sarah's confidences, though not the travelling. A true believer in the divine, she accepted without hesitation that Sarah was the new Chosen One, but Sarah did look to Alina for 'earthly' advice.

Judith, the planner and organiser, had been invited in by Sebastion as an ex-work colleague. He knew her qualities well. Now in her mid-thirties, she'd been through a difficult divorce and was another lost soul. Once he'd shown her the truth at a country event, she was enthralled and knew her path was set. She was the main player at finding the correct venues and audiences for Sarah. Before her arrival, the events had mostly taken place in churches or other similar small halls, but Judith had moved beyond this to a new and different audience. Through her wealthy family connections she was able to convince or bully many more moneyed and powerful players to attend small exclusive events at private venues or later at conference centres. Sceptical before arrival, all were convinced Sarah was the new Chosen One and without exception all were keen to be involved in the new phase of the journey to the enlightened pathway.

Lovage, so named by hippy parents, truly was a gift from God, attractive, mid-twenties, overflowing with charisma and with the face of an angel. She always addressed the invited audience before and after Sarah's appearance. The events were always beautifully stage-managed by her and carefully orchestrated to captivate, with so little, it seemed, effort. Magical to look at, a mesmeric voice, and when not presenting Sarah, always happy to turn her capable hands to anything, however mundane.

Sarah, with the help of the Almighty, had somehow been presented with the perfect four, plus Andrew, already deeply religious, the perfect overseer of her finances – so important up till now. Fortune follows the brave, and Sarah was that recipient.

Each one was one hundred percent behind Sarah and would lay down their lives for her. They would follow her path as they believed totally that she would take them on her pathway to the New Jerusalem.

Unknown to them, the word was beginning to slowly spread beyond her Watchers upon High

This of course had been foreseen by Freja Sarah.

*

Neil let Miles know by phone that it was another dead end at Marc's house. The only difference was a small scrap of paper in a bin, partially hidden so as not to be completely readable. He took a careful mental note of all he could decipher and would give a copy of it to Miles when they met at the pub later. He hoped he liked puzzles.

He was due to visit Lain's house shortly, but couldn't honestly say he was looking forward to it. It was a hopeless task when you really didn't have a clue what you were looking for. Even if he took Miles with him, which he obviously couldn't, he guessed the result would pretty much be the same: nothing of interest. How wrong he was.

Midday arrived. He was already in the chair. An early cleaning start saw to that. He now considered the cleaning as a way of being paid to keep fit rather than going to a gym. He was already partially dozing.

Checking his watch, he closed his eyes and instantly stood in Lain's hallway. All was quiet. Miles' information had been correct. Then, he heard voices upstairs. Dammit. So much for Miles.

He moved into the adjacent room where he could still see the stairs and hallway and faded out, still there, as Lain's wife (he assumed) came down the stairs, only partially clothed, followed by a young fit-looking guy in shorts. In the hall they gave each other a long embarrassing kiss as she told him she wished Lain would go away more often.

Hands all over each other, he agreed, and said how sorry he was to have to go back to the gym and give more lessons, rather than spend the rest of the afternoon with her.

That was enough for Neil. He was out of there in a flash and back sitting in his chair with a large grin on his face. Okay, he thought, it may not have been exactly what Miles was after, but for Miles to know Lain's wife was having an affair with her gym instructor would be music to his ears.

He couldn't wait to give the news to him later, but in a cruel, fun way. He spent a little while sorting out the half- readable scrap of paper and then went off for a proper afternoon nap.

*

They met at the pub bar later. A little earlier than normal, to ensure they were not interrupted.

"How did you get on, Neil?

"Well, a bit disappointing again, not surprised, only just been there really."

"Yeah. I guess you're right. What about at Lain's?"

"I'll come back to him later. I'll just get some peanuts."

Miles was already sunk low in his seat, eyes drifting into the middle distance.

"Okay, right," said Miles, looking at his pint, head hung low.

"I did find a small note on a scrap of paper that had fallen into the waste paper bin, but had wedged itself behind an old envelope so I could only see some of the writing. I took note of what I could see." Neil passed it to Miles.

"You can nearly make out a couple of words and the start, or endings of a couple of others. It'll give you something to do. I hope you like puzzles."

Miles screwed up his eyes, really trying to decipher

141

it. "I can read a bit. Is that all you could see?"

"'Fraid so. I tried from different angles but that was it."

"Fair enough, Neil. It may be something, you never know." He put it carefully in his pocket to study later. "What about at Lain's?"

"Nothing obvious, he seems like the careful, tidy type." Neil knew only too well the importance of timing and moved just slightly to the side of Miles. He waited until Miles put his beer glass to his mouth, took his first mouthful and said, "Did I mention that Lain's wife is shagging her gym instructor?"

Timed to perfection, a great mouthful of beer erupted from Miles' mouth and went everywhere. All the eyes of the pub went to Miles who was still out of control, coughing and spluttering.

Neil, kindness personified, said innocently, "Are you okay, Miles?"

Waiting till he had some control over himself, shaking his head at Neil, he said, "You bastard. You did that on purpose. Look what you made me do."

Neil couldn't stop laughing, nor could half the pub as the barman gave Miles a towel.

Further timed to perfection, Greig ambled up saying, "You okay, Miles? Something wrong with the beer?"

Chapter 20

I stood at the window, looking out at the Brighton view in front of me; if you liked car parks this was the hotel room for you. Dan promised a quick phone call home, but it was twenty minutes before he finally turned up. He'd rung me earlier to move the timing forward. I had no problem with that as my weekend had been on the boring side; my fault. Truthfully, I was eager to get the week ahead started and now we were.

On the journey down, he'd confessed that the electrical storm was just used by him as an excuse, as Jill had been having a bit of a go (his words) and needed some sleep and help with their baby.

He bounced in, clearly excited by the prospects ahead. "Princess Leia, sorry, Lucy."

I didn't laugh.

"You can 'leap' back at any time, right? So how about this afternoon? Let's see what it brings."

"How come on the first one you suggested the same time as the attack?"

"It was our first and I wanted to make it dramatic. Apologies, never again."

143

"Fine by me," I said.

"Okay, what about four o'clock?"

"Suits me, that's in half an hour, so let me change into my evening wear, relax and I'll see you later."

He left the room with a thumbs up.

I changed quickly and then relaxed into the chair, my mind still too active to doze, but closed my eyes anyway. Before too long, using my usual method of focusing on the time and place ahead for a short while and then un-focusing, I was there.

Steadying myself between the two shrubs at the front of the house, I checked the curtains were drawn and set-tled myself. There was a hazy darkness, no stars but a light moon and that, coupled with the streetlighting, was almost perfect for viewing. Across the road into the park, I could see perfectly well for at least half the distance I wanted to. No car had parked in front of me; there were double yellow lines on the opposite side and just a few cars parked on this side.

In the park there was no sign of movement, all still, but the road itself was a little busy with some cars in both directions, but mostly with a steady stream of cy-clists, maybe a group ride.

Two elderly ladies came by with their dogs, out to-gether. They passed quite close to me. I could hear them talking but neither looked my way. I was in deep shade in my dark 'uniform'. Then, from the park came a fast, fully lit cyclist who turned left at the road. I'd seen his lights from a distance so discounted him.

Then there followed a period of quiet. I wondered if

I'd got the right night, but knew better. I was tempted to try and get a little closer, but heeded Dan's instructions to stay hidden. A couple of cars passed but that was about it. I was still alert but beginning to think about the next and final visit, when I thought I caught just a glimpse of movement in the park but at the peak of my viewing distance. Now in alert mode, a touch of optimism went through me .

I held my breath – impossible – but that's how I felt, hypnotised to that area.

Then, I saw it was a portly, slow old man with a small light-coloured dog walking towards me.

No. I was sure it was the same old man I'd seen previously at the other park.

Coincidence – hardly likely.

As he walked towards me, I couldn't believe what I was seeing; I would have blinked my eyes if I could. The hunched, slow old man suddenly stood taller, and quickly increased his walking pace. He seemed to somehow raise the dog out in front of him as though the lead was rigid and the dog didn't seem to mind. With his free hand he somehow shortened the lead until the dog was by his stomach. The dog made no sound or movement and as they got nearer the road he had a quick look around, then opened his jacket and pushed the dog and lead under his armpit so both arms were free. Then, to top it all off, he pulled off his hair and stuffed it in his pocket. The penny dropped and I realised it was a wig.

As he stood to cross the road right in front of me, gone was the old man, replaced by a younger model; a young guy with a shaved head. Still furtively looking in all directions, he crossed the road diagonally to a car. I heard the key beep as he opened the rear door and threw his jacket with the dog inside into the back. No sound of protest from the dog.

Clever guy. Who would fear or suspect an old man walking a dog.

He started the car. I stepped forward onto the wall and found myself with a further step on the pavement. The car, without lights, moved out, going away from me, just as a cyclist came along in the same direction. With the help of the cyclist's front lamp, I managed to catch the last two numbers of his registration – HT.

I was sure of it. That was him. But he didn't allow for me. Before I realised it, my time was up. I was back in my hotel room. I left my chair, had a drink of water to help me collect my thoughts and then Dan arrived.

"Any better this time?" he said, with a touch of optimism.

By now I had managed to compose myself and went through the whole experience detail by detail. He sat there completely captivated by my story, or so I thought.

I leaned back as I finished and he said, "Let me get this straight. You're telling me that a young guy who impersonates an old man walking a stuffed dog on a telescopic metal rod is the rapist."

"That's it in a nutshell. Not only that, but I managed to get the last two letters of his registration plate, so all I have to do is get the rest and we've got him."

Shaking his head as though in disbelief he said, "If it

wasn't so far-fetched, Lucy, I wouldn't believe it, but I do. This is one very clever guy."

"But not clever enough. He won't beat us."

Dan sat thinking. I already knew what I wanted to do and wondered if Dan was thinking along the same lines – and he was.

"Can you 'travel', sorry, I mean leap, twice in one day. If so, how do you feel about either going back to where you've just been or going to the last scene, before the attack, just to see if you can find his car and get the full plate, and to check that he was responsible for all three attacks."

"That's what I was thinking. Let me go to the third scene. I only know the car was a grey saloon. I reckon that's enough if he's parked there. There can't be that many grey saloons."

"Let's go now and check the obvious parking places."

"Let's do that."

We arrived in the area and could see how crowded it was in the afternoon. It made sense; this park to the east of the town was full of activities that could be enjoyed well into the evenings, especially summer evenings. It seemed such a strange place to choose. Parking was virtually impossible along the roads, but it would be a lot quieter in late evening. I could see most of the parking was along a main road, with parking on both sides, and when I relayed this information to Dan, he decided we should concentrate on one section of about half a mile, between the two paths leading from the park.

"Can you walk that distance in the time you have, do

you think, Lucy?"

"Yeah. I can't see a problem with the distance. The only problem will be other people. To be on the safe side, I will have to keep changing sides of the road."

Dan had been searching continually for a spot for me to leap to that would be dark enough not to arouse any suspicion.

"What about over there?" he said, pointing to a gap between two gorse type bushes just off the path. "They're a bit prickly so you'll have to be careful."

I raised my eyebrows and glared at him.

"Just get on the path as quick as possible, avoiding dogs," he said smirking.

"Now we're on to a bit of success, are you going to be like this all day?"

"Okay, I'll control myself."

"C'mon, Dan, enough reconnaissance. Good word, I'm learning police talk fast. Let's go."

*

Back in the hotel coffee bar we were relaxing, probably for the first time on this 'case'. It was just after six thirty and fairly shortly I aimed to go upstairs for the leap. We'd agreed that the timing should be around quarter to ten on the assumption that the suspect would have to make sure his car was parked at the perfect spot for him. We both reckoned not too near a streetlight, but just another assumption on a night of assumptions. We went our separate ways, agreeing to meet around seven.

I sat down at last for a bit of peace and quiet without Dan on steroids. I think he could smell the sweet aroma of success and to be honest, so could I. This leap should be the easiest of the three: well-lit area, more people around, and all I've got to do is check car registration numbers. Book dinner, Dan.

*

It's amazing how the evening light can vary even at the same time of night. Moonless tonight, but still a light dusty blue, the stars just beginning to force their way through. The sun had set behind a large purple wave of a cloud. It was beguiling, too beguiling. Stop this, Lucy, remember what your first thought should be: 'the first step is the most frightening'. Stop being poetic. I was too comfortable, convinced this leap would be a 'piece of cake'.

From my shadowed position the light was mottled around me. I was well camouflaged. Nobody was near. In fact, I couldn't see anyone anywhere. That was a relief.

So, I carefully walked a few steps to the pathway; just a few more and I was by the road.

Turning left onto the path, a couple of girls were walking and chatting together coming towards me. One moved behind the other to let me pass. I'd passed the test, ordinary me, just like everyone else.

The road had an occasional car or bike going past in different directions; there was now plenty of parking and people here and there. I set off to walk the few hundred yards to the other path, the route I had agreed with Dan, checking number plates as I walked. No grey saloons in sight, so my pace was pretty good, when a man pulling a dog behind him came towards me.

Oh God.

My relief was palpable when a large golden retriever came around from the back of him. The dog looked straight at me, at about a cars length, so I stepped into the road and crossed with a car parked between us. Good. No problem with the dog.

Back on the pavement, but on the other side of the road, a couple of fast cyclists zoomed past, then in the distance, another dog walker. I was preparing to cross again but waited a bit, and a lone female came into view with a small terrier. Having seen how excitable those dogs could get around me, I quickly crossed again.

Couple more cyclists went past as I mounted the pavement and then a car pulled in behind me. I skipped forward to check the car in front, black not grey, when something just forced me to turn. The car was a grey hatchback with its rear door open, and there was a dog making a few excitable noises. There was a vibration that I'd never felt before – something wasn't right.

I was hypnotised by the sound of the dog and just about managed to force myself to look down to the registration number: GX15 YHT. A ripple passed through me. I could see my hands tingling and vibrating.

He closed the boot with a loud bang. I looked back to see the stuffed dog already on the ground, fixed to the lead-rod. I knew it wasn't a real dog on a lead, I knew it was fake, but the way he handled and moved it was really believable, even from a short distance. I could really see how the victims were fooled. He'd also put his old man costume on, the overlarge jacket and the grey wig and his practised slow walking stoop.

What a memorable performance. Before I was lulled too far into his act, he turned, and started towards me.

He raised his head slowly and looked me in the eye, very frightening, icy and cold. All I could think about was getting away, so I turned fast. He sped up. I didn't want to let him know I could just disappear, so I moved fast between two parked cars and crossed the road just in time in front of another car, forcing him to slow down.

If he managed to grab at me, obviously that couldn't happen, but I hoped it didn't come to that. I wanted him to think I was just one who managed to get away. I could see he was looking to follow me across the road.

He waited for a van to go by. As it went by, so did I.

What went through his head, I can't and don't want to imagine, but I was very happy to be back in my chair.

I called Dan and once he arrived, I went through most of the experience with him, but left out the strange unexplainable terror that I had felt in the man's presence.

The guy was evil.

Dan sat back with a contented smile, looked at me and said, "Really well done, Lucy, a great job. That really was a leap into the past – three times and, thinking about it, three leaps into the dark."

"Thanks, Dan, I know it's an old cliché, but I couldn't

have got anywhere near him without your planning – team effort."

"To more team efforts," he said, raising an arm with a pretend glass."

"We said somebody had to stop this guy and it was us," I grinned at him, though my smile hid the shadow of terror that still clung to me.

"Right, let me ring Kim and give her the news. Maybe they can get this guy tonight."

Dan went back to his room for ten minutes, I assumed to pack, and then returned to where I was waiting. He suggested we grab dinner, stay overnight and go direct to Cloud 10 tomorrow to have a look at the next case.

Over dinner, he took a call from Kim, who sent congratulations to us both. Apparently, the suspect was now in custody, helping the police with their enquiries. We drank to that.

Chapter 21

Make your plans, as Gods do,
But as ever, the fates decide.

After a morning meeting with Judith, Sarah now convened a meeting with all of the four after lunch, in order to get them to agree to her wishes. It started well and ended well.

Sarah started by admitting she had only a limited knowledge of London, only what she'd seen and read over the years. What she needed and asked for was their help.

"London needs events and London events need to be spectacular."

The four agreed on that and between them came up with an idea to have two or three targeted events with an invited guest list featuring only the London artistic set comprising of only the major players in film, TV, theatre and music. A carefully invited group that would not only enlarge Sarah's flock but more importantly prove very beneficial for publicity. These celebrities were followed by many on the internet, and featured in the press, and their endorsement of her could only help speed and strengthen the coming of the true path.

One subject agreed on by them all was that they must have no contact with the major religious leaders of the main denominations. These so-called leaders could never accept any deviation from their scriptures. Sarah would never be accepted as the new Chosen One; that was best left to their different congregations. They would deny what was before them as the devil's work. Her doctrine of 'accept me and learn' would be heretical to them. So they would be ignored.

The time was now, to enlighten the multitudes to the light.

It was time for the spectacular.

But first, the small and creative venues, and this was where the four could help. She needed to be where even the non-believers wanted to believe. They must yearn to be involved, to join with the watchers upon high, it must become their life as she knew it would.

Together they sat, as a team, the four believed, but to Sarah they were like worker bees, and she was Queen. They were there to do her bidding.

However, their knowledge of London life was needed – a world largely unknown to her – but for now her light would shine in London, just a steppingstone on her quest. Her message was quite simple: I must be followed, for we are not in times past, I am needed for times future. The spell was broken by Lovage.

"Freja Sarah, in my life before the chosen time, I had a good friend, a very musical friend here in London. He is well known and respected, a person I shall contact, he has many friends. He would listen and trust what I say."

"Thank you, Lovage. Please summon your friend and his friends to our gathering."

Alina then told Sarah that unfortunately she had no connections anywhere so sadly could not help, but would assist in any way.

Sebastion elatedly offered, "I have many relatives and connections in the theatre world. It's a very close-knit world of intimate friendships. If I invite one, many will wish to be included. I know who shall be in the selected few for the first event. We may have to offer another."

"Thank you, Sebastion, great words of encouragement. Once these new beginnings have been contacted, Judith will organise, as she does so well, two or three small gatherings. Lovage will address the audience in her normal sublime way, and I will make my customary appearance and address to them. Let us make these plans in haste as, once past, I intend to host a large gathering of many thousands in a London park, possibly Primrose Hill, according to Alina one of the most beautiful spots in London on a summer's day. Chosen ones, the days and weeks ahead will be world changing. Blessings to you all. Praise the new dawn on the horizon."

The meeting ended as it started: well.

*

Sarah hadn't quite expected the pleasure that life can

bring with just a simple change of location.

Now the meeting was over, and the four had their new tasks, Alina aside. Sarah needed her. She was an innocent child in the modern world and Sarah found her views on the way ahead a perfect foil. She was a just confidante against the difficult times ahead. For the unworthy will take no shelter in the coming storm. They must accept and learn what awaits.

Now for a short meditative walk to refresh her mind.

Sarah let the four know she was not to be disturbed, changed again into her street clothes, now with an added baseball cap with her hair in a bun beneath. Dark glasses completed the transformation. She opened her personal door to the world outside; for a while she would be completely free and unknown.

This time she decided to walk to Kensington Gardens, not too far through the energetic streets.

The gardens were laid out quite formally, but oddly this had the reverse effect on her thoughts. She was able to somehow tune out all sounds of the bustling city and move into a quiet meditative state. The noise and formality improved her transcendence. It was in these moments and shortly before she was fully awake in the morning that God spoke to her and it was no different today – thank the Lord.

The thoughts made her smile. Enough for an ice cream treat.

Sarah decided to have only two forthcoming events. One for the musical world and one for the theatre world. Both very important for the enlightenment. Then after the events she would give each group a 'happening' relevant to their lifestyles.

There would be no words that could describe the subtlety to them.

She could not thank God, the Almighty One, enough.

Chapter 22

Some might say the quietest week of the year is the third week in July, the week before schools break up for the summer holidays. That may be the case, but it didn't start that way for me and Dan as we entered Cloud late Tuesday morning to a champagne welcome, minus the champagne, as Nikki had substituted elderflower.

Darryl, Kim, Henry and Nikki stood to welcome us 'home', so to speak.

Darryl spoke. "Lucy, Dan, in your first week you've come good, exceeded all expectations so early. Absolutely well done. A toast to you both!"

We all raised our glasses at that.

"Don't think you'll have this every time, you two. That's it, everyone back to work," said Darryl, filling up his glass again.

"Take no notice of him," laughed Kim, "That was an ace result. Did you enjoy it? I know it's not a good thing to say about a rape, but did you enjoy the work?"

Dan motioned with his arm for me to speak.

"I wasn't sure, till we started, and then I really did. I began to think I was really doing police work."

"Absolutely," said Henry.

"You absolutely were, Lucy," Dan added, smiling proudly. "If that wasn't police work, I'd like you to tell me what is. You were superb, especially your powers of observation."

Kim followed his sentiments with, "You were amazing. Dan's already told me how good your descriptions of the scenes were, especially at night. The amount of detail was telling. Are you sure you haven't done this before?"

We all laughed at that.

"Kim," I asked. "How did you let Brighton police know without giving away any clues about our involvement?"

"That was easy. We have a telephone line, nationwide, managed 24/7, used for giving anonymous tips about any crime, past or present. We just passed on the tip to Brighton, and told them it sounded genuine. They took it from there, and quickly, to their credit. I heard from them later that they were pretty sure they'd found the guy. He is now helping the police with their enquiries; even the dog is in custody."

We all laughed again – police humour.

"Again you two, congrats, let there be more," said Darryl as he walked off to his office.

Kim and Henry sauntered off, then over her shoulder, Kim said, "Dan, a few more cases have come through, I've forwarded them to you."

Nikki collected the glasses, then headed to her desk.

By this point I was dying for a coffee, so I headed

downstairs to grab one.

"Do you want me to bring you one up?" I asked Dan.

"If you don't mind, but you go back down afterwards. It'll take me a while to read through the files Kim's sent."

As I walked into the galley, I found Nikki sorting out the glasses with Morry watching from the sofa.

"It went well then, Lucy?"

"Yeah, it really did. Once or twice it caught me off guard and was a bit scary. When I finally came face to face with the rapist, he gave me such a look of hatred and at the same time saw me, I think, as his next victim. I never realised there was so much hatred and anger in the world."

"Unfortunately, here, we get to see a bit more than we should," said Nikki.

"But it does give me a feeling of satisfaction that we got him. That easily beats the horror. I hope I never lose that."

"I don't think you will, Lucy."

Nikki left the room and Morry closed his eyes. I grabbed Dan's coffee and took it up to him. He said he was still looking through the files and would be for at least another hour, so I left him to it and decided to give Morry a bit of company for a while.

I was relaxed and enjoying a story in one of the galley's magazines when Dan came through the door. I'd completely lost track of time; it was a good story. Dan was obviously hungry as he pinched my last biscuit and said, "It's way past lunch. Do you want to go out and get something to eat?"

"I can't really be bothered, sorry, Dan. I might just get a sandwich and eat it here."

"Yeah, not a bad idea. I'll check with Nikki where to go. I can eat at my desk; it'll save a bit of time. What do you like?"

"Anything 'eggy', please."

And off he went. I remember him talking to Nikki. I was back in my story and the next thing I knew, he was back.

"That was quick."

"Yeah, really easy, just across the road. I suppose I never noticed the sandwich bar as we always come in the other end. There you go," he said, handing me an egg and cress. "I'll see you later."

Later turned out to be a couple of hours later and while I'd spent the time relaxing, Dan hadn't and looked quite hassled.

"Why don't we leave this till tomorrow?" I suggested. "We can go through it together then. You look a bit done in."

"Thanks for that. Maybe you're right."

"We can come and go here when we want, so let's go."

And on that note, we let Nikki know we were off and left.

I took the magazine home with me.

Chapter 23

Yesterday's evening at the pub with Miles had so far been the highlight of the week for Neil, but it was still early days, although looking at his diary nothing was going to change that. He needed a bit of stimulation. He'd sat around for most of the day and now was on his way to the Compasses, hoping for a bit of company other than just Miles. He needed a bit of rowdy pub culture. Bring on Ray and Greig, at least.

His walking pace was increasing, but being Neil he was always half-expecting disappointment. He walked through the open bar door and wasn't surprised to see none of his drinking mates were there. Too lazy to go to the Northern straightaway, he ordered his usual at the bar and to cheer himself he got a packet of pork scratchings, which he accidentally dropped on the floor. He just knew it was going to be one of those nights. He reached down, picked them up and raised his head, just as Miles, Ray and Greig walked in and towards him, still stooped.

"How many have you already had?" laughed Greig "C'mon get up off the floor it's only eight o'clock."

Neil, just happy to see them all, laughed along at

himself.

"What are you drinking then, lads, coke or shandy, and just to let you know, right now, I'm not prepared to share my pork scratchings."

Three more pints were ordered along with two packets of peanuts. Miles was always sniffy about salty snacks ruining the taste of the beer.

The banter flew thick and fast for a good while but in the end they quietened down and moved to a booth away from the bar, clutching pint number three. They leaned back just settled until Ray went for a cigarette outside and Greig needed the loo.

Sensing his only moment, Neil asked Miles, "Have you used the bit of info about Lain's wife?"

"No, not yet, I shall keep that ready until the time is right. I found out, through a lady friend, which gym she uses. I know it's a bit over the top and pathetic, but I had to find out the instructor's name."

"Why?" asked Neil with a puzzled look.

"I need to be fully armed for the future. What if she changes gyms or gets a female instructor? I needed his name. So I went to the gym as a potential member and on the notice board were photos of all the instructors. I took a photo of it. Hang on, I'll get it up on my phone and you can see if you recognise him."

"Jesus. Miles, are you sure this is necessary?"

"'Fraid so. I've got to cover all possibilities."

Miles opened and enlarged the photo on his phone, then passed it to Neil who straightaway recognised the guy.

"That's him, second on left, top line."

Miles enlarged again so he could read his name.

"Pepe Ornalitto. What sort of name is that?"

"Beware the continental," laughed Neil. "But truthfully, Miles, he sounded like he came from Essex."

"Whatever, Neil. That's a name I ain't ever gonna forget... Pepsi Canaloni."

"What are you two finding so funny?" said Ray.

"Nothing much, just about someone you don't know. Don't worry Ray, it wasn't you, it was Greig," said Miles.

"Thanks a lot," smiled Greig.

It was Miles' round, and after finishing his pint, he asked what everyone wanted, but the other three were only halfway through their pints. He agreed to leave it ten minutes and as he went to temporarily put the money into his shirt top pocket, the small piece of paper from Neil yesterday fell out from between the two ten pound notes and onto the floor.

Ray lent down to retrieve it for him. Miles quickly said, "Careful with that Ray, don't get it wet, it may be important."

"What is it Miles?"

"Just a little puzzle I'm trying to decipher, with no luck yet."

Ray had a good look at it, held it up, moved it about a bit and said, "That's easy mate, it's an address."

"You sure, Ray?"

"Look, I'm a builder, and like all builders we get given scraps like this all the time. Usually with coffee stains and worse. We have to work them out or we'd lose business. Builders aren't known for their handwriting skills."

"Can you read it, then?"

"Not all, of course. First word is either check or clock. I'd guess check. Second line might be clowns. Third line, wait, I'm good at addresses."

He then wrote across the empty space with a pretend pencil.

"It fits perfectly. I bet it's Covent Garden. Last line impossible."

"Ray, you're a genius," said Miles, taking back the bit of paper from Ray. "Has anyone got a proper pencil?"

Of course, Ray, the builder, had a small one in his pocket and passed it across. Miles grabbed it and wrote in the space 'vent Gard' and it fit like a dream.

"Ray, I'll say that again, genius. Let me get you any drink you'd like."

Ray stood, took a bow, in fact three bows, and settled for a brandy.

Neil looked across at Miles and gleefully said, "Put on those walking shoes."

"You betcha."

Greig, who'd just listened through all this, said, "I hope you've all finished now, Sherlock. That's all been kinda interesting, at least for Miles, but I've got something a bit better, well, might be. I've been invited to a special event this weekend, musicians only; not just that, the top echelon only."

"Well how'd you get in then?" said Ray, getting a bit

of revenge.

"I dunno, really. One of the bands I've been working with for some time, when invited, told them I was an important member. I have been on all their hits; don't worry, none of you lot would have heard of them. Anyway, I'm in as a special guest. Apparently it's some mystic thing; all bands love that kind of thing. I'm sworn to keep quiet about it. Oh dear... whoops."

Miles had tuned into this even though the others hadn't.

"You interested, Miles? It'll probably be another Derren Brown-type thing. I'll probably end up barking like a dog if you say the word beer."

They all bellowed at that – for too long.

When at last the barking stopped Neil tapped in, "Well, that's you two sorted out with something interesting to do this week. What about me and Ray?"

"Speak for yourself, Neil, I'm doing a lovely attic conversion, top price. Working for a cracking model type. Every time we go up in the roof, she goes into the garden for a bit of topless sunbathing. Thank God it's not November. I'm sure she does it on purpose. My mate's taken a photo from the roof. I'll show you next time I'm in."

"So it's only poor old me that's sad and lonely," moaned Neil.

"You could always see your girlfriend a bit more, you know."

"That's not a bad idea, Ray. I will. Whenever I arrange to meet her usually something else crops up."

At that, Ray headed off, making sure he got his pencil back from Miles, and Greig got up to leave as well, moaning about modern bands working during the day, not like the good old days when they'd played into the night

"What's happened to modern youth?" he sighed, shaking his head.

"Just the two of us left now, Miles," Neil said leaning forward, and carried on in a serious tone. "I don't want you to take offence at what I'm going to say, Miles, but I think we're going about this like a couple of amateurs. I know revenge sounds sweet, but I think we should change tack. We should start looking for fresh leads, not old stuff."

Miles sat back and Neil waited for the blast that didn't come.

"I hate being wrong and I have been, Neil. I have been a cocky, stupid sod and you are right."

"Let me take a couple of days to track down what I can in Covent Garden, and we'll rethink and replan. Are you up for that?"

He held out his hand to Neil, who shook it – a fresh new start.

Chapter 24

After such an amazing start to our time at Cloud 10, I guess the days following our trip were always going to feel like we were going in reverse. The weather was dull; the new set of case files were dull and spending all day going through them was even more dull. Not one of them stood out as being particularly important or life-altering. Dan proposed that because of the one quick success we'd had, the higher echelons in the Force were hoping that this was going to be the norm, so had inundated us with stale dross. Our early success would be difficult to follow, but that was for us to worry about later. All we could do for now was concentrate on today.

We went through the cases one by one, putting them in some kind of order – possibles, maybes and unlikelys; not exactly scientific but then what we were doing wasn't scientific. Despite the dullness, I was surprised at how well I took to the mundane side of police work; the kind of work that Dan had been undertaking for years… poor Dan. We decided to concentrate on cases inside the M25 corridor as there would be no need to leave London – I could just go upstairs. There were a couple of new cases that stood out, but none seemed quite as interesting as the kidnap of the German businessman Klaus Huber. So that was the one we decided to work on.

Though it seemed rather tame compared to some of the other cases, it was the lack of clues that intrigued us both. There were no clues; none whatsoever. Dan summed the case up as a well-rehearsed and choreographed piece of trickery, which may or may not have involved inside help.

On the morning he'd been taken, Klaus had been to the German embassy for a coffee with an old colleague. Upon leaving the embassy and walking back in the direction he'd come, he came across a car with a rear puncture (he assumed) and a person kneeling down sorting out the jack. Cleverly, the person dropped a spanner at Klaus' feet and asked if he could pass it back. As a good citizen, of course he'd leant down to hand it back. Immediately, another person had appeared behind him and both men had bundled him straightaway into the boot. They had then got back in the car, leaving the jack there, no fingerprints, and had driven off as though nothing had happened. No one had noticed anything – one slick operation. During the journey, the only thing Klaus could remember of any relevance was that he thought the car went over a bridge across the Thames.

When the car had stopped, Klaus had been told to put a hood over his head – if he didn't he would be shot. He took their advice. Once helped out of the boot, he was told to keep his hands in his trouser pockets and was then bundled into a ground-floor room with adjoining toilet; no windows. The whole escapade had taken about twenty minutes and although they had spoken to him, he had been unable to identify any particular accents. He had been told that he would be fed well as long as he kept his hood on. Of course, he complied.

He had no idea why he was being held, and when he was bundled back into the car and dropped off in Albert car park to the west of Battersea Park two days later, he had no idea that the reason for his release was because a ransom had been paid.

After fumbling with the hood over his face, he had finally been able to break free and make his way to a police station, though the car was long gone by then. Unfortunately, he had barely any information of value to give the police. All they discovered was that the ransom had been paid through a series of bank transfers across the world that morning; instructions had been given on an untraceable phone. It was a very professional job.

Dan looked up from the file. "I can't see there's much we can do on this one other than go to the scene where he was taken and where he was dropped off. We have good timings on both. What do you think, shall we go and have a look first?"

"It does seem like all we can do, but you never know."

Our plan agreed, Dan and I went down to let Nikki know.

"Sounds a good plan, Dan," she said, laughing at her rhyme. "Do you want to use one of the office cars?"

170

"This place surprises me over and over again. You have office cars?"

"Of course. Didn't they tell you?"

"Evidently not."

"We have two, both parked at the Shelton Road car park, about five minutes' walk, level three. Two Golfs, one light and one dark grey, take your pick. And you'll need this." She handed him an official notice for the dashboard. "Now you can park wherever you wish." She threw him the keys. "Don't crash."

"Thanks for the vote of confidence," Dan said, laughing.

It was as easy as Nikki said, and a short time later, we were parked near the German Embassy in Belgravia.

"What time was he here?" I asked Dan.

"He arrived for coffee with his friend at ten thirty and left at eleven fifteen." said Dan, "and my guess is, he was followed here, and they must have waited somewhere close. Someone must have had a bit of inside knowledge, from where, who knows."

"That sounds likely. You can't just guess on a kidnapping. It's a pity I can't leap to when he was taken, but there's just no cover and I'd stick out like a sore thumb. They'd see me instantly."

Dan nodded in agreement, and we drove to Battersea Park. Failing to get a parking space in Albert Road car park, we left the car outside with a well-placed police notice on the dashboard.

I followed Dan as he walked to the exact bay where the kidnap victim had been dropped off. There were a

171

number of trees nearby, and plenty of cover near one tree, so we decided on that spot. We knew the times of capture and release; now just to check out the weather so as not to be conspicuous, and to make sure we dressed accordingly.

A little while later, we drove back to Cloud, and ate the sandwiches we had picked up on the way in the galley.

"I'll aim to do both leaps this afternoon. If I can, which one shall I do first?" I asked Dan.

"Let's do them in time order. It was raining that morning, so you can walk around a couple of times without arousing any suspicion in a raincoat with your hat pulled down. Then do the car park later."

I nodded in agreement and went to grab another cup of milky tea, leaving Dan to head back upstairs. After finishing my drink, I went to the wardrobe, found a non-descript raincoat and hat, headed over to the leap, found my usual spot and lay down.

*

As all this was taking place at Cloud, Miles was taking his second walk around Covent Garden. He'd wasted yesterday wandering aimlessly with no success; not surprising as he'd been completely unprepared.

Not today. He'd done the research last night, printed off a good clear map and made himself a route that took in all the roads and small pedestrianised areas of which there were plenty. During the walk so far, he had been amazed at the number of small businesses tucked away in these little courtyards.

Something else had caught his eye and amused him. One of the roads was called Langley Street, and it still made him smile as he thought about it, as the Headquarters of the CIA in the US were located in Langley, Virginia. Perhaps someone with a sense of humour had named the street.

He rechecked his route, acting the role of a tourist, looking at the map carefully hidden inside the large tourist guidebook he'd obtained. He deliberately left the Langley Street area until last; he just had a feeling. He sat outside a bar with a beer watching the world go by, eager to go but savouring the moment. Something inside him sensed something.

He finished his beer and slowly, full of anticipation, walked to Langley Street. It looked a very ordinary road but halfway along it, he glanced to his left towards a café and his heart almost stopped.

There it was… Cloud 10. His head was on fire.

What to do. He took a couple of minutes to compose himself and nonchalantly walked up to the window, noticing the girl at her desk, and read the writing on the facia. Some kind of computer business. He reread the writing on the window, but it was written in some kind of computer geek speak. He didn't understand a word, why should he, but he knew enough to go home and read the website. He memorised the website name but once around the corner tapped it into his phone.

Home quick was his only thought.

*

I first noticed the drizzle, but it didn't seem to notice me. I was some way off the embassy, walking towards it along the pavement on the opposite side of the road. Walking slowly, taking in the moment. I knew what Klaus Huber looked like from a photo Dan had shown me: middle-aged, grey short and balding hair, dark suit and using a black umbrella.

I was about a couple of minutes' walk away, and could see the embassy flags hanging wet and limp, when suddenly, there he was, on the embassy side of the road. I sped up. Yes, that was definitely him. We almost passed each other but he turned right and up the steps to the main entrance. I slowed my pace and stopped in the pretence of altering my umbrella, noticing as I did so a BMW slowly coming down the street towards me. It came to a stop very close by, and the front passenger door opened. From across the road, a young blonde girl quickly crossed behind it, then got in fast.

As the car moved off, I calmly memorised the registration plate, before disappearing back to the leap. D.I. Firmin was on the case.

Dan was in the corridor as I walked out of the leap.

"That was quick."

"You bet. Blonde female following, picked up by BMW, registration plate HJ 69 LEF."

"What can I say?" Dan said incredulously.

"Coffee for me, telephone for you."

174

Dan grinned and disappeared, returning to the galley a few minutes later, looking glum.

"False plates, I'm afraid."

"Damn." Perhaps things had been going a little too well. "I'll try again at the car park in a while."

"Are you sure?"

"Yeah, yeah. Just give me an hour or so."

Dan went back to the office. For him, there was always more paperwork to go through.

Sighing, I headed downstairs to find Nikki.

"Sorry to trouble you, Nikki, but could you make me one of your herbal teas, the ones that make me really sleepy. If you're not too busy?"

"No problem, I'll be up in a minute. I need to get Morry onto those. He's been out for about four walks already today and I can tell he's looking for another."

"Try sleeping pills... or vodka," I laughed, heading back up to the galley.

Nikki came in a minute or so later. She'd talked Henry into giving Morry another walk, but only a short one.

"Same as before then, Lucy? A touch of déjà vu about today, isn't there?"

"Definitely. The same tea and a similar leap, I didn't do so well on the earlier one."

"Sometimes that's the way it goes. Your first case was so good it's probably better to have a small failure. Too much early success can have consequences. You'll be swamped with more cases; we'll have to get a larger office space, it could go on and on."

"Point taken. I'll make sure I fail," I grinned, taking the tea from Nikki as Nikki's phone rang. I carried on sipping my tea as she answered it.

"How do you spell Rogerson?... Oh, thanks, and your first name is Miles?... My colleague Mr Stephens is just out of the office. He'll be back shortly and will call you... You're a journalist worried about being hacked?... Yes, I'm sure we can help. I've got your number. He'll call shortly... Yes, thank you for calling."

As she finished the call, Henry came in with Morry. Nikki gave him Mr Rogerson's details and Henry said he'd have a quick cup of coffee and give him a call, which he did.

The weather on Thursday afternoon was pleasantly warm and bright, a normal July day, so I discarded the raincoat and swapped my dark hat for a large straw one, as I prepared to appear next to the car park. I had never tried to leap twice in one day and wondered if I would be able to, or if it might be different. Thanks to Nikki's herbal tea, I found myself alongside the tree just at the edge of the parking bays in the car park at Battersea in no time at all. Unlike earlier, there were a couple of empty spaces and just a few people milling around, and of course the dreaded dog walkers all bound for the park. Nobody seemed to look in my direction and the time drifted slowly.

Then, in came the BMW, reversing into the expected spot. Nothing happened for a while. All clear, they must have thought – I was out of sight. The passenger door opened and a well-built and well-dressed man stood quietly, surveying the scene, before speaking to the driver in a foreign language. He then went straight to the boot and in good English, maybe with a slight accent, told Klaus that everything was okay; there was nothing to worry about, unless he took his hood off. Klaus shouted from the boot that he would keep it on. The boot was opened, he was helped out, and told to face away from the car park, which he did.

The man got back in the car shouting, "Loss!"

They were gone in a flash and so was I. Straight back to Dan who looked up, giving me the high-eyebrowed quizzical look.

"You're getting very quick. Does that mean good or bad news?"

"You tell me, you're the detective. I think I heard the kidnappers speaking in German, or a language that sounded similar. I'm not sure, but what does 'loss' mean. Any idea?"

"I'll get it confirmed, but I think it means 'get going'. Anything else?"

"Well, I did get to see the passenger quite clearly. Maybe you could arrange for one of your police artists to contact us or I'll try and do an identikit picture."

"That's a very good result again, Lucy. Sounds like UK villains aren't involved; maybe some kind of inside job. Whatever happens, the Met are going to be happy with us. Well done, again."

"Thanks. I couldn't have done it without your careful planning and timing."

"Great work both of us then. I can't see much here for you to do now Lucy. Why don't you go home a bit early? I'll see you tomorrow. I've got a few phone calls to make. Just let Nikki know you're leaving."

*

On his way home a bit later, Dan stopped and let Nikki in on the latest news. He told her that Lucy had seen one of the men and he'd like a police artist to see her and get a likeness.

"Don't worry about that, Dan, I've been trained for that."

"Is there anything you can't do, Nikki?"

She just smiled.

Chapter 25

Miles was in deep conversation at the bar. He'd rung Neil after speaking to Henry at Cloud 10. He was pretty pleased with himself as an appointment had been made for him there at ten thirty tomorrow morning. He'd laboured on a bit, or so Neil thought, about all the traipsing around Covent Garden before stumbling upon the Cloud 10 offices just off Langley Street. Neil too was suspicious of that CIA coincidence.

He expanded on his phone call. He'd played the role quite well he thought, of the writer/journalist worried that his internet wasn't secure and could be hacked. Henry had assured him he could solve all his worries with a firewall and told him to bring all his devices with him.

For Miles, it all hinged on Friday morning, and Neil picked up on this. "So what are you expecting Miles? Have you any idea?"

"To be absolutely honest, haven't got a clue. But my journalistic nose tells me all is not as it seems."

"Well, at least it's something current. We're not chasing ghosts."

"Exactly my thoughts. Cloud 10's premises look just a little bit too substantial for a computer data protection company. Let's face it, these days you only need a desk to work from and sometimes not even that, but then again, what do I know about these things."

"Well, with a bit of luck and what we can do between us, we might be about to find out. I thought it might be an idea if I met you there to get an idea of what you're talking about. You mentioned a café nearby. I could have mooch about and meet you in the café afterwards."

"Good idea."

"What time's your appointment?"

"Ten thirty."

"Let's say I see you at the café just before ten thirty. I'll have a look around and see you back there about eleven. Half an hour should do it, if it's any longer you could give me a call as your pretend missus."

"If I'm right you'll have to see the place sometime. No time like the present."

"All agreed, another beer?"

Had anyone cared to look, they would have seen two very satisfied men sitting at the bar, and that's exactly what Greig saw as he came in.

"You two look like a couple of cats who got the cream. Lottery win? I must say it makes a change for you two."

"Hi, Greig, nothing special, you just caught us relaxing. We've both had a couple of days we're trying to forget. No Ray tonight? I wanted to get him a drink for his little favour."

"Not tonight, too busy, but I need a drink or two, same as you. If you or the public knew what poor musicians the young bands are, they would be shocked."

"Wasn't it always like that, Greig?" chipped in Neil. "Don't you remember The Monkees?"

"My grandad told me about them, Neil," he said with a wry smile, "but you're not wrong."

"Any news on your special event?" asked Miles.

"There is actually. Apparently, twenty special people involved in the music industry have been invited, virtually summoned, to outside the Abbey Road studios on Saturday night at eight o'clock. Whatever it is will only last about half an hour."

"Is that all you know?"

"Yeah. Everything. We've been told to keep quiet about it for our own benefit. If word gets out, too many will turn up and it could get out of hand so we're all keeping shtum, as you can see by me telling you lot. Keep quiet about it."

"How mysterious," said Miles. "I hope you're coming back here afterwards?"

"If you're gonna be here, I will."

"Okay, we will for sure," they both said, nodding their heads.

"Remember, you're sworn to secrecy about it and if I say the word beer you've got to bark," laughed Greig.

Another couple of their drinking mates turned up, but still no Ray, and the rest of the evening idled by in a good way, with the three of them all with something different to look forward to.

Nikki decided she had plenty of time before Henry's client turned up at ten thirty to undertake the identikit portrait of the car passenger. She pulled aside Lucy as she arrived at the office and told her to be ready at nine thirty. She told Lucy the whole procedure should only take about half an hour and to come on her own.

She'd commandeered Kim's office and set up the program on the computer, telling Lucy that she had full training for this and to just relax and remember the moment. She knew Lucy had very good powers of recollection and thought a good likeness was likely and began with a straightforward question.

"Shape of head?"

"Rectangular, but squarish."

"Hair?"

"Thinning, quite short, brown."

"Nose?"

"Ordinary."

"Eyes?"

"Blueish-grey."

"Okay," said Nikki, taking some time on the computer, muttering and moving about to get a better look. "I think I'm getting there," she said very seriously, and turned the screen to face Lucy, who nearly fell off the chair.

She found herself looking at a boxer dog with all of the characteristics she'd given.

It was a fantastic moment. They both collapsed in shrieking laughter and hadn't calmed at all when Kim opened the door.

"Up to your normal tricks again, Nikki?"

"Now I'll do it properly," Nikki smiled, tears of laughter still wet on her cheeks.

Twenty minutes later, Lucy walked down to her office and handed Dan quite a detailed hard copy of one of the kidnappers.

"Nikki sent you the same online."

"How close is this, Lucy?"

"Pretty close, I think."

"Great, I'll send it straight away to those who need to see it. Let's hope they can put a name to it. My guess is Interpol will come up with it and get the UK off the hook."

He took a couple of minutes to do this and in that time, Lucy went and made a couple of coffees and told him the full story of Nikki and the dog. He'd wondered what all the noise was about.

"That's me done then, Dan. What's next?"

They spent quite a bit of time going through a lot of mundane and probably unsolvable cases. A couple stood out slightly, one a mugging of an MP, the other a missing teenager, seen on camera getting into a car, but on a very dark road.

"Right, the mugged MP."

"From my quick look at the file, what you should say is the botched mugging of the MP and correct me if I'm wrong, we wouldn't be looking at this if he wasn't an

183

MP."

"Correct again, Lucy, we wouldn't, but if we don't sort this one out it might open the door to all sorts concentrating on the rich and famous. That would cause all sorts of problems for the mayor and the Met – publicity of the wrong kind."

"And they don't want that, do they?" Lucy retorted. "So what's the plan, Dan?"

Dan gave Lucy the look which said without words that he'd now heard that joke too often.

"Same as before. It's not far. We could go and have a look now at the scene. If we can find a safe vantage point you could have a little leap later."

"Nicely put."

"The Met thought they had the whole area under watch by cameras, but this spot slipped through. Another coincidence? Anyway, it's down to us to have a look," he said.

"Let's go quick, you can tell me about it in the car. I don't want to be late for lunch as last Friday in every month Nikki puts on a little treat. Today it's tapas."

On the short journey to Parliament Square, Dan went through the few details he had on the mugging. The MP had left a meeting at the commons bar at about ten. He'd arranged to be picked up by a family member across the road on Victoria Embankment. He had walked across the road by Big Ben onto a pedestrian crossing, leading to the riverside. That was where he was hit, and he felt the thief trying to grab his watch. In the melee he fell forward onto his arm and broke it. The mugger ran off and a bystander dialled 999. The police checked out all the cameras but found it impossible to see anything clearly on the, with all its traffic light poles, railings and metalworks.

They stopped and parked close to the Embankment, walking to the scene. Dan pointed out a statue raised on a plinth that Lucy could stand next to when she leapt later. Satisfied, they both headed back to the car, eager to get back in time for tapas.

*

Miles and Neil met outside the café just before ten thirty, both as punctual as ever. They both followed their agreed plans. A quick hello and Neil watched as Miles walked towards the frontage of Cloud 10 and then started his own walk around the area. He took a good look at the building, agreeing with Miles' assessment: substantial building in a prime spot. I wonder what's on the other side, he thought? He passed by Miles as the door was opened and watched as a spaniel came straight towards Miles, tail wagging as though meeting and greeting an old friend.

Miles saw the receptionist about to welcome him but was a little taken aback by the dog.

"That's not the reception I was expecting but it makes a nice change," he said, giving the dog plenty of attention.

"You're quite honoured actually, he never normally leaves his basket. Anyway, good morning, I'm Nikki,

I'm hoping you're Mr Rogerson."

"That's me and morning to you."

"Please take a seat and I'll let Henry know you've arrived." She clicked her fingers at Morry who went back to his basket. Miles took a seat but Morry hadn't finished with Miles yet and bounded over as Nikki left the room. Miles, not a dog person, refused to give the dog more attention as Nikki came back with Henry.

"Good morning, Mr Rogerson, seems you've made a friend there."

"It's not that often I get such a warm welcome, and by the way, it's Miles."

Holding the door open for Miles, Henry said, "Come this way, just down there to the left."

It all seemed very normal and business-like so far, thought Miles, but a large part of him was looking for anything out of the ordinary, but nothing so far. Henry motioned Miles to take a seat and collected the computer from him and asked for the password.

"Thanks, Miles. Following on from our phone conversation, could I just confirm that you want to ensure that the private work on your computer stays private."

"In a nutshell, that's it. My work as a freelance journalist entails sensitive details that need to stay private. In the wrong hands certain bits of information and misinformation could be highly problematic and I wouldn't want anything coming back to me."

"Very wise. We can do this quite quickly, and we do quite often; it's the world we live in. Won't take me very long. Would you like a tea or coffee while you wait?"

"Coffee would be great, milk no sugar."

Henry picked up the phone. Miles heard him talking to Nikki but couldn't make any sense of it.

Luckily, Henry explained. "Coffee will be a couple of minutes. Once a month, on the last Friday in the month, Nikki puts on a special lunch for us all here. She's at a crucial point in the special Spanish tapas she's organising today. If you're happy just sitting here, I'll start."

"No problem for me. I'm hoping it takes a while," he said jokingly, "I really like tapas."

But the joke was completely wasted on Henry who was plugging in and out various memory sticks. Miles wondered whether his Mr Nice Guy approach was worth bothering with. He carefully appraised the office – nothing out of the ordinary – as the door opened and in came his coffee with Nikki.

"Thank you very much; sorry to be a nuisance. I hear your tapas are legendary."

"That's the first time I've heard that," said Nikki, laughing and turning to leave. As she did so, Miles saw somebody coming down the stairs and heard Nikki say, "Dan, can I borrow you for ten minutes. Morry desperately needs a walk, would you mind? It's not far to the park."

Miles tried to hear the reply, but the door closed, so he just sat back and enjoyed the coffee, watching Henry in deep concentration.

"I'm going to turn everything off for a few minutes

and then back on again, then I'll check within our system that I can't gain access. Anything else I can do for you while we wait?" Henry said in his best charming voice.

"Well, I know it sounds a bit odd, but when I came through to your office I couldn't help noticing the heading on your white board. I know it's none of my business, but it really puzzled me; I'm a nosy journalist. It said, 'It's a crime to call a rabbit hair-brained'."

Henry shook his head. "It's our CEO. He thinks up these little sayings on a daily basis. It's his way, he thinks, of lightening up the office with his humour." He stopped to think. "Yesterday's was 'certain, as any idiot can be', and the other day it was 'wet birds don't fly at night'. I don't know where he gets them from."

"I get it; I suppose computer work can be a little boring," said Miles.

"You're right, of course, but funnily enough, geeks like me find it fascinating; it takes all kinds. Times up, let's see if I can hack in."

Silence resumed in the office as Henry tapped through the keyboard for the next few minutes, finally stopping and with a smile said, "All done. Let me check your phone."

Miles handed it over and let Henry fiddle for a few minutes.

"Anything else I can do for you?" Henry asked, handing the phone back.

"No, that's it. Thank you very much. Do you want me to pay now or do you send an invoice?"

"Take that as a 'freebee', Miles. If you can put anything our way that would be payment enough."

"Thanks very much, Henry, much appreciated." Miles waited as Henry called Nikki to come and take him back to reception. As she entered, Miles smiled up at her. "I'm sorry to miss the tapas, I hope you all enjoy it."

Just as she was about to reply, the door opened and in came Morry, pulling on his lead, followed by Dan.

"All okay, Dan, did you need the bag?" asked Nikki.

"No, thank goodness."

Miles looked at the dog, then at Dan. There was just a flicker of recognition there. He was sure he'd seen him somewhere before. He tried not to stare, but Dan had rung a bell with him. Where? He studied him again – smart, military bearing. Was he ex-military or ex-police? He had that certain look of some kind of training. Miles found it very hard to see him as a computer geek but looks could be deceiving… so who knew?

*

Miles left the building and walked over to the café where Neil was waiting inside.

"Anything to report, Neil, before I tell you how I got on?"

"Well, I had a good walk around. The main entrance is on the other side of the building which is shared with a music publisher. The whole building is clad, top to bottom, with dark bronze one way glass so you can't see anything inside, but they can see out. So, nothing to report. What about you?"

"It was very interesting; I'm really glad I went there. Henry the computer guy sorted out my computer in no time at all and no charge. Just wanted recommendations from me, so they are, on the surface, a genuine computer company, but I did see an interesting guy called Dan who just didn't look like he belonged there. He'd been coerced into taking their office dog, even that's odd, for a short walk to the local park."

"Yeah, I think I noticed him coming out as you were in there," said Neil.

"I've just got a vague feeling that I've seen him before. My nose tells me something's just not quite right. It just looks too large a building. I wonder if anything's happening on the other floors. It might be worth you taking a look one night."

"Okay, I'll take a look."

"One other thing, apparently the last Friday of every month, today, they have a special lunch, tapas today. If you've got time to spare now, is there anywhere on the other side of the building where you could wait and see if anyone else turns up? I'd do it but they might recognise me."

"I've nothing else to do, Miles. Let's walk back that way and see. Leave here separately and I'll see you round there."

They walked to the main entrance, but it was just a series of offices and doorways. Neil spotted an area of landscaped trees and shrubs about fifty yards away, the odd bench scattered between the trees.

"I'll sit over there and fiddle on my phone and let you know what happens, but as it's a joint entrance it won't be easy to see who's going where. Anything interesting, I'll let you know."

They said their goodbyes and Miles went home, leaving Neil to sit for as long as he could without looking suspicious. A few people came and went but nobody stood out.

Chapter 26

Nikki couldn't wait for them to come in, it was nearing midday and although she would tell them it was nothing, just a lunch, she had spent hours making the selection: roasted peppers, aubergine delights, various cheese and potato dishes and much more, and her *pièce de résistance*, her frittata, her own recipe for Spanish omelette and always her number one. All washed down with a specially selected rosé. She had put the phone system to answerphone and hoped the next hour would be special for them all.

She'd kept everybody out of the galley, including a very miserable Morry, and there it was laid out beautifully in front of her. She knew it was one of her best. She heard voices outside the door and hoped most of her work colleagues had made the effort to turn up.

The door opened and the small crowd began to make their way in. Naturally Darryl was first but just behind him came Grace and Hilton and the even Jay had made it. Everyone milled around the table giving her only compliments.

Smiling broadly, she said, "I'm so happy you could

all get here, I hope you'll like the dishes."

Darryl, as always, the first to speak, already with plate in hand. "Nikki, you've surpassed yourself this time."

Then from towards the back, Dan piped up, "As I've already said, Nikki, is there anything you can't do?"

There was no end to the compliments, but they stopped fairly quickly as it was all hands to the tapas and rosé. Plates and glasses filled, everyone moved into small groups.

Darryl said to Lucy and Dan, "Let me introduce you to your other 'comrades in arms'," and waved across the room for Grace and Hilton to come across so he could formally introduce them to each other.

Hilton said, "As it's Spanish time here, for the next hour, please refer to me as 'Hiltonio'," to much laughter as the others tried and failed to give their names a Spanish twist. Only 'Henrico' succeeded.

Grace said to Lucy and Dan, "I'm really pleased to meet you both at last. We don't get into the office that much as we have to spend most of our time at society bashes, keeping our eyes and ears open. They can be a funny lot. After lunch let's get together, the four of us."

"I'd really like that," said Lucy. "I'd really like to speak to you about what we do."

At that, Darryl came up with Jay. "I think you've met Jay but time to meet him again."

"Hi, again. Even I come here when it's one of Nikki's specials."

For the next hour there was a lot of general small talk

and work-related subjects seemed a no-go area, which Dan and Lucy picked up on. Indeed, the food was so delicious that it seemed to be the centre of the conversation. The time just disappeared and before too long, when most of the food was gone, they let a sulking Morry in to finish off the leftovers. Gradually, the room emptied, and Grace beckoned Lucy and Dan upstairs with her and Hilton.

It would be strange to see how the conversation went, thought Dan, and decided he would be a background participant.

Hilton, it seemed, had decided the same. "Dan, as these ladies have got quite an unusual gift in common, and so have we, why don't you and I pop out to the local hostelry for a pint and leave them to it?"

"Good thinking, Hilton, I think we might be a couple of lemons here." They got up to leave and Grace said, "Thank you both, we'll see you later."

*

I sat quietly, looking at Grace, expecting her to start the conversation. She was attractive, a woman of the world it seemed, in her early thirties perhaps, maybe older.

"Lucy, I'm really happy to have you here at Cloud. There's been nobody else I can talk to about our gift. I call it a 'gift' loosely, but that's not altogether true, is it?"

"No, you're right there. I'm already dealing with some horrible dodgy characters. At least you're not coming up with the people I meet."

"Actually, you'd be very surprised how many people in the Royal Family and their hangers-on are nice and how many more are not. There's a tremendous amount of bickering, infighting and jealousy going on and everybody expects to get their own way. In fact, we have a number of nicknames, some very rude, for some of them. We call the Queen and the Duke of Edinburgh 'heads' and 'tails'."

"That's very good," I chuckled.

"And another pair we call sweet and sour. I bet you can guess who they are?"

"Yeah, that's an easy one."

"Most of our time is spent socialising. It can be a bit tiresome hearing all their moaning. Hilton likes to say occasionally 'we spend our time at society bashes', as one does, don't you know, just listening out for rumours. You'd think with all their money, privilege and power they'd be happy and content, but it doesn't seem to work like that. If you're a miserable sod, I think you're a miserable sod, rich or poor."

"Dan's easy to work with. Hilton looks the same... is he?"

Grace nodded. "He's really very good. As far as our acquaintances are concerned, he's something in a city bank and I inherited a bundle, so we work as a couple even though we're not."

Small talk over, we switched to talking in detail about our 'astral travelling', as Grace liked to call it. It turned out that we could do similar things. Grace could travel for twenty-one minutes, but could only go back in time

195

for thirteen days. Apart from that, it all seemed very similar, but due to the infrequency of trouble in the Royal circles, Grace didn't need to travel very often, so a trip to the office was a rarity.

I couldn't resist pushing a little further. "Grace, you don't have to answer this if you don't want to, but if you could travel back further in time, would you go back and find out what really happened to Lady Diana?"

"That's a very good question and I have brought that up with our 'overlords' and what you wouldn't be surprised to learn is that if anyone was able to, it would be a treasonable offence. As I was told in no uncertain terms, 'certain things are best not available to the public' – so the mystery continues."

"They haven't said anything to me yet, but I won't bring the subject up. Do you have any idea if and how many other people can do what we can – any clue?"

"There was a lady here before you and I. She could do certain things, probably different, but I could never find out more. Apparently her powers diminished as she aged and she left. That's all I know. It does make you wonder who else could be out there. I've heard Kim say that your powers of observation are outstanding. I never need that as the people I deal with are just too obvious and rather than do any physical harm people would just prefer to embarrass them in the media and that's quite easy to get stopped."

"I just find it easy to remember things, that's all. Anyway, if I can be of any help to you just let me or Dan know."

"I will, Lucy, and thanks. Let's go and find our men."

Walking across the road to Hilton's favourite watering hole, we spotted them walking back. As we caught up with eachother, Dan, focused on the job as always, reminded me that I had one more leap to make. I rolled my eyes at him, and we parted ways with Grace and Hilton, heading back to Cloud and up to the leap room. Leaving me to change into my normal night attire, Dan headed back to his office, and I settled down to attempt a leap to the plinth we had spotted earlier. I'd decided on a kneeling position, which would keep me out of sight but still give me good vision.

Closing my eyes, I prepared to doze, focusing on all the positive things that had happened today. But I couldn't. Perhaps it was just the busy day. I tried again, calming my breathing. Nope, still at Cloud. I tried again, then again, but still no.

Panicking, I got straight up and went to Henry's office.

"Sorry, Henry, to barge in, but I've just tried to leap and haven't been able to."

"Don't worry, Lucy, we've come across this before," he said reassuringly "It's one of two things – either too busy a day or too many leaps in a short space of time; you have been busy."

"But it's never happened before to me."

"I've seen it before, honestly. Just go home, have a relaxing weekend and don't worry about it, it won't help."

"Thanks, Henry," I mumbled, and went off to break

the news to Dan.

He was supringly calm about it.

"No worries, Lucy, I thought this might happen sooner or later; you've been really busy. Go home, like Henry said, and relax. I'll see you Monday."

Chapter 27

I am the bringer of light,
Forward to the New Jerusalem

Sarah's week had been exactly as she'd hoped, quiet and reflective. Andrew had called yesterday and arranged to meet the four regarding the properties he was about to purchase on their behalf. He had all the details on his computer but had arranged to have paper copies of these at his disposal and was glad he had. The four were keen to look at these and passed them between each other eagerly.

Sarah expected to be at the meeting for some time but it soon became apparent that this wasn't necessary. She checked this with Andrew who confirmed what she thought, made her excuses and left. She went to her annexe after leaving instructions that she wasn't to be disturbed for any reason.

She had plans to make and these plans would be far more ambitious.

She quickly changed into everyday London gear, now with a shoulder bag holding her phone and purse.

She now epitomised the everyday modern girl in town and left the house via her private exit.

She hailed a cab to Abbey Road and got out in front of the famous music recording studios of EMI. Alina, encouraged by her, had given her more of a recent history of London which included The Beatles. Sarah, of course, had listened to their music as her parents had been fans and did know of the famous studios, but she hadn't realised they were a top tourist landmark until now.

Both the studio and zebra crossing, made famous as an album cover, were alive with sightseers; the zebra crossing teeming with tourists all trying to copy the walk of The Beatles across the road. It was now an icon of the music world.

Listening to Alina talk about it had given no inkling of its popularity, and her initial thought that it might be too obscure was gone. It was absolutely perfect for a spectacular, and Sarah, delighted, left for her next destination, London Zoo.

Alina had only mentioned the zoo in passing but something clicked in Sarah's mind, some kind of divine intervention, she surmised. It was 'summer busy' with parents and children everywhere; a very nice place to be on a sunny morning. She went past many different animals and at last made it to her destination, the large lion enclosure, which was very impressive with a large number of animals. She took a careful look across and around it, found the spot she was looking for and left.

With a bit of time on her hands, instead of going back

to the house, she took a cab to Oxford Street and meandered along, fixated by the fashions and styles. The shop windows were full of promises of love, happiness and romance, things that had never occurred to her.

In the circle she had created, the majority of the men were poor and ineffective, more the feudal peasant than the modern man. This fact had only just entered her mind. London really was the centre of a different universe for her, something that she was now coming to terms with. It was changing her outlook on life to some degree – in a good way.

Some of the young men she was now seeing were to her like confident peacocks, full of themselves, but as she now began to think – not unattractive.

Stop, stop, she thought, enough. I've no time for this.

She was correct, but a small weakness was beginning to show itself and she wasn't comfortable with it. She went into, now, one of her favourite stores for a couple more pieces of clothing and another pair of summer shoes. These were specifically to go with the outfit she had decided on for this evening's events. She needed some gold-coloured shoes to go with her dark green dress, but with one added extra. On her recent walking expeditions, she had come across a shop specialising in party outfits and masks. There before her, in the window, was a gold half-mask, covering all but her mouth, with thick black eyelashes and from beneath one of the eye holes was one large tear. This would have a dramatic effect on her sermon which, she hoped, would be uncomfortable listening for her audiences.

Not only that, it would preserve her anonymity and add to her slightly sinister presence. London was a very different place to rural Suffolk. City folk were very different and would expect something out of the ordinary. She needed added effects even beyond appearing and disappearing.

She was soon back at her new headquarters and immediately contacted Judith. She wanted to make sure her events went without a hitch and while her previous followers had always held her in awe, she wanted to make sure this new audience did the same. To ensure this, Judith was arranging for a couple more of her most trusted to join her this evening, to assist in the smooth running of her performance. She had the utmost confidence in Lovage, who had a tried and trusted way to ensure order by consent. Judith confirmed that Hayden and Simon had arrived and were being updated on this evening.

*

The time was now.

Still in her ordinary clothing, Sarah went to the main house where they were all ready and waiting. Judith in charge had the full itinerary. It was an hour before Sarah would appear and the six would now make their way to be in front of the mound inside the enclosure. Most of the day visitors would have left and the invited few had been told to ensure they were not late.

Lovage would meet and greet, introducing herself

and welcoming them all to a visitation by the new Chosen One. She was expecting a certain amount of ridicule and cynicism from them and knew the timing would have to be perfect, and it would be. From past experience, they knew Lovage could hold the audience purely on her own looks and personality, and the remaining initiates would ease the invited into positions where they could all see the miracle of materialisation. They all knew their roles, the taxis arrived, the weather was good, but as usual there was an air of anticipation as they prepared for the event, which even though they had witnessed it before always gave them a sense of wonder, like nothing else on Earth.

Sarah withdrew to the annexe to become Freja Sarah, changing quickly. She looked perfect, hair, dress and shoes perfectly balanced, and with the mask – perfection. She settled and waited to be beckoned.

Chapter 28

Hair of burnished gold
Comes our lady lifetimes old

Getting there was no problem for the six as they purchased their tickets and entered the zoo, making their
way to the lions' enclosure. The crowds were indeed beginning to thin and Judith pointed out the mound in the
enclosure which they stood in front of, as tourists and
animal lovers. There were more lions than they had expected, mostly sitting, with a few walking about. The six
had no preconceived idea as to how these wild animals
would react as Freja Sarah materialised – another mystery to behold.

Before too long small groups of the 'invited' began
to arrive and spotting these was not that difficult for
Lovage and Judith, who both took the time to greet them,
talking to each individually. Both letting them know it
wasn't a fool's errand being here and to keep an open
mind as they would all be witnessing a mind-blowing
event.

How many did arrive of the invited or came along

with the invited was difficult to work out, but did it matter? There now was a substantial group of men and women of indiscriminate age standing before the six facing the enclosure. Lovage, with her experience, knew the moment had arrived to start proceedings. She motioned to Judith to make her call, which she did. Standing before them she went into her script, only changed slightly for this literary and bohemian set to pander slightly to their egos. She could see in their faces how well it had worked but that most of them were taking her talk of the Second Coming, The New Jerusalem etcetera with the proverbial 'pinch of salt'. She guessed they had heard it all before, but because they enjoyed her oratorical power, her unbending belief, they went along with it on a sunny afternoon. It may have been very different on a chilly day. She could sense she was losing her audience with the odd grumbling from the back of 'get on with it' and asked for just two more minutes of their patience before this outstanding moment in their lives. They quietened down, silently agreeing to hear her out.

Freja Sarah had taken the call and, now rested, was ready to go. She closed her eyes, felt the mask was correctly in place, employed her usual technique, and within a minute she was there, on the mound.

She stood, upright and regal. they would likely show hostility towards her, or run and hide. The lions were absolutely terrified and ran in every direction, snarling and growling in their panic to move away. The noise and panic of this was a magnet of course and made everyone in a wide field look in her direction, even a couple of keepers some distance away. The noise of the frightened bewildered lions contrasted totally to the stunned silence of the invited gathering.

The muttering of discontent had turned into complete disbelief, jostling, shaking of heads, cries of "What!", "Can you see this?", "I don't believe it!", now the new order of the day. The six moved back to let the sight of Freja Sarah, a shimmering entity, both simultaneously attractive and menacing, be there in front of them. Far from the very nearly bellowing crowd just a minute before, these hardened thespians were lost for words and it needed Lovage, who had moved to a position behind them, to speak.

"Behold, look before you. For who you see is The Almighty's New Chosen One, Our New Blessed who has come at our time of need to lead us to the Light. Listen most carefully."

In a crystal voice as if from heaven, Freja Sarah spoke. She managed to utter just one simple word 'welcome' when she noticed, as did her audience, that two large male lions had quietly crept up on either side of her. They crouched ready to pounce. The already quiet crowd hushed more, only the quiet click of the camera phones could be heard. The atmosphere was electric.

Unperturbed, she slowly raised each arm as in a cross, towards each lion. What power she had over these animals was unearthly. Both animals, ready to attack, made no attempt to move towards her, in fact, they both retreated in unison, still in the attack pose, watching her intently till they stood some distance away and ran back to the rear of the enclosure to the rest of the cowering pride.

Completely unperturbed by any of this, Freja Sarah again spoke in her ghostly velvet voice, but this time, instead of quiet murmurings, her onlookers were transfixed, hypnotised by what they had just witnessed. All eyes were upon her as she spoke.

"Welcome all, bards, scholars and members of the artisan world, to my small sermon upon the mount. You, the favoured few, specially selected leading players in your fields, should be ready for change. You are here as my witnesses, as it is written, to the start of the new beginnings of the road to salvation. You should have no fear or apprehension, for fear is the weapon used by our enemy, the unbelievers. For those who deny and issue falsehoods I say, prepare, and take shelter from the coming storm. For although Judgement Day beckons and nears, I have no desire to be an Avenging Angel."

Sarah paused, looking upon her audience with such dignity and grace that many began to lower themselves to the ground.

Sarah smiled. "Faith and love will conquer all, seek out and look forward to the Divine Destiny that will await you all. For what awaits us all is the new glorification of all mankind, for I am the goodness and light. And you are amongst the favoured first to witness the miracle of the Almighty's Chosen One. Now, my believers, rejoice in the faith, rejoice, for the time has come, for I am she, God's Chosen One."

She looked at the assembled before her, her new congregation, some now on their knees, others as turned to stone. Slowly, very slowly, she disappeared before their eyes.

Slowly the crowd dispersed, there was nothing to say.

The six, led by Judith and Lovage, gave the audience a short while to recover, answering questions where they could and informing the now new followers (there were no dissenting voices) that more would be asked of them as it would undoubtedly be a rocky road ahead and help from them as they were major players in London would be required. They were all keen to offer any assistance they could. Once the last stragglers had left the zoo, the six headed for Abbey Road.

Sarah, meanwhile, had returned to the annexe, pleased with the way the afternoon had gone, and prepared herself for her next and final event of the day. For the first time since moving to London she had the house to herself and she took her time and relaxed with a snack, prepared by herself (a rarity), and just waited till eight o'clock for the next event at Abbey Road.

The six had over an hour to wait before they were required at the steps of the EMI Studios to take their places. After the afternoon's event most of them needed to recuperate, for although they had seen the spectacle of Freja Sarah before, each occasion deeply affected them as well as the invited. Judith, less affected, at least to the eye, quite matter of fact about the happenings, suggested a stop somewhere, which they all agreed to.

She was particularly looking forward to the evening

event. Always a fan of the music of The Beatles, she had never been to where it all had happened or the famous zebra crossing. They sat relaxing in a restaurant and chatted about tonight's event. The plan was to be quick and easy as this was a much younger audience with a shorter attention span.

The plan was for the six of them to form as large a semi-circle as possible around the main entrance to the studio just before eight o'clock and for Freja Sarah to already be in position and to 'materialise' within that space just in front of the main door. With good planning, the audience would not notice, and the 'happening' they would see would be Sarah dematerialising halfway across the zebra crossing. Sarah would give a short, sharp talk to them and hopefully, if it went well, Lovage would give the main talk and explanation afterwards. They would be instructed to follow Sarah and the six to the zebra crossing and position themselves along either side of it across the road. Judith, during the week, had four posters printed that four of them would hold up in front of any traffic which said:

PLEASE BE PATIENT
FOR JUST ONE MINUTE
FILMING TAKING PLACE

Time raced ahead, as it sometimes does, as the six mingled around the front of the building, which luckily was quite deserted. Soon a few groups of young men and women arrived and started chatting amongst themselves. From what the six could overhear there was a certain amount of healthy cynicism and joking as a lot of them knew each other quite well, but all were thinking it was a bit of a waste of time and were waiting to be offered something to buy and planning where to go next.

The six took their designated places in a tight semi-circle around the main building entrance at just before eight o'clock. Lovage in the front facing outwards, keeping the small crowd amused with a few well-rehearsed jokes, a little flirting and massaging of egos. Judith had planned this event with Sarah but had no idea at all what she would say. She hoped it would be short and sweet. They'd hoped that Sarah's spectacular finale would be so impressive that once it was over, and the audience recovered, that Lovage would be able to make something of an explanation and introduction to the movement.

With perfect timing, Sarah materialised, standing from her crouched position. She was wearing full London street-style clothing, a baseball cap and dark glasses. Nothing that would give the audience any unease. The carefully orchestrated bunching had ensured that nobody had noticed her arrival – so far so good. The six parted in two groups and stood diagonally angled slightly in front, so that Freja Sarah was now centre stage.

Judith now said in a commanding voice,

"Everybody, please come closer so you can hear

Freja Sarah clearly."

Sarah took a step forward, positioned perfectly at the apex of the two lines. The audience then naturally stood in a semi-circle facing her.

In a clear voice she said, "Thank you guys, for coming. I suspect that you probably think this is just some kind of stunt to get you here for another purpose. It's not. There is a deep and serious reason for you all being here, which will be clear to you once you have witnessed the event."

That brought forth a few 'thank God for that' comments but to their credit the whole audience largely kept quiet and waited.

"You might think that what you are about to see is some kind of magic trick. It is not, and I would ask you to believe your own eyes. After what you witness, my friends here will be able to answer any questions, but before that I would like you to listen to what my good friend Lovage has to say."

Lovage took a little bow. "Better than keeping you longer than necessary, please do exactly what Judith asks."

Judith took a little bow, then said, "If everyone would like to follow us down to the famous zebra crossing, you will witness something beyond your understanding, beyond spectacular. I can guarantee, as you will see for yourself, there cannot be any trickery involved."

Right on cue, to add to the musical showbiz feel of the evening, Sebastion turned on his musical player and at a singalong volume that all could hear came forth

211

'With a Little Help from my Friends' by The Beatles. Any discordant murmurings from the crowd stopped; they were caught up in the moment and all sang along to the famous song as they walked to the crossing. The song was not quite finished as they arrived.

Four of the six stood on the crossing and opened up their posters on either side and the few cars stopped. Everyone took their places along the side, all with a good view of Freja Sarah as she stood ready to cross. Timing again was everything, and she listened to the song as it began to get to its end, waiting for the exact moment to cross, and as all eyes fell on her she said, "Are you all ready and watching?"

She took another pace forward, looked up and smiled, and set out. She was halfway across as Ringo's voice finally ended the song, and she faded out before their eyes.

The sound of silence.

A couple of the group went to the place where Sarah had been and looked to the sky, in disbelief, looking back at their friends, shaking their heads, but to each and every one of them it was just mind boggling.

The overall silence, with just a few incoherent mutterings, was a well-known effect and Judith knew the time was right.

"You chosen people have been witnesses to a modern day miracle. You will want us to explain this and answer all your questions. This we can do. Can we all go back to the EMI studio entrance."

Once there, Judith took her place where Sarah had

stood and tried to explain in everyday language who and what they had witnessed. The audience struggled to find just a simple question to ask, which Lovage picked straight up on.

"Please don't believe you're foolish to find difficulty in what you've all witnessed. You were the chosen few, invited by us, because of who you are, some of the shining lights of the music business. People we believe we can trust and who can inspire others, for as always, the media will avoid the truth, and with good reason, as they have much to fear, but you can keep our faith and be purveyors of the truth. There will be further events in the coming time and all we ask is for you to remember you were amongst the first to witness the Second Coming of God's new Chosen One, here on Earth, not as an Avenging Angel but as the Miracle of the New Messiah, to lead us towards the Light and far from Judgement Day. For we know the people are seeking more; God has decided you have suffered enough."

She then listened to many questions, all she had answered many times before.

Chapter 29

Neil sat with Miles at the bar. Miles had been there some time until Neil turned up. Where was everybody else tonight? After all, it was Saturday. They'd talked by phone, at some length, about Cloud. There was nothing suspicious as far as Neil was concerned, it looked as clean as clean could be – and he should know. However, it was a different story for Miles. Neil just knew he would bring it up again, and he did.

Neil gave him the 'don't please' look, but he knew it was coming – he wasn't wrong.

"Neil," Miles said very slowly. "Look, I've just got that feeling about Cloud, maybe something else goes on in the building. Something just doesn't hang right."

"I know, Miles, it's your nosy nose at it again," he said exasperated. "Go on, what do you want me to do?"

"As a last favour – and the drinks are on me tonight – will you just take a little look, just a tiny look to keep me happy?"

"Last favour, okay, just to stop you going on about it, but I'm looking for something out of our partnership as well, you know. I can't just keep doing this just for your nose or one of your hunches."

"Just trust me on this one. I can't tell you how, but I just know something's not right."

"Okay, to keep you happy, and save on beer money, I'll toddle along there one day next week. I can go in the front reception office."

"What if all the doors are closed?" Miles said, already looking for problems.

"Don't worry, Miles, a little thing like that is nothing to me. I sorted that out years ago. I just reappear on the other side of the door arc. All offices, well the ones that I've been in, have their doors open inwards. It's not easy to put anything in front of the door as you're going to close it. Even if it did open outwards, who would leave anything there that they had to move to get back in?"

"Yeah, I get your point, clever thinking."

"Monday night then, just to keep you happy and give your nose a rest."

"Okay, just do this last favour for me. If I'm wrong, you have my solemn promise never to play a hunch again."

"Promise?"

"Definitely. Remember, drinks on me tonight."

"Then I'll have a chaser with my pint."

"Done deal, Neil."

They sat, problem resolved, and the conversation while not exactly riveting did move along in different directions. Neil did ask if there was anything else looming that might interest them, politicians aside, but seemingly Miles' nose hadn't sniffed out anything. All seemed very lacking and quiet.

It was about thirty seconds later that the pub entrance door crashed open and in came an ashen looking Greig.

"Christ, Greig, are you okay?" said Neil.

"You look like you've seen a ghost," countered Miles.

"I just have," he said, staggering to a spare chair. "For God's sake get me a drink and I'll give you the story of your life."

"Elvis is alive and living in Grimsby," joked Neil.

"For Christ's sake, Neil, look at the state of him," said Miles.

"Sorry, Greig, what's happened?"

"Let me have a drink first. I need it."

They all replenished their glasses, sat and waited for him to continue.

"Well, you remember I was invited to this 'Derren Brown' type of event at eight at Abbey Road."

"Sorry, Greig, forgotten about it," said Miles. Neil nodded in agreement.

"I got there with a couple of the band just before eight, seemed a bit of a crowd were already there. I knew virtually everybody, so it started with lots of jokes and laughter. We really weren't expecting anything and were already making plans for later. Then at the front of the building some bird stepped forward, just ordinary, who told us to follow her and her friends down to the crossing. Quite good. Next, one of her lot started his music player with The Beatles' song 'With a Little Help from my Friends' which, of course, we all knew and started to sing along with. Good fun. The girl had told us something great was gonna happen, but we ignored that really. You know what we're like. Anyway, we got to the crossing and stood in two lines across it. They'd stopped the traffic with posters. She walked across and just the second Ringo stopped singing, she just disappeared – right in the middle of the crossing."

"Sorry, Greig, what do you mean disappeared?"

"Exactly what I said. She was there one second and gone the next."

"A trick, it's got to be a trick," said Miles.

"That's what we thought, but we walked up and down, looked up, everywhere – she'd gone."

"What happened then?"

"They told us to go back to the EMI studio entrance, where all would be revealed. I was really blanked out; I've never seen anything like it. I could hardly walk, I still can't."

"And?" said Neil, leaning forward.

"Well, this other girl gave us a talk about Sarah, the one who disappeared, and told us very sincerely that Sarah was the New Messiah, God's new Chosen One, come to save us, and all that gubbins. Apparently, we were amongst the first to witness her miracles and there would be more coming."

"Are you havin' a laugh?" said Neil in his best geezer voice.

"I promise you it happened. You can check, it's gonna be in all the papers tomorrow. You just watch."

"What did she look like then?" asked Miles.

217

"It was hard to tell. Young, dressed ordinary, but with a baseball cap and sunglasses. Hard to see much. Dark hair, I think. Nice figure and spoke well. That's it."

"What did everyone else think?" Miles asked.

"We chatted about it afterwards, everyone felt lost and amazed at what they'd seen. Do you think it's true?"

"God only knows," said Neil, pleased with his clever comment. "Miles, do your thing and see what you can find out?"

Miles wouldn't normally leave his chair on Saturday nights, only for the obvious, but went straight outside, on his phone as he walked out. Greig and Neil sat and waited, as there was nothing left to say. Greig was just staring into his glass.

Miles came back in pretty quickly shaking his head and said, "Just been on to a couple of contacts. Greig's right. It did happen and not only that, it happened to a group of thespian types earlier."

"Same place?" said Neil, now showing more interest.

"No, they went to London Zoo, and met in front of the lions' enclosure this afternoon. The woman appeared on a small hill at the front. The lions all scattered away. She told them to believe in her or they were done for. Dark red hair, dark green dress, but for that show she wore a gold mask."

"Doesn't sound like the girl I saw," said Greig.

"Looks and costumes can be deceptive."

"Christ, Miles, I'm surprised she didn't get eaten, like the Christians in Rome. What's that biblical story, Daniel in the lions' den."

"Not this time, Neil. Seems the lions all made a run for it. Then she gave a little speech saying that she was the new Chosen One come to save us all etcetera, or something along those lines and then disappeared before our eyes."

"Jesus, now I'm scared of saying Jesus," said Greig.

"What do you think all this means? She certainly is a girl for the dramatic exit."

"Haven't a clue," answered Miles, "but I think we're going to find out. What do you think, Neil, any ideas?"

Neil, not really a believer, thought quietly before answering, "Sounds a bit to me like something I've heard about before. What do you think, Miles?"

Miles got it immediately, by the look in Neil's eye.

"You could be right, Neil," he said enigmatically, in a way that said he knew what Neil was thinking. All this went over Greig's head as he sat drinking and looking at all the texts he was getting. It hadn't taken long before some of his friends, who had witnessed the 'miracle' were thinking they'd been duped. How, they didn't know. It was some kind of trick and it wasn't going to spoil their weekends.

Greig took off to the toilet and Neil looked at Miles.

"I could do it, with the right planning. What we've got here is one deluded lady."

"I'll drink to that, Neil."

Chapter 30

Anxiety. I think that one word sums up my weekend. A couple of my old girlfriends had been in touch and we got together; had fun reminiscing about old times. One of them had an invite to a party Saturday night and one phone call enabled us all to go. Ordinarily, I'm a bit of a party animal, and although I did enjoy myself there was a black cloud hanging over me that was difficult to shake off, but I made a good pretence at having a good time.

My parents both sensed, correctly, that things weren't quite right. They didn't ask any direct questions, but arranged for Uncle Pete to call in on Sunday. He assured me that failures were quite normal, well, normal for us travellers, until our personal sequences were worked out. Apparently, it was all connected to the Fibonacci curve and how the numbers related to me. The same thing had happened to my grandmother at the start and that had worked out fine as it would for me. It was just a case of numbers and frequency and Henry was the man for this. He and his predecessor had plenty of experience with curve numbering and coming up with what you could and couldn't do. Once we had it worked out it was just a case of sticking to it.

He sounded convincing enough, and I went along with it.

Nevertheless, on the morning journey to London it was still hard to think of anything else. I still felt I'd let them down and hoped Henry would be able to come up with the solution or the key to the problem so I could leap and help them again. I hoped and prayed I could still do it.

Once there, my confidence increased. Nikki and Dan didn't mention it and Morry wasn't interested. Within a short while, Dan and I were in front of Henry who started things off with a large smile.

"I expect you had a pretty rubbish weekend, eh, Lucy? Don't worry, let's go through the numbers and sort it out. It's always the numbers, or frequency. I've come up against it before and no doubt will again."

"Have faith," said Dan. "As Darryl would say, there are no problems, only solutions."

"Thanks guys. What do you want to know from me, Henry?"

"Okay, let's go," said Henry, getting his screen up and running.

I suspected it was always up and running, but I liked his forthright manner. I already felt better.

"Tell me, how many times have you leaped lately?"

"I've been going through this in my head already. Tell me if I'm wrong Dan. We did two for the kidnap, three for the rapist and before that I did two in the office.

One for Kim and one for you, Dan."

"That's exactly right."

"Right," said Henry. "Seven. So according to the numbers, we're wrong somewhere. Seven just doesn't work. The only numbers we're not totally sure about are eight and thirty-four. Let's start with eight."

"Is it always the numbers, Henry?" asked Dan.

"Absolutely always, Dan." He put his pen to his mouth as if to emphasise his words. "It's always the numbers."

"On that Italian-sounding scale," said Dan.

"Correct, Dan. I've been here for about six years and the person before me, at least twenty. It was a good changeover period and we went through everything many times. Always the numbers. Lucy, about how many times have you travelled in your life. Just a guess and about what frequency?"

"Well, I've been doing it from quite an early age, so probably about a hundred or so, but spread out over lots of years."

"So, since joining us, this must be the most you've done in a short space of time."

"Yes, definitely. Usually I just do it maybe once or twice a month, sometimes a few months between."

"Okay, so let's discount the number thirty-four for the time being and concentrate on the number eight. Go over them again with Dan."

Dan and I went over them again, while Henry listened intently. We knew we were correct the first time. Henry then asked me to think back to the last time I'd done it before joining them.

Then the penny dropped.

"I've got it. Two or three weeks before joining I'd tried to watch Jimi Hendrix at the 1970s Isle of Wight Pop Festival just to tease my father who always regretted not seeing him."

"So how did that work out? All right?"

"No," I laughed. "I mistimed the leap and ended up watching Joni Mitchell."

That lightened the moment.

"Try and remember when that was, Lucy," said Henry.

"I can only… no, hang on. I came from university at the end of May. I remember thinking about it for a while and doing a bit of research. That was easy because it was all available on film. So I reckon it was about ten days or so into June."

Henry's eyes lit up .

"I think I've got it. It's all in the numbers. Let's say it was around the tenth, that leaves about twenty days in June, add that to the fourteen days you've been here. There's the number thirty-four appearing. Add that leap to the seven you've made here." He paused. We know your limits. I would say with all my experience that you can take the leap eight times only in a thirty-four-day period. That fills in the two blanks on the Fibonacci sequence perfectly."

"Thank you, Henry, but can I be sure of that?"

"Well, we don't know the exact date you went to the festival. We can never be sure. My suggestion is, you have another try today and every day this week until you have success. Then we'll know when the thirty-four-day cycle starts."

"Christ, Henry. That sure is a result."

"Now's as good a time as ever Lucy. Let's see if you can take the leap that you failed on. If not, try tomorrow."

So on the advice of Henry, that's just what we did. We went to the office and double-checked timing and my position.

Dan said, "From now on, Lucy, no more ridiculous cases, someone's favour or ego trip. Now knowing we have a finite number of leaps in a certain time, we'll only look at the important ones where we have a good chance of making a difference. From now on, you and me will have complete control."

"Agreed. I'll just do the last one again and see what happens."

I went off and changed into my dark clothes outfit and made my way upstairs, passing Nikki on the stairs.

"How'd it go with Henry?" she asked.

"Just great, thanks. He really knows what he's doing, doesn't he? I'm sure he's got it right for me. I'm just going to repeat the leap I tried before. I'm confident if it doesn't work today, it will in the next few days."

"He's the man, Lucy. Good luck."

I assumed my position, now with a greater confidence than I felt earlier and closed my eyes.

I think it may have been the troubled sleep I'd had over the weekend that made it so easy to doze off, because before I was expecting to, I was crouched, high

224

on a plinth, but with a good view of the crime scene.

All seemed normal as it always did, just a few passers-by, still lots of traffic but no sign yet of the MP. However, it wasn't long before I noticed him walking towards the Embankment zebra crossing. Just out of the corner of my eye I spotted movement. Just on the steps leading up from the Thames path. I saw a man looking towards the MP waiting to cross. He moved at some pace and the mugging started. It was over in no time at all. The MP on the ground clutching his arm, the attacker gone, down the steps.

That was it. No clues whatsoever, just a guy in dark clothes and a large hoodie.

No point staying. I was back. Back at Cloud with a large smile.

I couldn't have been gone long because as I opened the door where Dan was still sitting, all I got from him was, "Already?"

"Yes, complete success and complete failure. No problem with the leap and no chance at all of any clues. Just a hooded guy who came and went via the Thames path steps."

"Great on both counts. I'll ring the date on my calendar. Seven to go in the next thirty-three days and no more wastes of time. Go and tell Henry," he said.

I did, and watched him mark the date as Dan had. I could tell how happy he was for me by his comment.

"Go on then, back to work, I've got things to do," he said, with a grin all over his face.

Chapter 31

Driven. That summed up Miles for Neil. While they were both near or at Cloud on Friday, both had checked the office hours and it seemed unlikely that anyone would be there two hours after it closed, so he was set for seven. Yet again Miles had sent him on another 'fishing trip' with no idea what he was looking for, just anything that seemed like an anomaly. Miles had assured him that his nose had never let him down. Well, of course he would say that, wouldn't he. Though Neil had to admit that even he thought maybe, just maybe, Miles might be right. He would soon find out.

He closed the blinds in his room and sat comfortably. His plan was quite simple; he'd used it many times. His position on arrival would be just inside the exterior doorway of the front office, in his invisible mode. A quick look there and then he would move in front of the interior door, which he assumed would be closed and maybe even locked. Then he would materialise in full, directly on the other side in the door arc. There was still plenty of light at this time of year, enough for him to go room to room, observing, looking for abnormalities. It should be fairly quick, plenty of time to meet Miles later.

Standing there, inside the main building, his plan accomplished to perfection, he stood motionless, listening and watching for any sound. He'd had the odd scare in the past not being aware enough of sights and sounds, so he was careful to check that he was on his own. Satisfied, he set off towards the first open door. Nothing unusual as such: magazines, papers and usual paraphernalia for drinks, though there was sufficient seating for at least twelve people. Miles had only come across two or three, where were the rest?

As he walked back into the central staircase area, his eyes flicked towards the office white board. Again, nothing much, only an idiotic scribble about cool heads and hats – idiotic. What he did notice was a partly rubbed out 'Henry help Lucy with her travels'. Could be nothing. They knew Henry, but not Lucy. Another anomaly for Miles.

He moved on, noticing the downstairs toilets, then headed left for the first floor. No, he thought, let's ring the changes and start from the top and work down. Arriving at the top floor, he was astounded to see the whole area had been converted in what looked like four identical hotel rooms, furnished but empty and seemingly unused. Again, very strange.

Moving down to the next level, his system of transferring himself the other side of the door was working perfectly, but this time not needed as the door was open.

"Jeez," he said, out loud. A mistake on his part as silence was golden.

It looked like a set from a sci-fi movie. Either side of the long room, attached to the wall at about two foot off the ground, lengthways, were six beds, three on each side. Not really beds; there were no blankets, just a pillow and side table, all empty. If you wanted a sleep or rest during the day, this was it. If you wanted overnight, it was the top floor beds, no question. What was going on here, he wondered.

Crossing to the other side of the building, he found two identical well-equipped offices, both in use with the usual personal bits and pieces, the odd plant and books, nothing much of interest. The first was very tidy, too tidy… even the waste basket was empty. There was no chance of him finding anything there. The other one, however, was a little more promising; definitely a room in use. A notebook had been left on the desk with a few scribblings and crossings out. He could only make out for sure 'Lucy sorted' and the numbers 'eight' and 'thirty-four', followed by a tick. Again, nothing at all in the wastepaper basket. How tidy these people were, he thought, or were they making sure to hide everything away?

Down again to the next floor. The doorways were all closed, so he had to use his transference skills to get through. He started with the largest room: all desks with adjoining tables and chairs; three computers. Two of the workstations were completely blank, looked unused, but the third had a drawer left slightly open. Not enough for a good look but he saw a pile a manila files and the words 'Metropolitan Police' scrawled on some paper next to an illegible number. Where was Ray when you needed him, he thought. Last look round, nothing. He guessed the room was only used in full occasionally.

Off to the middle-sized room. Manager's by the look of it; there was better class furniture, nice easy chairs in one corner, but it was altogether too neat, too clean and too tidy. He'd cleaned enough offices in his life to know this was not the norm. He had to agree with Miles, something wasn't quite right and what he didn't yet know he was about to find out in the small room on this floor.

Neil wasn't expecting anything in the small room, maybe just storage, and wasn't really bothered as he felt he had enough suspicions already, definitely enough for Miles. The door was closed, so he entered on the other side of the door to find himself in a semi-darkened room, lit slightly by a small quarter-size window near the ceiling. Not good, but it gave him just enough vision to make out the obvious: floor to ceiling wardrobes along one side, mirrors and a dressing table for make-up – by the look of the stains – on the other. One of the doors had been left completely slid back and the inside was crammed with dresses, trousers, in fact everything for a change. The same clothes were in a number of sizes. He could only think perhaps the other cupboards held even more. He felt bemused; what was this all about? Time to tell Miles.

*

Neil and Miles sat together at the bar as Neil went through everything he'd seen. Miles, to his credit, just sat and listened.

Neil finished off and said, "Miles, you may be onto something here. Let me give you a piece of advice – insure your nose."

"If I could, I would, Neil. Now, what are we gonna do?"

"I think it's down to you. Of course I'll go back again if I need to, but my guess is I'll find it pretty much the same as I did tonight."

"Yeah. I think you're right. You leave it for now; leave it with me. I've got some good contacts who know things they shouldn't. I'll have a quiet word."

Over the next few days that's exactly what he did.

Chapter 32

Sunlit clouds abound, showing the path,
Echo of the past reborn

Satisfied. That's the word that summed up Sarah sitting in the garden without a care in her world. Her two small, but very theatrical, events on Saturday with the invited major players in the London arts scene had been perfect and all there had been sworn to secrecy, which was in fact the very opposite of what she had hoped for.

She'd spoken and taken the advice of Judith, who knew modern times better. That the press and media would assume she was just another illusionist, of which there were many fine ones. She knew she had planted the seed, which now needed feeding and watering to make it grow slowly and strongly. She knew enough of human nature to know that the so-called celebrities who had witnessed the events would be unable to dismiss them so easily and would dwell upon them, and they would grow rather than fade in their memories. In fact, one or two mentions had already appeared in some newspapers, only because of who was invited rather than the mystical events.

Rather than do anything similar she'd decided to hold a major, more traditional event for her followers this Sunday morning. She would hold a Peace Event whereby she would do nothing magical, just a gathering of thousands, she expected, of her flock. This would be an opportunity for the 'watchers upon high' to come together on a Sunday to celebrate the coming of the new Chosen One and listen. To assure them they had not been forgotten and were indeed an important part of 'Pathway to the New Beginnings'. She had instructed Judith to organise her four to contact all of her followers, no matter the distance, and command their appearance. They all needed to be there. This was their chance to show the power of Freja Sarah and her force against the unbelievers.

She had also asked both Judith and Alina to go to the top of Primrose Hill and seek the perfect spot where she could give her sermon, looking down over the slope where she would give her flock exactly what they wanted. Sebastion was to be in charge of ensuring she could be heard by all.

Once her sermon was over she would sweep slowly through the crowd giving them all the chance to be near her. She knew that this would probably be the last time she would walk amongst them, for the time being.

She arose from her seat and walked to her annexe. Her work at the house done, it was time for a little relaxation on her part. She informed the house that she wished not to be disturbed as she was praying and seeking further divine guidance. She changed into her street clothes, donned her hat and dark glasses and left by her private exit. It was her time now to relax and collect the specially made crown she had requested from the shop where she had purchased her mask. Not a crown of thorns, but her new crown of flowers.

Chapter 33

Nikki arrived to open the front office door, early as usual, and was about to enter the code and thumb identification when Morry cowered back, whimpering and snarling. Just another normal morning she had thought, but normality seemed to have ended. What was going on? Morry never behaved like this. She looked behind her, just in case it was another animal that had upset him but there was nothing.

She dragged him inside and closed the door behind him, pulled Morry further in and pushed him through. The galley door was open, always left ajar overnight, and she had to force him inside. Nothing had changed for him, and she looked around herself to see if she could notice anything different from when she left last night. Everything looked the same. Let's try the rest of the building, she decided. She picked him up and carried him up the stairs. This seemed to calm him down somewhat, but as soon as she put him down near any of the doors he started howling again. She opened the three doors in turn to check the rooms where unchanged and he restarted his antics. All seemed unchanged inside.

She was unable to entice him inside and picked him up to carry him to the two remaining floors. Again, he wouldn't enter and showed the same reaction – panic and fear.

Something had happened in the office overnight, that was the only solution. She went back downstairs to the front, pacified Morry enough that he sat trembling in his basket and got straight on the phone to Darryl.

"Darryl, you'd better get here as soon as you can. Something's gone on in the office overnight. Nothing that I can see, but Morry's sensed something and completely lost it, snarling and whimpering everywhere he goes. Come to the front."

He confirmed he was on his way and within fifteen minutes he'd arrived.

"Morning Nikki," he said and walked over to Morry, who'd managed to calm a little. Darryl knelt down and made a fuss of him. "Hello, Morry, you okay now? Are you going to show us again?"

"He will if you drag him."

"I'll let you do that, Nikki. Don't tell me any more. I want to see what happens myself."

Nikki picked up the still shaken dog and Darryl opened the door. Once again, all hell broke loose. Morry jumped from Nikki's arms, ran around the corridor and finished at the door of the galley, barking and snarling. They went from room to room with the same reaction. It was only while on the actual staircases that he calmed down. After they had finished on the top floor they returned to the front office, Morry pleased to be back again in his basket. Nikki and Darryl sat down.

"I wondered if and when this might happen, Nikki. I think, in fact, I'm fairly sure, we've had a visit from another traveller."

"Really, Darryl, what makes you think that?"

"Of course, I can never be one hundred percent positive, but I think Morry has picked up on it. Animals in general seem to be finely tuned to astral travellers and suchlike. Something us mere mortals cannot do. I'm sure he sensed it."

"And there I was thinking you just really liked dogs." She laughed ironically. "Do you really think someone else has been here?"

"Yes, I do. No way to absolutely prove it, but have you ever seen him behave like this?"

"No, never, ever. Well done, Morry, I guess you did deserve all your treats."

"Yep, clever boy," said Darryl. "If you noticed, he also told us that the intruder spent some time in each room and none on the stairs. Why would you walk up and down stairs when you could materialise on each floor?"

"I never thought of that. I'll get him some special treats now."

"Right, Nikki. Can you contact everyone and make sure whatever they were doing to drop it and be here for an important eleven o'clock meeting. No excuses."

And there were none.

*

At the specified time they were all seated, if a bit cramped, in Darryl's office, waiting for his appearance, with not a clue between them what to expect.

He came in followed by Nikki.

There was a hush of anticipation and some anxiety, as nobody had the slightest idea of what this was about. Darryl stood before them with Nikki at his side and went through the morning experience with Nikki nodding where necessary.

It was very serious for them as a unit, very serious. The consequences could be horrific if it got to the press/media. D notices could be slapped on but the damage would be done. Darryl confirmed how diligent they had all been and there was nothing that showed in any way that the traveller could know that they were anything other than a computer company, but nonetheless somebody had made a connection with them to something else. He hoped it wasn't to the Secret Service but they must take that as the most likely. He told them to carry on as normal and although he knew of nothing that could be done at this time, he would speak to MI5 to see if there was anything they could suggest. He finished and asked, expectantly, if they had any questions. Not surprisingly, they all started at once.

"One at a time, please."

Everyone raised their arms. Darryl pointed to Henry.

"Thanks, Darryl. Is it not possible to have some kind of electronic alarm that comes on automatically once the building is closed, nights and weekends, to inhibit infiltration? What do MI5 and MI6 do?"

"Good question, Henry. The other services have built into their buildings a low-level vibration field. This was put in when the buildings were either built or renovated, which makes it impossible to materialise within. I only wish we had the ability here, but the construction prohibits it and also it could make it difficult for us to function."

Dan asked, "I expect you know the answer to this, but is there any way that travellers can be filmed? Is there any special film that could be used?"

"Unfortunately, not yet. We're on the lookout all the time for anything new that arises.

"Just be extra vigilant in all you do. I know you will anyway. And give anything from your waste baskets to Nikki."

"On another tack," said Jay. "This may be related. What about those two things that happened over the weekend. I don't know if you've all heard about them. The London Zoo and the Abbey Road things. They both featured out of body experiences. Well, they looked like it to me. Do you think they're related?"

"I've been told about these, Jay, interesting. I've received video clips of her in action. I'll show you all in a minute. She sure looks like she's doing what some of you do. We've always assumed, from the get-go, that there have to be others out there with your gift, but we hoped most of them would just assume they were having an odd type of nightmare. I think she may also have the ability, from what I've been told, but it seems she may believe she is something extra special; some godly being."

"If she does, Darryl, we are dealing with one deluded chick," said Hilton.

"I personally think that it was someone else; maybe we have two on the go," said Darryl. "Somebody who's more interested in the establishment side of things. Maybe they already tried the two main service buildings, got nowhere, and somehow got a whisper about our little obscure offshoot. Either way, everybody keep a careful eye out for anything that seems a little bit unusual, however obscure. Let me know straightaway."

"Could it be one of us from the future?" said Henry.

"Pretty unlikely. Why would they bother? I think we can discount that one. Also, remember only a few can go back in time – it's rare. We must assume someone is interested in us. Let's have a look at the videos I've been sent. They're not great – they were taken by two different people on their phones – but they do show her effect."

Darryl turned his screen to face them and they all moved until they had a view and he showed them the short clips of her in action. The London Zoo one was from a distance but did show clearly part of her message and her disappearance. The Abbey Road one was clearer. She didn't speak, or it wasn't picked up, but it did show her face clearly on the crossing before she too disappeared.

"I've got to say," said Hilton, "Assuming she was the same girl in both, they were very well choreographed pieces of work. Nothing that we couldn't do, but still, pretty exceptional."

Grace said, "Also she presented herself beautifully, perfect for her different crowds. Certainly for The London Zoo event, if you were expecting the new Chosen One, that's what she gave you, mask and all. Also liked her choice of clothing for the other event, just a casual girl, till it finished. Somebody or a team put a lot of work in here and got it spot on. Any rumours about what she's going to do next?"

"Not yet," said Darryl, "but we're pretty sure she calls herself Freja Sarah."

Hilton started to laugh. "I had a girlfriend called Freya, difficult girl, but that's another story. She was forever telling me what Freya meant in Scandinavian – The Goddess."

"Another master stroke," said Grace.

Lucy had just listened so far without comment, just absorbing all the new information and now came up with, "As Morry picked up on the visit here, and I know animals can sense such things, what about leaving a dog here at night? At least they might be put off."

"Good idea, Lucy. Maybe we could get a full-time nightwatchman with a dog. Everything is an option," said Darryl. Seeing questions over, he said, "Thanks, everyone. Just carry on as normal but keep to the easy and mundane stuff for the time being. I think you're probably the exception here, Jay. I can't see it as terrorist linked but you never know. I also don't think it will affect Grace and Hilton, but Lucy and Dan keep to the easy and obvious for the next couple of weeks. While we're trying to get more of a handle on it here, all of you take a few days off here and there. Let Nikki know and be sure to keep in touch with her every day."

And that's pretty much what they all did.

Chapter 34

Even in the quietest moments of the quietest days, there are organisations, most totally above board and some nefarious, collecting the world's data. Insignificant scraps, rumours, predictions, of no obvious use to anyone, but some of these were of interest to one of the shadowy Belgian news agencies owned and overseen by Nicolas Peeters.

Word was seeping out from London about the escapades over the weekend of Freja Sarah and had reached his ears. The Belgian media magnate ran a shadowy network, with links to the European Royal Families, Russian oligarchs, American billionaires and high-profile politicians of all persuasions.

Unbeknown to the world, setting aside the 'conspiracy theorists', there had always been a secret organisation, 'The Alchemati' with their invisible hands behind all governments, running the world for their own benefit, and he was part of the higher echelons. Now, not just content with total influence over the world's population, these unscrupulous beings had set a new primary aim of the pursuit of longevity and ultimately immortality, not content with a normal lifespan, and had many clinics throughout the world. No small task but a series of experiments had brought both nearer.

Not a fellow to let even the remotest possibility pass him by, he had seen the videos of Freja Sarah's events over the weekend and while poor quality, had satisfied himself that further investigation would be required, especially if she considered herself to be the new Chosen One – however unlikely. She may have something, and he would not let that chance pass him by.

He had immediately contacted his London associates and before long he was given the name of the owner of her base, a Christopher Wilson, completely unknown to him, and most importantly an address in Holland Park. Seemingly a gift of residence from one of her followers. The area was known for its wealthy residents and exclusivity and there were also a good selection of life prolonging and enhancing clinics for the privileged, specialising in exclusive longevity treatments, via which Nicolas had some connections.

Freja Sarah was put under twenty-four-hour surveillance from an apartment opposite, easily arranged by Nicolas. She had been seen secretly leaving the house on her own, by her own private door, on a number of occasions. She had been professionally followed and while considering herself the new Saviour, had been found to have many aspirations of a normal young girl, considering the number of clothes and make-up stores she visited. Standard young girl with all the normal emotions, as far as Nicolas was concerned.

Just how to capitalise on this?

He wondered what his young team had come up with. He had no need to worry, as the team had hatched a plan. No problem, according to them – The White Knight Rescue. The plan was afoot already. She would be the victim of an attempted mugging. A passer-by would come to the rescue and see off the muggers. Young, handsome Richard Anthony had been chosen for the role as he worked nearby in a local clinic. Just a passer-by doing a good deed.

Perhaps Richard could conjure up a romance. What a start he'd been given. According to his track record, if anyone could, he should be able to. From that, everything led. If she fell under his spell, he could then find a way to move her towards the dark side, unless of course, she was God's Chosen One, in which case he was in a lot of trouble.

She would have the power over the people, to get for them the substance they were most short of – adrenochrome – by the bucket load, and that's what Nicolas wanted.

Chapter 35

It was a standard midweek night at the Northern, where the usual array of drinking buddies normally met up. There was no formal agreement to meet between Miles and Neil, but both being creatures of habit, that's where they knew they'd be. Both enjoying a bit of down time after the last few weeks, only for that to be altered by Greig and a mate who blustered in.

Instead of joining in the chat about the usual and not even bothering to order a beer, he said, "Look here, I've got a video on my phone of her, in fact I've got two. Somebody who was there at Abbey Road had the sense to get his phone out and record it, sent it through, not great quality, but amazing. You can even hear a bit of her sermon on it."

He held the phone in front of Miles and Neil; his mate Keith had already seen it and got the beers in. They both leaned forward in feigned amazement. He got the video playing, a short section on the steps, then nothing until she reached the crossing, then gone.

"How could she do that, Neil? It's impossible," said Miles, with a quick knowing look to Neil

"God only knows. Perhaps she really is the new Saviour," said Neil.

"It's a pity we couldn't hear more, but another one might surface," said Miles.

"Well, I believe it," said Greig. "Wait till you see what she does next."

Greig took back the phone and got the London Zoo one up.

"Not a great view, but the bloke was at the back. You can see she's in the lions' enclosure and all the lions are running scared. You can hear a bit more of what she's saying. Watch, watch and what happens again, she just disappears."

Miles and Neil carried on their double act, now getting into it.

"Just not possible. I can't for the life of me see how she can pull off a trick like that," said Miles. "Did anyone check afterwards for wires, a trap door or mirrors? I've seen those used on disappearing acts before. Covent Garden, I think," and gave Neil a sly look.

"It's a bloody lions' den, Miles. Who the bloody hell was going to go in there? Are you mad?" said Greig, as his beer appeared. "Thanks, Keith. I just don't know what to believe. I've spoken around. No one kept schtum, and we all feel the same, totally gobsmacked."

The conversation went on in circles till finished by Neil. "I always hated that song by The Beatles, 'With a Little Help'. Couldn't she have chosen something better? What about 'I Saw her Standing There'? That's more her."

This statement was followed by a combined roll of eyes. Typical Neil.

"Are you going to go to church now Greig?" said Miles.

"I dunno, makes you think. I'm wondering what's gonna happen on Sunday morning."

"Sunday?" piped Neil.

"Yeah. She's going to have a bit of a rally on the slope on Primrose Hill at eleven o'clock. Apparently she's got thousands of followers. They're all gonna turn up there for her sermon."

"Like a sermon on the mount, Greig?"

"Yeah. Just like that. A big peace event, that's what I've heard."

"Well, she's done Daniel in the lions' den," said Miles.

"Anyway, I'm going, and so are a lot of my mates. What about you two?"

Neil answered, "Do you know, Greig, I will, just in case, you know, she is the real thing, then I want to be on the right side of her. What about you Miles, coming along?"

"I've got nothing else on, hope it's not raining."

They agreed a time and place to meet. Keith was not coming as he had something else on. It was settled, all three would be there at the peace rally.

"I don't know about you, Neil, but I'm actually looking forward to it," said Miles.

Greig and Keith went out for a 'fag break' which was opportune timing as Neil said, "This could be interesting,

Miles, but I'm not expecting her to do a vanishing act. If she's anything like me, she's time constricted; both her tricks at the weekend were short. That is unless she really is the New Messiah, then we're all in trouble. "

"Too right."

"Any news on Cloud?"

"Yeah. I should hear this week from a disgruntled ex-MI5 worker. All very hush hush. He won't, obviously, talk on the phone; I'm accidentally bumping into him at a café in a tube station."

"They've certainly put the frighteners on him then."

"Yes, they have, all my other sources have blanked out. Hold on, Greig's on his way back. I'll let you know what I hear, but I've got something else to ask you, so hang on till they go outside again."

It seemed, as these things do, like an eternity till Keith asked Greig to go outside for a cigarette, but at last they left for the garden again.

"What's on your mind, Miles?"

"Well, I was just wondering if you can do your trick but at the same time go back in the past? I don't imagine you can go in the future, but have you tried going back in time?"

"No, I haven't. In fact I've never even thought of it."

"Well, why don't you give it a try. You know the exact time and place of, let's say the Abbey Road one, eight o'clock, Saturday. Why don't you check it out and give it a go? You never know till you try."

"I don't think there's any chance really, but why not?"

"It would be a game changer. Then you could do the

future and get me the lottery numbers."

"Dream on, Miles, one thing at a time."

"Okay then, give it a go."

"I will," and with that, back came Greig and Keith.

They carried on drinking till late in the evening, the three of them looking forward to the Sunday Service, which from a group of drinking buddies was not something you heard very often.

Chapter 36

Pete stood looking out of the window at the side door the girl would leave from. It was a nice second-floor flat that they had been given the use of, courtesy of one of Nicolas Peeters' London colleagues, but no matter how comfortable, it was difficult to relieve the tedium of constant surveillance. He'd watched and waited all day yesterday, but no sign of her. Today the weather was brighter, just perfect for a nice walk and shop; perhaps the cloudy, muggy weather had been off-putting, at least that's what he was hoping for. It was the perfect day for a young girl with things to buy. He hoped his motorcycle team, waiting below, were not arousing the suspicion of any of the flat owners, but at least they were not able to be seen from the main road. Richard was also ready, just five minutes away, in a management position at the clinic, so able to move at a few minutes' notice.

The plan was simple, but like all plans, easily messed up by the simplest thing, but it had been tried and tested before, with great effect. They would wait for her to leave the house, the two lads would stay in position, still out of sight. He would then leave the flat and walk in her direction and watch for her return. As lookout he would tell both the lads and Richard when she was about to arrive. The lads would wait for his signal that her return was imminent, Richard already set. The muggers would attempt to steal her handbag, Richard would run to help her making his 'white knight' appearance and see off the attackers. Of course, they were under instructions to be noisy and aggressive, but under no circumstances were they to put her in harm's way and make sure the mugging failed. Simple. But for the time being, they all had to just sit and wait.

At last he saw movement at the door. He was sure he'd seen the door start to open, then close, then nothing. He'd given it a couple of minutes, then just about as he was going to make a coffee, it opened.

She was alone, dressed in her normal street clothes, jeans and a t-shirt, the white baseball cap the only item to make her stand out. She was normally gone for around one and a half hours. He rang the boys waiting by the bike and told them to go to amber alert – she'd just left – and gave Richard the same message.

All were now ready for action. As with most things in life, it was the waiting that really dragged. Pete left the apartment and followed in the direction she'd gone. She'd been watched before and both times she'd returned the same way. Third time lucky?

Pete was now about two hundred yards away, near a small garden, where he waited for her return. He leaned by the railing, took out a paper, kept checking his watch and looking down the road as though waiting for a lift.

251

He liked the acting; he felt he was a part in a play, and this was Act One.

Again time slowed down, but at last he saw her coming, walking towards him and on the side of the road he hoped for. She carried a big carrier bag, with her handbag over her shoulder. He rang Richard and the boys and told them to get ready and note the large carrier bag. Action in about two minutes, when she was nearer her house and Richard could appear from the side street where his clinic was situated and run from there to her defence.

What could go wrong?

Well, nothing actually. It went like clockwork. The strangest thing about it all was how shocked she seemed at what was happening to her. She just sat down with her legs splayed out making a peculiar moaning noise. The boys overacted to perfection, making a good pretence at trying to get the bag off her shoulder. In fact, it had fallen off and they were about to go for the carrier bag instead, when thankfully Richard turned up. With arms flailing in the air and a good series of threats he managed to see them off, just like the hero in Act Two. They roared off up the road swearing and shouting insults to him and gave Pete a thumbs up as they passed and the curtain came down.

Pete now came along and asked, "Is she okay? Shall I phone the police?"

"She'll be okay, just shocked I think. Don't worry, I'm actually a doctor, with a practice just a short way up the road. I'll take her back there and get her checked.

Probably too late for the police. Those guys are long gone," Richard added with a wink.

"Right, I'll leave you to it," Pete said with a smile.

Sarah still sat on the pavement, legs splayed, stunned by what had just occurred in the last thirty seconds, her thoughts in turmoil. For they were life-changing seconds, as nothing even remotely like that had happened to her in her whole cocooned life. She had taken it for granted that she was somehow invincible to the woes of ordinary people. After all, she was the new spiritual being, the new Chosen One. She didn't understand why, but this must be a test from the Almighty, and if so, she would be up to it.

With all this confusion running around in her head, she had failed to notice who had come to her rescue and now looked up to see the person who had intervened.

As she did so, he leant over and said, "Are you hurt anywhere? Check before you get up. Take a minute and be sure."

She checked herself for any pains, but knew only her mind, not her body, had been affected. "No, I seem to be okay."

"Then let me help you to your feet, slowly." He moved behind her and carefully helped her to her feet. "I'm glad you seem to be all right after such a horrific experience. I should tell you I am actually a doctor with a practice just over there," and he raised his arm and pointed a short way away. "Lucky for us both, I think, that I was just out to drop off a prescription. I insist you come back with me. I'll get one of my nurses to give you a quick once over. Then I want you to sit and relax for a few minutes, till you're fully recovered and then you can be on your way."

She was still in such a bemused state of mind that she would probably have done anything at the time. She agreed and they slowly walked across to his clinic. She started to feel a little better and clearer headed, and for the first time she noticed what a young and attractive man he seemed.

The door opened automatically at the clinic and he led the way, shouting for a nurse. He explained the situation and she was led by the nurse into a treatment room. Plan A was under way, he thought. He waited in his consultancy room for her to be brought in if everything was okay, which he knew it would be.

They entered, the nurse confirming no damage done, just shock, and Sarah was shown to a chair where Richard sat beside her.

"Can I get you a drink of something?" said the nurse.

"That would be lovely. Coffee, milk and one sugar please."

"I'll have my usual as well, Brenda," said Richard.

"I must thank you for coming to my aid." She considered using the word 'rescue'. "I don't know what would have happened if you hadn't been there," she said, trying to stop herself admiring his looks and general persona.

Richard, a professional in these matters, could already sense a slight flickering in her eyes and hesitation in her speech, and he wasn't wrong. She was succumbing. After all, she was just a mere child to him in the art of seduction and he was a master.

The longer she spent with him, the more comfortable she became. They talked for a while, taking their time over the coffee, Richard carefully keeping clear of the mugging and talking more of where she had been and London generally, avoiding any mention of her personal life. He was his open, smiling and very attentive self and with his effortless sense of timing, he said to her earlier than she was expecting, "Let me walk you back to your home now."

"There's no need for that, I'm fine," she said, with a hint of regret.

"Of course I will. I wouldn't be doing my duty as a doctor and gentleman if I didn't. I also want you to come back here tomorrow, to check you're okay, just to put my mind at rest. If you feel uneasy about coming to the clinic, we could always have a coffee in the hotel across the road. Much more pleasant and relaxed. Shall we say eleven o'clock?"

She nodded slightly bashfully and her 'yes' reply was only just loud enough to be heard.

"I'll be waiting on the corner for you, just to make sure the muggers don't return."

Which of course they wouldn't.

Chapter 37

Miles was like a dog with a bone. Neil knew there was no chance of him letting go of the notion that he might, however unlikely, be able to go back in time and in fairness he was keen to have a go himself.

He decided the sooner the better, and had spent some of the morning at London Zoo. Already he had enjoyed his time there. He couldn't actually recall if he'd been taken there as a child. He had small, vague memories of being near animal cages, but really, as far as he was concerned, this was his first time.

He took his time wandering around, before ending up at the lions' enclosure. He spotted the mound where the girl had materialised then dematerialised and could only applaud her sense of theatre. Daniel in the lions' den. Standing in front of the mound, now with a lion sitting on it, he stood facing outwards across where her captivated audience had stood and looked out beyond, hoping to find an obscure place for him to materialise unnoticed with a good view. Nowhere. He would try Abbey Road.

A short while later, he stood on the steps of EMI Studios and felt a strange sense of history creeping over him. He had seen many photographs of The Beatles and was quite an admirer of their music, because of his father's influence. Unfortunately, his father had died a few years ago, but had spent much time with him listening to their songs while they did other things and he couldn't remember any other music ever played in their car. Feeling nostalgic, Neil left the steps and walked down towards the famous crossing.

Once there, he looked across from where they had started their iconic walk across and was still surprisingly enchanted. He was still deep in those days when a car stopped, thinking he was waiting to cross, and he crossed. He noticed, ahead of him on the other side beyond the pavement, was a small hedged garden. He could travel to there without any problem as all eyes would be on the crossing and the vanishing girl. That's what he would do, later today, before seeing Miles that evening.

He wondered if Miles had met up with his MI5 contact yet. Neil was beginning to feel he was a part in a book unfolding before him that he had no control over, not that he wanted any. How the last couple of weeks had changed his life and what the next few weeks would bring was completely unknown. Unstoppable, that was the word that came to mind.

As he settled in his chair, he was confident he'd done the correct research. He knew the exact time, date and place. He would try his best, but was expecting nothing.

He would materialise very slowly. If any eyes were in his direction, he would just remain unseen. He only had to be there a couple of minutes, if his timing was as accurate as he'd planned.

Here goes, he thought, and closed his eyes.

*

Miles was already seated at the end of the bar. It seemed to Neil that he may have been here a while as he spotted an empty dinner plate to his side.

"If I knew you were eating Miles, I'd have joined you."

"Sorry mate, spur of the minute thing, quite tasty. So, how'd it go, are you the new Doctor Who?"

"You tell me first. The clandestine spy meet, has it happened?"

"I'm really struggling to pin him down. I think somebody's put the frighteners on him. I'm working on him in a light way."

"What do you mean light? That's not like you, Miles."

"I made sure I accidentally bumped into him, took me three attempts. I know where he has the odd drink and told him I only needed a positive hint. I didn't want to push it too much and he suggested Friday."

"That's good, hope it comes off."

"So get on with it. What about you?"

"Well, I went to both places, London Zoo definitely out, nothing but grass. Abbey Road seemed better, so I gave it a go."

"And?"

"Yeah. I managed it."

"Bloody hell, Neil."

"Yeah. That's exactly how I felt. I just got there in the nick of time, saw her stop at the kerb crossing, start walking and kazoom – gone. You should have seen their faces."

"That's fantastic and fantastic for you. That changes everything."

"I gotta say, Miles, I'm truly amazed. Once we get through this Messiah stuff, I'll try it out some more. Do we know what her name is yet?"

"I don't. I'll ask Greig if I see him, but I expect we'll find out on Sunday."

"Anyway, well done, Neil, fantastic. Actually it really is fantastic. I wonder if you're the only one with this 'magical' power," he said in his best pathetic spooky voice.

"No more jokey voices, Miles, just another pint, then I'm off as I've got an early start in my real job."

"You got it, Neil."

How true that statement was.

Chapter 38

After taking Darryl's recommendation and spending a few days away from the office, I was really at a loose end. My parents had asked a few harmless questions, easily fended off, and most of my friends were busy, so when a late-night call came through from Dan asking if I would go in the next day, I couldn't wait; it was the escape I was looking for. He told me that he'd been sent an unusual case that required action from us urgently. Frankly, I couldn't wait to get there.

I walked straight through the office to see Nikki, the font of all knowledge, and seeing her giving Morry a treat said, "Any more strange action from Morry?"

"No, he's been as calm as calm can be. Sorry, re-phrase that, he's been as calm as Morry can be; you know spaniels."

Dan must have seen me arrive as he came into the office overhearing and said, "So, no more visitors. Any other developments?"

"There's a few minor bits and pieces," said Nikki, "but I'll leave them for Darryl. I don't want to spoil his moment. He's probably rehearsing now."

This was encouraging news. I was getting used to the lulls and rushes of the job. It was always calm then edgy, what we were doing, and I was beginning to really like it.

Dan said, "I don't know about you, Lucy, but I'm glad to be back in. I suppose I should be more of a modern man, but a couple of days looking after a baby was hard going, but Jill enjoyed the break, so it's only fair."

"Shame on you, Dan, but honest," laughed Nikki.

"We'll go see Darryl and then I'll go through the case with you, Lucy."

Nikki said, "You two go up, do you want me to bring you up a coffee, Lucy, as you've just got in? I know Dan has had one."

"Thanks, Nikki, if you don't mind."

As we were leaving the front, Grace and Hilton arrived. Hilton, his normal self, gave a royal bow towards Nikki, saying to us all, "Greetings one and all, fare thee well?"

"Yes, me farest well," said Nikki. "Howest thee?"

"Okay, enough, Hilton," said Grace, who sounded like she'd heard this banter from him too many times. "We're both fine, like you, wondering what this is about."

Before any of us had a chance to speculate, Darryl came in overhearing the last line. "You need wait no longer. C'mon all, come up."

Which we did, and creatures of habit, we all took the same seats as we did at the previous meeting.

"Thanks for coming in. All settled? Yep. Good. We've been doing a bit of research. Actually, there's

261

quite a lot available on public record on Freja, with a j not a y, Sarah, or should I say, Sarah Childrake."

"Ah ha," said Hilton. "Methinks the plot unravels."

"Enough dramatics, Hilton, we're not at The Globe," said Darryl.

I could imagine that Hilton was having one of those days that Grace had mentioned to me, when he'd rather be in Shakespearean costume spouting the Bard. Grace just about had him in slight control with the occasional elbow.

"So," said Dan, "she has some history."

"Nothing…" as Darryl started to speak, in came Jay. Darryl, a bit surprised to see him turn up said, "I didn't expect to see you here this morning, Jay."

"Well, Darryl, I've been thinking about it and seen it in the papers and I believe I should be totally involved in it, as I think it might escalate and have serious ramifications in the wider religious communities. I foresee unrest."

"That's good thinking, Jay. I'll pass that on. If she carries on in the 'I'm the new Chosen One' theme it will lead to a lot of unrest in some quarters. Take a seat."

Which he did, as Darryl made a note and underlined it on his prepared sheet, before carrying on.

"Okay, I'll restart, Freja Sarah, as she's now known, was christened Sarah Childrake and spent most of her life at her parents' manor house in Suffolk. She had a very privileged upbringing with no sign of what we are witnessing now, or none that surfaced, but a few years ago her parents were in a tragic car crash on the estate, and both died instantly. For some reason, a mystery to this day, the car left the road, hit a tree and both were killed. They were not wearing seat belts. The subsequent investigation found no mechanical fault in the car and both parents in good health and no adverse weather conditions – accidental deaths verdict. She had no siblings, was made a ward of the court and entrusted to the estate manager and his wife until she was eighteen, two years ago. Both have subsequently left their positions of employment at the manor."

Dan asked, "Did the police have any reason to think of foul play?"

"If they did, there's nothing on paper, Dan."

"After that, things began to take a different turn. She began to bring in a different set to run the estate and began to make a series of, let's say, 'appearances' throughout the county and beyond, in churches, religious and fringe meetings, stating she was the New Messiah and must be listened to and followed. These have grown over the last two years with word of mouth and her 'appearances' as the new Chosen One, come to save them all. She now has many thousands of followers who call themselves 'watchers upon high'."

"It's strange that before this week I'd never heard of them," said Grace, "and I know some really weird people."

"You've no idea about weird," said Jay.

"I think we all do," said Darryl.

"I don't," I said. "I feel I'm missing out."

263

"Moving on," said Darryl. "She has a small team behind her, of which we know little about, and has been given the use of a large house in Holland Park by, we believe, a benefactor for their use, from which she now operates. All clear so far?"

We all nodded in agreement except for Hilton who said, "Is it going on much longer? If so, can I get a coffee?"

Darryl ignored him and carried on. "You're probably wondering, should we be taking this seriously? And the consensus is, yes, we should. Any more questions?"

I think we all had questions but decided to keep quiet rather than look an idiot asking something stupid, but Dan asked one I was thinking,

"She's now in London, upping her game. Have we anyone inside or is it too late? Also, how's she getting her message out other than the theatricals?"

"Right, first point, no, and probably too late, though we'll try. We don't know fully who's in her team."

"I'm not surprised, it's all been quick," said Dan

"Second point, She is excellent at using social media. One of her inner circle is very professional with her output. She looks on camera exactly like you would expect her to look. She does have a mesmerising look and her use of biblical language is excellent. I'll give you all her sites afterwards."

Hilton asked, "Are the public buying into this? Over the years there have been so many so-called new Saviours, mostly from the US, who eventually came to nothing. Isn't she just the latest?"

"She does seem to be hitting a nerve here, Hilton, even the media are warming to her. I suppose it's the theatrical stunts and the media always like a 'looker'. What she does next will show us the direction she's going and whether the public will let her."

A second's gap enabled me to get my question in, the one we were all thinking,

"Does anyone here think she's one of us? But doesn't know it or really believes she's more, perhaps honestly thinks she's the new key to the future? I mean, maybe she is The One, but at this stage we don't know, do we?"

"True, Lucy, only time will tell, but we can't afford to wait. So, my plan is, we'll all go to the service on Sunday either individually or in pairs. Nikki will also be going. At least some of us might be able to get close enough to hear what she has to say or if she tries another of her 'miracles' we'll get to see for ourselves. Let's go and see."

We all agreed to go. I would go with Dan, who as we left said, "Come up to the office, Lucy, we've got one to work on before that."

That was just what I wanted to hear and followed Dan to his desk.

"I've got a good one here, one where I think we can make a difference."

"Go on, Dan, I'm all ears."

"Right. A young woman landed at Gatwick, three days ago, got into a car and hasn't been seen since."

"Surely there's cameras everywhere to get the registration plate?"

"You would think so, but due to an unbelievable set of circumstances, they have pictures of the car, but the number plate's always blocked. He came into the pickup zone between two buses, double-parked, stopped in the road, picked her up, followed a bus out, and was tail-gated by a van. Four cameras were unable to get the plate."

"What about cameras afterwards?"

"Same situation. Followed a slow bus with the van virtually on his bumper. We're looking at all motorway footage but nothing."

"Our help is needed, Dan. Let's go and get that number plate."

It was a relief to get out of Darryl's office and be working on something tangible. We collected a car from the garage and before long were pulling off the motor-way onto the dual carriageway to the North Terminal. Dan had given me a set of photographs of the missing woman, including ones at the airport, to study en route. She seemed a very happy and attractive lady in her late twenties, dressed on the day in jeans and a reddish jacket with a dark wheeled suitcase.

Pretty easy to recognise, and all I needed was the car registration number. Easy, I thought; makes a nice change and in daylight.

We parked out front, Dan putting the Police Parking Permit on the dashboard, and walked to the position where she boarded the car. Behind us on the left was a workman's hut set out just enough from the wall for me to materialise in the space. Work done. Back to the office with plenty of time to do the jump today.

*

We were back by three, I double-checked the time and date when she disappeared and said, "You go and have a coffee in the galley, I'll go upstairs, do the leap, and join you in about twenty minutes."

It was that simple and that's exactly how it turned out to be.

I positioned myself in my now usual spot, closed my eyes and soon found myself behind the builders' hut. No sign of any prying eyes. I checked my watch, all good, and walked across to a position where I could see everyone exiting.

It was a very busy day at Gatwick, so I had to use all my 'police training' to stay observant. Then, there she was, reddish jacket, dark case, and coming in my direction towards the double-parked car. A few women had looked similar, but she was the one.

Except she wasn't.

The photographs I'd been given were very clear and while this lady looked very similar, facially she was less attractive and with a much larger nose. Nevertheless, I tracked her to the car, same car, and while she put the case in the back I memorised the car number.

Job done. I retreated to my original place and with no eyes in my direction returned to Cloud. Still repeating the number in my head I went down to the galley where

Dan was relaxing and reading the paper and gave him the registration number, which he put straight on his phone.

"Jeez, Lucy, that was quick. I've only just finished my coffee."

"Yeah. It was fairly straightforward."

"Well, looks like another one solved."

"I'm sorry to disappoint you Dan."

"Why?"

"It wasn't the right woman. It was the right car and she looked like the correct one in a reddish jacket and a dark case, but she wasn't the one in the photographs you gave me."

"Sorry, give me that again," said a puzzled-looking Dan.

"It was a different woman. We're chasing the wrong car. I think you'd better get in touch with your police contact now and get them to check, but I'm sure you'll find I'm right. I don't think they have anything to do with it."

Dan stood up and phoned, retold the story and sat down with a sigh. It gave me enough time to get one of Nikki's special teas. I needed it.

"They're on to it as we speak. They'll get the registration address and go there straightaway. They promised to ring back as soon as they know for sure. I think I'll hold on here, Lucy, till I hear back. It shouldn't be long."

"Fine by me, Dan, I'll see if Morry needs a walk."

I went to Nikki's office.

"I've got an hour to kill, Nikki. Does Morry want or need a walk?"

"Morry always wants a walk," she said, and put on his lead and gave me the usual doggy plastic bag.

So I took Morry for a walk, or perhaps what I should have said is Morry took me for a walk. I took my time, luckily not needing the bag, and as I was walking back, I saw Dan coming towards me.

"I couldn't sit and wait till you returned. You were right. The police called to the house in Sevenoaks and she was sitting having a cup of tea with her husband, who had picked her up from the airport. She'd been to see her sister in Spain. It all checked out."

"Well, that's good news and bad news. Missing woman still missing, Dan."

"Back to square one for them. They were sure she was on the plane, but now…?"

"I hope they get a lead."

Dan agreed, and the three of us walked back to the office to see what else was new.

Chapter 39

The holy piper played her tune,
The light unfolding joy for all

Lovage noticed a small change in Freja Sarah, nothing she could pinpoint, after finding the damaged and scuffed jeans, ready for washing. She'd asked how it had happened and all Freja Sarah had said was that on one of her walks she'd tripped over a kerb. This sounded perfectly reasonable, but Lovage noticed a slight hesitancy in her reply, then thought she'd imagined it. But when Freja Sarah asked if one of her favourite normal-wear dresses was washed and pressed, as she'd like to wear it today, Lovage knew something was up.

Lovage tried to dismiss these trivialities, but together they nagged at her. Why did she need that particular dress? Why not just put on one of the others? Then she thought that perhaps Sarah would like one of the four to accompany her for a change.

"Freja Sarah, would you like one of us to walk along with you today. We know you need these walks to refresh and seek guidance, but if you'd like Alina or my-self along, we'd be happy to do so."

"Thank you, Lovage, for your lovely offer, but I need these solitary walks for my soul. I have ceased searching, for I know the true path that I must follow, but the path may be rocky and I must be shown the way."

Lovage accepted this as a good enough reason and Sarah felt she had placated her small concerns. She dared not mention her close call with the muggers or her meeting with Richard or how much she was looking for-ward to meeting up with him this morning. Sheer mortal longings would be totally unacceptable to her initiates, even though, she thought, Jesus was married, and there-fore mortal, so why not me.

"You have nothing to be concerned about; nothing to fear but fear itself, Lovage. You and the others are part of my life and have much to do in preparation for our great event on Sunday."

"Thank you for your wisdom, Freja Sarah. You're right, I must go and help."

With that, Lovage left, fears allayed, at least for the time being, and went back to the main house where the others were hard at work. Sarah was correct, they really had a tremendous amount to do, contacting the thou-sands of Freja Sarah followers to let them know they were needed for Sunday. There were phone calls to be made and emails to be sent. Sebastion had made a short film of Freja Sarah enthusing her followers and encour-aging them to be there and encourage their friends and family who weren't yet in the fold to consider going.

The short video spread throughout all the social media outlets. It was a major challenge, but they were up to it, of that she had faith.

At last on her own Sarah, now dressed in her best normal clothes, left 'number 26' as the group liked to call the home. She opened the door to the pavement, hesitated for a couple of seconds, then walked towards her rendezvous with Richard. Looking ahead, she saw him on the corner, waiting.

Her heart raced. He was so handsome; it made her legs buckle just to look at him. Emotions that she never thought possible flooded her mind. She wondered if he felt anything for her, or was she just another patient.

Whatever her doubts, as she got nearer he gave her a broad smile and said, "Sarah, I'm so happy to see you. How beautiful you look and no signs whatever of yesterday's trauma."

She was virtually tongue-tied but managed to say, "Hi, Richard, yes I'm fine. Thank you for the lovely compliment. I'm really happy to be here too."

Without a second thought he took her arm. She was astonished how natural it felt to be arm in arm as they walked towards the hotel. Richard was equally astonished how readily she accepted. Nicolas had been in touch and was at pains to tell him not to rush anything, just to take it slowly. She wasn't to be one of his usual conquests. This girl was special, how special they were yet to find out, but if she was a fraud, she was a very good one and from all the news that was coming his way, Nicolas thought she just might be the real thing. Let's take no chances, he'd told Richard. He was adamant. Richard knew how powerful he was, so he would be the best Richard Anthony that was possible. It wasn't hard to play the part: she was a lovely and attractive girl and he was drawn to her. This was a task that was really no task at all.

They sat together having coffee overlooking a beautiful garden with a pond full of flowers, butterflies and birds. He felt like he was in a film scene written for them and as the moment wore on it seemed difficult for them to keep their hands off each other, forever just touching and it was beyond his control not to lean forward and give her a small kiss. He apologised immediately.

"I'm truly sorry, Sarah. I don't know what came over me. I should never have done that. Please forgive me."

Sarah had been caught completely unawares by the kiss, which had scrabbled her brain, but she managed to get herself together and before she knew it said, "Richard don't worry. It was a lovely moment that I shall treasure forever," and she leaned forward and gave him a kiss.

Richard was lost for words, his thoughts in turmoil. While this was technically just a job for him, he was realising he was actually beginning to fall for her.

"I'm lost," he said. "I didn't expect this to happen. Sarah, I honestly only had your welfare at heart, at least until yesterday, but today…" He left the rest of the sentence unfinished and sat just looking at the table and shaking his head in disbelief.

There seemed nothing left for either of them to say,

it was enough to leave it unsaid – they both knew.

Their drinks finished, they agreed to meet again, just for a coffee, before leaving the hotel, arm in arm. They walked towards the corner where they had met, and would part ways, at least for now. As they reached the corner, across the road, Sebastion was making his way back to the house after a short errand. It was quite busy all around and he just happened to look across and thought 'wow, that girl looks just like Freja Sarah', but it was so ridiculous to contemplate her being with a man that he dismissed the thought immediately.

Chapter 40

Was it just providence that the tumultuous thunderstorms that had raged over London on the Saturday had, by Sunday morning, become only menacing cumulus clouds skirting the far distant horizon? One could be forgiven for thinking divine intervention had saved the day. That was certainly what Freja Sarah and her close initiatives thought.

The week's hard work now a distant memory, the followers had been contacted, as had the press. Freja Sarah stood waiting for Sebastion to finish loading the PA system and small portable stage into the van. He would make his way to Primrose Hill Road at the top of the hill where he would be aided by two strapping lads, capable of heavy lifting and also overseeing some semblance of simple crowd control as thousands of her flock tried desperately to touch her. There were now many who believed she could heal the sick and dying. The position chosen on the road enabled them direct access to a diagonal path which led to the paved area overlooking the complete slope down to Regents Park and provided a perfect view of the London skyline.

They hoped this would be the greatest religious rally of all time in London. Some had called it a Peace Rally, but Freja Sarah felt such a name was dated and totally incorrect. It was a rally for the people. A Ceremony of Hope.

It was all down to a question of perfect timing and delivery. She would follow Sebastion along the path after just five minutes. He had assured her that was all the time he needed to set up. They had all practised their roles, delivery and positioning to perfection, though there had now been a late addition to the programme. A world-famous actor, who had been a witness to the lions' enclosure event, had appealed to them to be able to speak. His wish had been granted.

Lovage would open as usual, but with a much shorter introduction, thanking everyone for being there. She would then 'notice' a world-famous British actor in the front of the audience and ask him if he wanted to say a few words and from that moment they fully expected the day to be theirs.

*

Down by the main Camden Market, at about the same time, Neil, Miles and Greig were counting their lucky stars that they had decided to take a cab, rather than battle the thousands swarming onto the tube, otherwise they might have missed the start.

*

Neil and his drinking buddies were not the only ones who had arranged to arrive in good time. The staff of Cloud were also there, in pairs or individually. Even Darryl had thought it wise to go along.

Dan and Lucy had positioned themselves near the top of the hill, which was still only sparsely filled by Sarah's followers, but as Dan looked out across the growing crowd, he realised the action would be taking place further down the hill. Gesturing to Lucy, the two of them moved slightly downhill, passing beneath the paved area now entirely taken over by Sarah and her group.

His mind focused on finding a good spot, it took Dan a while to realise that Lucy was no longer beside him. Turning, he searched for her in the crowd. She had stopped just a few metres away and stood surveying the scene of thousands of eager-faced people beginning to fill the whole area down to the canal. All waiting for the moment to begin.

Dan caught up with her. "Hey, I thought I'd lost you there."

"Sorry Dan, I just realised something." Lucy grinned. "You're not going to believe this, but the last time I stood looking at such a scene of happy people with a fantastic view behind the was…"

He interrupted her sentence with, "The London Olympics?"

She laughed out loud. "No, it was the Isle of Wight Pop Festival in 1970."

"You're joking."

"No, honestly, my father always wanted to see Jimi Hendrix, but Jimi died before he had the chance. I travelled back, I wanted to tease him about it, but I mistimed it and ended up watching Joni Mitchell. I met some really nice guys there. It's hard to believe they're probably now in their 70s."

"When did you do that?"

"Just before I joined Cloud. It was that leap that caused the problem I had; it was the one too many I had forgotten about."

The conversation finished there as they heard over the tannoy somebody testing to make sure it was working, which it was, loud and clear.

What they had come to see was about to begin.

*

Lovage climbed the steps to the stage, her initiates took four seats in front and one each at the side of the stage platform. A single rope had been arranged in an arc around the setting to allow some space; it also enabled the whole of the stage to be seen by the audience as they stood down the slope.

Lovage stood before the microphone, herself a beauty to behold on this momentous day, and a hush came over the assembled throng. She thanked them all for coming to such a day, the first of days celebrating Freja Sarah showing herself to the world in all her glory. She then thanked her associates for their help in making it possible, turning to bring forth Freja Sarah to the front.

As she turned, with impeccable timing, as one would expect, a gentleman from the front pushed forward and raised his arm and pleaded, "Please let me speak just a few words, for I have witnessed the miracle of Freja Sarah."

Lovage, knowing that this had been prearranged, pretended to look back for instructions on how to proceed, and heard Freja Sarah say, "Let him speak."

The crowd gasped; they recognised the famous actor Sir Giles Arbroath step over the rope and make his way to the microphone, dressed in his usual dignified country squire attire as he raised his hands to quiet the crowd.

As they did so, he said, "I will not keep you long waiting for Freja Sarah, but I must share with you that I was amongst a privileged few who witnessed a miracle, an unearthly event, only just recently. Some of you may know of it. I am here as a convert, a new subject to the word of Freja Sarah, for I believe she is the new Chosen One, and urge you to listen to her words. For she alone, in this world of increasing darkness can show us the path to the light."

A gentle hum of acknowledgement rose from the crowd. Giles held the moment till full quiet returned and continued,

"Please believe, as I do, that God believes we have lost our way. We should suffer no more. We have suffered enough through these dark times. Her course will be clear. I am asking nothing but for you all to listen and follow. For as I see it, if ever there was a time for God to help humanity, it is now, before we fall into the abyss."

The crowd erupted.

He had full mastery over his audience; held them for just a little longer then with his usual perfect timing said, "We need a bringer of life. We need Freja Sarah."

He left the stage to possibly the largest ovation of his life, as Freja Sarah moved forward to deliver her speech.

"Jesus… That was some warm-up act," said Miles.

"She's gonna have trouble following that," Neil said, shaking his head.

"Shush," said Greig. "I really want to hear again what she says. You two better keep quiet or I'm moving off."

Before any of them had time for another smart reply, Freja Sarah started speaking. Somehow the amplification had made her voice both clear and haunting and it seemed to perfectly match her green dress and red hair. All in all a strange but perfect combination.

She had the audience in the palm of her hand. She spent most of her sermon going over her usual diatribe of the modern world and moved onto encouraging her followers to wait and watch as now she would show the present leaders of the world, the controllers of the people's money and the modern churches of all denominations, that she was about to change their worlds for ever. They must prepare for this or face their day of judgement. Most of this had been said before and it was music to the ears of her flock. Only towards the end did she talk about what was to come…

"For my followers, the path is clear and true, but many have yet to find this path. There are many lost down many paths and I am God's messenger to guide to the true course. This will be shown. I have no wish to be God's Pale Rider, to be the Avenging Angel. In coming times, the way will become clear. A chain of miraculous events will unfold; all unbelievers will see the truth. For I am everything. For I am everywhere. For I am she, God's Chosen One, sent on God's mission to cleanse your souls. You will become kings and queens of this world."

She outstretched her arms to make a holy cross. Her followers cried out in ecstasy, "Freja Sarah!" and thousands dropped to their knees. She backed off the stage to a mighty adulation and Sebastion came forward, his arms making quieting gestures, calming the noise, addressing the crowd and TV cameras.

"She is not gone, she will return. Freja Sarah will make a number of miraculous appearances in the coming weeks. When these are to happen, I shall inform the world. She is the one you seek and will be accepted as that, for we are no longer in times past. She is needed for times future. For she alone is God's Chosen One. The Freja Sarah."

As quickly as Sebastion left the stage, Freja Sarah reappeared. The sound of the crowd could get no louder as she said, "I shall now walk amongst you."

*

Miles, relieved that the 'sermon on the mount' was over, turned to talk to Greig and couldn't help but notice a huge rolling wave of a cloud moving ominously in their

281

direction, hung high in the sky but coming their way at some speed.

Sensing a possible drenching, he said to the others, "Look, it's finished here. Have you heard enough, Greig? Just look at that cloud coming our way."

Greig looked and nodded.

Neil said, "Let's get down to the canal if we can. It's not going to be easy."

"That cloud looks unnatural," said Miles. "It looks like something from 'War of the Worlds'. Did you guys know that in H. G. Wells' book, Primrose Hill was the last Martian base?"

"Is that right Miles?" said Greig.

"Yeah. So it's another 'end of the world' as we know it story," said Neil.

"C'mon you guys. Let's get going."

*

Freja Sarah had left the stage and was safely enclosed by her initiates. She was heading down towards the canal to a prearranged pickup point at a nearby church, but was making slow progress against the dark cloud which was beginning to blacken the sky. Many in the crowd had noticed it and were dispersing in all directions, but some still followed Freja Sarah, including at least half of the Cloud team.

It seemed to take an eternity to shuffle down the slope. At one point, Miles and company were bundled nearer Freja Sarah than they expected.

Neil was the nearest to her and could just about make out her saying, "I shall liberate the oppressed. Seek the path, see my light," all of which left him cold.

The cloud still lingered above them, but to their relief it had not yet opened. Miles, Neil and Greig had fallen in with a group just behind Freja Sarah as the park narrowed towards the canal, and then suddenly everything came to a standstill.

A group of lads were barring any further progress and shouting at Freja Sarah, typical laddish comments. "Ooh, look. There's Jesus' sister," and various other jibes.

Freja Sarah stood and looked them in the eye, unbowed, as various members of her entourage tried to move them on with, "Listen to her and you shall be saved."

Unsurprisingly, this 'preaching' did not go down well at all, and prompted even more barracking.

"Go on then. If you're the new God, you should be able to walk on water. Go on then, walk over the canal," and all started laughing. They thought it was hilarious and even Miles and Neil couldn't help but chuckle.

She replied calmly, "So you'd believe in me if I walked on water?" but before it could be taken any further, the strength of the crowd pushed the lads even closer to her in what seemed like an intimidating way to the onlookers.

This was an unexpected end to the morning, but what happened next was even more unexpected. Out of the crowd, a man pushed to the front saying, "I'm a police officer. Move back or I'll get reinforcements. I've got you on my camera."

Amazingly, they did so.

Miles watched, very impressed with the show of authority by the man, then suddenly realised he was the man he had seen at Cloud, now confirming his role.

Dan had saved the day, but his troubles were only just starting.

Chapter 41

There was a sombre edge to the meeting on Monday with Darryl. I couldn't help but feel it from everyone.

Trying to dwell on the positive, I commented, "At least we reached the car before the heavens opened, that sure was a downpour."

"Well, you can count yourself lucky. Grace and I got soaked," said Hilton.

"I went along with Henry," said Jay, "and the crowd was so bad outside the tube station that we were stuck in it as well."

"You should have seen the state of Morry," said Nikki.

Before anyone else could comment, Darryl entered and sat.

I'd seen and heard from Dan how much he bitterly regretted stepping in at the canal's edge. I'd watched him drop his head and push himself back into the anonymity of the crowd when he'd realised he might be photographed. The last thing he needed was his face to be shown in the newspapers or worse, on the news, and I guessed he knew what Darryl would open with. He sat pensive as Darryl spoke.

"Welcome, all. Well, that was a bit of a do, wasn't it?"

There was nothing anyone could add to that. We all just nodded.

"Dan."

"Yes, Darryl, I know."

"What came over you?"

"Years of police training. Before I knew what I was doing, I'd done it. I can't apologise enough."

"You're a lucky, lucky boy. The TV cameras hadn't been able to get down there. We've checked photographs in the newspapers and everything so far online, but not one clear photo of you. I guess it was so quick and crowded, nobody could get their phones out fast enough and from what she said I think you'll be old news soon. What did the rest of you think?"

I came in, trying to rescue Dan. "To be honest, I think the lads' comments were quite funny, especially the one about her being Jesus' sister."

"And the one from the guy who held up a safety pin and said 'if you prick me with this, will I become holy?'," said Grace.

We all laughed, even Darryl, and happily the sombre mood lifted.

"I didn't see you there, Grace?" said Dan.

"I was right near you but with a long wig on, just to be safe."

"Okay, let's move on," said Darryl grinning. "Is she or is she not The One?"

Henry said, "That's for us to find out."

Everybody agreed with that and said so. There were then a number of comments about how gullible the public were, and some in the public's defence. There was some agreement for both.

Dan came back with, "It seems to me that we can do nothing more at present. She's got some big plans and that's where we'll catch her out, if she's catchable. Do we all agree she's catchable?"

We all agreed as one that she was and left the room.

Back in our office, Dan again apologised, but we agreed to forget it for the time being. Then his computer sounded: an email from his hotline at the Met.

"One's just come in, I'll open it up."

"No rush, Dan. Seems I've got all day."

After a couple of minutes he said, "No, you haven't. We're off to Newbury. I'll tell you about it on the way."

*

"Told you," said Miles, sitting in Neil's lounge. "I just knew when I saw him at Cloud there was something about him."

"Your nose again?"

"Naturally, but I've had years of coming across these people. I can just kinda smell them. I suppose it's something to do with their training – slightly military, they know how to conduct themselves, or it's their facial expressions. It's just something they give off. Plus my brain, being a journalist's brain, is wired to consider the unexpected, not just the obvious. I've spent years not believing the obvious."

"Well, let's hope he didn't spot you."

"Nah. I was always just out of his main view, by accident, not design. I was just another face in the crowd and that was a hell of a crowd, wasn't it?"

"So, what are we going to do now?"

"Nothing."

"Nothing? That doesn't sound like you."

"I think we should let things develop with Freja Sarah. It's all winding up. She's gonna do something dramatic. I just know it. She did say she had big plans. We'll see."

"Got anything else? I'm kinda bored. "

"Well, I do have something actually. Something that could get me, sorry, us, some real brownie points."

"Showing your age there, Miles."

"You know what I mean."

"What then?"

"Did you read in the papers, over the weekend, about the car crash where a young child was snatched from the car while the mother was unconscious in the front?"

"I don't read the papers anymore. Sorry, Miles."

"Well it's big news and the police are appealing for information as they have no leads. Everyone's going mad trying to find the other car and get the child back."

"When did it happen?"

"Saturday night."

"Well, that's not a problem now, but I need time and location."

"Location, Newbury, but time not exact, a bit vague,

around six thirty on a country road. On her way back from a supermarket. Didn't seem planned, no marital problems, but you never know. All they have is that it was a white vehicle. They probably know more as there are many versions of white in the car trade, but they're not telling us. All we need to get is the registration number and description of the driver. Easy, eh?"

"Aren't they all, Miles," he said sarcastically. "Though why not, I've got nothing on."

So off they went to Newbury.

*

"You should have told me, Sarah," Richard said with a look of disappointment, as they met on the corner.

"I wanted to, Richard. I really did. But I just never had the chance, not over coffee in a hotel. When I'm with you, I can't think of anything else but you. There, now I've said it. I'm sorry. I suppose now you don't want to see me anymore?"

"Yes, of course I do. I feel the same for you, Sarah. I don't understand how it's happened to me as well. I just feel... I just feel deflated and lost."

"I'm truly sorry, really. Please... please don't leave me."

"I couldn't if I wanted to, but you must tell me. Are you the new Chosen One? I really need to know."

"Well, part of me is, Richard, but a part of me I never knew existed isn't. I didn't think in a thousand years I could feel like this."

"C'mon," he said, "Let's go and sit in the park. I'm not in the mood for a hotel coffee, are you?"

"Yes. Let's do that. I'll tell you anything you want to know, and any question you want to ask. Anything. I don't want to spoil this."

Richard listened attentively to Sarah's absorbing story. She told him virtually everything, even some things best untold. He was torn apart. He'd fallen completely for her, with no reservations. This was something totally out of character for him, but he knew it wasn't going to be easy with the black cloud of Nicolas hanging over him. He dismissed that thought.

Richard wasn't a religious person as such, but there was something spiritual and compelling about Sarah. He could see how her followers believed. He'd never met anyone who had the effect on him that she did and was sure he was never likely to do so again. What a line he must tread.

Sarah had the good of the whole of mankind in her heart, while Nicolas only thought of riches. What turmoil. What if she really was the New Messiah? If so, he only had an eternity in hell ahead, but if she was only a mortal with some unusual power, then she was the one for him. Either way, he wished his plight on no man.

She could see he was troubled and said, "Richard, are you still with me?"

"Forever, Sarah."

"But my followers must never know I have a mortal side. So you must remain, for the time being, a secret. But I shall soon have the house to myself. My associates, my close four, have each been given their own home. A place that they can go in troubled times, and they may lie ahead. They will be furnishing and settling into these during the rest of this week."

Richard looked bemused.

"My home will be empty, and you will be free to visit, when you wish."

"I need more time with you, Sarah, real time, not just coffee time. I love you, Sarah."

"And I love you, Richard."

They embraced in a long, deep hug, and promised each other it would soon be much more than that.

It would have been the perfect moment, but Richard couldn't help but think back over the conversation he'd had earlier with Nicolas and the gentle reminder he'd been given.

"Richard, excuse me for saying, but are you falling into her web? Just make sure you don't get entangled. Don't forget our objective."

If there was one thing Richard knew, it was this: no one crossed Nicolas.

Chapter 42

Getting to the crash scene for Dan and Lucy was a proverbial 'piece of cake', having been given the postcode and exact location courtesy of the Met. Unfortunately for Neil and Miles, the same could not be said. Neil's older car lacked any features and Miles' map reading left a lot to be desired, but perseverance won out in the end.

Unbeknownst to Neil, he missed Lucy by a couple of hours, but both reached the same conclusion. There was a nice field hedgerow from which they had a perfect view of the corner where the crash took place.

Returning to London, Neil decided to revisit the scene later that day, hoping the time he had chosen would be correct. Little did he know that his timing would soon be the least of his worries.

*

After visiting the crash site, Dan and I returned to Cloud, checking in with Nikki to see if there were any new developments from the weekend. Sadly, nothing had come up, so we headed upstairs to the office. I couldn't shake the thought of the missing child, what they must be going through. This case couldn't wait. I needed answers, now.

"I think I'll go upstairs and travel back as soon as I can. This case is a bit unsettling. The sooner we try and help the better."

"Yes, I'm totally with you there. What time are you going to leap to?"

"I reckon the six thirty is as good a time as any. I've got around thirteen minutes and if I'm too late or early, I can always go back again later today."

I left Dan in the office and headed upstairs, laying down in my favourite spot. But the crash and abduction were playing on my mind, so it took a long while for me to relax enough to leap. Eventually, I felt myself going, and seconds later I had materialised by the crash site.

I froze on the spot.

Standing next to me, against the hedgerow, was somebody else. I could tell instantly by the static electricity between us that he was also a traveller. He looked as shocked as I felt, but gathered his senses quicker.

"Who are you?" he asked sharply. "What are you doing here?"

"I just..." I stuttered, unable to speak.

"Have you come for the crash?"

I nodded.

"Well, you're too late. You missed it. And lucky for you."

Part of me wanted to disappear back to the safety of

Cloud, but I couldn't move; I was transfixed.

"It was a grisly affair. If you've got the ability I've got, don't come back again. It was awful. Here's the registration number," he said.

I was barely listening, and when he recited the number I couldn't take it in. My mind was a jumble.

"Did you get that? It was foreign. Eastern European. A nasty bloke who got out, spoke with the driver and grabbed the kid who was screaming. Put the child in a box in the back of the van and just drove off. I've given you all you need, here's the number again: AL 63 2 JHP. Have you got that? Remember. Don't come back."

I looked at the scene in front of me: the crashed car, the unconscious mother inside... I turned back towards him, but he was gone. I disappeared seconds later.

Chapter 43

"I've just met another like me."

"What?" said Dan. "Quick, come and sit down and try and get yourself calmed down. Nikki, get her one of your teas."

I sat down just looking at the cup for a few minutes, going over in my mind what had happened. I just managed to blurt out the most important bit of information.

"AL 632 JHP, white van."

Dan wrote it down immediately and said, "Nikki, look after Lucy while I rush this through," and he left the room.

Nikki sat in silence. I could tell she was patiently waiting for me to start speaking but I was still trying to get my brain in some sort of order. Then Dan came back in.

"How is she, Nikki?"

But before Nikki could answer, I said, "I'm okay, Dan, I'm back with the living. It was just such a shock. The last thing I expected was another like me."

"Man or woman?" asked Nikki.

"A guy in his late twenties, with light brown hair. I'm

sure I'd recognise him again."

"As soon as you're finished here, we'll do an identi-kit of him," said Nikki.

"He seemed quite a nice guy. I'd missed the abduction. He said it was really grisly and gave me the registration number twice so I wouldn't forget it and told me twice not to come back as the whole scene was just too horrible."

"So there's more than you out there, and the holy one," said Dan. "We must try and find out who he is and what he's up to. I'm going straight to tell Darryl what's happened. You sure you're okay?"

"She'll be fine, Dan," said Nikki. "It must have been a hell of a shock. Something none of us expected. I think I'll go and get the kit while the man's face is still fresh in your mind. What do you think?"

"I'm sure that's a good idea, but I don't think I'll ever forget his face."

I sat there, trying to get myself together. The scene was just running round in my head. I was just relieved that he seemed to have my welfare at heart and thinking about it again, I thought I'd like to thank him in person, his real person that is. Just when I needed a bit of actual bodily contact, Morry saved the day by jumping up and sitting next to me, putting his head on my lap. Nikki came back.

"You seem to have made a friend there. I've never seen him do that with anyone. I've always thought that dogs can sense emotions and I think that's the proof I needed. Well done, Morry. You seem much better now,

Lucy."

"Yes, I am Nikki, thanks."

"Okay, let's get this guy's face."

We went through the procedure. I knew the way she worked, no jokes this time. It seemed only minutes and there he was. Perfect.

Dan came back in the room. He'd got Darryl up to speed with my experience and told Nikki to get everybody into the office nine a.m. sharp the next morning, no exceptions.

"We've got nightwatchmen who now come in on a shift basis," said Dan, "but Darryl suggested that we spend the night here upstairs as it's been a day like no other and he needs us here early."

Nikki said, "I'll stay as well, with Morry. We'll go get something to eat, then come back and stay."

I agreed, phone calls were made, and the night passed without incident.

Chapter 44

The very moment that Neil returned to his chair he grabbed his phone and dialled Miles.

"Miles, you gotta get over here now, it's urgent. I can't tell you over the phone, just get here."

"On my way." He quickly called a taxi and within twenty minutes was in Neil's lounge. Neil put a glass of brandy in his hand. Neil was already on his second.

"Okay, I'm ready, tell me."

"I went to the accident scene, no problem and perfect timing. Within a couple of minutes, the van tried to over-take the car, scraped the side which pushed the car into a ditch. I watched the passenger of the van get out, run back to the car, have a quick look, then he ran back to the van, spoke with the driver then ran back to the car. He grabbed the screaming child from the back, opened the rear door and stuffed him in a box and they both drove off. I got the plate number, foreign."

"So what's the problem?"

"As the van drove off, a girl materialised next to me."

"What?"

"Yeah. That's exactly what I thought."

"Who the hell was she?"

"I didn't get to find out. She was as shocked as I was. I guessed she might have something to do with the police. It was a terrible scene so just in case she tried to come back I gave her the reg number and told her it was a white van. Made sure she remembered it and left instantly. I hope she did too."

"This is getting crazy, Neil. First I thought it was just you, then we come across that Sarah and now another. What's going on?"

They sat for a few seconds in silence, trying to get their heads around it. Neil leaned forward and topped Miles' glass up. Neil was already on his third.

"But now she knows about me, that there are others. Where's this going to lead to?"

"God knows," said Miles. "Let's ask Sarah."

"It ain't funny, Miles."

"You're right, sorry. I think we should keep a low profile for a while. Let's see how it settles, but prepare ourselves for anything."

"Gotta agree, Miles. It all seemed so straightforward just a few weeks ago. What are we getting into? Let's be extra careful, not breathe a word of it, not that we do, and hope we can get away with it."

"Was she pretty?"

"She was actually."

*

They were all there by nine, Nikki with the prepared

identikit picture that Lucy thought was a very good like-ness.

A furrowed Darryl said, "Looks like we've got more company out there besides this Sarah. Any suggestions, anyone?" He looked directly at Dan.

Before he could answer Hilton replied, "Somehow I think the kettle's beginning to boil."

"Shut up, Hilton," said Grace.

"No, I think he's right." said Darryl.

Dan seized the moment to enter the conversation. "Well, we can't exactly give the picture out to the media, bearing in mind the circumstances, and our visitor the other night. It may be a coincidence, I don't think so. I think it's safe to assume it's one person, not two. He must have some knowledge of us or be working with a partner who has the knowledge or suspicion. So, how did they get the info?"

"That's a good starting point, Dan. Henry, you see everyone. Go through all the visitors that we've had over the last six weeks with Nikki and Dan. Everyone else, go over the last few weeks and anything, and I mean anything, that was just slightly out of the ordinary or with hindsight now seems a little odd; bring it to our attention."

Henry left the room fast and they all followed him out through the door, but while he went to his office, Nikki beckoned the rest to join her in the galley.

"Darryl's correct, just take some time here talking amongst yourselves," Nikki suggested. "Maybe some-thing will turn up that might ring a bell, an alarm bell."

Half an hour later, Henry put his head round the door. "Dan, would you come up to Darryl's office? I've got the list."

Dan nodded, and the two of them headed to Darryl's office. Henry held centre stage as Dan and Darryl listened.

"I've got names which may be of interest to us and I think there are four to check out. There were obviously more but I've discounted these at this stage as they all worked for major companies who had made appointments for them, whereas the four were just individuals."

"Right, Henry, give me the list," said Darryl. "I'll get them put under surveillance for a few days, then we'll bring them in."

Henry went through the names, then said, "There is one name that stands out by a mile – Miles Rogerson – freelance journalist, who, when I think back, came here on a flimsy pretext, so flimsy I didn't invoice him. Just wanted a firewall on his computer. Fair enough, you might think, but there was something odd about him, but I let it go as most journalists are odd."

"Thanks, Henry, he'll get special attention. Let's find out who his friends and associates are. Perhaps we can match him with the photo kit we have."

"Leave it with me for a few days."

Chapter 45

Comes the dream still to be seen;
Destiny awaits its call

A small gap in the curtains was enough to let an early morning ray of sunshine fall upon Sarah's face and she woke. She raised her head off the pillow just slightly and looked at the two sets of feet at the bottom of the bed, also bathed in light.

The previous evening and night had been more intense than she could possibly have imagined, but her unending joy of looking at Richard's head resting peacefully on the pillow knew no bounds. She lay back, wondrous at her happiness.

The previous day had made all this possible. It had started with an early morning visit from Andrew.

He'd summoned Alina, Judith, Lovage and Sebastion, sat them before him and said, "Let me first say, this is due entirely to Freja Sarah, but the power of money is immense. It makes the impossible, possible, for in this short time, I now have homes for each of you. Freja Sarah is determined that the troubled times ahead must not befall you, and we can only praise her for her foresight, for she insists on your wellbeing."

Looking at the disbelief on the faces of the four that such a wonderful gesture could be happening to them, Judith said, "Can this really be true Andrew, so quickly?"

"Yes, Judith, money rules the world, at this time. Only when the word of Freja Sarah is accepted by all, throughout the world, will this cease to be, but until that time comes, I'm afraid to say 'money rules'."

"Hallelujah. To that day," cried Lovage, and to that they all agreed.

"True for now," said Sebastion, "but this is about to change."

Andrew continued. "I deliberately sought out only properties that were empty and as you can imagine, in a city like London, there were many. I have chosen, with help from my team, only homes in good neighbour-hoods, within a mile or so of here, so you are able to come and go from here as necessary. Each flat consists of two bedrooms, a lounge, kitchen and bathroom, all to a very high standard."

"When will we be able to see them?" said Alina.

"All in good time, Alina. Freja Sarah and I were so pleased with all of them, that we have decided you should each choose a key and whichever key you choose will be the key to your new home, for all time."

Andrew opened his briefcase and put four sets of keys on the table in front of them and after some hesitation, one by one, they took a set.

"Do not be unsure of your choice, be happy, as each

is perfect. There are small differences, none of which will affect your enjoyment."

They looked at each other, still slightly unsure whether they had made the right choice, but they had chosen and looked at Andrew in gratitude. Their thoughts were with Freja Sarah.

"Also, my team and I have taken the liberty to partly furnish each flat with all major items; obviously your own personal items are still here. We hope you like what we have done, we certainly do."

In actual fact his team had worked every hour available to them and were highly pleased with the results. The effort he'd put in was worth it, just to see their faces, full of happiness and glee and he only regretted not being there when they opened the doors.

For Lovage and Alina, in fact for all of them, they looked in shock. It was beyond anything they could have envisaged just a few weeks ago, and so fast. Judith said, "Andrew, I speak for all of us, I know. This is truly wonderful and we want to thank Freja Sarah from the bottom of our hearts. Please do so from all of us."

As if on cue, Freja Sarah had entered the room to a warm, loving response. It took some time to quiet them all down and then she spoke. "You are my close ones, my friends, my only wish for you is to be happy and later today Andrew's colleagues will show you your new homes, not just places of refuge, but yours forever. Go and stay there for a few days to make them yours, but for now I must ask for your help and assistance."

They all responded positively of course.

She continued, "I have decided that as we reach dramatic times, dramatic events are necessary."

There was a short silence. What could she possibly have in mind after last weeks' events.

"The young lads by the canal last Sunday were correct. I must become beyond jokes and laughter, and so on this coming Sunday afternoon, I will walk across the river Thames. They wanted to see me walk on water and now the whole world will see it happening and I hope that they will also."

There were gasps of amazement and Lovage said without thinking, "Won't that be dangerous with all the boats?"

Freja Sarah laughed. "There will be no danger for me, only for the boats."

This time they all laughed.

"I hope Andrew and Judith will organise the when and where, but somewhere a large amount of people can watch, to be televised and seen by all. I want a boat with steps down to the water, so I can walk down and up to and from the water. Is this practical for you to organise in a short time?"

"Anything is possible for you, Freja Sarah," said Sebastion. "Please let me help Andrew get a boat in time."

"I certainly would appreciate your help, Sebastion," Andrew replied.

"This will show the world. They will see the truth," said Freja Sarah and everybody agreed. This was their moment.

They all had work and packing to do and left. Lovage

checked whether Freja Sarah would be all right on her own in the house. She confirmed, in a motherly way, that there were plenty of provisions, but if she needed anything just to contact her.

Sebastion told Andrew he could be ready in next to no time to help him with the boat, but Andrew told him to relax, go enjoy his new surroundings. He would contact him when required tomorrow.

With that, they all dispersed and within a couple of hours Sarah was on her own and had picked up the phone and called Richard, with planned bliss ahead. And that's exactly what it turned out to be for both of them over the next couple of days.

She now lay next to the love of her life, morning had broken, and she was free to enjoy this secret mortality of hers, at least for a short while.

Richard was in fact awake with his eyes closed, thinking much the same of his life with her, but mostly how was he going to carry on this life he loved with Sarah and how he was he going to get out of this, with Nicolas like a monkey on his back.

They both had serious problems.

Chapter 46

Perhaps it was just the cycle of the moon, but there seemed to be an air of uncertainty and suspicion seeping across the land, or was it just a low pressure system giving a series of unending grey days?

Miles and Neil had decided to keep a low profile after what had happened, keeping their own company for a few days to see if anything developed. Neil stayed at home but Miles still went for the occasional drink, keeping an eye out for anything vaguely suspicious.

Darryl had been to a lengthy meeting with the Intelligence Services, who had already spoken to two of the names on Henry's list and discounted them. Of the remaining two, the money was on Miles, as a journalist, whereas the other was running a dating agency which seemed genuine. A street camera on Miles' road had been remotely repositioned to pick up any comings and goings and was being monitored constantly, as was Miles, his movements tracked and traced by professionals.

Gone were the days of single male spies hiding in

shop doorways or sitting in pub corners reading a newspaper. Now, in the modern world, spies were disguised as unobtrusive couples, just everyday people enjoying an evening out in each other's company. Brenda and Dan, not the Dan from Cloud, were the youngest of the couples assigned to watch Miles at the start of the evening in the Compasses, soon to be replaced by an older couple, Colin and Joan.

Miles, drinking at the bar with a few friends, was in a subdued mood, noted by everyone.

After a pint and a half, he claimed a headache, gave his apologies, and left for home with a lot on his mind. This was the cue for Colin and Joan to leave and go their separate ways, to be replaced by a trio of younger girls who bought drinks and stood at the bar chatting.

After a while, one of them said to the barmaid, pointing to her friend, "My girlfriend here had a date with a nice guy from round here. She lost his number, and he hasn't rung her."

She got a photograph from her bag, doctored by the services from the identikit, showing Neil standing in front of a bar with a beer in hand.

"I know him, that's Neil. He's in here all the time."

"You couldn't pass her number on to him, could you? I don't suppose you have his number?"

"Hang on, I'll ask Chris."

She walked down the bar and spoke to the guy changing barrels. "Don't suppose you know Neil's phone number?"

"Do you mean Neil Bland?"

"Yeah. That Neil."

"No, I don't, but I know he lives in Wood Green."

"Thanks, Chris."

She walked back to the girls, took the number down and told them she'd make sure he got it.

They thanked her, finished their drinks and left saying they'd be back as it was such a nice pub, very friendly.

Miles came in the next night, his mood unchanged. Trish, behind the bar, told him what had happened the previous night.

He knew immediately the game was up and telephoned Neil with the bad news. It wasn't going to be a restful weekend for them; they were due a visit, that was for sure.

They both knew it was just a case of when.

*

At Cloud, nothing seemed different, at least on the face of it. I was late getting in because of delays on the train, but I found Dan and Kim chatting amiably in the galley.

"Morning, Lucy, we've got some very good news for you," said Kim, smiling up at me. "The police have got the child back, completely unharmed."

I let out a huge sigh of relief. I had been doubting myself for days, starting to wonder whether in my shock I had heard the number plate wrong.

"Thank heavens for that. Well done that guy. Tell me more."

"Well, it was no surprise that the vehicle wasn't registered in the UK, but the whole of the Police Force had been monitoring every motorway and road camera continuously and at last it turned up on the M4. Very quickly, they managed to get an unmarked police car on its tail. Eventually, it turned off the motorway and led them to a suburb of Swindon."

Kim took a deep breath and another sip of coffee, then continued.

"APB followed and within minutes the house was surrounded. Swat team broke the door down. The surprised occupants offered no resistance and just pointed up the stairs, where the child was fast asleep."

"What great news."

"Yeah, apparently one of the guys, supposedly builders, had a sister living there, who was desperate for a child. 'Simple as that'." Kim sighed, exasperated. "What happened to legal adoption?"

"At least they're behind bars now," Dan offered.

"I don't care about that, Dan, I'm just happy for the mother."

"The child's back with his father; the mother is still in hospital recovering and hopefully the child won't remember a thing. Good job, Lucy," said Kim with meaning.

"Well, let's be honest, I know I could have gone back, but we've got to give the mystery man some credit. Any news there?"

"I think there is," Kim said. "I spoke with Darryl earlier. They've narrowed it down from four possibles to two and now one."

"It's all happening here," said Dan. "Who is he, did Darryl say?"

"No, though he told me they are currently following both this guy and the man he's working with, who happens to have been here before because of some 'computer issue', a bit of fishing, as they say," Kim clarified. "In fact, he's due back in later this morning on something Henry's trumped up. A mistake on our firewall and could he bring back in with him his computer, should only take ten minutes. We think he's bought it. Well, maybe he did, we'll find out soon."

*

Miles' weekend of worry was not going to happen. He took the phone call he was expecting and decided he had no real choice but to go. He would try and bluff it out, that's what he would do. After all, he and Neil had done nothing wrong.

He kept that notion in his head as he waved to Nikki, who smiled and let him.

"Mr Rogerson, they're waiting for you," she said ominously, and he was shown up to Darryl's office. Darryl sat with Kim beside him.

He tried a bluff, "I've brought everything you asked. Is Henry not here?"

"Miles, can I call you Miles? I'm Darryl and this is Kim."

"Of course, Darryl. Hello, Kim," he said, ready for

311

anything.

"Miles, are we going to keep up this charade? Because we know all about you and Neil Bland, so there really is no point in trying to pretend."

Miles sat stupefied.

"Before you say anything, let me first say you've done nothing at all against the law and we really appreciate you coming in at short notice. You are completely free to get up and walk away now, if you desire, but I think we may be able to assist one another."

Miles sat for a second of thought, realised the game was up, thought about leaving, then said as cool as possible, "Okay, I'm listening, Darryl."

"Let me say, hypothetically, we may be engaged in similar activities and could benefit from cooperation. I don't want to say too much more at this stage, only that it would seem sensible to have your partner here also. Do you think that's a possibility, Miles?"

"I think it's highly likely, yes, I believe so."

"Okay, shall we adjourn here now and meet again on Monday?"

"Let me take a minute, Darryl, and give Neil a call, perhaps a little privacy."

"Of course," said Darryl, and he and Kim left the room.

Miles rang Neil, telling him to sit first, went through the whole thing, adding a bit of colour here and there as only he would, but made it perfectly clear it was positive rather than negative.

Neil felt he had no other option than to agree, but at

the same time he saw it as another move forward. At least, he hoped so.

Miles opened the door where they were waiting and asked what time would they like them to be here on Monday.

If they all knew now what the weekend would bring, they wouldn't believe it.

Chapter 47

Dark waters recede, the light becoming clear,
But only the sure-footed know the path

It was the day. The day everything would change for Sarah. Plans had been made. Plans had been checked and were ready. Only the final performance remained. Sarah and her four sat waiting. Waiting for the morning to end.

Sarah, with the event of her lifetime in front of her, thought only of the fact that due to the planning she had not been able to meet with Richard. Judith couldn't wait for the time to pass; she knew today's event would be the making of her. She had informed the now hundreds of thousands of Freja Sarah's internet followers when and where the 'Miracle on the water' would take place. That was enough. She had checked and the press were geared up for a multimedia happening and she knew they often avoided the unpalatable truth, with good reason. This would receive world coverage.

Lovage and Alina looked upon Freja Sarah in wonderment and at the same time loving concern.

Sebastion had checked and double-checked the timings. Knew when the tourist boats were not moored and where on the river, and also at what time the river would be at its highest. He had arranged with Andrew to pick up the boat at a place called Pier 39 upriver near Fulham. The steps on the side of the boat were fitted and the inside cabin curtained. It was ready to go, and so was he.

All in all, the four, plus Andrew, had done first-class work in their own way and were eager to see the successful outcome.

Andrew called and collected Sebastion first to collect the boat. The others would make their way by taxi to the join them at the riverside and Freja Sarah would materialise in the cabin.

At the prearranged time they left, and Sarah went and sat down in her annexe waiting for the call.

As in all complicated plans, there was a slight hitch as another boat containing Freja Sarah's followers had moored their boat where Sebastion needed to be. He explained to them the situation and of course they moved and then he needed to get the boat facing downstream with the cabin in the exact, already marked space. It all took just five extra minutes. He looked along Westminster bridge from the water; it was thronged with crowds, as were both riverbanks. He couldn't help but notice the number of TV cameras. The time was now.

He made the call.

*

Freja Sarah walked from the cabin and stood on the small deck. Her initiates and Andrew had moved to be along the side to ensure that she was in full view. She was dressed in a diaphanous light blue dress, cut to above the ankle so her feet could be easily seen. The crowd erupted into a tumultuous roar, then she took her place above the steps leading down to the water. As if on cue from above, the clouds slightly parted and the sun gave her a light and delicate shimmering effect, highlighting her red hair over the muddy Thames water.

She took her first step onto the water. The crowd hushed as one. She proceeded to walk slowly towards the South Bank. The crowd then took up a low chant of "Freja Sarah" as she started across. As she reached roughly halfway, Sebastion noticed another boat heading towards her, still some distance off, and motioned to Andrew, who threw off the moorings and took the boat out to the centre of the river, forcing the other boat to manoeuvre behind him, where Freja Sarah had already walked, as he held steady.

Sarah was oblivious to all of this. She had her eyes set on the spot of her retrieval and her walking, which was the same on land as on water. She was actually thinking of Richard and when they would meet again.

The crowd were still chanting a reverent "Freja Sarah", with individuals shouting "Messiah", "Our Chosen One" and various other terms of adoration, but still she moved on. Andrew had now positioned the boat with the steps facing her and all in the boat watched her, either in a state of rapture and amazement or keeping their heads clear to ensure no slip-ups. At last, she reached the steps to an even louder roar, climbed up and walked into the cabin, not to be seen again.

The riotous crowd were mad in awe. There were no words to describe what they had just witnessed. They stood as one, completely unsure what to do next, just staring at the river. Andrew had already moved off to return the boat. Flabbergasted could best describe the quiet audience now searching for meaning and answers, all mesmerised and wondering what in heaven was all this leading to…

Chapter 48

In the history of Mondays, there had never been a Monday like this.

The press and the media had a field day with the 'Miracle on the water', making all sorts of prophecies and even more conjecture. Nevertheless, for the government and leading religions it was becoming a problem and only likely to get worse as things progressed. She wasn't going away, that was clear. Many in the country were beginning to take her very seriously and further events, it was believed by those in power, could lead to civil unrest.

There had already been a lot of dissatisfaction and discontent in the air before Freja Sarah had started her fight against the oppression of the people. to lead them to a new promised land.

Her words of comfort and her certainty of a new path from drudgery as the new Chosen One, the new Bringer of Light, had been music to the ears of the general populous. Civil disobedience was a distinct possibility, for now things were under control, but for how long? It depended on her and the unfolding of events that she promised would happen.

For now, she came across as an 'Angel of Light' but who knew, would she become a 'supergirl' with the powers of obliteration? The government had to know, and called upon MI5, who in turn called on Cloud10, who intended to get to the bottom of it, one way or another.

*

Miles and Neil walked towards the tube station on their way to Cloud and talked about the 'stunt', as they called it, over the Thames.

"You sure it was a stunt, Neil?"

"Yeah. Totally. The giveaway was the cabin. It was blacked out so she couldn't be seen, Miles. Obvious."

"What do you mean?"

"Well, if she was truly the Daughter of God, she'd have just turned up with her crew, taken the applause, walked across, taken more applause, got in a car and been driven off. But she had to have somewhere private to materialise and dematerialise on the other side – the blacked out cabin on the boat. Did you see how quickly the boat scarpered? I wonder where that went?"

"You sure?"

"Absolutely, Miles. I could have done it myself, easily. Just a case of getting the boat to the right place."

"Right, just good planning then?"

"Dead right. I bet if we could have seen her gang there beforehand, they would have been measuring up or something."

"What if she'd appeared slightly off-centre, Neil?"

"Well, like me, she might be able to be invisible to people for just a short time when she travels. She probably can in an emergency. Her team are good though."

"Aren't they, and what a good idea. I reckon she pinched it from those lads by the canal, Neil."

"Yeah. I remember hearing one of them say, 'why don't you walk across the canal' or something like that."

"There you are then."

"Looked good on telly though."

"I wonder if they clocked it at Cloud."

"Yeah. I also wonder how we're gonna get on there, Miles?"

"It'll be fine – my nose says so."

*

It was beginning to feel like a regular occurrence: all of us sitting in Darryl's' office.

"Well, what did you all make of that?" said Darryl.

"Very clever piece of work," said Hilton. "I still think she's a very clever fraud, but one with a really good team behind her. Whether they know she's a fraud or not is another question."

Dan chimed in, "I think he's right, Darryl. Lucy could have done that; so could Grace and Jay."

"I don't think I'd have the nerve," said Grace.

"I think I could, just about," said Jay, "but I've not had any of that type of experience. I'm usually at the back of a room or looking through somebody's belongings in their bedroom."

"I could have done it," I said confidently. "In fact, if you want me to do it, I'll do it with you guys planning it."

Hilton looked at me thoughtfully, as though seriously considering it.

"That won't be necessary, Lucy," said Darryl. "But thanks, anyway."

"Spoilsport," muttered Hilton, grinning at me.

Grace shoved her partner's shoulder playfully.

"Right then," Darryl continued, "what are we going to do about it? I want some good ideas and others, no matter how absurd they sound. Apologies now. I've got to cut the meeting short as we've got the 'other two' coming in shortly. I wonder what they made of it? We'll regroup after lunch, when they've gone. Remember, ideas, please."

*

Miles and Neil were let in by Nikki, who asked them to wait while she checked if Darryl was ready for them.

Within seconds, Darryl opened the inner door with a smile and said, "Gentlemen, good morning, would you be so kind as to follow me."

They did, both with eyes everywhere, but there was nothing of note. They sat in front of Darryl. Henry or Kim would join them if necessary.

"Hello again, Miles."

"Hello, Darryl. Joining us today is my friend and 'partner in crime', Neil."

"Pleasure to finally meet you in person," Darryl smiled amiably, though Neil felt there was something ominous in his choice of words.

"You first, Darryl," said Miles, gesturing towards their host.

"Certainly, though I would be a lot happier if I was confident I was talking to the right person." He pointed to Neil.

"I've no problem with that. If you'd like to bring in the girl I almost bumped into at the accident, that should satisfy all of us."

Darryl picked up the phone. "Nikki, would you mind asking Lucy to pop in for a jiff?"

Lucy knocked and walked into the office, looked across at Neil and said, "Nice to see you again, and thanks again for your help."

Neil smiled; in fact, they all smiled.

"We must do it again some time, but next time under better circumstances."

"Okay, Lucy, thanks," said Darryl, dismissing her, but not before she had time to turn to Neil and say with a twinkle in her eye, "See you later."

"Oh, Lucy," said Darryl, as she was about to close the door, "Can you ask Kim to come down with the two forms for us."

"Sure, no problem."

Neil grinned. "Well, I think that answered all your questions, Darryl."

"Without any doubt," he said as Kim entered the room.

Darryl moved his chair slightly across so Kim could put a chair next to him, but as she looked towards a chair, Miles quickly interceded and put it there for her.

"Kim, let me introduce you to Miles and Neil who have, it seems, some of the attributes of our team here."

Kim thanked Miles for his gentlemanly act and then said, "Morning, guys. We've got some good news and some bad news. Which would you like to hear first?"

Neil spoke before Miles had the chance, "Let's hear the good news first."

"We've seen your talents in action," said Darryl. "Did you have a good look round the other week, Neil?"

Neil laughed and said, "The only thing I actually enjoyed were the funny sayings on the notice board. None today."

"Too busy today, but I've got lots more, if you're interested. Perhaps another time?"

"I'll let you know, Darryl," said Neil.

"Okay, cards on the table time. We'd like you both to consider joining us here at Cloud to assist us with what we believe will be a formidable problem. That is Freja Sarah and whatever shenanigans she has up her sleeve. We can foresee some unrest in the country and the more help we can get the better."

"And the bad news?" asked Miles.

Kim held up two sheets of paper and put them in the middle of the table and said, "If you agree to help and join us, for no matter how long, you'll have to sign the

Official Secrets Act. After all, you will be employed by MI5. We have full authorisation to offer this to you both."

The smirk on Neil's face had to be seen to be believed as he rolled his head towards Miles. "Sounds perfectly reasonable to me. Don't you agree Miles?"

Miles, completely taken back by Neil's reply, could only stutter, "Just let me think about it for a minute."

Kim came in immediately. "Miles, your journalistic talents are well known and will be put to good use here, along with your partnership with Neil assisting the rest of our team with our immediate problem. I can see your reticence, but there is no alternative I'm afraid. And we pay very well."

"Okay, I understand, pass them over."

Which she did and they both signed.

Chapter 49

It was a time of reflection throughout the country and beyond for all who had witnessed Freja Sarah perform her 'miracle' or had seen it streamed into their homes. None more so than Richard, as he rolled out of bed leaving Sarah still sleeping.

All who had observed the event, no matter who, had their own adjectives to describe the momentous piece of theatre, staged to perfection, most good adjectives, but obviously not all. There were always disbelievers to everything.

It would be correct to say Richard was confused, and rightly so; he felt adrift in a sea of emotions. Helplessly smitten by his love for Sarah he was deeply afraid of what the consequences might bring, and what effect it would have on Nicolas, should he find out. The ever-menacing Nicolas called Richard to offer his congratulations with his work so far and insisted he take his offer of the flat opposite Sarah's headquarters, empty now the initial surveillance was over. Only towards the end of the call did his tone change with a gentle but firm reminder that he pulled Richard's strings and expected full success with his dark mission and anything less wouldn't be tolerated, said in kinder words but the meaning was clear. Richard felt threatened, and rightly so, the flat being the only bonus of the conversation.

Richard told Sarah that the flat was owned by his family and was between tenants, and would be for a few more weeks. She, of course, was delighted to have him so close when not working at the clinic. He'd taken some annual leave and cut his hours down to a basic 'call me if you need me' and knew no calls would come. She had his number and no moments when her initiates were spending time in their new homes would be lost. Luckily for her they were frequently away, but not frequently enough. When Sarah managed to get the house to herself, she wasn't prepared to be on her own for long.

As he stood by the bed, dwelling on his problem, he glanced through the window blinds and saw two of the four house members returning early for an afternoon meeting at the house.

He quickly dressed, shared the news with Sarah and collected the rest of his belongings, preparing to leave. Sarah kissed him goodbye, knowing that they would be back together when they could.

Soon, he thought, he might be forced to come clean with her, but only maybe and not for some time yet. As he stood pondering his dilemma, he opened the door to check the coast was clear, and heard her intercom buzz as he went one way and she the other.

He decided to call at the clinic just to check there were no problems and all was running well; with his quality staff he knew everything would be. In his office with a morning coffee, he forced himself to call Nicolas and check whether there were any new developments. Nicolas was all sweetness and light and informed him that they were about to clear part of a larger clinic in his area in readiness for the final part of the plan. This unnerved him slightly as he could see how quickly things were moving. He told Nicolas it was all going to plan, leave the timing to him, to have faith, but Richard had no faith, only hope. He sat after the call staring at the wall in front of him, but the call had finished well.

Back at '26' all were now back for the meeting and quite rightly seemed pleased with themselves, wondering what would happen next.

Judith, her forthright self, asked, "Where do we go from here, Freja Sarah?"

"God has shown me the path, Judith. We must take our time and prepare well, for the establishment and the ruling classes have yet to understand that the world is about to change for them, and for all time."

"Is there anything we can plan for now?" said Sebastion, "as I normally need some time to get things together."

"Actually, I do have a task for you, Sebastion. I will be making four separate appearances for the people, breath-taking, I hope. Nothing more than that but in highly visible places and after each we shall send to the government, the so-called rulers, one demand. Piccadilly Circus at rush hour will be the first and I would just like you to confirm to me there would be no problems."

327

"I can certainly do that for you. Now?" he said, puzzled, but as keen as ever.

"No need to rush. Tomorrow will be fine."

As far as she was concerned, Sarah had dreamed vividly this message from God. The four appearances in the centre of London were essential. Whether this idea was indeed a message from on high God only knows, but they were fixed in her brain.

Judith then asked what she could do and Freja Sarah replied, "Judith, your task will be very important. You will let the people and the media know what will take place and afterwards I would like you to contact the government with a demand from me, also let everyone else know the demand. On each appearance, I will make a different demand."

"Do you yet know the first demand?" she asked.

"Yes, the first demand will be that the armed forces be phased out. We will see the outcome of the demands as the events progress. I expect it will take some time for them to agree, but we already have God and when we have the people, they will have no option other than to concede. God has spoken through me. I have no wish for them to see me as the bringer of their Judgement Day, but God must be obeyed."

"I fully understand, Freja Sarah. You have no wish for confrontation. Do you wish to meet them in person?"

"Yes, Judith, if that could be arranged, so much the better."

Sarah knew there was no one more capable than Judith to make this happen. She had connections and had always been a trustworthy person and had friends who, if believers themselves, would make it happen.

"Is there anything Alina and I can do?" said Lovage.

"Just to have you both behind me is enough. Just carry on as you do, relax and enjoy your new homes. That goes for you all. With all your help I shall start the new events in the next few days. I shall tell you well beforehand what is needed from you. Come and go as you wish as the path is now clear."

They all thanked her profusely for her love and help, and told her that although they had small personal plans, they assured her they were totally available at any time. She told them to take their time and hoped they would so she would have more time in Richard's company. In fact, she encouraged them to go as soon as possible as she was so keen to call him as he was so close and she missed him already.

Chapter 50

To my complete surprise, and to the surprise of everybody else at Cloud, Neil and Miles' arrival had been a breath of fresh air. It wasn't that they took the work lightly; in fact, the reverse, but somehow they added a lightness to the atmosphere, something that Darryl had tried, but failed to install. Perhaps it was their lack of deference to MI5, but whatever it was, they slotted in perfectly.

I loved the fact you just didn't know what would happen next.

Miles had found kindred spirits in Hilton and Jay. The three of them were often to be found in their favourite spot in the galley, frequently joined by Nikki and only sometimes Morry, and had been told more than once to keep the noise down a bit.

I'd sat in with them for a coffee earlier and it was fun listening to them. Jay had said that the Sarah problem made a change from hunting down a lone gunman and Hilton countered with even that's better than some lunatic who wants to use the Queen's toilet. They were all relishing this new challenge.

Neil had moved in with Dan and me on a more or less permanent basis, as keen as us to crack the case'. Neil, in a playful moment, had crossed out Darryl's inane saying on the notice board and put his own 'You can't overcook kale' and promised more. Darryl took it in good humour. It was now a joyful place to work, despite the seriousness of our current case.

"So, where do we go from here?" Dan asked Neil.

"We can't do much until we find the base she's operating from. Maybe Darryl will have some news on that later."

I piped up. "If so, then perhaps you and I can leap there and have a sneaky look."

"What's this word 'leap' doing there?"

"It's the word we use when we go off on one of our dream travels. It makes more sense to just use one word for it. In fact where we do it from upstairs is called 'the leap'."

"I can't see me getting used to that, is it an MI5 word?"

Dan and I shook our heads.

"Just easy slang," I said.

"Oh right, that's what I thought. Let's go and have a look. My guess is we wouldn't learn much; I didn't get anything when I came here."

"That's because we're MI5," I said, and we all laughed.

"Yeah. Right," said Neil.

Miles had told me that Neil was known amongst his friends as a 'miserable git' but there was no sign of that today. He seemed to have undergone a complete personality change, which I liked.

"I wonder if she's taken any precautions, like having pets, like you do here with that dog," said Neil.

"She must know how animals react to her," said Dan, "otherwise she wouldn't have done the 'Daniel in the lions' den' impression."

"Yeah. I suppose not. So what else can be done?"

"We wait. That's the coppers way," said Dan, "and hope she makes a mistake or upsets one of her team. Then we might get a tip-off."

"We need something," I said. "The press and the TV are all over it. I can only see matters getting worse."

"I tell you what though," said Neil, "I loved the way her dress shimmered over the water. It made her feet look like they were skimming across."

"You're right. She really has a way with theatrics, or reads the Bible a lot."

Again, we all laughed loudly.

"Come on you lot, do some work," said Nikki, overhearing the joke.

"If we had something to get our teeth into, we would, but we're having to sit around helpless and hopeless until something happens and one way or another we're sure it's going to," I told her.

"If you're not working, you may as well be eating. Anyone for lunch? I've made sandwiches and some special drinks for you down in the galley. Let's go."

She didn't have to ask again, and we all headed down to the galley, until we were all summoned by Darryl around half an hour later.

"Welcome, all," he said. "I've got no news, so good-bye."

We looked at each other as the seconds passed.

"Take no notice of him today," said Kim.

"Not really. Stay there. I may have something later, once it's checked and verified. I should have her London base. One of the Met boys has been given a lead by a trusted informer, who apparently has already done some surveillance there. It's being checked as we speak. It should here soon."

"Some good news possible then," said Kim, "but in the meantime anything from you?" And she swept her arm around the room to deathly silence.

Dan spoke eventually, "Nothing of any significance. We've been over all the footage available and now have some idea of those working with her. There seem to be three other girls and one or two guys; we're not sure yet what roles they have. There's one guy we know called Sebastion Edwards who seems to be a tech and equipment guy. The girls are harder to place. Two of them were definitely with her in the days of her running a spiritual commune in Suffolk, not sure on the other. Once we get names we can run full background checks."

"We said it earlier, but really we're waiting for her to slip up and make a mistake that we can work on," said Neil.

"What do you think this is for? What's her aim?" asked Darryl.

"Power," said Neil.

"Undoubtably. But she also wants adulation in the guise of helping people in their fight for justice," said Dan.

"Dan, you're starting to sound like her," I laughed.

At that moment, opportune for me, Darryl's phone rang. We stayed quiet and listened as he said, "Yes…yes…yes… Right, I've got it," and wrote something down.

He finished the call and said, "Right. We have her address and it's on round-the-clock surveillance. Let's see what that brings. Okay, anyone got anything else to say?"

We all agreed 'no' by the shaking of heads.

"I'll let you know what transpires."

We left him already on the phone to somebody else, obviously important, as he didn't start talking until the door closed.

"Let's all go down for a drink," said Nikki.

Which is what we all did, except for Henry, who had some real 'work' to do for a client.

We sprawled over the galley with nothing much to add, until Neil said, "Anyone watching anything good on telly?"

Only Neil could come up with such an inane comment to bring matters down to Earth.

Chapter 51

Fly through the haze dream into the blue,
Where the mystic waters flow

Sebastion came back to the house after mingling with all the tourists at Piccadilly Circus, having had a really good look round, expecting to find the house empty. To his surprise, he found Lovage watering the pots of flowers she had put around the front of the house.

"I didn't expect to find anyone here except Freja Sarah."

"I needed to collect the last few things for my flat and saw the flowers needed watering and thought I'd do it now before they all die in this heat."

"I assume Freja Sarah is in. Have you seen her?"

"No, I haven't, but the funny thing is, as I was watering the pots over by her annexe, I thought I heard a man's voice in there."

"No, I'm sure you didn't, perhaps the TV or radio."

"You're probably right."

"Funny thing is," he said, "last week, coming back from collecting some printing paper up the road, I thought I saw her on the corner across the road with a guy."

"Nah. Can't have been her. Must be our imaginations working overtime."

And that's how it was left. Lovage finished the last pot, picked up a couple of carrier bags by the gate and said, "See you later, Seb."

"Yeah. See you tomorrow," he said, went into the house and buzzed through to Freja Sarah.

Sarah had been spying on them through the blinds from her upstairs window and said to Richard sitting on the bed, "Sebastion's just come back. Lovage has just left. I'll have to go across and see him. Be careful you're not seen as you leave."

"Till later, my love," he said, collecting his belongings as she answered Sebastion through the intercom.

"Hi, Sebastion. Have you been already?"

"Yes, Freja Sarah, I've had a good look."

"Okay, I'm coming over."

She checked in the mirror that there were no tell-tale signs of Richard, straightened her clothes and walked over, impressed by the watering of Lovage. Sebastion opened the door for her and they sat studying the photos he'd taken. To double-check, not that Sebastion wasn't thorough, they opened up the computer on images of the area. Nothing seemed even remotely different, which was what she expected.

"What's your idea, Freja Sarah?"

"Well, I haven't decided exactly. I thought I'd wait until tomorrow's meeting and listen to what you all say.

You may have ideas that I can use. Have you fully settled into your new home and are you happy there?"

"Yes, it's absolutely fantastic. Thank you again."

"My real pleasure, Sebastion. Go and enjoy it."

They both left to go their separate ways. Sebastion to the tube and Sarah to the phone.

The next morning they all sat together in the house to discuss the coming afternoon's event at Piccadilly Circus. Judith was the first to speak on the subject. "After all the complications of the last events, this one may seem a little on the tame side. Don't you think that everybody will be expecting more?"

"You're right of course, but remember, this is only the first of four occurrences that will happen quite quickly in central London and more importantly, after each one, we shall make a different demand for change to the government. Each will be difficult for them, but I hope now we will have the backing of the people to force them to concede to the demands."

"Do you think they will though?" asked Judith.

"It won't be easy for them. That's why we need the people, the press and media to be with us."

"So what's the first demand?" asked Sebastion eagerly.

"Something I hope to get the whole world to do eventually."

"Tell the truth," said Sebastion.

"You're joking. That's too much to expect," said Judith.

337

"No, I'm going to demand that the country's armed forces become the Peace Forces. No more arms. The Forces must do only good work in the country and over-seas. No more fighter planes, ships or guns – just peace."

"Wonderful," said Lovage. "Wonderful."

"Thanks be to God," said Freja Sarah.

Alina then said, "Why not just tell the press and TV about this afternoon? That's all you need to do and let them ask you a few questions, then the whole world will see the truth. A kind of question and answer session."

"Truly inspirational, Alina," said Freja Sarah.

Judith then said, "Tell the press about four thirty. That's plenty of time for them to get there before five and by five the roads will be gridlocked, resulting in quiet, or quieter traffic."

"That's exactly what we'll do," said Freja Sarah. "You are such a wonderful team; I could never manage without you all."

"Of course you could," said Lovage, "because you are God's new Chosen One."

"Didn't Jesus have his disciples, Lovage, to help him though his difficult and trying times? You four are in ef-fect my disciples."

All four of them bowed their heads in homage and thanks to her and held the silence for just a short time as if in prayer.

"Okay," said Judith. "Leave it to Sebastion and me. Exactly where will you appear, Freja Sarah?"

"Sitting, reading the Bible on the plinth beneath the statue behind the metal fencing."

"Just perfect," said Lovage, and they all agreed.

*

The press and TV stations were notified by Sebastion at four thirty about the forthcoming event. Freja Sarah waited till just before five and sat, clutching a Bible, ready. Five o'clock came and she was already dozing and on cue was sitting on the plinth, head down as if reading the Bible. Judith was correct, the press and TV vehicles had jammed the area. Traffic police were trying to clear the roads but it was impossible.

It would have been fairly quiet but for the invited who clapped in astonishment at her presence. There was a great push forward as all the reporters with microphones held high tried to get Freja Sarah's attention.

Freja Sarah held her hands out before her, facing them in an attempt to quiet them, and they responded. A reverential hush descended.

"If you shout at me, then I shall leave. If you are respectful, I shall answer a few of your questions."

They responded by holding their arms aloft in the air and Freja Sarah pointed to one of them at the front saying, "Please address all your questions to Freja Sarah," and then proceeded to take questions from them in turn.

"Freja Sarah, can you tell us your aims?"

"My aims are simple. The people are lost down many paths, yet I alone can guide them to a land beyond their oppressors, whatever form they take, and when they follow me I shall lead them to a world devoid of corruption, cleansed of evil and full of God's light, to a land of joy and happiness for all."

"Freja Sarah, when will that be?"

"Only God knows when, but the path is becoming clearer."

"Freja Sarah, are you really sent from God?"

"I am not the Son of God that was before. I am the Daughter of God that is now. I am the Final Coming. Look upon me. For I am the new Chosen One. I am the Bringer of Light sent to save you, for I am the last and final Chosen One. There will be no other."

"Freja Sarah, can you cure the ill and dying?"

"Once the people of the world have accepted the New Beginning, all will be possible."

"Freja Sarah, where will you appear next?"

"There will be three and only three more. After each, I shall issue a demand that must be accepted by those who have assumed control over the people. People in turmoil, people who are seeking help from their oppressors and search for the light. They have not been abandoned. We move towards the Day of Reckoning. It cannot be stopped."

"Freja Sarah, what were you reading in the Bible?"

"I was reading Revelations 6. I have no wish to be a Harbinger of Doom, an Avenging Angel with a Fiery Crown, but I say to those who deny, I say people, prepare, take shelter, take shelter from the coming storm. Deniers, I will summon the Angels of Order, for love shall be the New Order."

She looked down towards her Bible, but actually

340

glanced at her timepiece and saw her short period there was nearing its end, looked up at her congregation standing before her and said, "You have heard my words. Tell your leaders to listen."

Then very slowly, she started to fade out before their eyes, but not before one of them shouted, "Do you think you're the only one who can do this? We're coming for you."

Neil looked at Miles and said, "That got her, I bet. Did you see her face twitch before she disappeared?"

Chapter 52

"Miles, Miles," said Darryl, exasperated. "For Christ's sake why didn't you let us know?"

"I just didn't have time. We were just about to get on the tube to go home when I got the nod from a mate in Fleet Street. We just had time to change trains and run to get there. Honestly with not a second to spare."

Darryl lent back in his seat, slowly shaking his head.

"We had absolutely no chance at all," said Neil, "but we got through to her, I'm sure."

"Look, I've got all the coverage here, let's put it on the large screen and watch it through," said Darryl. "I hope you're right, what you said to her Miles."

The picture appeared on the screen. It was fairly short but Neil wasn't happy watching it all.

"Come on. Let's move it forward. I've listened to her rubbish enough."

Darryl moved it forwards a little and watched till the end, when Miles had shouted at her. Even as she was fading out, they could see her glance in his direction.

"Look again, you can see her flinch at what he says. Wind it back and slow it down," said Neil.

Darryl did exactly that and it was clear. She definitely twitched at what he'd said. "I'll give it to you, Miles; that was quick thinking."

"She's beginning to get on my nerves, Darryl. I just had to do something."

"Okay, let's get Lucy and Dan here and try and work out a plan."

Dan and Lucy arrived and were shown all aspects of the previous day's film in slow motion. They agreed that she'd heard it.

"It wouldn't have affected her like that if she really was God's daughter, would it? She's all human and pushing it."

"Not exactly how I would have put it, Miles, but nevertheless, spot on," said Darryl and continued more seriously. "As you left the last meeting, I took a phone call from the home secretary. He informed me how seriously the prime minister, the government and all opposition parties are taking this. They are very worried it could lead to total civil disobedience soon. All the press and TV companies are stoking it up, and fair play to them – it could be world changing. Obviously we believe differently, but I haven't passed that on yet. We need something more tangible, more definite than a hunch and a few seconds of film."

Miles said, "What else can we do? What's happening at her house?"

"It is under surveillance and we have a few early leads in a different direction but nothing I can tell you yet that might help us," said Darryl.

"We have to wait still, said Dan, "but going forward, sorry, I hate that phrase, I think we should find a way to put Lucy up against her."

"But how?" said Lucy.

"We don't know yet, Lucy, but if it happens, will you be okay to try?"

"Yes, of course. It sounds the best of our few options at present. I can't see any harm coming from it, at least I hope not."

"I'll also do anything I can," said Neil. "We'll be okay as long as she's not the Divine One and I don't believe that for a minute."

"Thanks, both of you," said Darryl.

Miles said, "I personally think she's going to spring these appearances on us without much warning, so we must be ready at all times or at least during daylight hours, at least for the next week or so."

"Agreed," said Dan "We should use the four top-floor flats. They're always ready, and we haven't the luxury of time travelling to-and-fro from home."

"I'm not too keen to actually stay here," said Miles.

"England expects," said Darryl. "Look, it won't be much of a problem for a short while. She'll do another trick soon. You've seen the flats – they're all self-contained and you can come and go a short distance from here, as long as one of you remains. Don't panic, Miles, you'll still get your beer."

"Fair enough, but we'll all need to go home tonight, pack our stuff and come back in the morning."

"Yeah. And I'll have to break it to Jill," Dan sighed.

"That isn't going to be easy."

"Promise her a holiday, Dan," said Neil. "I hear that normally works."

"Tomorrow's fine, I can't envisage anything happening that quickly, but if it does, I'll be here," said Darryl.

Everybody was happy with the plan, despite it being rather open-ended. Miles and Neil went up to see the rooms, as neither of them had taken notice when shown before and were perfectly happy with what they saw. In that brief interlude, Nikki had brought them all drinks and they resumed where they'd left off.

"Back to the plan," said Miles. "I would say we mustn't underestimate her. Take yesterday, with her opening up reading the Bible. She must have expected a question on that and she was ready. Revelations 6. I looked it up and read it and guess who appears?"

They all looked blankly at him, Darryl a bit embarrassed as he should have checked that, not Miles.

"The Four Horsemen of the Apocalypse. She didn't mention them by name or what they did, but we all know that they weren't very nice people."

"A bit of an understatement there I think, Miles," said Lucy.

"But she did tell people that they might need to take shelter, a clever small threat. I'm just surprised that it wasn't picked up by the press," said Miles.

"They were too busy with the first of her demands," said Dan.

Neil then asked if he could have another look at the last couple of minutes of the film again in slow motion.

Darryl put the footage on where Neil had specified, and they all sat watching and wondering what it was Neil was looking for.

"Can you zoom in a bit so we've just got her sitting?" he said.

They all watched through it again. Nothing seemed to stand out. Then he asked, "Okay, watch again, where she finished the Bible bit. Wait until she finishes her answer, then watch her glance down."

Darryl did as requested, then Dan spotted it.

"She looked down to check the time," said Dan in amazement. "Jesus, Neil. Well spotted."

"I'd never have spotted that," said Darryl, "but I guess you have to have some experience at travelling to know."

"You're right, Darryl, we have to do it quite frequently. I've a number of watches that look correct for the year I'm going back to," said Lucy.

"Timing is everything," said Neil. "We've got her. Definitely. She's a fellow traveller but with delusions."

Chapter 53

The waters swirl, the currents concealed;
The clouds begin to mask the sunlight

"Are you okay, Sarah?" said Richard, as he could see something was on her mind.

"It's only what that last guy shouted out at Piccadilly Circus. I can't get it out of my head; he seemed so vindictive."

"You shouldn't worry about him, just another typical loud-mouthed journalist, trying to get a reaction, but he left it too late."

"I expect you're right, Richard. Sorry, but you better go now. Andrew is calling here. Apparently he needs to speak to me urgently."

"Okay, I'll see you later, I hope."

"You will," she replied, and he left in his normal cautious way, proceeding back towards the clinic, but then crossed the road and double-backed towards his flat. He was down to ring Nicolas that morning with the latest update and needed no interruptions.

Sarah had so much on her mind she didn't

acknowledge his leaving. She tried to get the journalist out of her head, as she knew Andrew was very matter-of-fact and she needed to be her normal level-headed self. Lovage buzzed to let her know that Andrew had arrived and as she walked across the drive, Andrew met her at the door.

"Good morning, Freja Sarah. I'm here with some really terrific news. Your website is on fire with donations. The events and short videos have had a tremendous effect on your followers, now in the millions."

"What do you mean exactly, Andrew?"

"We're inundated with donations, in the millions and growing every minute. We probably need to discuss what to do with the money. It really wasn't expected."

"Well, I don't want it. Let's give it all away."

"Freja Sarah, are you sure? All of it?"

"Yes, all of it. I've got enough, haven't I?"

"Yes, I've put enough in a personal account for you that only you can access and anywhere in the world."

"I shall never need it myself but I may need it to help others along the way."

She thought for a brief moment.

"What I'd like you to do Andrew, as soon as possible, is to get together a list for me, of worthwhile charities across the country, absolutely not just London. I'd like many different and maybe unusual causes and give them £1 million that they must spend directly on their causes. None of the money must be spent on administration, that only causes problems and resentment. How quickly can we do it?"

"I have £40 million available now and the way the money is coming in, another five to ten million a week."

"Excellent. Get together a list of about one hundred charities and we'll take it from there. Mix them up so the money goes to all parts of the country and all different charities. Sorry to repeat myself, but that's very important."

"Okay, leave it to me. I'll get my whole office on it."

"How soon, Andrew?"

"Tomorrow, Freja Sarah."

"Perfect," she said, shaking her head in disbelief. But what a bonus, that had never occurred to her. God Bless. Sebastion then entered the room with a knock as Andrew was just leaving.

She told him every detail of Andrew's news and he suggested to Freja Sarah, "Let's make a short video about all this money being donated to charity and I will release it tomorrow. Are you about to do another appearance? I could include that as well."

"Yes, that's a very good idea, Sebastion. I will do a short appearance tomorrow, just so I can make another demand on the government. Then stop appearing for a while and see how things settle with the people."

"Shall we go and do it now, Freja Sarah?"

"Why not?"

They left for the small studio Sebastion had fixed up. She told him she was going to appear on one of the two tall chimneys, by the river at the Battersea Power Station. Told him to release the video just after midday and she would appear at one o' clock. He could follow her brief appearance on the screen, telling them this would be the last appearance for a short while, but they would get ample warning of the next, but also remember to take binoculars for this one. He would make more of the charity donations, reflecting that this appearance was basically to give the government another demand from her, for the people. Sebastion filmed Freja Sarah and set about sorting out his own appearance, which he knew would take some time.

Sarah left him to it, she knew how capable he was, and went and sat with Lovage, Alina and Judith for a coffee and a snack. All of them seemed very relaxed and delighted with the charity donations.

Sarah asked them, "Is there anything, anything at all you need?"

There was a general shaking of heads.

"Remember, anything at all, just ask Andrew."

Judith said, "I know I speak for us all here Freja Sarah, but we're happy just to be here and help and serve to the end."

"Thank you all, you've made my life here easy and that makes it easier for God's will to happen."

"Praise be, to that," said Lovage. "I just follow as you do."

Sarah smiled, then, with their coffee finished, she suggested they all go to their new homes, which one day she would love to visit, and come back for Andrew's meeting in the morning. This they would do, but Lovage just had some sorting out to do in the house and then the annexe before she could go.

Sarah suggested she do the house, then come across to the annexe. That would give her enough time to ensure that there were no tell-tale signs of Richard.

She checked the annexe. It was Richard-free. She gave him a call to let him know the timing for this evening.

This time he seemed under a little stress as his boss Nicolas Peeters was coming to London the following morning for a general check and to see all was in order and that Richard was happy with everything. He told her he may have to curtail some of their meetings over the next few days.

He was disappointed and he expected Sarah would be too, but such was life, he thought, and told her they would have many, many more days together, or so he hoped.

Chapter 54

The mood at Cloud hung low like a sea mist and with some justification after everything that had happened recently. Spending our days and nights stuck in the same place had done nothing for our enthusiasm, and with no new leads, all we could do was wait. Then, finally, as we were lounging around the galley, something happened. A video flashed up on Freja Sarah's website, a very clear and concise message directly from her. She would appear on one of the two tall chimneys at Battersea Power Station on the south bank of the Thames at one o'clock. It was only just after midday; she really hadn't given her followers much warning. Still, at least there was enough time to put our plan in place.

The idea was that I would appear on the opposite chimney to the one Freja Sarah was due to appear on, wearing white and holding a cross. We were hoping Freja Sarah would appear in her normal darker colours, giving me a more religious look.

Miles had been the instigator initially of this idea, with Dan the brainwave behind the matching cross held high. It was the perfect plan to ruffle her feathers and cause some confusion in the minds of the public over who was the Chosen One. This plan wouldn't give away anything about my role at Cloud, but it would put a question in the mind of Freja Sarah, which was what we needed.

All of us were eager for the action to begin, and anticipation was high. Darryl had already spoken to the authorities, and they had confirmed that the tops of the chimneys were boarded over, so I didn't need to worry about falling through one, not that it would hurt me if I did, but we needed to ensure that our plan would work. The weather was still very poor, but as long as Sarah and I were both visible, that didn't matter. I could be there in a blizzard without it affecting me.

At about twelve thirty, I went with Nikki to the wardrobe and we chose a particularly religious looking white gown. Meanwhile, Dan, with some wood, material and a staple gun, managed to fashion a cross that from a distance looked pretty good. Nikki applied a finishing touch by putting a white headband across my forehead. I was ready for action.

Heading upstairs, I lay down ready, with about ten minutes to go before one o'clock. Nikki passed the cross to me, gave my final appearance a onceover, wished me bon voyage and left the room. I could see the exact time on the wall clock from my position, and as it neared the top of the hour, I dozed, ready to go.

Seconds later, I was shocked into awareness as the door burst open.

Nikki rushed in. "She's been and gone!"

"What!"

"For some reason, she appeared at five minutes to one and left after five minutes. She stayed just five minutes. It all happened so quickly, we were all caught by surprise and sat there like dummies. She just went, out of the blue, she was gone."

A wave of disappointment washed over me, and Nikki's face told me she felt much the same.

"Don't blame yourself, Lucy. You didn't have a chance."

"I'm not, Nikki, but that would have been a great chance, a chance now missed."

"Come on, let's go and get you changed, then go see the others."

Ten minutes later, we walked into a room of gloom with comments flying across the room.

"That's the only time she's missed the spot," said Dan. "Is she on to us? She can't be, can she? Can you check with your surveillance team and see if there's been any unusual activity? Anything different."

Miles said, "I sense a change. She planned it or was it the weather?"

"Let's watch it again," I suggested. "I haven't seen it yet"

We all watched intensely, hoping to get some clue, but even with the best camera lenses she was too far away in the rain. Even if I had managed to get there, we both would have been too far away to make any real impact. I needed to confront her nearer a crowd.

Dan said to Darryl, "Would you mind just checking

with her surveillance. Has anything happened this morning, or late this morning, out of the ordinary?"

Darryl rang straight through while we waited, but he put the phone down shaking his head. "Absolutely nothing out of the ordinary, in fact quieter than normal."

"Can't you or Neil travel back and ruin some of her appearances? Just turn up and spoil them?" Miles asked.

"Miles, let me explain simply. If we went back, we couldn't do anything to alter the past as it would alter the future. Remember the *Back to the Future* films? It would alter time and we wouldn't be necessarily sitting here now. Don't you think we would if we could? It would be impossible."

"Sorry, Lucy, just ignore me. I'm already trying to get my head around the impossible and it's not easy."

"That's okay, it's an easy mistake to make."

Darryl's phone rang and he listened intently.

"We've just got the latest demand from her. Basically, it's just for a fairer distribution of wealth throughout the country."

"That's a bit of a cop-out," said Neil, "and that's not gonna happen."

"Agreed, that's just a bit of old soap," laughed Dan. "Everyone always asks for that; perhaps she's running out of ideas."

"She may be," said Darryl, "but just look. In this short time the internet's gone viral with her latest romp. We may know one thing about her, but the rest of the country think they know something else. We're not getting very far are we?"

"No, we're not," said Dan and Miles virtually together, but Miles carried on, "but things you're not expecting always happen when you least expect them. We've just got to be patient, as Dan said last time, just wait. Our time will come. My journalistic nose says so."

"You and your nose, Miles, but to be fair, it hasn't been wrong since I've known you," said Neil.

Jay entered the room. "I thought I'd just see what had happened. Apologies for being a bit late but I've just had an interesting tip from an informant."

"I'm glad you're here, Jay," said Darryl. "I'd also like your take on what's happening in the other religions other than the Christian ones. You've a better street feel than we have stuck here."

"Well, they are absolutely agreed. It seems the Jews, Muslims, Hindus and other non-Christian religions are in total disbelief at what's going on. They see it as some sort of trick of the West and as we see it, they're not wrong. Also I've just had a tip that someone might have a go at her with a rifle, although that may be just a rumour."

"Apart from the gunman, that's exactly what I thought," said Darryl.

"I haven't heard whether you've any more information about this guy she's secretly meeting up with, a Richard something?"

"I was just about to talk about him Jay, good timing. Full name Richard Anthony, aged 28, UK resident, fully qualified doctor specialising in life-prolonging and enhancing treatments at a local clinic. We've been monitoring his phone and he's had a couple of international calls from a very dubious character, a multimillionaire in Belgium called Nicolas Peeters who has very dubious links in several areas, one of which is to supply the elite with life-lengthening treatments. That's all we know about him. How he became close to Sarah is still a mystery."

Dan said, "Shouldn't we be putting effort into that? It doesn't sound like a coincidence; maybe it was somehow contrived. Does the Belgian have any financial interest in anything else that might be involved?"

Darryl scrolled through his computer. "He's also a director in a couple of maternity hospitals, including St Saviours Maternal clinic, here in London."

"My nose is twitching, Darryl," said Miles. "That needs checking."

"Hang on. Jesus," said Darryl. "I've just been sent a list of fifty charities that she's donated one million pounds each to. She's always one step ahead. This is really getting on my nerves." He turned his screen round so that we could all have a look, but the screen writing was too small, so he rang down for Nikki to run off hard copies.

*

Downstairs, Nikki was also reading the list, sitting quietly reading through it slowly, a smile beginning to show on her face. The charities ranged across the country and

357

top to bottom, but one stood out for her. She gave a lot of her free time to a charity on the North Downs in Surrey, which specialised in the rehabilitation of old and mistreated racehorses, and this charity was now the recipient of £1 million pounds. She decided to keep quiet for the moment and ran off the copies then took them up.

As she left them all looking at the list, she overheard one of the men say, "She certainly knows all the tricks. We're gonna have to bring her down."

That was something she wasn't expecting to hear in such a direct way, and for a number of growing reasons it wasn't something she wanted to hear.

Chapter 55

The reason Sarah gave her associates for going a bit early was that she'd only glanced at the clock and misread the time, but the true reason was that she had just wanted to get it over with; it was boring.

Life was tedious without Richard. He had been due to see her later that day, before his nemesis Nicolas Peeters had called and let him know he was flying into London that afternoon from Brussels. He was expected to meet him at Heathrow and spend rest of the day with him. He'd told Sarah as soon as he could get away he would try to get to see her, but unfortunately with Nicolas he couldn't be sure.

That gave her the rest of the day with nothing else to do but kill time and hope he could make it. She went over to the main house, thinking everybody had left, but found Lovage still cleaning. Seeing Freja Sarah she stopped and they both sat with what seemed like a cloud of aimlessness over them.

"Is anything wrong, Lovage, you look in low spirits?"

"Not really, Freja Sarah. I think I've just got used to the routine here with everyone here most of the time, but now it's all changing so fast and I'm having trouble adapting to the quiet."

"Don't worry, Lovage. All's going well, the path is clear and in a short time now those in charge will really have to listen to our demands and act. The people will demand it. Perhaps it's just the awful weather, gloomy days and continual rain, but this will give way to sunshine and all will seem better. Just wait."

"It would certainly help. You won't leave me will you, Freja Sarah?"

"Never. Put that thought away forever."

Sarah then tried to lighten the mood into something more positive, asking Lovage about her new home.

"It's truly lovely, absolutely perfect, but when I'm there, alone at night, I get very lonely and miss you all."

Sarah knew herself how alone she felt at night when Richard wasn't there, but didn't miss the others not being around, quite the reverse.

"It's not forever, just a short while. Let's go for a walk in the park."

*

Richard met Nicolas at Heathrow as arranged and they were soon sitting in his suite at the hotel.

He couldn't help feeling slightly troubled. No, to tell the truth, he was frightened as Nicolas' humour had high expectations.

"When are you going to put our needs to Sarah?" he asked over drinks.

"Soon, I promise you Nicolas, when the time is right. It's all going to plan and beyond but as you know yourself it's all down to the right moment. It will come. There will be trouble along the way and when that happens, I'll be there for her, her support, and then and only then will I put our requests."

"You mean demands."

"No, no I mean requests. I know her well. We've both fallen for each other in a deep way. A demand would shake our bond."

"I'm glad to hear that, Richard, and I'm pleased for both of you for what you have found. I'm sure you know best. I know you'll never let me down."

"I've promised, Nicolas, and I always keep my promises. When the moment comes, you'll know at the same time. There'll be a hiccup, and that's when I'll catch her."

"Agreed, Richard. I'm happy, happy and hungry. Let's go and get some dinner. I hear the food here is excellent, as is the wine, and I promise not to bring the subject up again."

*

The rain was pouring down as it had done so relentlessly all day, as a well-covered woman with a large umbrella walked past the main entrance to number 26 and paused at Sarah's private doorway. Pretending to stumble and drop her bags, she hammered at the door. Knowing she was being observed, she started loading one bag clumsily and as soon as she heard some movement the other side of the door she banged again and shouted, "Message from Richard!"

Sarah, on the other side of the door, thought the whole thing very odd as he always phoned. Perhaps it was difficult with Mr Peeters there, and this was the only way he could get a message to her? She wanted to, but she couldn't ignore it. Against all of her logic, she opened the door slightly and the woman pushed in and closed the door behind her.

"What are you doing?" shouted a very confused and worried Sarah, as the uninvited guest put down her umbrella and took off her coat very quickly.

"I need to speak to you. Can I come in?"

"You're already in and I want you to leave."

"Not until you've heard what I have to say. It's important, very important."

That wasn't enough for Sarah. "No, I want you to leave. Now. You haven't a message from Richard. You were lying just to get me to open the door."

The woman said, "If it wasn't important, how would I know about Richard?"

"Okay, tell me quickly and then leave."

"I will, but believe me, I'm a friend."

Sarah stood her ground, not letting her beyond the hall and waited.

"I work for the Secret Service, MI5, and our department is trying to bring you down and I don't want that to happen. They already have this house under constant surveillance and all your phones are tapped, otherwise how could I know that Richard exists? Your housemates don't. Do you still want me to go?"

Sarah stood shaken. "Is all that true?"

"Yes, all of it," and she followed Sarah through to the lounge where they both sat across a small table.

"Why are you here, then? How do I know it isn't some trap?"

"Why would I come, risking my own position? I had to get to see you, and without them recognising me. I don't believe in everything they're doing to stop you. I think they're wrong about you, maybe not everything, but I believe in your goodness. Your message is good and the money to charities a wonderful gesture; it included one I'm involved in. I believe."

"Thank you for believing in my message. I was expecting some trouble from those who run the country, in government and the elite who think they're superior, but there is nothing to find in my past. I only work for our future."

"If it was only that. They want to stop you completely, no matter what."

"There is nothing I can do about that, and nothing I need to. I have God on my side."

"But I believe there is. I have an idea that might bring them to understand," she said and opened her bag and took out two brand new mobile phones, which could never be traced and put them on the table with a folder. "It's an unusual and extreme plan and if you say no, I shall leave now and tell no one about visiting you. Consider this, materialising in our office in the middle of a meeting about you. You can then answer any of their questions. You can explain God's mission to them, that he is working through you."

"Would that work? Would that stop them? Is there a chance they would see the pathway to the New Beginning? If it would, or even if there's a chance, then I must take it, but I would want to know where I'm going, lots of information. Do you have what I need? If you show me what I need, then I will."

"I have all you need here," the woman said, and she opened the folder and took out a selection of many different angles and plans of the building and most importantly Darryl's office. She had thought of everything and had on her phone a video of the building which she showed Sarah first and then went through the photographs individually. She hadn't missed a thing.

Sarah was completely at ease with all the information and had already worked out where she would appear, at the back of Darryl's office, but had one last important question:

"What about the timing?"

"Take one of these phones. The meeting will start around eleven o'clock. When I'm sure it's about to start, I will ring you and just say one word: 'now'."

"How long will I have to appear?"

"The meetings last at least half an hour. Will that be enough time?"

"Yes, easily. I will be ready."

"Once you're there and they accept that you are, I expect you'll get a gruelling set of questions to answer from your enemies, because that's what they are. If it becomes too difficult or nasty, you can just leave. I believe you can have some success with some of them, not all, but maybe enough of them to make a difference."

"Can I ask your name?"

"I won't tell you that, but maybe I'll be there. If I am, don't show any sign of recognition, as I will still be able to pass information to you. We may have more to do together, and if it came out we were in contact, I would be imprisoned and that wouldn't help your cause."

"I'll do it tomorrow. I'll be ready."

The woman put back on her coat, hood up with the umbrella well down and left, quickly walking to the tube station, checking and rechecking she wasn't being followed, eager for tomorrow.

*

At last a night in the pub. It felt like freedom for Miles and Neil to be almost relaxing with the usual crowd at the bar, the dark clouds pushed away by the banter of Ray and Greig.

Ray, his usual self, started it.

"Haven't seen you two in here much lately. Still cleaning, Neil?"

"Yeah. Still cleaning," he lied. "People are so filthy, but I suppose if they weren't I wouldn't have a job. I'd be on the dole."

"Same with you, Miles. I began to think you two might have gone away together on holiday somewhere."

He laughed at his own joke and in fairness they all

did.

"What have you been up to, Miles?" asked Greig.

"Same old same old. Chasing down leaks that lead nowhere. The whole country seems on hold with all this Sarah business."

"This bird, Sarah, The Almighty One, well, she is a bit to me," said Greig. "When's she gonna spring up next?"

"Want me to tell you?" said Ray, feeling full of himself after his previous success.

"I bet better brains than yours are hard at it now," said Miles.

"Yeah, but they're not London builders, are they?"

"Well, she's done Piccadilly and Battersea," said Greig. "What's next?"

"She must have a plan," said Ray. "Show me on a map where they are."

Miles couldn't really be bothered, but Ray insisted and to shut him up, he got a map of central London up on his phone and handed it to Ray.

"Show me where she's been, Miles. Anybody got any glasses? I can't see it; it's too small."

Greig passed over his glasses and Ray studied the map for about thirty seconds.

"You're gonna owe me a pint, Miles. Did I use the words, 'bleedin' obvious' last time? If not, it's bleedin' obvious. Those clever sods can't see what's in front of their eyes. The two she's done make a vertical line."

He paused and showed the map to Miles, who still didn't get it. Neil and Greig also had a look. Still no joy, all completely lost.

"Give it back," said Ray. "Can't you guys see it? Put a line across from Buck Palace to Westminster; see, that's horizontal? Put them together and what do you get? I think that's a song. It makes a cross. My guess is the balcony at Buck Palace and Big Ben; she likes a bit of height."

Miles and Neil just looked at each, rolled their eyes to heaven before shaking their heads in disbelief.

"Elementary," said Ray. "Pint, please, Miles, and a chaser."

Chapter 56

After the long, tedious dinner laughing at Nicolas' poor jokes, Richard managed to say goodnight to him and though it was close to midnight, he sent a text to Sarah apologising for not being able to get there. He said he'd be there early tomorrow, God and Nicolas willing. He was surprised to get an instant return text as she would normally be asleep by now. She said she'd missed him and couldn't wait to see him in the morning. He would let himself in, hoping to surprise her in bed, but could only stay till late morning. This suited her perfectly because of her impending appointment with the 'enemy'.

It all went nearly as planned, but Sarah thought that Judith and Lovage wouldn't be at the house until the afternoon, so she told Richard to stay upstairs, out of sight, but on her way across to the annexe Judith felt sure she had seen another figure upstairs as Sarah opened the door. A mistake she thought, as there was no one it could be.

"We're almost ready, Freja Sarah, come over in about ten minutes."

"Thanks, Judith, ready when you are."

Judith went back and said to Lovage, "Odd question, Lovage, Freja Sarah hasn't a visitor, has she? I thought I caught a glimpse of somebody there."

"Not as far as I know. I've never known of anyone else to go in there, other than one of us, but I thought the other day, I heard voices. Can't be."

"I'm sure you're right. Let's get on with the final planning of our 'picnic in the park' this weekend."

Freja Sarah had thought it might be a nice idea to give her multitude of followers an afternoon of pleasure. Then to offer them the option of a march on Parliament in support of her. Judith had checked with the authorities that a picnic in the park would be something they were happy with, and they had no objections. She didn't mention the spontaneous march that would follow.

She'd also checked with the Met Office and a warm and clear day was forecast and now they were just waiting for a late Sebastion to record a short video of Freja Sarah inviting them to the park with her to enjoy an afternoon picnic.

Sebastion turned up. Traffic problems, so he said, and Judith went across again to the annexe to collect Freja Sarah to come across for the recording. No sign of any movement upstairs. She went in and sat down while Freja Sarah did a final check on her appearance.

Unbeknown to Judith, the visitor was still there, hiding, but as he was collecting his bits and pieces strewn across the room, he slipped over a shoe and knocked into the bedroom door, causing it to slam.

"What was that?" said Judith, puzzled.

With quick thinking and in a calm voice Sarah said, "Oh, I must have left a window open and the breeze closed the door." She was fuming with Richard for his clumsiness, but still remarkably calm on the outside and said to Judith, "Let me go and close the window, then we'll go."

She went upstairs to where Richard was hiding and said in a whisper, "You must be extra careful. I've got Judith downstairs and she's not stupid. She mustn't know you're here. What happened?"

"I'm sorry, Sarah. It was just an accident. I tripped over a shoe. I'll leave as soon as you do and call you later. Sorry again. What did you say?"

"I said I left a window open and it must be the breeze blowing the door closed. We must be extra careful, my love. I can't risk my four knowing about you. They just wouldn't understand our love. It would cause massive problems for them."

They embraced passionately, both confirming their love for each other and Sarah telling him how much she wished Nicolas would return to Belgium and it could be like it was before.

She went downstairs and left the annexe with Judith, who couldn't help but notice there was no hint of a breeze, the air still. Sarah had regained her composure and was the epitome of calm as she warmly greeted Lovage and Sebastion. She took her place in the studio and in one take had told her millions of followers about the Saturday picnic, and returned to the annexe to await the call.

*

Over at Cloud, the morning started as usual with coffee in the galley. All were there, Miles and Neil looking and sounding really pleased with themselves, but giving nothing away, but for Dan and Lucy just another day of waiting, or so they thought.

Darryl came to the top of the stairs and shouted down, "When you're ready, everyone."

They finished their drinks and started upstairs, and Nikki went to the front. She took a phone from her bag and started to dial a number, just as Kim put her head around the door to say, "When you're finished, Nikki, the meeting's about to start."

She'd finished the dial and heard it was answered, looked up towards Kim and in a questionable tone said, "Now?"

Kim nodded and Nikki got up to follow, but then Morry started to whimper slightly. Nikki grabbed this as the excuse she was looking for and said to Kim, "I've just got to sort Morry out. I won't be very long but tell Darryl to start and I'll be there shortly."

Kim agreed, went upstairs and told Darryl to start. They all sat as usual facing Darryl and Kim, Miles and Neil barely able to keep still.

"Good, you're all here. Nikki will join us. I've got a bit of interesting news."

Miles straightaway interrupted, "And so have we," and motioned towards Neil.

371

"I wish we had," said Dan.

"Who's gonna go first?" said Darryl. "Is it good news or bad news?"

"All good," said Neil.

"Okay, let's hear it. And I don't want to be disappointed. I'm not in the mood."

"You won't be," said Miles. "Neil and I have been studying the map of central London and we think we know what she plans in the short term. Let me show you."

He produced an A4 size map showing a heavy black line drawn between Piccadilly Circus and Battersea Power Station. With a red felt tip pen he drew a line across between Buckingham Palace and Westminster. He showed it around the room so they could all see. It showed a perfect cross.

"How about that!" he said triumphantly. He took the silence in the room as wonder that he and Neil had come up with this and continued. "We think she'll appear on the famous balcony at the Palace and, as Neil says, she seems to like heights and putting on a show... hence Big Ben."

"That's genius," said Darryl.

"Wait. There's more. We don't know which order she'll do them, but we've come up with a plan for both, if you agree."

"Come on, tell us then," said Dan like an eager schoolboy.

"Neil, to be ready for the roof of Buckingham Palace, dressed with a beard and white robe as Jesus, and Lucy ready for the walkway at the top of Big Ben dressed as an angel with wings or Mary Magdalene. Let's think alternative."

Just as they were about to get a thunderous applause – it was that good an idea – Darryl stood up and took a pace forward. "Brilli—"

His jaw dropped, his eyes virtually left their sockets, he was speechless as…

Sarah materialised at the back of the room.

Kim managed to point and they all turned as one. All completely flabbergasted. The room was completely silent and immobilised for what seemed like an age as she stood regally in front of them.

Dan was first to collect his thoughts and composure and said, "Hello, Freja Sarah."

"Good morning, everyone. I thought as you're making such an effort to see me, that I'd come to see you and save you any more trouble."

Darryl, who thought he'd seen everything in life, said, "Freja Sarah, thank you. That's very kind of you to save us the trouble. What can we do for you?"

"Before we go further, you may ask or say anything to me, but all I ask is, please treat me with respect, as I shall you."

"Of course, we shall, of course," Darryl said meaningfully, but nobody had listened to him as questions were fired at her from all points. Darryl turned and quietened everyone down and carried on. "Okay, guys, let's be civilised."

No sooner had he said this than the whole rigmarole

started again, all of them firing questions simultaneously.

Darryl motioned again for quiet saying, "Let's be sensible here, one question at a time. Apologies, Freja Sarah, you've caught us a little unawares. We will question in turn." He turned and looked at them all. "Won't we. I'll start. Why are you here now?"

"I am here to let you know that I spread only the word of God, that which is written in the Bible, of love and understanding. I wish nothing for myself. Can you not see there is a better path, a chance of a new life for the people of the world? The people are lost down many paths; I am here to show the way, to save them."

Dan's turn came as motioned by Darryl.

"Freja Sarah, seriously, what can this achieve? I see only a defenceless nation. Its traditions and lifestyle would be under threat from any other country, at their whim. Will it not lead to irretrievable harm and upset to millions, the ruination of a nation?"

"I see now only turmoil, hardship and unhappiness for many, who yearn for new beginnings. Can we not agree on that?"

Darryl then turned to Miles, much to the annoyance of Lucy.

"Freja Sarah, what do you expect to achieve? I see only total anarchy, the breakdown of law and order, misery and pain, like my colleagues."

"You don't understand yet, but all will be made clear. My message is quite simple. Follow God's teachings and the path to the light will become clear, all will be revealed. I cannot fail as I have the hand of the Lord behind me. For I am the Chosen One, sent to save you. Believe in me. All will be well."

She could see that they, like many others were having difficulty accepting a new faith, then some questions came that she hadn't allowed for.

"Freja Sarah, speaking only hypothetically," said Lucy, getting her question in quickly before anyone else. "What would you feel if you found out there were others with your unique ability to appear where you want? For example, if I had your gift also."

"Then, I would say to you, are we not sisters under God's Righteous Glory? Isn't it our divine duty to work hand in hand? Be guardians to the Pathway of Light? Jesus was sent by God as a man, now it is the time of women."

The questions were coming thick and fast, but Sarah seemed more than capable to answer with ease, perhaps a rehearsed ease, that was until she heard from Neil in his best 'London barrow boy' voice.

"You can stop all this Bible talk for me, darlin'. I don't believe a word of it. Why are you really here, luv, and why shouldn't I try and stop you? I like it the way it is, thanks. Go and try Mars."

All heads turned towards Neil. Most looked horrified with his aggressive manner, but Miles and Dan were quite in awe, and Lucy looked thoughtful.

Sarah began to feel the irritability start to rise within her once again and just managing to hold her anger back said, "I can see I'm talking to a bunch of Philistines. Am

I now not getting the very same problems that Jesus had to suffer? Do you not see what happens to those sent by God to do his work? I can see you have no wish or desire to join my quest but I have no malice towards you. I have no fear and that's what you shall see in the coming times. May God help you see the way, for you shall see I am no false prophet. I am the new Chosen One."

And on that note she disappeared.

"Well," said Darryl, "that was unexpected."

"Talk about understatement," said Kim. "It's just a pity she went before I had the opportunity to ask the question that should have been asked first. Sorry, Darryl."

"And that was?" he asked.

"The obvious. How exactly did she know about us in such detail? How did she know when our meeting was taking place and how did she know the exact place to appear? That's what I'd like to know," said Kim forcefully.

"You're one hundred per cent right, Kim. How on Earth did that happen?" said Dan.

"My nose is on high alert," said Miles. "There's something fishy here. I think the fish tank's sprung a leak."

"Always take note of Miles' nose. I know from experience," quipped Neil.

Before anyone could comment further the door opened and in came Nikki and very cleverly feigned surprise at the state of everybody in the room, but said in all innocence, "Sorry I'm a bit late. Have I missed anything?"

"Only Freja Sarah. She popped in for a chat," said Miles.

"What? How?" she said in a surprised voice.

"That's what we'd like to know. We're open to ideas," said Dan.

Darryl quickly got Nikki up to date with an abridged version of events, then Neil said, "What a performance that was. Sorry I put an end to it but I wanted to see if I could get a rise out of her and I think I did."

"She just about held it together," said Miles, "and that was a very well put question Lucy; that also threw her."

"Thanks, Miles. I was just trying, like Neil, to get a reaction from her. I didn't want to let her know about us but at the same time I wanted to give her a bit of doubt."

"Yes, Lucy, it was really clever. I hope it gives her something to think about, maybe just nag away at her over-confidence," said Dan.

They all belatedly agreed that Freja Sarah had, to her credit, pulled off her audience in front of them and Darryl spoke for them all when he said, "That was enlightening, but enough. We've got a bit of a quandary here now. I need you to put your thinking caps on again. How has this happened? Find out."

"Didn't you have a smidgen of news, Darryl?"

"Oh yes, come to think of it, I did."

"Enlighten us," said Miles.

"Well, it seems yesterday early evening, according to

377

surveillance, there was a disguised visitor to her annexe. It was raining but the female was hooded with a large umbrella, obviously not wishing to be identified. She stayed for about ten minutes, left hurriedly, and we tried to follow but she was too fast and we lost her at the tube station."

"Egg on their faces," said Dan, "but they must have got a photo."

"Yes, but no help," said Darryl and put it on screen. They all agreed, useless.

"No help at all," said Dan. "Could be anyone, male or female. But events are moving fast; let's make sure we don't get left behind."

"There's her picnic tomorrow in the park to look forward to. I need you all in for that. She'll add something to it for sure. Just in case, let's get Lucy and Neil down to theatrics in the morning; that should be fun for us all."

*

Sarah had put the diversion, as she liked to think of it, at the sceptics' office behind her and had moved on to the picnic. She hoped she might get a glimpse of the woman who claimed to be with her, but she had rung Sarah to apologise for the idiots at the office and promised to help when she could, and it followed therefore she must be involved there. It mattered not what the unbelievers planned for. With God's guidance, nothing was beyond her, and with Richard as her chosen one, she felt magical.

Now all she needed was to see Richard, but first tomorrow.

She'd arranged her four would be there for the afternoon and they were. She'd contacted Sebastion earlier and asked him to visit Buckingham Palace, which would be her next high-profile appearance on the Saturday evening to finish the day on a high.

She asked him, "How did your visit to the Palace go?"

"Visit went well, but I've never seen Buckingham Palace look like it does. I checked and apparently the president of the United States is on a stopover here in London and tomorrow night is having dinner with the queen. The whole of the frontage is draped with the American flag. It's absolutely covered. A bit over the top, I think."

He took out his phone and showed Sarah a photograph he'd taken. She could see that her plan to appear on the famous balcony would be no good as flags had half-covered it. It would have to be a rooftop appearance.

"Actually, they've done it rather well," she said begrudgingly. "Now, about our picnic. Judith, is the weather going to be good?"

"Yes, it's going to be a lovely day. A lovely day for our picnic," she replied. "Are we going to do anything special there, Freja Sarah?"

"No, we'll just walk amongst them, just ourselves, just stop and talk."

Then Lovage asked, "Do I need to make a picnic for us?"

"No need for that," said Freja Sarah. "I'm sure we'll

be offered more tasty snacks than we can handle, more than enough for the 'March of Light' that follows."

"Are you going to tell them about the march on Westminster before the picnic, Freja Sarah?" asked Alina.

"No, I thought it might be good if we just mentioned as we walk around that we are going and see if they follow."

"I don't think we're going to be short of company, do you?"

"I would be very surprised," Sarah said, and stood up ready to leave. "If there is nothing else, I suggest you all go home, it will be a long and happy day tomorrow."

Chapter 57

A feeling from on high, a guiding hand,
She walks amongst us with gentle grace

Richard rolled over in bed towards Sarah.

"Are you awake, my love?"

"Yes, did you sleep well? No more thoughts of Nicolas?" she replied, leaning into him.

He looked deeply into her eyes.

"Sarah, I want to marry you, if that's even possible. If you were to say yes."

"Richard, it's my dream also. Yes, of course I would, and I see no reason why not. It's widely believed, and by me, that Jesus took a wife while here on Earth."

He wrapped his arms around her and gave her a loving, passionate kiss.

"Thank you, my love, forever."

"However, we may have to wait a short while until we are beyond the awakening. The time for us will show itself, it should be soon."

Another momentous day ahead of her, she blew him a kiss and left him there just gazing at her. Today would be a day of all days. Finally the establishment would see they must bow before her. She showered, dressed and left Richard dozing in bed and went across to the main house, awaiting the arrival of the four. Idling she turned the television on, and found every news station was fixed upon her and the day ahead. They talked of nothing else. Everyone interviewed, eager for the day to start. Little did they know that the picnic was only the prelude to even greater events, but they would find out in due course.

The front door opened and Sebastion and Alina came in together. As they lived near to each other, Sebastion had taken to giving her a lift. The others would arrive shortly, but it gave her time to record a short video about her appearance at Buckingham Palace this evening. This would be uploaded to all her social media outlets at six o'clock. She had calculated the picnic and march would end around this time and Sebastion had already parked a car in nearby Belgravia for their return here, giving her plenty of time to prepare for the evening's appearance.

Once back in the lounge she found Judith and Lovage enjoying their coffees.

"Good morning, my best and loved. What a day ahead." She was pleased to see they had all followed her instruction to dress in white so as to be highly visible to her ever-increasing flock. "I feel ecstatic about today and I hope you all do."

As if one, they all agreed it would be a blessed day.

Judith, always the practical one, said, pointing at the window, "Look at the sunshine; truly we have God on our side. Tell me, Freja Sarah, what time would you like to set off?"

"My idea was to walk from here about one o'clock, through the gardens, which I'm sure will also be busy, and into Hyde Park. Let's take our time on the walk, talking and meeting, having time for all. We should be through the park and ready for the March of Light about four. Then we'll tell our followers about the walk to Parliament Square and if they'd like to join us and be sure we are back here by seven o'clock. Sebastion has transport parked nearby for us."

"That all sounds a good plan, Freja Sarah," said Judith. "I can't add anything to it. Let's have a small lunch before we set off."

As they moved into the dining room, Richard was getting himself ready to leave. Opening the door to the road, he noticed a few more people than usual just hanging around, talking, and it crossed his mind that somehow the press might have got wind of where Sarah was operating from. Unlikely, he thought, as he closed the door behind him and walked away, failing to notice across the road behind him a photographer pointing a long camera lens in his direction.

Sarah and the others took their time over lunch, all being extra careful to keep their white clothes white and once finished left the house and walked off towards Kensington Gardens.

The gardens seemed as usual, not crowded, but once past the large house, ahead of them far into the distance, all they could see were thousands, perhaps hundreds of thousands of people picnicking on the grass. The press had caught up with them at the entrance, and were following their party at a short distance.

"Wow! Just look at all those people, Judith. I've never seen so many at the same time, there's hundreds."

"A bit of an understatement there, Lovage. There must be a million at least," and she wasn't wrong.

Freja Sarah set forth with the others either side of her. She smiled to herself as her assumption that the crowd would part and open up in front of her was correct. She walked slowly as nearly everyone had something to say or ask and she took time to connect with them all. It seemed to her that most were telling her just how happy they were to be there in her presence and valued her in their lives. Some wished to be blessed, which of course she was happy to do.

A little further along, they came across a lady in a wheelchair who asked, "Can you perform a miracle for me, so I can walk again?"

Sarah put her hand upon the woman's head and said, "All these things will be possible once the New Beginning comes to pass. Have faith a little longer. The Lord knows of your suffering and you will be cured."

This was the essence of her words to all that came forward, and there were many looking for a healing miracle.

They were offered tasty morsels by whoever they passed, and some so delicious-looking it was difficult to decline, the temptation occasionally too strong to resist, but they kept their intake to a minimum. They next came to a shady area where many mothers with babies had congregated to escape the burning sun, when the unexpected happened. A mother came forward with her baby and offered it to Freja Sarah.

"Freja, please bless my baby."

Sarah took the baby from her arms and kissed its forehead.

"Of course, I shall be delighted. God bless the pure spirit, for these children will have no boundaries to meet. They truly shall inherit a new fresh and joyous world where all are equal under God."

No sooner had the first baby been blessed, she was inundated with mothers wishing the same for theirs. She was surrounded on all sides and Sarah was trying in vain to bless each one. The mothers were ecstatic, but the time involved was taking it's toll. Judith noticed first and managed to get hold of an attractive coloured glass beaker, not unlike a chalice from a nearby family, the Lord's work, she thought. She filled it with water which Sarah blessed, and this enabled her to sprinkle a few drops on each baby's head while blessing them. However, that wasn't the end of it. Mothers started to offer their children to Sarah to take back with her, cries of "please take my baby and let my child stay with you" became commonplace, catching Sarah completely by surprise. In fact it unnerved her that so many wished her to have their children, for even a short time.

The sprinkling of the holy water worked extremely well, and she was able to move on, the cries of the anguished mothers still ringing in her ears. Eventually the gate at the east of the park came into sight.

She was expecting some ribbing and banter after the incident at the canal, and sure enough she came across a small bunch of young lads with their girlfriends and one of the boys called out, "Freja Sarah, we've run out of food. Are you going to feed us like feeding the five thousand?"

Quick as a flash she answered, "You're all too fussy nowadays. Would you be happy with just a bread roll?"

His girlfriend chipped in, "What about turning my water into Prosecco!"

"I would, but I don't think it's a good idea in this hot sun. Come and see me tonight."

Laughter exploded all around. For many it was a welcome relief to see that Freja Sarah had a sense of humour and wasn't always serious. It reminded some of the painting of Jesus laughing. This moment, she thought, was the time to tell of the 'March of Light' to the crowd.

The four started telling all around them about the proposed walk to Parliament Square and to pass on the message. As far as they could ascertain, virtually everybody was going to do it, and around them could see people packing up their picnic, ready to follow.

Eventually, they left the park at Hyde Park Corner and looking behind could see many were already following. The time seemed right to start the walk and they left the park gates leading a throng onto the main road and across the large roundabout. All the traffic was forced to come to a stop and although there was much beeping of car horns and insulting language, nothing was going to stop them. They made their way through Green Park and St James' Park to Parliament Square.

The march was largely uneventful as such, some on-lookers confused with what was happening, but the crowd started to chant "Freja Sarah" very loudly, only drowned out occasionally by the press helicopters. Only a small proportion of the hundreds of thousands of people drawn to her event actually managed to get in the square, the remainder filling the two parks. Sarah hoped the message and size of the demonstration would finally make the government listen and when she thought that the job had been done, she decided to end it.

She asked her four to pass the message around that the march was over and would they mind all backing off as she needed to prepare for this evening.

The crowd were largely cooperative, but it was still not easy to get to Belgravia. Sebastion motioned to the car and with his help she stood on the door sill and thanked them all for coming. A large cheer went up from the crowd as she settled into the back of the car. She hoped today would have the desired effect that she wanted, especially with tonight's appearance.

Chapter 58

"I've got to admit, that was a spectacle," said Miles grudgingly, as the six of them sat watching Darryl's newly installed large screen television in the galley.

Kim nodded in agreement saying, "What will she do next? She seems always one step ahead."

Dan, seeming particularly depressed by his own shortcomings said, "I should have seen this coming. I've dealt with people like her before who never know when to stop."

"Come on Dan, none of us can work out her mind," said Kim. "She's on a different wavelength. She really believes she's the New Messiah."

It had been a long and frustrating day for them all, and a terrible start to the weekend. Darryl and Kim had come in specially, in light of the spectacle, but they had decided to leave everyone else, including Nikki, to enjoy their weekends at home.

Sensing everyone's mood was low, Darryl was about to suggest they call it a night when the phone rang. After speaking down the line for a few seconds, he threw up his arms in disbelief, almost shouting, "My God! I've just heard, if it wasn't enough for her already today, she's doing Buckingham Palace tonight!"

Miles, laughing, said to Neil, "You better go and suit up, Jesus. It was a good idea with the flags, Darryl."

"Yes, the lads did a good job there blocking off the balcony and making it look natural. I've also made them give instructions that under no circumstances is anybody allowed to go onto the roof. I want it clear for you, Neil, to approach her. Have you worked out what to say?"

"I won't go into it, but I've a number of things to call her out. It depends how she opens the conversation. I think she'll be shocked to see Jesus there."

"I wish she'd chosen Big Ben first," said Lucy, "but if you don't get through to her as Jesus, Neil, I'll make sure I do as one of God's angels, one way or another."

"Go get her, Neil," said Darryl.

Neil got up and left and Kim followed to give him a hand. Kim had contacted a costume agency and had acquired a wig and beard that took some time to fit correctly, but eventually they managed it. After that, Neil donned sandals and a brown tunic, which were an easy fit. To add effect, Kim had also hired a wooden staff that, once in Neil's hand, completed the look. With Neil ready to go, they headed back to the galley to show the others.

Miles, of course the first to comment, went down on his knees. "Jesus. Or is it Robert Powell?"

"Trust in me, for I am God's guiding hand. At least I hope I am," said Neil.

"That is fantastic," said Darryl and everybody agreed.

"One question," said Dan. "Are you able to take the staff with you?"

Lucy laughed. "You still don't quite get it, do you Dan? If we believe the staff is in our hands, then it is."

"I had just one moment of doubt there, as I opened my eyes. Just for a second, Neil, I thought I really was seeing Jesus. Kim, you've done a really fabulous job. I can only hope Sarah falls for it and I can't see any reason she shouldn't," said Darryl. "I can't wait to see Lucy as an angel."

"The costume is pretty angelic, if I say so myself," said Kim.

"Perfect," said Darryl. "There's about an hour to go before lift-off. Let's have another drink and try and relax. Neil, don't spill anything."

*

Time is relative and the next hour was relatively slow. Neil, with staff in hand, went to one of the four flats – where the bed was larger – and waited till just before eight to doze. He could get into the dream state quickly with all the practice he'd had. Trying to think as Sarah would, he had decided to materialise on the central section at one edge, as he believed she would appear in the middle by the flag.

Down in the galley, all eyes were on the screen looking at the mass of crowds awaiting the event. Darryl turned up the volume. Using the tune to the French song, 'Frère Jacques', some bright spark had changed the words to 'Freja Sarah, Freja Sarah, we love you, we love you'. The whole crowd had caught on to it and were singing along. It was definitely a party atmosphere there. A number of food and drink vans had positioned themselves around the far edges of the large roundabout, and a Highways vehicle was trying to undertake a repair, with workers having taken a manhole cover up and cordoned off an area between the road and the path.

As the time neared eight o'clock there was a restless anticipation throughout the crowd, all eyes on the palace roof, awaiting just a glimpse of their New Messiah. The workman near the open manhole cover appeared to be putting an instrument down, while asking the surrounding people to move back if they could.

At last, Freja Sarah appeared on the mid-section of the roof near the flagpole, with her arms towards them. She then raised them to heaven. As she did so the workers' van raised its roof that had been obscured by the high-sided panels. To the casual passer-by, the disguised camper van passed the test, but any observant person on another day would have noticed that although the rear doors had the usual high visibility stripes and blacked out windows, the oversized side panels with 'Highway Emergency Services' written bold and clear were obviously fake. The workman stood by the passenger door as though writing on a clipboard and inside a gunman began to take aim at Freja Sarah with a high precision long range-rifle.

On the roof, Freja Sarah was accepting the adulation she was expecting when she noticed movement to her right. She was startled to see a figure appear near her and just for a few seconds she believed it to be Jesus, until he said in a voice that still had a London accent:

"Sarah, why are you taking our Lord's name in vain?"

But before she had time to answer, two shots rang out and part of the wall near her exploded into pieces. Horrified, she realised straightaway that shots had been fired at her and instantly disappeared. Neil, equally quickly understood what had happened, saw there was no further chance of a confrontation with her, and did the same.

The shooter lowered his gun and the roof of the camper van fast, and at the same time out of the manhole cover came smoke, where his partner had dropped just seconds before an incendiary device, timed to perfection. The workman shouted to the nearby people to leave quickly and panic set in immediately, which was what he wanted. The van reversed, beeping loudly onto The Mall. There was pandemonium everywhere, panic and fear had taken over. Their ruse had worked perfectly and as they drove down The Mall they watched as dozens of police cars, lights flashing, passed them in the opposite direction.

*

Neil walked down to the galley in dismay, his chance gone.

Darryl put his hand on his shoulder. "How could we

have expected that, Neil? What a pity the attempt, although ridiculous, on her life was so soon into her appearance. Did she manage to say anything?"

"No, I just asked her why she took the Lord's name in vain and then bang, bang. She never had the chance to reply although I saw how shocked she was to see me as Jesus. I think she thought I was Jesus."

"You had no chance," said Dan, "but I remember Jay said something last week about a lone gunman, although this sounds pretty well organised. The police report should be interesting when we get it. That van looked suspicious to me."

"I don't think it'll happen again, at least, I hope not," said Lucy.

"We're not done yet," said Miles. "Look at the way she scarpered. She didn't hang around, although she could have done. I'd like to be a fly on her wall tonight."

They all agreed on that.

Chapter 59

The sun lost behind the clouds will return
For like herself it has no choice

Sarah jolted upright from her chair and for once in her life felt both despair and loneliness.

Was this another of God's tests? She remembered briefly that God had tested her before and thought back to the fate of her parents. God can be ruthless, she thought, but I still have much to do for him, to fulfil his wishes for a better and more just world.

Richard was due that evening, but because of that madman she would spend even more time on her own. She sat stupefied, the same thoughts going round and round in her head but, amazingly, with all that had happened, she fell into a calm sleep; a sleep of no dreams, something extremely rare for her, only interrupted as she heard a key in the door. Richard at last.

He rushed into the room and held her in his arms.

"Are you even slightly okay after what you've been through? What is wrong with the world? You're only acting as God's messenger. Can I do anything for you, my love, anything at all?"

"Just hold me and tell me you love me." Which he did and for what seemed like an eternity they sat embracing and then moved to the bedroom, both enduring uneasy sleeps.

They were still lying together in each other's arms when Sarah heard the buzzing ring from the main house. It was Judith.

"You'd better come over, Freja Sarah, as soon as you can."

Sarah sensed some anxiety in Judith's voice and wondered what could be so urgent. She dressed quickly, telling Richard to dress but stay where he was, and she crossed to the main house.

Judith had an expression on her face that Sarah couldn't identify and said, "Look at this."

She held up a copy of the cover of a Sunday paper to show her the headline: 'Who is the mystery man?'. Beneath were pictures of Richard entering her annexe. Sarah collapsed on the nearest chair.

"And it's all over the television," said Judith, awaiting Sarah's response.

"Judith, I'm so sorry. I tried to keep it a secret, but I'm just an ordinary mortal here on Earth trying to do God's work. I need to eat and sleep, and I also feel the need for love. I didn't ask to be chosen, I didn't ask this of God. It was his will and I'm sent to do the will of God, the best I can."

Judith sat with her and put a comforting arm around her shoulder.

"I do understand, Freja Sarah. Perhaps, for you, it might have been easier to tell, rather than we find out in the news."

"I was frightened Judith, frightened of what you'd all think and say."

Judith hesitated then said, "I have been in contact with the others and they are all making their way here, but take a look outside, the press have the house surrounded, ready to pounce on them. I've told them to rush though the side gate and not say a word."

"Thank you," said Sarah and sat quietly.

"Let me get you a cup of tea and we'll wait together. I'm sure it will be fine."

One by one they turned up and saw Freja Sarah sitting, just waiting, expectant of their judgements of her actions. Alina was the first to break the silence.

"Freja Sarah, to be honest, we've all had our suspicions over the last few weeks. We've all had some idea that you have a special friend."

"Is he nice?" said Lovage.

"Yes, he's wonderful. Would you like to meet him? He's here now."

"Of course we would," said Alina, speaking for everybody.

"Okay, give me five minutes to let him know what's happening and we'll come out together." Sarah went back to the annexe, told Richard his face was all over the newspapers, and that the four were in the house ready to meet him. They were both shocked that he had been spotted, but both believed honesty was the best policy, as if they had any choice now.

Judith opened the door to them and they walked into the unexpected. All seemed genuinely happy for her, and Richard gave them his most charming self, saying, "It's been very difficult for me, the secrecy, but can you imagine the anguish that Freja Sarah has been in, having to live a lie to you. I know she loves you all and doesn't want you to feel let down by her, but I, like you, believe she is the new Chosen One, here on Earth to gives God's message."

They were all captivated by him and understood the dilemma he and Sarah had faced, answering that it would make no difference to them. They just wanted to help towards the new pathway for the people.

Sebastion changed the tone of the conversation by asking,
"But what are we going to do now? Our house is surrounded and they're not going away. What can we do? We must find Freja Sarah a safe place. We all have ours."

Richard knew his first moment had come. "We may have a solution for you, at least an option. I am a qualified doctor working in the maternity departments of a number of clinics and hospitals in West London. I could make a call to my CEO and see if we have any spare capacity for you all, just on a temporary basis. Would you like me to try?"

They had a talk between themselves and realised they had no other option. They put their trust in him and asked him to make the call. He left them waiting and called Nicolas.

"The first moment has arrived, Nicolas. I need to move them fast. You mentioned St Saviours before. Is that still on?"

At the other end of the line, Nicolas confirmed one wing was completely empty and asked if he should send a car for them.

To which Richard replied, "Wait for my call. I have a plan."

Richard walked back to see their hopeful faces.

"One of the wings in St Saviours in North Kensington, has just been completely refurbished and is empty. A car could be sent for you, as soon as you are ready. The hospital has many exits and entrances, so you could come and go as you wish. How does that sound?"

They all agreed as Richard had hoped. Sarah went to the annexe to get what she'd need and Sebastion went to the studio to collect the equipment he would need for further videos.

Then Judith said, "But how are we going to get out of here without being chased?"

Richard even had a plan for that, and a mighty good one. "I shall leave the annexe by its door, where most of the press are waiting. I'll arrange for a car to pick you up from the front of the building while I'm at the side. After all, I'm the one they want to talk to."

He rang Nicolas and arranged a car to wait near the front of the building and to collect them as they appeared, in about ten minutes. He told them to go outside and look for a large grey Mercedes parked nearby, open the gate and run to it. A simple but genius plan.

Richard checked over himself to make sure he looked the part. His idea of being casual was an open white shirt and chino-style trousers. Just to make it perfect, he'd borrowed a pen and pad for his top pocket. For the press, he was every inch a doctor.

He stepped outside to solid shouting. He put his arms up to quieten them and said, "I'm here to answer your questions but before you all start to shout at once, let me say a few words. My name is Doctor Richard Anthony. I'm based at a small clinic nearby and I am also Freja Sarah's personal physician."

Someone interrupted with, "Did you stay there all night?"

"I most certainly did. Freja Sarah was the victim of an assassination attempt yesterday evening and was in no state to be without medical care. It would have been a dereliction of my duty to have left her on her own under those circumstances. Would anyone disagree?"

Someone else shouted, "How well do you actually know her then?"

"She is my friend and confidante, nothing more. And I think that's all, gentlemen." He then walked off towards his clinic.

The press were completely thrown. A wasted day for most, and no one even noticed the Mercedes drive off from the front.

Chapter 60

Coincidence, probably, but the weather changed almost immediately overnight. Gone were the sunny days. The sky had darkened considerably. Now safely settled into a lovely suite of rooms with Richard, Sarah once again felt safe from the outside world. There was a small private terrace and she and Richard sat waiting for their lunch to be delivered. Although the clouds were heavy, it was still very warm.

Richard's phone rang and he silently mouthed to Sarah it was Nicolas and moved into the lounge to take it. This gave her time to think back over the last twenty-four hours with horror and dismay. Had God forsaken her? She couldn't believe the possibility of that and looked to the positive. She was relieved to be away from the attention of the press thanks to Richard's quick thinking and the offer from Nicolas, perhaps part of His plan.

She hoped that the homes of her four hadn't been discovered. Alina, Judith and Sebastion had decided to base themselves at their homes, knowing that they could be with her quickly if she needed them. The exception was Lovage, who had been more cautious and wanted to stay close to her. She had been given a nice but smaller suite next to hers and Richard's and Sarah was pleased to have her nearby.

Richard returned with a request from Nicolas that he would really like to meet her and would it be possible for the three of them to have dinner together that night.

"Would you mind doing that, Sarah? I know Nicolas is aware of who you are and would love to meet you. He is a charming person, and it would mean a lot to him. You can see how much help he's been."

"Yes, of course, Richard. I'd like that as well, to say thank you for what he's done."

"I'll let him know after lunch, but can we talk about last night? I'm really confused over what happened at the palace. Are you happy to talk about it? If not we can another time."

"No, it's fine by me. Even I find it confusing. Probably a good idea to talk about what happened; it may become a little clearer."

"Okay, so what actually happened on the roof, I couldn't see? I've had a look at all the news footage and all I can see is you turn around and look behind you, as if startled, hesitate, and then the shots rang out. The odd person interviewed thought they may have seen a hazy shadow behind, but were not sure."

"I'm pleased about that, because if they saw what I saw, they wouldn't know what to think, because I didn't know what to think."

"What do you mean?" he said bemused. "Was there

401

anybody there?"

"You'll find this difficult to believe, as I did, but I saw Jesus standing there, as we think of him, long hair and beard, cloaked and with a wooden staff."

Richard almost laughed, shaking his head in a puzzled motion. "Jesus?"

"Yes, Jesus, and he spoke to me. But I was, and still am, in such a shocked state at seeing him, so astounded, that I can't remember what he said to me. I've tried and tried to remember. It was something about the Lord's name, but that's it."

"Did he speak English?"

"Yes, I remember thinking that was funny. He spoke good English, but it sounded like he had a slight London accent. I always imagined, if I met him, he would just send the words to me, sort of telepathy, or at least with a Middle Eastern accent. It's not something you really think about."

"Perhaps he'll appear again and repeat the message."

"I hope so," she said and sat in deep thought, just gazing ahead.

Then Richard said, "The other thing is, I've had an idea which might help you."

This was the moment of all moments for him, and he knew he had one chance to get it right, or it was all over.

"I watched all the footage of the lovely picnic, and what struck me as important was the way the mothers were wanting you to bless their babies. Some even asked you to take their babies. Has it occurred to you taking babies might be another way of bringing the government to heel?"

"I don't understand?"

"Well, just think about this. We've got a complete empty wing, here at St Saviours. You could get willing mothers to bring them here and leave them with you for a couple of days. We have wonderful nursing staff who would look after them and you could take time to bless them over and over again if you wanted. If you sent out a video, you could ask them to bring them here. I think we would be inundated. Who wouldn't want their babies blessed by you?"

"What would I tell the mothers?" she said, not really taking it in fully.

"That you would bless and bestow each innocent child with enhanced life qualities. They would always be special, as they will have spent time with you."

That was his best pitch. He couldn't have done any better and awaited the response.

"I'm not sure."

He casually said, "It was just a thought, to be able to do more good and give happiness to the young mothers."

He could feel it wasn't a definite 'no', but before he could add anything else, lunch arrived with a knock at the door. They ate lunch without mentioning the subject of babies and when finished he went and called Nicolas. He confirmed the dinner for three. Nicolas asked how the plan was proceeding and Richard asked for his patience just a little longer.

Nicolas told him in no uncertain terms, "You're going to get me the adrenochrome I require. Do I make myself clear?"

Richard confirmed it was about to happen and prayed to God it would. He knew what happened to those who let Nicolas down. He went back and found Sarah sitting, having just finished a call to Sebastion. She looked up to him and smiled.

"Richard, you were very clever with the press yesterday, and having thought about your latest idea, I can see you're right again. I can see the joy it would bring to those mothers. It would add a complete new dimension to my work as I still have much to do; there are still unbelievers. In fact, I've just been speaking to Sebastion and he's on his way here to set up a small studio. Do you think it's too quick if I put out a video and ask the mothers to bring in their babies tonight? I feel invigorated. There's so much more I can do."

"Yes, let's start," he said, hardly able to contain his relief, wanting to shout from the rooftops 'Nicolas, I've done it!'. Instead, he calmly said, "I'll go and arrange it now. We'll get a new switchboard. There will be a lot of calls, and I'll arrange with the nursing staff to get things ready and be on hand to settle the babies in. How many at a time do you think you could bless individually?"

"I've thought about it and if I give each one a couple of minutes, I think sixty at a time. What do you think?"

"Yes, I think that's a good number, say sixty a night for three or four nights, otherwise it might go on forever. Shall I sort it out with the hospital, or would you like to be involved?"

"I've faith in you, Richard, just tell me when and where. I'll wait for you to give me the telephone number for them to ring and then film the video with Sebastion and put it straight out and wait for the response."

"I'm so happy you're doing this Sarah, for you, the mothers and the babies. Let me know when Sebastion arrives and I'll give him the number. I'd better go and get started; lots to do."

He left the room and straightaway called Nicolas. "Dinner's off this evening. But all systems go for the babies, starting tonight."

"I expected nothing less from you Richard, well done."

"I'm about to arrange a new switchboard for the mothers to call. Sarah is putting out a request for them shortly and we're expecting the first batch of sixty this evening, so you'd better arrange for your team to be ready."

"Already taken care of Richard, they're on standby. Sixty is a good number for them; they know what they're doing."

"They must be extra vigilant. One of Sarah's four is staying here, Lovage, who mustn't get a whisper of what's really going on."

"Don't worry, Richard, it will all happen in the middle of the night."

The call ended. Richard could at last relax slightly, then Sarah called to say that Sebastion had the studio up and running. She in the meantime had put together a

405

short script for the mothers, basically saying that she'd listened to them yesterday in the park and agreed to their request. She asked them to please bring their babies, for she was their future and she would enhance the spirituality of each one. Rejoice for them, for they would receive only pure comfort and enlightenment. It was God's will for them to receive a gift beyond all others.

Richard came through with the number and the video was posted at four o'clock. The switchboard went straight into overload and the first babies were being welcomed by Sarah at six o'clock.

Sarah met each mother and could see how much joy it gave them to hand the baby to her and she in part blessed each baby in turn, helped by a delighted Lovage who held a chalice of holy water sprinkled over them, as part of the welcoming ceremony.

When the blessings were over and the babies sleeping peacefully, darkness fell, and new medical staff and technicians took over. It was then a different story.

The wing was now off limits to the ordinary staff and security guards were posted to keep everybody else out. An array of ceiling lighting was put up across the whole of the babies' ward. All windows were blackened; no one could see in or out. A sound system was put in that played only loud, very loud claps of thunder, and the lighting was set to imitate lightening. It was enough to frighten anyone, let alone sixty babies.

Meanwhile, the doctors and nurses began inserting very tiny butterfly needles into the heel of each baby to collect blood. Not just ordinary blood – this would be blood filled with adrenaline from which adrenochrome could be extracted. The doctors would take only a small amount from each baby, no more than ten millilitres maximum, and using the heel, the mark of the butterfly needle would not be noticed. It was a tried and trusted method.

Someone hit a switch. Thunder and lightning raged across the ward, the babies were terrified, and the harvesting began. It lasted for only five minutes; this was enough to collect the first five millilitres. The nursing team took time and soothed all the babies until all were once again asleep. Medical research had shown it was best to do this twice and ten minutes later, it started all over again. It was amazing that the medical staff could cope with performing such torture on innocent children, but such was the power and fear of Nicolas.

At last, it was all over, the needles were taken out, blood safely stored and the storm abated.

All this torture for a few more years of life in the dark world of Nicolas and The Alchemati.

Chapter 61

Darryl and Kim tried to muster some enthusiasm for the meeting ahead, but with another failed attempt behind them – who could allow for a shooter – and not much else to go on, they were expecting a drab affair. Unless something happened out of the blue, they were down to Sarah's appearance on Big Ben, if they were right.

Dan broke the glum silence. "Okay Darryl, big day, get us up to speed."

Once a remark like this would have raised a laugh, now it didn't even get a smile.

"I've a few questions before you start, if that's all right, Darryl, if you don't mind, while they're still in my head."

"Go ahead, Miles."

"Have you any news on our leak? Somebody gave us away."

"Not a whisper, I'm afraid. Just keep our plans between us, as I know you're all doing. Something's not right, even I feel it, let alone your nose."

"Any news on the shooter? Has Jay come up with anything?"

"Nothing, cameras lost them in the traffic. They stopped somewhere and took off the side panels and stripes. There was little chance anyway with a million people on the streets and traffic chaos. That said, they had it well planned."

"Lastly, what have you got, Darryl?"

"Bits and pieces only, I'm afraid. Firstly, MI5 followed the Mercedes with Sarah and her cohorts from the front gate to St Saviours Hospital in North Kensington, while the doctor kept the press busy."

"That was a well-executed getaway as well, very well planned," said Dan. "Do we know anything about their destination?"

"We know it's a private hospital, owned by a multi-national company that's fronted by a Belgian businessman called Nicolas Peeters; I'm told he's a very dubious character, who's managed to stay whiter than white. He's got many fingers in many pies and is closely associated with an elite society for the ultra-rich and powerful and some members of various royal families. MI5 are trying to work out his angle in this. I'll let you know what that is, as soon as I know."

Dan said, "That's something, at least a lead."

Neil smiled, "I've thought of something about you, Lucy."

"Only nice things, Neil, I'm not in the mood."

"No, it's just a play on words, but you never know, we might be able to use it. It's about your name, Lucy Firmin. Has anybody said to you if split it up a bit, it becomes Lucifer, as in the devil?"

She shook her head. "Only you could come up with that, Neil. Nope, never heard it before, but I like it, sounds good."

"That's worth remembering," said Darryl, writing it down. "Well done, Neil, you never know, it may be useful with all the twists and turns. Anything might be worth a try if we don't move forward, but back to the immediate issues. MI5 are going to have a friendly chat with her associates. We now know who they are and where they live, that's ongoing as we speak."

"That's taken too long to find out," said Dan.

"You're right there. One of them has stayed with Sarah at the hospital, so that's a bit tricky, but the other three will definitely receive some friendly fire."

"You never know what that will turn up," said Dan.

"How are the government reacting? You must be getting some stick," said Miles.

"Too right," said Darryl, but we've told them that the investigations are moving forward fast and for them to hold back on any communications with her, no matter the pressure they're under. To keep their cool. Well, not exactly those words."

That raised a smile from them all and Miles said, "Knowing that lot, as I do, they wouldn't know what 'keeping their cool' meant."

"Okay, as regards you guys, she usually does her thing in the evenings, so why don't we all meet mid-afternoon, get up to date with what's going on and just wait till she does or doesn't release a video? We've got one last chance at Big Ben unless anything happens before that, and my guess is sometime this weekend. You guys happy with that?"

That seemed to go down well; it was the logical thing to do. Meeting over, they went down and sat in the galley. Almost immediately, Morry came running in and lay his head on Neil's knee. As the person least interested in him, it was only natural that Morry had gravitated towards their newest recruit. Neil had slowly begun to soften towards him.

"Neil, you wouldn't mind taking Morry for a walk, would you?" asked Nikki, joining them. "I'm really busy and I can see he likes you."

Miles joked, "Go on, Neil, we can all see you've become a dog lover; don't say you haven't."

Neil ignored the jibe completely and said, "Just for you, Nikki." And off they went.

*

At the closed-off wing in the private hospital, each baby was due to be picked up by their mother between four and six o'clock. Each baby had been meticulously checked by Nicolas' nursing staff to ensure there was no sign of bruising or inflammation on their heels. It was very rare as the medics were incredibly skilled, but occasionally it did occur. None were showing any signs but some of the babies were more subdued than normal, unsurprising after what they'd been through.

Sarah and Lovage took a break before the hand back

started, which gave Lovage a moment to tell what had happened to the other three. They'd all had a friendly and cordial visit from an official, they weren't sure where from, who tried to get information about Freja Sarah and also what was going on at the hospital. They refused to give any information and just told them that at the requests and demands of the mothers the babies were all being given a special blessing. They were as faithful as Sarah expected.

Four o'clock came and the mothers arrived at their allotted times. A few of the infants were still slightly subdued and Sarah reassured the mothers they were only quiet as they were absorbing their new life qualities. The look of joy on the mothers' faces was extraordinary.

It all went like clockwork – it had to with Nicolas orchestrating everything – and before too long the next batch had arrived for their night of barbarism.

Chapter 62

Life in the private ward, in the private wing of the private hospital had settled into an established routine. After a couple of days, everybody knew their place and time. Lovage, who had once had ambitions of nursing, had eased herself into that routine. With little to do for Freja Sarah, she had slowly made herself indispensable to the nursing staff. She was now on first-name terms with virtually everyone and was used to hearing 'Lovage can you…', 'Lovage fetch…'. It was all music to her ears. She was now in effect part of their team and was having the time of her life. It was a major part of her personality to want to help and nowhere had she found that more than here.

Sarah was pleased to see her so happy and content. Earlier she'd had a surprise call from the as yet unnamed Nikki and her spy, as she liked to think, who gave her name and apologised profusely for not giving her any information about the Jesus figure on the palace roof. She confirmed that the figure dressed as Jesus was in fact one of her colleagues. That was a weight off Sarah's mind; it had niggled away. A thought kept cropping up

413

that it just might have been Him, but now she knew the truth. If only she could remember what he'd said. Still, it couldn't have been important. Nikki told her she would have to be extra careful at the office, as they knew someone had leaked information, but still had no idea who. She promised if she heard anything she would ring and told Sarah to ring her about anything, if she needed to. I'm always available to you, Freja Sarah, she said, and decided she would be and take a few days off, if she could. Sarah found comfort in the call and sat thinking.

She'd begun to really enjoy meeting the mothers and babies and even more so when handing them back. The happiness was infectious from them, though she was glad to be having a night off to spend with Richard. She and the nursing staff needed a break, so tonight would just be the mothers collecting. Sarah thought the next morning would be a good time to meet up with the four, if they could make it, which of course they could.

*

The next morning dawned bright and warm. It was good to see her chosen four again, even after just a few days, and to catch up. Sarah went through what she was doing at the hospital, but they all seemed to know as it was all over the news, in a positive way. She took time to congratulate Lovage on her role, and everybody seemed really happy with the new turn of events. Alina now had a love interest in her life, a close neighbour she'd become friendly with, and they all wished her well.

She asked Sebastion if he had time to film a short video for release on Friday at six. He was of course delighted and she explained: Friday would be the last of the four dramatic appearances, but the important news was that she'd felt God's guiding hand again, and very strongly. God had told her to send a last message to those unbelievers who supposedly ran the country, to tell them that, from Friday, they would have seven days, until Sunday 13th, to accept her teachings; to agree to follow the new pathway of fairness for all. It would be a day to remember. God had told her: for those who deny, I say beware, take shelter, take shelter from the coming storm. Heed the four horsemen. He had told her that he only wishes peace and has no wish to be an Avenging Angel. The path is clear, yet they do not wish to see.

Events were unfolding beyond her control and she said to her four, "These are strong words, direct from God."

Judith asked what they meant as the four all looked worried.

"I am not sure myself, but the faithful should have no fear."

This was stunning news, but deep down, they'd hoped for something more; they knew not what but something, as a feeling of stagnation was beginning to set in especially since the government had shown no desire to move.

They had a final drink together and wished each other well, before Judith and Alina returned to their new homes and Sarah and Sebastion headed to the studio.

Once Sebastion had finished filming, Sarah looked forward to her afternoon with Richard. They would have lunch somewhere, maybe take a walk, relaxing and enjoying each other's company. Then the evening would come, and unbeknownst to Sarah, the evening regime would begin again.

Chapter 63

Sarah was as pleased when Thursday evening came, as much as Lovage was disappointed. Lovage was in her element, looking after the babies and being everybody's best help. Although the nursing staff had made her keep her distance early in the morning, while they checked for tell-tale signs on the heels by their procedure, she didn't know that. Once that was over, the babies were all hers and she went from one to another comforting and feeding them in turn.

She was bouncing around the ward offering to do anything. The nursing staff had the equivalent of all their helpers in one with her there. She chatted away as she worked and although it was ending tomorrow for her, she wished it would last forever. The nursing staff seemed to think it would last another week, but weren't sure, they just carried on until told to stop. In her meanderings across the ward, she sometimes overheard snippets of conversations but one word, which seemed out of place, turned up three or four times. The word was 'show'. Odd, she thought, but just let it go.

The departures went as normal, but a couple of mothers mentioned that their babies seemed a little pale. Sarah eased their minds by telling them that a few of the babies were unusually receptive to their new found enhancement and were absorbing the gift more deeply.

She said nothing to the staff, but did wonder why. She knew nothing about babies and surely the nurses would keep them in if there was anything wrong. They'd all been checked. It gave those mothers even more joy to think theirs was even more special. She watched and held all the newcomers and left.

Lovage stayed longer, savouring every minute, and as it was the last night, she didn't want it to end. She went for a cup of coffee and decided to take one back to the attendant, who always sat by the doorway of the corridor leading to the ward. They'd become quite friendly over the last few days.

She passed him the coffee and asked, "Do you take sugar? I've some here if you do."

"Yes I do, one sachet is great. How are you, Lovage? Not finished yet?"

She passed him a sachet. "No, there's always something for me to do. I've turned into the general gopher."

"Gopher?"

"Go for this. Go for that."

He laughed and said, "Well, you better drink that quickly. The show's nearly over."

Totally bemused, she quickly picked up on the word 'show' but countered in a calm voice while sipping her coffee, "The show's still on?"

"Pardon?"

"You know, the show."

"Oh, yeah. That show."

"What time does it finish?"

"About now, in a couple of minutes."

"I'll just go in now, catch the end, and be ready to help out."

"Right you are. Take your earmuffs."

"Got 'em," she answered, and went through the first automatic doors into a small corridor, pushed the next set open and stepped into Hell.

It was appalling. Flashing lights. Thunderclaps, and worst of all, babies screeching in pure fear. Her babies. The babies she'd cuddled. Her babies being tortured. On the verge of collapse, she just had the wherewithal to get her phone out and video the dreadful scene. She finished filming as the show did and noticed under the now normal lighting that each baby had a tube coming from its heel. They were taking blood. Why?

She turned and left the room, composed herself between the two sets of doors, wiped away a few tears, and walked through.

"Leaving already?"

"Just for a minute," she managed to say without looking at the guard. "Forgot something, be back in a minute," and turned into the corridor.

The nursing team passed her by. Look at them, not a care in the world, she thought. What do I do? Does Freja Sarah know about this?

Mind instantly made up, she left the hospital, hailed

a cab, and made a call to Judith.

"I've got to see you urgently. Now."

Judith would know what to do.

Chapter 64

It was definitely the morning after the night before at Judith's flat. Lovage had told Judith the whole story, in fits and starts, tears in her eyes, but eventually she got the gist of it. Lovage was short on details, but high on emotion and the adjectives, 'horrific', 'terrible', 'insane', and more. Judith was unsure how much of it was true. It was hard to imagine, but she didn't have to imagine anything when Lovage took out her phone, got the video up and passed it to her. Then she realised the full horror of it. She could understand how truly horrific it must have been in person. Poor Lovage. This was serious.

She comforted Lovage as best she could and told her there was nothing they could do tonight, nothing could be changed. They would sleep on it and act decisively first thing in the morning. Judith also insisted that Lovage sent her a copy of the video, so no matter what happened the following day, there was another copy. As they didn't know who they were dealing with here, they also agreed to keep the footage a secret.

Judith found the card given to her when she had been

visited by the government or the police, she wasn't sure. She remembered the lady had been very positive about who to ring if she needed to speak about Freja Sarah. She had been given a general number, but if it was really important, she had been told to ring a different number and insist on speaking to Darryl. Apparently, Darryl was the 'top man' as she'd put it. That was who she'd call, once Lovage had left.

She'd told Lovage that she must confront Freja Sarah with her discovery.

Lovage finished her coffee and said, "I'm frightened, Judith, frightened for myself."

"No need to be, Lovage, be frightened for the babies."

"I'm sure Freja Sarah would never let this happen. If she knew what was going on, I'm sure she'd be heart-broken, after putting her trust in Richard."

"Lovage, there is only one way to find out, and you know it. Speak to her; you know her better than anyone. Do you think she'd agree to this barbaric torture? I think you know the answer to that. I think she's been duped by some very clever people. She's always relied on you; help her find the truth. Don't let her down and let me do what I have to do. Keep quiet about it, and whatever you do keep quiet about the video. It could be dangerous for you if they know we have it."

"You're right, Judith. I love and trust her."

Judith rang for a taxi for her. Lovage was not keen to go, but she knew what she had to do."

*

422

Darryl stood looking out of the window, not at anything in particular, just looking. What would the day bring? Something, please. Anything. The waiting seemed to go on forever. It was an old saying but 'something's gotta give', he thought. A knock at his door broke the spell and Nikki came in.

"Darryl, I need a big favour. It's short notice, but I need the rest of the day off. It's really important to me. I've been trying to get a place on a weekend course on Yogic Flying. It's always full, but someone's cancelled at short notice and they've rung me. It starts this afternoon in the Cotswolds."

"Yogic Flying?"

"Yes, you know me."

"Yes I do. And yes, get going. It's quiet here. Nothing going on. You're free, go fly, but mind your knees."

"Thanks, Darryl, I'll see you on Monday. Now I've got to see Neil."

"Neil?"

"I've got no one to look after Morry at such short notice."

"Good luck with that one," Darryl joked as Nikki left to see Neil and Darryl resumed his place at the window.

*

"Neil," Nikki said in the best little girl voice she could muster.

"What do you want?" he said quickly but in good humour. "If you want me to try any more of your tea experiments, the answer's no."

"No, it's easier than that."

"Come on, spit it out."

"I've been trying to get on a course this weekend. It was full but they've just rung me to say they've had a cancellation and can I make it."

"Well, go and enjoy it."

"I don't know what to do with Morry. You wouldn't look after him, would you?"

"I don't know anything about dogs."

"This isn't just a dog, it's Morry. He really likes you. I've got all his stuff here and you can ring me if you have a problem."

He thought about it, shaking his head as if to say no and said, "Okay, till Monday, and only because he's the only dog I've ever liked."

"Thanks Neil! Everything is here, food, his lead and bedding and even a few green bags."

"Okay, it's a deal, on one condition. You don't tell Miles."

She was still laughing when Morry bounced in and sat next to Neil – a pair of buddies.

*

Kim came into Darryl's office to see him staring into nothing, but before she could say anything, his very private phone rang.

He picked it up and said, "Yes, Darryl speaking."

"Hello, Darryl, my name is Judith and I'm one of Freja Sarah's inner circle."

"Just hold a second, Judith while I close the door."

He immediately put the phone on loudspeaker and motioned shush with his finger to Kim.

"What can I do for you, Judith? You can speak freely to me, I know who you are."

"Right. You are Darryl. The top man investigating her?"

"Yes, I am, and I know quite a bit about you, Alina, Sebastion and Lovage. Convinced?"

"I am. I think she's in trouble. I think she's been duped into condoning something she's not aware of at the hospital."

"Exactly what, Judith?"

"Before I go into any more details, let me send you a short video, taken last night by Lovage. Where should I send it? Then I'll put the phone down and ring again after you've watched it in about five minutes. That should be enough for you and you'll see what I'm talking about."

He gave her what she needed. The line went dead and he said to Kim, "Well, well, what have we got here?"

"We're about to find out, Darryl, any minute now."

Within a couple of minutes, the video was playing and they both watched aghast at what they were seeing. They watched it again; it seemed even worse the second time. The phone rang again.

"Absolutely disgusting and horrific isn't it?" said Judith before Darryl could speak.

"It beggars belief," said Darryl. "It was beyond horrific. What are we dealing with here? What depraved mentality?"

"Lovage also told me how she'd stumbled on it. She'd been helping the nursing staff during the day and the word 'show' cropped up now and again when they thought she was out of earshot, and she wanted to try and find out what they were on about. She wheedled her way into the ward, when it was closed off, not knowing what to expect, and nearly collapsed but had the hindsight to film it as she thought no one would believe her."

"What a girl. That took some guts."

"She also told me that when it stopped and the main lights came back on, she thought she saw a small line coming from the babies' heels, as though they were taking blood or something."

Kim mouthed to Darryl, "I think I know what's happening."

"What are you going to do about this, Darryl?" said Judith. "You must do something."

Kim asked, no, demanded Darryl to give her the phone, which he did and she said, "Judith, I'm Kim. I work with Darryl. I think I know what they're doing. These are dangerous and ruthless people involved here, and if they find out about what you know, you could be in a lot of danger. Judith, just for our peace of mind, and I believe your safety, can I send a car for you and Lovage and bring you here?"

"Lovage has already gone back to the hospital to confront Freja Sarah."

"That's a pity. We can't help her, but we can help you. Let us bring you in here, please let us. It's a big, comfortable place and you will be safe and made welcome."

"You really think it's that serious?"

"Yes, I do. These people have no scruples. I'll explain when you get here. Please pack a bag and we can collect you. Be ready in ten minutes. A police car will get you."

The line went dead.

Darryl was on the other line organising. They of course knew her address and the police confirmed they would be there very quickly. Darryl turned to Kim and said, "Okay tell me."

"There's a deep organisation that works for the very rich and powerful. It supplies an anti-ageing compound called adrenochrome which can only be found in stressed babies. The organisation is deep underground, but worldwide. It's rumoured, but not proven, that children have been killed in America on a large scale. It's ongoing but nobody can get to the bottom of it. They have friends in very very high places."

"God, that's awful. I had heard those stories. To think, they'd do that to babies just for a few more years of life for old rich people. They must be depraved."

"You know as I know, the world's not a very nice place. You can see how Freja Sarah's message of hope works. I hope they don't harm Lovage."

"Nothing we can do about that, unfortunately. Now, let's concentrate on what we can do. Let's get everybody in, as quickly as possible. There's only Neil in now."

He rang down to Nikki to ring them, but she'd already left. Kim started calling them in and Darryl took his place by the window, only this time with plenty to think about.

Chapter 65

Lovage sat in a chair in the corridor outside Sarah's suite, waiting for her and Richard to return. How she wished things were different. How she wished they were as before, but they weren't. It was the complete reverse. She summoned up all her courage to confront Freja Sarah, but really she just wanted to go home, not to her new flat, but home with her parents. She wished the last few years had never happened.

At last she heard them coming and forced herself to get to her feet. Sarah saw her there, puzzled by her demeanour, her shoulders slumped, her face sad beyond description.

"What is it, Lovage? What's happened to you?"

"I've got to speak to you Freja Sarah. It's really important."

"Richard, you go. Come in," she said, opening the door for her.

"No, I'd like Richard to stay," she said, somehow her confidence increasing, and they all moved into Sarah's lounge and sat with Lovage, facing both on the sofa.

"I don't know if you know what's going on here, either of you; at least I hope you don't."

Richard sensed the worst and started to look pale, the blood draining from his face. He hoped he wasn't going to hear what he thought he would, but feared the worst and said, "What's this all about Lovage?"

"Well, you know I've been helping with the babies a lot?"

"Yes, you've been wonderful Lovage," he said hesitantly.

Lovage looked away from Richard and spoke directly to Sarah. "Freja Sarah, did you know they've been experimenting on the babies?"

Sarah shook her head, puzzled.

"When I was working, some of the nurses and doctors, when speaking to each other, kept mentioning 'the show' but stopped if they thought I could hear. I couldn't help wondering why and in the end my curiosity got the better of me, so I turned up earlier than usual last night and managed to trick my way into the ward and found out what they meant."

A tear fell from her eye, but she wiped it away and continued.

"They've been doing horrible things to them. Thunder and lightning, really loud, it scared me. All the babies were screaming. It was torture and I think they were taking blood from them."

"Don't be stupid. No one would do that. You must have had a nightmare that seemed real," said Richard.

"No. It was real."

"It can't have been," Richard continued. "I know the hospital well and everyone who works here; they wouldn't do that. It was just a bad dream. It couldn't have happened. I would have known. Let me give you a sedative and you can go and have a little nap."

"No, I was there, I tell you."

She could see Sarah didn't believe her, and contrary to Judith's advice, she took out her phone. They waited, puzzled, as she held the video up facing them.

"Now do you believe me?"

Sarah was completely taken unawares and started screaming and shouting. "No…no…no…"

Richard, on the other hand, tried to feign horror and ignorance of the scene in front of him, but Sarah saw though it. He knew something.

She looked him in the eye and said, "You knew about this, didn't you, Richard?"

She still had a little hope he could come up with an answer she believed, but all his composure left his face. He felt his only option was to come clean and put the blame on Nicolas.

"I didn't have a choice, Sarah. I'm so ashamed. Nicolas made me do it. You don't know what these people are like, Sarah. They would have me killed if I didn't do what they wanted."

"I don't care. You saw what they were doing to the babies. Look what they've done to me. I'll never be forgiven. I've failed God. Now I'll face the wrath of God. How could you do this to me? I thought you loved me but you just tricked and manipulated me."

"I do love you, Sarah," he said, knowing it wasn't recoverable. It was all over.

"It's too late, Richard. Just get out of here. I never want to see you again."

She sat sobbing with Lovage trying to comfort her and he left to face Nicolas.

"I knew, Freja Sarah. I just knew you didn't know. I just want to know what they were doing to them."

"Don't worry, Lovage. I'll find out if it's the last thing I do."

*

Richard, consumed by fear now, walked to where he knew Nicolas would be, at his private suite having drinks with a few of his cronies. He pressed the buzzer, said his name, and the door opened for him to see a happy Nicolas at his bar. This was the worst day of his life.

"Hello, Richard," beamed Nicolas. "Everything good? Surprised to see you here at this time."

"Hello, Nicolas. No, a problem's come up, I'm afraid. A big one."

Nicolas ushered his guests from the room; no objections from them.

"It's all over, Nicolas."

"What do you mean, 'all over'?"

"Sarah's found out about the blood collection. She's finished with me and she won't stop until she's found out the full story and tells the world."

"That's not what I want to hear, Richard. I want more. I demand more blood! You haven't a clue how many people are going to be disappointed, really important people. Sort this out. I want more blood. It's not enough."

To make his point even stronger, Nicolas punched Richard who fell over a chair onto the floor clutching his nose.

"I'm telling you, Richard. Make it happen. Let me down at your peril." And he left the room in search of Sarah. If Richard can't make it happen then I will, Nicholas decided. I know the truth about her. New Chosen One? God's gift to the world? I don't think so.

*

To calm and console themselves, and to get away from the hospital, Sarah and Lovage were walking hand in hand in a nearby park. It was a sunny afternoon and the park was full of happy playing children and mothers and babies. This only made matters worse. There was no consoling Sarah and Lovage.

"I'm going back to see Nicolas. I want the truth and I'll get it."

They started back, but unbeknown to them, Nicolas had already sent out anyone he could to find her, once he had found out she had left the hospital. They were spotted walking back and Nicolas drove off to intercept them. He spotted Sarah straightaway, pulled up beside her, and opened his window.

"Get in," he commanded.

"Why should I?"

"Because I'll tell you everything."

She got in, telling Lovage not to worry, and the car raced off. Fearing for her safety she said, "Don't forget, Lovage saw me get in your car."

"Nothing's going to happen to you."

"Why?"

"Because I still need more blood. Next week should be enough and that will be all I need. Then it's all over for you; one more week and I'm finished."

"I won't do it. I don't care what happens."

"Look, young lady, you'll do what I say. You're already just a bit player in all this. You haven't a clue, have you? You've been played right from the start."

"What do you mean?"

"You don't think that mugging was real, do you? I set it all up, so you could fall in love with Richard. He does everything I tell him."

She started crying, thinking what a fool she'd been, now knowing fully that Richard had let her down.

"Don't play that game with me. You might fool the stupid public but you haven't fooled me. I need more blood."

"Why? Why is it so important?"

"Money. I can produce a chemical from frightened children's blood that lengthens old peoples' lives. It's worth a fortune. I've got plenty of buyers and you'll get it for me."

She was frightened, speechless and at a loss to know what to do. Then she did the unexpected, at least as far as Nicolas was expecting. As the car slowed in the traffic, she quickly opened the door and jumped out – well, fell out. With just a few bumps and grazes, she ran off and sat opposite on the kerb between two vans, out of sight. Nicolas was forced to move off by a barrage of car horns.

What could she do, who could she turn to? Only one person came to mind. She took out her phone, luckily undamaged, and rang Nikki and said, "Please help me, Nikki."

She saw a large petrol station with an attached shop opposite, gave Nikki the address and said she'd be in the store, somewhere at the back, till she arrived. She tucked herself at the rear with a coffee that she was unable to drink and waited the twenty minutes that Nikki said she'd take.

Nikki had somehow foreseen strange events unfolding for her, but not this one. She raced to the petrol station, picked Sarah up and took back to her own house. Sarah checked the time in the car, it was too late to contact Sebastion and cancel tonight's appearance. She told Nikki what she needed this evening in the way of solitude and silence and Nikki obliged willingly.

Chapter 66

Everybody had at last turned up at Cloud and been introduced to Judith, who seemed to fit in quite well. They'd watched the video released at four confirming the appearance on Big Ben. Darryl congratulated Miles and Neil for their correct prediction. All had been told by Kim the exact reasoning behind the baby torture, to produce the end result, adrenochrome.

Miles put it best when he said what they were all roughly thinking.

"There have been quite a few people I've wished had never been born, but I really mean it for Nicolas Peeters."

That covered it in one sentence.

"Do we know the whereabouts of Sarah after she got in Nicolas' car?" asked Dan. "We know he came back alone."

"No, she's gone off our radar," said Darryl. "Something may have happened at the hospital. We're still trying to find out what, but my guess is something serious. Lovage has gone back there, but for how long we don't know, maybe just to collect her possessions. We really don't know."

"I just hope she appears tonight," said Lucy. "I'm really looking forward to it."

"I bet you are," said Neil. "I wish it were me. If you're having any second thoughts, Lucy, I'm prepared to do it in drag, even if I look like a pantomime dame."

"Thanks, but no thanks," said Lucy.

"The very thought of that, Neil, has put me off any dinner I was planning tonight," said Miles.

Judith smiled. After being included in the afternoon meeting, she already felt part of the team and said, "You all seem very upbeat and positive about tonight."

"That's because we've had it planned for what seems like forever. We knew the format of the appearances, the four points of a cross, and we were very unlucky at the palace. Neil and Lucy can do the same type of travelling as her, but neither of them think – well, they haven't said so – that they're also the Chosen Ones, unlike her," said Darryl.

"She was very convincing, if you knew her," said Judith. "If only I'd known about you two, I wouldn't have got myself mixed up with her."

"No, we're lucky you did, Judith, and you'll be here to see her finally exposed," said Dan.

"How are you going to do that exactly?"

Miles spoke, "That's down to me, Judith. I've made really good contacts in the press and TV over the years and I've arranged to meet them after her appearance. However that goes. Then I shall give them a dossier on what she's been up to and a copy of the video you kindly supplied, well in time for tomorrow's press and tonight's news. That should do it."

"I guess I had better go get myself ready," said Lucy, grinning.

"You go with her, Kim," said Darryl, and they left for upstairs, accompanied by a loud shout from Neil:

"See you on Big Ben!"

Chapter 67

I followed Kim to the changing room. The costume designers had been hard at work on my white angel dress. The wings were flat when I lay down, but unfolded as I stood. I also had a small white cross that I could point in her direction. We'd checked Big Ben and there was a walkway close to the top with railings, and we expected her to appear there; there really wasn't any other choice.

It was getting towards eight o'clock and I moved into my usual position, helped by Kim with the wings. I relaxed and started my doze. I only hoped I would remember all the lines and phrases that I'd practised with Neil for so long.

I appeared to the side of her, out of her view. I knew she was there as I could hear her taking in the adulation of the crowd, "Freja Sarah, Freja Sarah".

I was sick of hearing those two words.

It should have been, to quote one of Neil's jokes, 'Fraud Sarah'.

I walked forwards and saw the crowd stretching across all the streets and just for one brief moment that happy crowd in the evening sun brought back memories of my recent few minutes at the Isle of Wight festival.

Sarah saw me and turned.

I held my cross high in hand and said, "Sarah, I am an angel from God sent to speak to you."

"I am Sarah," she said proudly. "God's Chosen One."

"I wish that were true, Sarah."

"I am She. I am God's guiding hand here. I am here to show the way to enlightenment. I still have much to do, God's Angel. Why not join me here on Earth? Together we can change the world. Let us be God's authority here and now for the benefit of all mankind."

"Sarah. Am I an angel from God, or am I actually just a mortal being? I am Lucy and I work for MI5, the Secret Service, and I am here to tell you the dream is over. Did you not meet my colleague, dressed as Jesus? Do you not understand?"

Sarah was at once confused and dumbstruck. I looked over the railings at the now silent crowd watching us, I should think pretty confused themselves. She seemed unable to speak so I finished what I'd rehearsed.

"You're finished here, Sarah. I know the truth and soon will the people. You can change nothing, for you are just a mortal, like myself. Tomorrow's news will show the truth, the full story with photographs of the barbaric treatment of those babies. You will be unmasked. There is no way out for you, it's over, accept it. Your dream is over."

I was really pleased with the way we'd put that speech together, I could see the pain and suffering in her eyes. I wondered how she'd react. Fight or flee, I still wasn't sure, but I was about to find out. She opened her mouth and I thought she was about to say something, when she leaned forward over the railings, outstretched her arms and did the most beautiful swallow dive down to…

The last sun ray lost behind the cloud, gone forever.
The lady walks amongst us no more

EPILOGUE

Nicolas Peeters denied all knowledge of what went on at the hospital. Richard took the fall and is in custody.

Nikki failed to turn up on Monday, whereabouts unknown.

Miles became Press Officer at Cloud and Judith joined as his assistant.

Lovage started a nursing course. Alina and Sebastion went back to previous careers.

Neil and Lucy spent more time together, walking Morry.

Outside a café in Chinatown, New York, famous for its speciality teas, two young women, one with newly cut and lightened hair, sat planning their future.

In a way, Sarah was a gift from God. Since the public had been told the truth of her, the talents of those at Cloud and others had become public knowledge, and crime had dropped significantly. The fear of much more easily being caught made the world a little safer and fairer, and it was spreading from nation to nation. Perhaps the saying that 'God moves in mysterious ways' is true after all.